FROM WITHIN
THE WOODS

T. INMAN

Cover design by Patryk Olas
Intermission art by Nicolas Denis
Edited and typeset by SassyEdits.com

CONTENTS

To the lovers of folktales and myths, this is for you.

PART ONE: THE HUNT

CHAPTER ONE

PREYING

The crisp evening wind bristled along Elena's bare arms as men from the village of Innorin marched her over the threshold of the forest. There was an ominous sense of finality to it, knowing that her decisions over the course of the next few hours would be crucial—and whether they were for this life or the next could only be known by the gods. Her hands were bound tightly behind her back, the coarse rope burning as it scraped her skin raw with every movement. She found herself digging her nails into her palms despite the pain in a desperate attempt to steel her nerves for whatever was to come next.

As the men chattered eagerly amongst themselves to distract from their superstition of the forest, Elena found herself drawn to what little was known about this place. Unlike the Southern forest across the valley they used for hunting, this one remained nearly untouched. Superstition had gripped the surrounding villages, and no one set foot into the forest without a very good reason. She wondered idly if she should laugh or be honored that they thought she was worth the risk of angering whatever lingered here. Some said it was haunted by a malevolent spirit or plagued by monsters, and others said it was a god with a taste for blood. Some said it held magical beings behind the borders, protecting the lands and keeping them pure so long as people did not cross the threshold.

Whatever it may be, the end result of the superstition remained the same; one should not disturb the forest, lest it decided to never let you leave.

But what if that was the intention to begin with? What if two men were walking someone to her death, and she was never destined to see the sunrise of another morning? The men had discussed this earlier, trying to ease themselves into the knowledge that they would be the ones delivering her and justifying it to themselves.

"It will be good to finally be rid of the witch. I don't know about you, but I am ready to put this mess behind us," one had said decisively. Elena recognized his voice as a man named Poe, whom her father had once trusted.

The other man, whom Elena did not immediately recognize, shushed him with urgency. "Lower your voice! You are going to attract whatever lingers in these woods," he hissed through his teeth. A twig snapped at that moment, and he flinched, quickly turning his head around to make sure nothing idled in the shadows cast by the looming trees.

"The forest knew we were here from the second we set foot into it without iron strapped to our skin," he said dismissively. "The point is not to avoid what lingers here, it is to deliver the soul. The forest will steal the spirit and keep it captive, so it may never reach us. It does not like to let things leave," he finished decisively.

The other man thought about this and frowned. "Then why would it let *us* leave?" he countered in a still-hushed tone. Elena thought he made a good point—as much as their superstition would allow, anyway.

It took Poe a minute or two of silence masked as trying to figure out the right words before he finally seemed to settle upon his reasoning. "Well, we are just delivering a sacrifice to it. It gets to keep the tainted spirit and we get to be rid of it. Even the old gods like sacrifices," he declared, and then they began to talk about other things to change the subject away from the topic at hand. The other man, becoming more relaxed from Poe's confidence, soon fell into the comfortable chatter.

Better not to think too hard on things they dared not try to understand, Elena thought, and then wondered which of the three of them was truly the blind one.

After they could no longer hear the soft chatter of the village over the wind that billowed too high above them in the trees, they began her torment. As they walked on, one of the men hooked his boot around Elena's ankle, causing her to trip and fall onto the damp ground of the forest with a sharp gasp hissing through her teeth. She had tried instinctively to brace herself, only to remember how feeble the effort was with her hands bound the way that they were. She grunted as the wind was knocked out of her but relished the cool feeling of the earth beneath her skin.

A heavy boot stepped onto her back, dampening her dress with mud from the recent rain as he crunched into her spine. She winced in pain and squeezed her nails tighter into her palms until he pretended to remember she was there. He grabbed her by the wrists and yanked her from the ground as quickly as she had fallen. Struggling to get her feet under her again, she was vaguely aware of him scolding her for being so clumsy to fall whilst the other man snickered.

She listened to them hiss the word *witch* as they leered at her, trying to provoke a response, so she bit down on the inside of her cheek to keep from saying something that might make her situation worse. She also found herself too tired to deny the label any longer. Her body ached from the weight of the man and from the trauma she had been through the past couple of days, and while she was not ready to give up just yet, she knew her energy was better spent thinking of a way out of this mess. She only needed her mind to focus, but their taunts persisted.

These had been men her father had once bonded with. She knew Poe from when her father had brought his son porridge when he had come down with a fever. Had he forgotten everything good about her and her family? Or had he chalked her current state up to her own actions and decisions, reasoning that whoever she was now was not the same girl whom he knew before? She wanted to scowl. She wanted to yell at him and remind him of all of the times her family had helped the village, but in the end, she knew it would do no good. She was walking to her death, and these men would not be swayed lest their conscience break under the weight of their judgment.

Her mind wandered to thinking about the animals these men would hunt for their village. Did their prey ever realize their fate before they died? Was it a slow chase where the creature began to dread and tire? Or was it afforded a quick and painless death, blissfully unaware of consequence until it no longer mattered? She wondered if she had been born a rabbit if she might not have been so scared as she made her way through this forest. She wondered if she would have been better off not knowing the murdering ways of the village she had once called home. The idea that they might have afforded their meals more mercy than her, was all she needed to know about them.

What good would have come of trying to convince them of her innocence now? She had tried that for the past two days, begging and pleading for them to hear her. To stop and just *listen* and consider they had made a mistake. She had tried to simply talk, and when desperation began to set in, she had cried until her throat was raw. None of it mattered. She would not be able to convince these two of anything anymore because they thought of her as less than the meat they consumed.

A year ago, life had been much simpler for Elena and her family. If she had learned anything from this, it would be that life was anything but consistent, and change would come whether you were ready for it or not. Life would move forward with or without you, and it would not hesitate to remind you the past was a place you may never return to aside from your ever-changing memories. So, that was what Elena did—her mind returning to the day her father said goodbye, unwittingly forcing her to say hello to a future without him in it. If she were to die tonight, she wanted to remember when things began to go so terribly wrong, starting with the first time she had stepped foot into the forest that would soon become her gravesite.

CHAPTER TWO

WORMS

One summer, back when she had just turned seven years old, her father had woken her up early one morning after the sky had wept in a massive downpour overnight. He swept her into his strong arms and carried her sleepily on his back, talking quietly about wanting to show her something. Slowly and drowsily, as he carried her, Elena had become aware of her surroundings only to gasp and cling to her father tighter. There they stood at the edge of the forbidden forest, dawn just barely cresting over the horizon.

"Papa, no!" she hissed through her teeth, eyes wide as they scanned the looming trees and fog that settled in scattered patches on the ground.

Earlier in the previous day, her teacher had warned her about the things that were inhabited here, speaking of the different layers of danger that enveloped these woods. The terrain was dangerous and unforgiving, and some said the forest warped its shape in order to make you lose your way. The beasts that roamed were more ferocious and blood-thirsty than of any other forest, feeding off of the potent magic in the air and, according to her teacher, poisoning themselves over time. What was worse, though, were the gods and spirits that threatened to steal you away forever, kept back only by the invisible boundary line surrounding the trees. Elena had come home that night and cried into her grandmother's arms, scared of things escaping to hurt her and her family.

Her father chuckled, the timbre of his voice still thick with sleep as it pulled her back into the moment. "My darling, do you not trust me? I would never let something hurt you," he said in a matter-of-fact voice.

Elena had frowned at his gentle chiding for her not trusting him, but she willed her protests to stay down and clung tighter to his back instead as she peered around them. She could feel the warmth of his body through his tunic as she held on, focusing on the sensation of warmth and listening to the dull sound of his heartbeat. The two fell into a comfortable silence as she took in the blue-tinted hue of the world in the quiet early morning, making their surroundings feel ethereal.

They walked just barely out of sight of their village before he swung her off of his back and plopped her on the ground. Her toes sank into the mud with a squishing noise, and she made a sound of surprise and protest before she realized he, too, was barefoot and happily wiggling his toes in the mud.

Was this man truly her father? Her father had always leaned towards being more quiet and serious, but in those twilight hours, he had looked like a brand new man had replaced him and erased all of his worries. He plucked something off of the ground and thrust it into her hands with a grin that took up his entire face, even with his facial hair.

Something wet gradually started to move in her hands, and she glanced down at it before her entire body tensed. She did not cry out or fling the small earthworm wriggling in her hand, but she was unsure how to feel about it. She let it writhe around, searching with no eyes as it looked for the dirt it had been picked from.

Her father had explained that the worms did important work for the earth deep beneath the ground, and while they were not always seen, their work was very necessary. When it rained, however, they crawled their way to the surface to worship the moisture the gods provided them.

He told her the forest provides for them and, if it can be so kind to something as small as a worm, why should they fear it for things people simply do not understand? The magic of this forest would not harm them so long as they respected its presence. It did not poison things. It merely existed beside them. But death was a part of life, and it was inevitable, whether you were inside a forest, in your home, or even in the church.

They spent the next half hour running through the mud, gently lifting falling branches of wood to find snails and worms, and even a frog at one point—which Elena had managed to wrangle into her hands and place very neatly on a mossy rock after saying hello. They laughed quietly, shushing each other as the echoes carried their voices away from the village. When the sun threatened to rise fully, her father pulled the sleepy-eyed and muddied Elena back into his strong arms. He carried her easily through the terrain as she nestled into the safety he provided and talked about the worms she had named as her excitement settled back into contentment.

When they went back home, her father explained that they should not tell anyone outside of their home about their trip to the forest. He told her the best secrets are the kinds that exist purely to the people involved and no one else. When Elena asked if she could tell her mother, he said her mother was the exception because even if they didn't tell her, she would still find out.

She saw her mother that day when they walked through the door, barefoot and covered in mud, just as the sun was beginning to rise, and Elena thought she was going to be angry at them. Instead, she merely huffed and chided them for going to the forest *without her*. Then Elena talked all about the creatures she had seen and proudly announced how she was no longer scared of the forest.

Elena kept the secret close to her chest, unwilling to utter even a whisper of it to anyone. She did not know why she felt so compelled to do this as normally she would have loved to share things with her friends throughout the village and provide them the same ease that her father had brought her. Still, something in her father's voice when asking her to keep the secret sank heavy inside of her like a stone. It would be her family's secret and one she would not betray, even if she did not understand his hesitation at first.

Eventually, however, she did come to understand.

One evening, not too long after visiting the worms with her father, Elena left her home to go play with a girl named Mara, who lived nearby. As she walked amongst the dirt roads, she hummed a lullaby her mother and father had sung to her. She had not gone far when she heard her parents' names being spoken in hushed tones, instantly making her soft hums fall silent out of curiosity. She walked closer to the open door of the fabric shop, listening to a man and a woman silently discuss her family.

"I am telling you, it was Anya and Mikhail. He was guiding her out of the Northern forest. Her hair looked like it had not even been *brushed* that morning."

"There is only one good reason why someone goes off into that forest. She was lucky he was there to pull her back before it was too late and it took her soul. Did he look concerned?"

"No, he seemed to be smiling. He was probably just trying to soothe her, though."

They said something else, but Elena could not bring herself to hear their mumbled words. As she heard the movement and slow shuffle of their feet, she inhaled sharply in surprise and ran to the side of the building, her heart thrumming in her chest. Whatever she had just heard, she suspected it was not intended for her ears. Unease settled into her stomach. *Was mother sick?*

Elena ran back to her home quickly, forgetting about wanting to play with her friend.

Once she barreled through the door, panting from running the short distance, her father looked at her with raised eyebrows. His demeanor was calm and stoic as usual, the light-hearted and joyous man she saw in the woods absent from his eyes as he waited for her to tell him what all of the fuss was about.

After telling him about what she overheard, the worry crept back into her voice at seeing his lips sink into a small frown.

"What is wrong?" Her voice was higher-pitched than she had intended, sounding unsteady.

Her question pulled her father back to the moment, and he looked at her with a small smile as he stood up. "Nothing is wrong, little cricket." He gently ruffled her hair despite a grunt of protest. He began walking to the door then, still speaking. "Your mother and I had just gone for a walk this morning. It seems our neighbors are merely being a little bit nosey. I think I will go talk to them, just to set the record straight."

With that, her father left their house. Elena frowned as she stared at the wooden front door. Their neighbors were always nosey—the entire village was, according to her grandmother—but it had never warranted her father going to immediately speak to them or clear up the confusion about simply taking a walk.

No longer feeling the urge to want to play, she found herself walking out to her grandmother's garden to help her pull weeds. Her grandmother would not ask questions, and Elena did not want to talk for the moment, so she knew she would be in good company. She pulled the weeds from the ground leisurely, pausing as she glanced down at the patch of soil for their garden. She slowly ran her fingers along the dirt and noticed the change in the texture compared to the outside of the garden patch.

The soil inside of the garden patch was similar to the dirt that she and her father had found worms digging through in the forest, and it was different from the soil of Innorin. It was cooler against her warm hands and felt soothing to the sharp edges of her mind as she touched it. It was also darker in color, with less mulch surrounding it, and finer in texture as it crumbled against her palm. Elena had played in the dirt around town far more than was typically considered appropriate for a little girl—though the townspeople had chalked up the action to following in her grandmother's gardening footsteps—so she was surprised she had not noticed the subtle differences before.

Elena started shoving her hands deeper into the earth to pluck the weeds out, surprised to find comfort in the idea that it was from the forest rather than feeling hesitant.

Her grandmother merely smiled at her new tenacity in pulling weeds.

When her father came home, he said that the talk had gone smoothly with their neighbors and it was merely a miscommunication, and he was seemingly more jovial than when he had left. Elena felt like she was finally able to breathe again. It felt like her family had avoided something, but she was unsure of what it could have been. Gossip, perhaps.

Elena found out only months later that her father had threatened the two shopkeepers, warning them not to spread such silly rumors about his family. He had told them that their eyes were wrong, and since her father was such a standing member of their village, they believed him. He was one of the most respected and skilled hunters that had taught some of the other hunters how to properly track when he had first moved to this village. So when he spoke, telling them the rumors were false, no one dared to even consider disagreeing. They even apologized for thinking such silly things. Her father made sure those rumors died quickly. He would not stand to hear talk like that begin to take place while he had any say in it.

However, gossip, just like the weeds, never truly goes away forever.

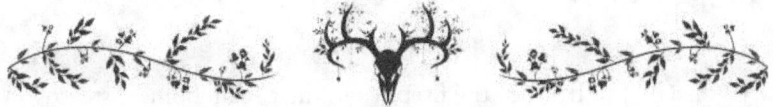

CHAPTER THREE

A YEAR
BEFORE THE FALL

E lena sat in front of the fireplace in their small home, listening in
silence as she pretended to practice her stitching on a wash rag
her mother had accidentally torn a hole in. Elena didn't think it needed
to look pretty as long as it was still functional, but her mother had
insisted she practice. *Your intent always matters, and if you intend to
do something, you should intend to do it properly,"* her mother had said
to her one evening in response to her protests and gripes. On this day,
however, she suspected that the necessity had less to do with stitching
and more to do with the fact that her mother wanted her to be out of
the way while she bustled around the house, gathering any last-minute
supplies.

Her father sat in his chair on the opposite side of the fireplace, lacing
his boots so tightly that Elena thought he might cut off his circulation.
She watched him out of the corner of her eye as he twisted the laces
around the top of his boot before tying them in the front with an
intricate knot that he had promised he would teach her later. It wasn't
quite proper for ladies to wear boots like his and even less so to tie them
in such a way, but her father said it was good to know these things. He
had jokingly told her that if her husband was from their village, he might
very well need her help in tying his own boots.

Her father had taught her many things that were not considered to be entirely proper for a lady. She often wondered if he had perhaps wished he had a son to share these things with, but the one time she had asked him, he grew so serious it surprised her. He told her he would never want anyone else aside from who she was, and just because she was a girl did not mean she should be barred from the knowledge of life and its happenings. Elena had very much liked this answer and had walked with her shoulders straighter for an entire week after that, determined to learn everything she could.

Now, as her father sat by the fireplace, she found her stomach twisting at the idea of him leaving for the hunt, and she found herself truly believing this one was different. All of the hunts made her nervous. Sometimes they caught nothing and came back upset. Even worse, sometimes, they came back with injuries from the terrain or animals or accidents. They were never nice easy trips, it had seemed, but her father was an excellent hunter, and he said it was his duty to help as he was able. The sense of fresh unease that turned inside of her made her frown at the possibility of disaster.

"Must you go this time?" she asked quietly, her voice barely above a whisper. She knew her father had heard her as he paused for a moment and then glanced at her with a look of curious weariness.

"Is there a reason I should not?" he countered in an equally quiet voice, as though they were sharing secrets or conspiring together.

Elena frowned a little bit, shifting uncomfortably under the weight of his knowing question. She hesitated before deciding on honesty. "No. I mean, I don't know. I feel like something bad is going to happen. Can't you just let them go this time and stay with us? Grandma might need extra help. You could—" Her father held up a hand to silence her.

"Your mother is more than capable of handling your grandmother, and if there is danger in the hunt, then it is all the more reason to go. We are better in numbers. I know you are worried, but things will be alright, my little Cricket." He smiled easily at her as he stood up, just as her mother padded into the room, handing him some last-minute additions of rations, clothing, and an extra water pouch.

Elena could tell her mother never liked it when her father left either. She would get quiet in the days leading up to the hunts, staying close to him like a watchful dog. Elena was sure that if her mother could turn invisible, she would have snuck away to trail her father on these hunts just to try and protect him as well. Elena had seen her mother when she was protective. She was also sure that if her mother had managed to go on those hunts, the earth itself would not dare to try and cross her. Her father had once said she would also scare the animals away with her motherly instincts, to which her mother had cursed him quite colorfully while he laughed.

Her mother placed an extra wrapped bundle of food into one of his hands as the other wrapped around her mother's small frame and tugged her to his chest. He kissed her full on the mouth, which, even now at seventeen years of age, made Elena smile softly and look away. He pulled away and grinned easily at her mother.

"I will be home soon," he said to both of them softly. He went to kiss his own mother on the cheek, warning her in vain to try and be pleasant to people if they came to visit before he walked out the door. Elena would turn eighteen in three days, but her father would never get the chance to see it.

T he hunters from her father's group returned one week later, two fewer men than they had left with. As they marched into town, the village seemed to fall quiet in silent questions and then mourning realization. They took in the faces that had returned, bloodied and dirty but recognizable. They were almost as recognizable as the two of them who *weren't* there any longer. The hunters did not go home immediately, but rather, one of them had gone to the Novak residence, and the other one had walked straight to Elena's house.

Elena was making tea for her grandmother when the knock came. Her mother, having just finished dishes, wiped her hands sloppily on her apron, then went to the door and opened it. She would never forget the wailing sound of her mother's screams as she fell to her knees. Elena ran to her, trying to console her and figure out what had happened, though she already had tears running down her own cheeks as her stomach sank. She did not want to acknowledge the suspicion creeping into her mind.

"Bring him back to me!" her mother screamed at the man in their doorway, calling out her father's name as if he was simply hiding around the corner to pull a terrible joke on them. After the second time crying out for him, her face twisted into despair.

"M-Mikhail?" her mother croaked his name as a question—a plea—looking up at the man with desperation in her eyes.

The man shook his head slowly, frown deepening. "I am sorry, Anya. I will... leave you to grieve with your family."

With that, he turned and left Elena cradling her mother on the ground of their home as the door creaked close. Elena's suspicions confirmed; she felt the world distantly, holding her mother tighter as she wailed louder.

The next couple of months went by in a blur. Since the villagers were unable to retrieve the bodies of the two fallen hunters, Elena found it hard to find closure. It didn't feel real, and despite the weight of knowing he was truly gone, she could not often bring herself to admit it until months later. The remainder of her small family spent many nights huddled in a shared bed to prevent themselves from feeling so alone. They cried together silently as if trying not to wake each other up despite knowing none of them were truly asleep.

Elena, for the most part, managed to keep herself together during the day. Her mother was distraught and barely contained herself most days despite trying to put on a brave front, and her grandmother had closed herself off to the entire village as if Elena's father was the only thing tethering her to them. She became distant to them and spiteful, putting up a front of anger and bitterness to most—but Elena and her mother still saw the cracks in her facade when she would water her garden with silent tears.

During the night, however, when Elena was alone as she cleaned up after dinner and when her family had already gone to sleep for the night, the reality was harder to suppress. Elena found herself shaking as she tried not to let the thought creep in. *He is gone,* her traitorous mind whispered to her. She blinked hard and tried to hide from the thoughts as if she could make herself invisible to them.

Eventually, they got louder, impossible to hide from as the weight of the thoughts crushed her chest. Her fingers began to shake so hard that doing her stitches was nearly impossible, and her breathing came out in short gasping breaths at times when she became overcome with emotions. She wanted to scream at the thoughts inside of her mind and fight them. She wanted to say he wasn't gone, not really, but she knew better. She couldn't make the thought form correctly without imagining his pale, stiff body being absorbed into the earth where the worms he once loved would consume him.

The image was too much to bear, and one night in particular, when her mother and grandmother were already in bed, too exhausted from their own grief to hear her walk outside, Elena walked toward the Southern forest. She got right to the edge, the trees towering over her, when she realized she was crying. Hot tears streamed down her face as she felt the suffocating grief tear her lungs to shreds. She had no plan, and she barely recognized her feet moving beneath her, but she had wanted to see her father. She had to know for certain he was gone.

One of the hunters from her father's group was walking home from the tavern late when he saw Elena, distraught and making her way to the edge of the forest as if she had planned on burning it all down, if it meant finding him. The sight was enough to sober him slightly as he approached her like a wild animal.

"What're you doing, Miss Elena? It is awfully late for you to be out here."

Elena did not respond as the tears burned her eyes. Instead, she clenched her jaw and forced her feet to continue forward. Upon seeing her move to enter the forest, the man came up and grabbed her from behind to stop her.

"Let me go! I need to see him!" she screamed. She thrashed wildly in his arms for a minute, but his vise grip around her chest made it hurt to breathe. Twisting then, she fell to her knees in his arms, defeat evident in her wailing. She cried and screamed into his chest, barely recognizing his warm tears drop onto her hair.

"It's going to be alright, darling," he said, his voice raspy and slurred but clear enough. A couple of other people had come out from the tavern to see what the screaming was about, but Elena didn't notice. She stared at the forest, screaming and wailing until her throat was dry and raw. It was that night she came to truly understand why banshees in the myths and legends always screamed at night. How many other women before her had been mistaken for these beings as their own crushing grief finally found purchase in the nights when they no longer had to feign strength for others?

Once she settled enough, the man managed to walk her home, despite his own slight sway to his step. They gave each other a small nod of acknowledgment and a silent swear to never speak of each other's tears before he, too, left her alone. She sank into her parents' bed, wiggling between her mother and grandmother, who welcomed her sleepily into their arms. That night, for the first time since the news, Elena was too exhausted to even have nightmares.

Soon, the tears began to dry, though. The grief never really went away completely, taking up a permanent residence in their hearts, but eventually, it did become easier to breathe. Slowly, they were able to say his name again, and they reminisced about his laughter and how he would want to be remembered. Her grandmother said he would have scolded the lot of them for crying so much over something so natural but would have held them anyway in a silent understanding until they had finished. He was a good man, and it would break his heart if they remained so broken over him for so long, so they tried their best and worked through the bad days.

The bad days were only just beginning for them, though.

Eventually, men and women from the village began to come to Elena's mother, whispering to her in the other room where they thought Elena or her grandmother could not hear. Elena would sit with her ear pressed to their thin walls and spy for her grandmother since she was not as mobile these days, and Elena was better at crouching. She had always been curious, and her grandmother had realized it would be pointless to try and tell her not to do something, so instead, she simply said, *"As long as you tell me what you hear, I will keep your secret."* They were quite the mischievous pair when left alone together.

Eavesdropping would yield pointless, though, as her mother would come straight in and tell them almost everything after the people had gone away. Her mother paced angrily or washed dishes with extra vigor as she explained that people thought it was 'unnatural' for the three women to be alone. She said they were pushing for her to remarry to have a man to provide for them, but she had assured them she was more than capable on her own. Their garden provided enough food for them as well as enough to sell at the local market, and she was known for her mending in the town, with no shortage of people willing to hire her talent. Mostly, she told them she was still grieving, and she might always be grieving, so with or without another man to provide, she would endure.

Elena noted what details her mother left out when telling them things, though, and would tell her grandmother later on. Like how the village was also adamant Elena marry since she was now of age. The idea terrified her, but her grandmother reassured her that her mother would not let it happen so soon under the circumstances, especially since her father had hated most of the village boys around her age and had never given his blessing to them.

Elena asked her grandmother what the villagers meant by saying it was 'unnatural' for the three of them to live together on their own. She was greeted by a snort from her grandmother as she rolled her eyes skyward.

"They think women are good for nothing, merely for pushing babies out of their cunts," she said, an edge to her voice that warned Elena this was a topic her grandmother felt particularly strong about.

Elena frowned, scrunching her eyebrows together in slight discomfort at the imagery.

Her grandmother did not stop there, though, and continued with her explanation. "They think any woman that has the ability to sustain herself without a man is equal to that of witchcraft. They wouldn't know a witch if one spit in their face, but they make themselves feel better by explaining away the things they do not like by calling them evil. Apparently, the only way a woman can be happy on her own is if she has sold her soul to the devil. Independence spits in the face of their ideals from their false prophets and new gods."

After a moment of consideration, Elena loosened the reins on her curiosity ever so slightly. "Then, wouldn't men also be considered witches?" she asked quietly, knowing there were men who lived in town alone. Those men had never taken brides and had been single for much longer than Elena and her mother. "Or shouldn't they be more concerned with finding and *keeping* a bride?"

Her grandmother cackled at her remark, and Elena gave a small tentative smile despite the topic. She liked making her grandmother laugh, and it seemed as though it had been so long since she heard the genuine sound fall from her lips, unless it had been a sarcastic sound disguised as one. Her grandmother did not answer the latter question but instead leaned in with a wicked gleam in her eyes.

"Who says they can't be witches too?" she countered in a soft voice, winking at Elena before her mother came into the room once more to help her grandmother to the bath. Elena was left to ponder the idea of male witches, wondering why the stories never spoke of them. Elena had many questions about male witches, but she decided to ask the question burning at the forefront of her mind.

"Are all witches evil?"

"Witches are no more evil than mankind is. There will always be extremes, of course, no matter what kind of creature you are. One dog can be rabid while another friendly, so trying to judge an entire group based on one or two is only going to make you more ignorant by the end."

"What makes someone a witch if not independence?"

"Goodness, child, you ask so many questions, don't you?" Her grandmother let out a slightly exasperated sigh at Elena's curiosity, but Elena could see the smile in her eyes, so she did not waver. Her grandmother leaned back into her chair once more. "There once was a time when magic flowed freely in the world, and humans were able to tap into its source. This was the gift of the old gods. But times change. Nowadays, it is said the only witches alive are descendants of the first wave of magic users. Some of their magic may lay dormant throughout their entire lives without ever needing it. Other times, it awakens in them early. There have been a couple of times throughout history, however, when magic will awaken in someone with no heritage of it at all. But all of this is just what gives a person magic. What makes someone a witch is their soul. They must respect the earth in which they live, and learn that their intentions are not mere figments of the mind—they can become tangible and volatile things. Now, go on and do your chores and leave me to rest."

The way her grandmother had spoken gave her more questions rather than answers, but she was content to let them simmer for now rather than try to push her luck. More often than not, Elena knew her curiosity could be tiring to others. Elena knew witches were real but had never paid much mind to the idea of them before. As she left her grandmother,

Elena's mind continued to wander with insatiable questions dying to be answered. Though, she supposed she could understand why men feared independent women and likened them to witches. With how cruelly she had seen some men treat their wives, it seemed to make sense they would fear the darker intents blooming as a consequence of their unchangeable actions. If they chose to oppress others who learn to think independently and then fight back, perhaps they deserved a little fear.

By the end of winter, as the year crept into spring, the villagers had all begun to treat them with hostility after continuous courtships for either Elena or her mother were turned down. Despite the pressure from the townsfolk, Elena was thankful her mother understood how little she wanted to marry anyone from the village and never tried to persuade her to do so. Though, it was getting harder to ignore the way people began to look at them.

It started out small enough, as occasional whispers or sideways glances. As Elena walked down the streets, she could feel the eyes lingering on her in disapproving ways or the hushed gossip of the town that her father had tried so hard to shield them from. He was no longer here to advocate for them, and so the gossip grew like a wildfire catching the breeze. Elena had distanced herself from her friends as she grieved, but then as she saw them in passing, they began to make feeble excuses for being unable to talk before they scurried away. She could feel the tension building within the town over her family, and her mother and grandmother's stories were similar, if not worse.

Then things got progressively worse as people began to critique Elena's mother for being 'too much' of things.

Too Loud.

Too Bold.

Too talkative.

Too abrasive.

Too headstrong.

*Too **much**.*

In the end, the consensus came down to her mother simply being too similar to a witch. She was all of those things, but those were the reasons why her father loved her. Now that he was gone, she was still all of those things, and now too alone. Only witches wanted to be alone, lest their new husband recognize their treacherous ways. Then the rumors began, which made everything far worse.

What should have been a healthy beginning to the spring crops and harvest was almost completely decimated by an unexpected late-season freeze. What was not ruined by the freeze was almost certainly blighted by a small infestation of insects not but two weeks later. The harvest had been wholly ruined in the patches of fields near the Eastern side of town. The Northern side, where Elena's family lived, was seemingly brushed over as her grandmother's garden managed to survive. Her grandmother complained it had been due to the negligence of the townsfolk who did not properly care for their crops, but her chiding did nothing to soothe the villagers' nerves as they scrambled to mend the crops and salvage their losses. Some began to claim her grandmother had hexed her garden selfishly or cursed others' gardens to spite them.

Matters only worsened when hunters came back empty-handed. They claimed it was as though every animal they came across simply knew they were coming. Frustrations were beginning to rise as the fear set in. This was not the worst spring their village had seen, but the tension surrounding Elena's family began to cause tension and superstition to override reason.

As soon as the villagers began suspecting her mother of witchcraft, they soon began to suspect her grandmother as well. Soon after, the rumor became they had conspired to kill her father and make it look like an accident by casting spells and cursing him. The villagers began to say her mother and grandmother had started a coven and would soon start to influence younger generations to break traditions and do unsavory things and become creatures of the occult. Most of the rumors seemed to leave Elena out of it—she had always been too quiet and soft-spoken to bring much attention to herself to begin with—but not all of them.

The first time she had been called a witch was by a group of young boys that she had passed by on her way to deliver some of the vegetables from her grandmother's garden to the market square. The boys, all younger than ten years of age, hissed the word at her as they scampered away, hiding behind crates. Elena had not thought much of this event, though she couldn't deny the unease settling inside of her.

The bakers began to give her mother only burnt or stale bread. The butcher gave Elena scraps. Her mother and grandmother's garden was able to help sustain them, but this seemed to only make the village angrier. Those who could rely on themselves were dangerous. In their eyes, people needed a community, even if that community was the one that turned their backs on them to begin with.

Elena noticed the glares of women and the way men turned their noses up when she walked by as if they were practicing looking down on her and her family. They had chosen to denounce the village customs and pressures, so she would be damned if she let them suffer alone—even if the sudden hostility was indeed beginning to scare her. She didn't understand the repercussions of that decision until the day her mother almost died.

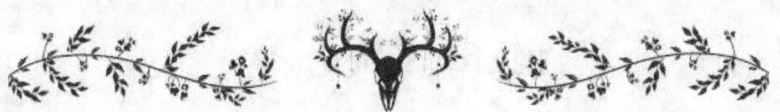

CHAPTER FOUR

DROWNING

E lena's mother woke her up on a particularly chilly spring morning, just shy of a year after her father's passing. There was frost coating the windows of their home, and the air was crisp enough to see their breath as they spoke in hushed whispers. Elena groaned quietly as her mother shook her shoulder. Her eyes fluttered open, blinking away the sleep before her heart skipped a beat. For a brief moment, with the sun behind her mother's back, Elena swore she could see her father's smile on her face. She was taken back to years ago, being woken up barely before dawn, and she felt her fingers shake, wondering if it had all been nothing but an awful nightmare.

Her mother tilted her head slightly, and the dawn sun was cast onto her face, removing any of the darkness and shadows that maintained the illusion of her father. Elena's stomach sank, but the blow was not as heavy as she expected it to be. Her mother's smile was warm, and she had a childlike excitement to her this morning. Elena quietly pushed herself up and avoided her grandmother shifting beside her under the quilts.

"Let's bake some bread before she wakes up. It is the perfect morning, and she has been hounding me for it," her mother whispered quickly before Elena could speak.

"She was complaining about her bones hurting from the cold. Maybe this will help cheer her up," Elena whispered back as she rubbed her eyes with the palms of her hands to try and focus more.

Her mother replied with a vigorous nod. The two women were then scurrying off to the kitchen in the next minute, excited whispers filling their home as they began the process. They kneaded the dough together just like they used to do. They laughed as they got themselves covered in flour and dough and then promptly shushed each other for the sound, moving silently around each other as if dancing a memorized routine.

As they waited for the dough to rise, her mother noticed how low they were running on flour and frowned.

"I'm just going to go run a few houses down. Miss Olga has always been kind to us. I am sure she can spare an extra cup or so if I can catch her after her husband has gone to work," she said decisively, already taking off her apron and moving to put on her shoes.

Unease flooded Elena's mind at the idea of asking the neighbors for anything with the recent tension, but she knew better than to attempt to argue with her mother once she set her mind to something. She watched her leave their cottage and then busied herself with the cleaning, trying to get everything ready for when they would put the bread into the oven when her mother returned.

Time began to tick by, and Elena watched the door carefully, silently wishing it would open at any moment. With the chores completed, she wished she was kneading the bread again, if only to have something to do with her hands. She remembered the uneasy feeling that had come over her before her father left and was struck with a sudden chill throughout her entire body. Her father had told her that things would be fine, and they hadn't been, so why should things be any different now?

She set her jaw and then huffed stubbornly before she pulled a cloak over her shoulders and slipped from the cottage, closing the door tightly to keep the cold out. Her grandmother would be fine alone in their home until she could get back, but her mother was gone for too long, and Elena was tired of waiting for things to simply happen.

The sun had risen and was beginning to melt the frost on the windows of houses. Her mother was nowhere to be seen, but as Elena walked closer to Miss Olga's house, she saw a familiar shawl lying in the dirt path and ran to it. She swiped it up into her hands, and then her eyes scanned the dirt on the ground. She saw what looked to be drag marks, and she followed them like a hound catching a scent. The trail led to the edge of the Southern forest, and then Elena broke into a run. She did not have time to stare at the ground and try to piece together what had happened or where the trail would lead. She simply ran as fast and as far as her feet would carry her until she heard the familiar sound of a creek and the horrifying sound of her mother begging.

"Stop it, please! I can't swim, and I am not a witch! You are going to kill me! Please, think of Elena! She can't lose both of us!" she shrieked. Elena hid quickly behind one of the trees, her heart hammering in her chest as she peered around and saw her mother thrown over the shoulder of one of their neighbors named Alexei.

"I'm doing this town a favor. All of ye witches will not be poisoning our minds any longer! If ye be innocent, then ye will die for a noble reason. And if ye are what I suspect ye to be, ye will swim away, and we will burn ye at the stake!" he roared with a righteous voice, speaking in an older tongue. He wasted no more time arguing before he tossed Elena's mother into the deep river. The current was not too strong, but her mother sank with a horrifying quickness.

Elena was moving again before she could properly think. She did not know how to swim, but she knew with an unexplained certainty that the river would not hurt her. She ran past Alexei, startling him as she removed her cloak swiftly and plunged into the river. Her moves were not exactly graceful as she dove in, floundering for a second with disorientation from the sudden shock of the chilled water surrounding her. Her eyes frantically searched, not wanting to waste any more time with the shock, and then found her mother's body staring up at her with wide frantic eyes.

Elena thrust and kicked her body forward awkwardly, closing her eyes tightly for a moment to try and focus before opening them once more. Her arms extended in front of her, and she clawed through the water down toward her mother. Her mother's face twisted with shock—maybe it was horror or dread—but the water had blurred and burned her eyes too much to tell for sure. Elena let her body take control, pushing her mind away and only focusing on her mother as her limbs moved automatically.

She couldn't explain how she knew what to do. Her mother and father had never taught her how to swim, and all she knew about it were the stories that her father had mentioned of it from his hunting trips. Women simply were not allowed to learn and risk being improper. Risk being too much like a witch.

Elena hooked her arms around her mother's waist and then pushed up from the ground, propelling them upwards. She felt the cool water glide along her skin until they breached the surface. Both of them gasped for air, her mother clinging to her. Elena coughed and kicked her feet to the edge of the river. She let go of her mother once she had pushed her up and out of the freezing water and onto the grass of the clearing. Shortly after, she hoisted herself up with shaking arms.

Elena sat on her hands and knees, taking the air into her lungs gratefully but remembered the man standing a few feet away. She slowly lifted her head to look at him, her long brown hair hanging loosely around her face. She met his eyes with a fierceness that she did not know she had in her, ready to face him if need be.

Alexei looked at her with wide eyes and a pale face as if he had seen a ghoul and stumbled backward. "Witch!" he cried out. "Demon! You are nothing more than an imposter to the true gods!"

Elena shakily pushed herself to stand, staring at him with false confidence, trying to make herself bigger like the animals of the forest did to ward off attacks. To her relief, he stepped back a few steps before breaking out into a run. She had earned the title her family had been given in the past couple of months, and she was perhaps the only one of them truly deserving of it.

As soon as his back was turned, she bent down, helping her mother to stand as she finished coughing up the water from her lungs. "How did you.." her mother mumbled, shock and confusion in her eyes, but as she looked at Elena, she seemed to have decided against asking as a knowing look came over her.

Elena answered her question anyway. "I don't know, Mama. I do not know." Her voice was raspy and quiet as she spoke, and she did not trust herself to speak more than that as she wrapped her discarded cloak around her mother's shivering body.

They walked home and were greeted by her grandmother, looking as though she wanted to make a sarcastic remark before she stopped and truly looked at them—soaking wet from head to toe and shivering.

"What in the gods... Why do you two look like drowned kittens?" she asked incredulously.

Elena looked down, feeling ashamed for a reason she could not quite name. She had saved her mother, hadn't she? So why did she feel like she had done something so incredibly *wrong?* She didn't understand why that man had done what he had or why her ability to kick and thrash ungracefully in the water made him suddenly fear her so much. Elena, who could not even bring herself to step on caterpillars when other kids had found them crawling along her path, had scared a man three times her size by flailing around and saving her mother.

Her grandmother got them blankets, and her mother started a fire in the fireplace and put the bread into the oven so as not to waste the dough—though the magic of baking with her daughter had now obviously been replaced with a tense urgency. Elena shed her wet clothes and hung them up to dry before getting into clean, dry clothes and staying silent, even under her grandmother's watchful gaze. She looked at Elena as if she knew what had happened without having been told, and Elena shifted under her scrutiny, wishing she were a ghost to disappear through the walls.

Her mother came back into the room after she, too, had gotten into new clothes. She had a look of determination in her eyes, letting everyone know she had come to a decision. Elena looked up at her apologetically, despite knowing her mother was not upset with her. She knew her mother would love her no matter what the consequences were. No matter if she was truly a witch or not. Still, it did not ease the sense of dread when her mother finally spoke.

"We are leaving. Tonight."

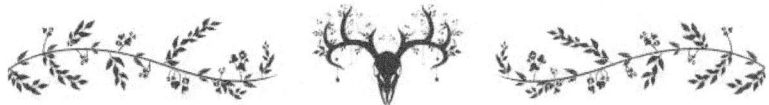

CHAPTER FIVE

THE WITCH HUNT

They moved quickly in making preparations for the three women to leave Innorin and put it far behind them. Elena listened to her mother's commands obediently, packing one extra set of clothes aside from the dress she currently wore. She also prepared food that wouldn't spoil easily or take up room in a small burlap sack.

Elena's grandmother sat in her rocking chair, trying not to waste any precious energy they would need to run for their lives. Elena's mother had told them she would steal a horse from someone in town so her grandmother would not have to walk much, but they would have to move fast and would have no time for resting once they started moving. Not entirely a fan of stealing, but seeing no other way, Elena promised herself that she would do everything in her power to at least make sure the horse remained safe with them. She would feed it her rations if need be.

Throughout the chaos, she had not noticed she was crying until her mother grabbed her shoulders, looking at her sternly before softening her gaze. Her mother cupped her face in her hands, stroking away the tears with her thumbs carefully. Elena made a choking sound at the gentle touch, and her mother smiled sadly at her. "You are going to be alright, my little Cricket. You have done nothing wrong. This village had grown far too small for our family a long time ago."

"Was he right? Am I a witch?" Elena asked quietly, looking into her mother's eyes. Now was not the time for gentle conversations, and Elena had a fierce need to know something for certain.

"I do not know what makes someone a witch, my dear. You and your father—"

"Father was a witch?" Elena interrupted, the realization crashing down onto her and knocking the wind from her lungs. Elena felt slapped in the face, though not betrayed. She had always known they were different somehow and had an understanding of each other, but to be witches? "Why did he never tell me?"

"Your father did not dare to call himself anything other than father, husband, and son. You must learn to do the same, Elena. Swear it to me. Promise me that you will never give these people the satisfaction of knowing you are anything but you. Lie and be adamant about it if that is what it takes to protect yourself." Her mother spoke urgently now, leaving no room for discussion in the matter.

Elena hesitated but nodded all the same, trying to come to terms with the new information. She was a witch, taking after her father. A new idea popped into her mind, and she looked at her grandmother with wide eyes only to be met with another knowing smile. She nodded to the silent question, and suddenly, Elena felt like laughing. The situation was not particularly funny, but she was flooded with relief despite the circumstances. She had found her certainty.

Elena's mother gave her another small smile, her relief palpable at knowing Elena would not admit she was a witch to these people. "This is not how we wanted you to find out. You have always had such a deep connection with the world. Your father used his skill to help the hunts, but you could do so many other wonderful things should you choose.

You are not unnatural, and you are certainly not evil despite what these villagers would have you think if they were to find out."

With that, they continued their preparations. Elena was lost in her memories, thinking back to all of the times her father had shown her the connections of the world. His love for the forest and forbidden things, his insistence on her to learn things despite if it was proper or not—all of them were because he had the same inclinations as her. She thought about the consuming feeling of safety she felt when she was in or near the woods. She wondered if it had to do with the comment her mother had made about her connection to the world or if it simply was because she was free to be a little bit closer to her true self out there without any watchful gazes.

The evening was gradually approaching as the sun had set over the valley, melting the orange sky into a deep indigo blue. Elena's mother had remained by the window as she peered through the curtains, keeping watch and waiting until it became dark enough to slip out under the cover of night. Her breathing hitched in her throat with a sharp gasp that immediately made Elena's head snap up in attention.

"What is it?" her grandmother asked quietly, clutching Elena's hand tightly.

"They're coming, and they brought the torches."

There was a sudden tense calmness between the two women as they looked at each other in silent understanding. Elena's grandmother squared her shoulders back, nodding slightly as she eased back into her rocking chair. She took a deep breath and kissed Elena's hand before letting go of it. There was a breath of silence before she closed her eyes and smiled.

"Be a dear and make me a cup of tea? From the fresh herbs I picked this morning from my garden?" her grandma requested, opening her eyes and staring at her mother with a newfound fire in her eyes.

Elena's mother obeyed silently with a nod, deepening her frown as she quickly ran to the kitchen. Elena was incredulous that her grandmother wanted tea at a time like this and more so that her mother was obliging her. She ran to the window, barely pulling back the fabric to see there was a group steadily approaching their house from down the road. They walked slowly and with purpose, as if they knew there was no way they could all escape. Elena's mother had not yet stolen a horse, and they had no carriage. Her grandmother could not move, much less run, and they were now sitting ducks.

Elena's heart raced inside of her chest, and she ran back to her grandmother. She knew she would not give up so easily. "Please, what do we do?" she asked softly, taking her grandmother's frail hands within her own and giving them a small pleading squeeze.

Her grandmother smiled down at her, a genuine one, but Elena could see the sadness in her eyes. "*We* do nothing, my dear. *You* are going to run like your life depends on it because it does. I love you, my sweet," she said softly and pulled her hands away in order to take the tea from her mother's shaking hands. She drank deeply, and before Elena could protest, her mother grabbed her shoulders, tugging her away so she could look into her daughter's eyes.

"Elena, listen to me. Our plans have changed, okay? We do not have any time to argue about this. You are my daughter, and you will do as I say. I knew that having a daughter would be the best day of my life, and when I looked into your eyes on the day you were born, I knew you were perfect. My beautiful little girl. Your father and I made a promise to you to protect you no matter the cost, and I have never been happier to do so."

"Mama, please—"

"No, my Cricket, no. It is time to listen to me. The people outside are no longer our friends. They are coming here, and they intend not to let us leave this house. You are to go to the bedroom window, and you are to crawl out of it. Run as fast and as hard as you can. Go towards the forest and don't look back. Keep running until your feet hurt, and then go farther. When you reach the next town, don't stay long. Don't tell them what happened. Say you were lost or anything that you can in order to get help, but you leave and keep going until you get far away. Rely on your senses and when you get stuck, just listen."

"Mama, I can't leave you," Elena choked out, her voice breaking as fresh tears poured down her cheeks. Her mother gripped her arms tighter.

"None of that, Elena. It is up to you now. There is a time for tears, but not now. Honor our memory by baring your teeth and claws. Show them that you will not go down without a fight. Honor our memory with your bravery and run." Elena's mother had her own tears sliding down her cheeks, but she smiled. "I love you. We both do. Now go, quickly now."

Elena hesitated a breath of a moment to memorize her mother's face for what could be the last time, but the loud pounding on the door snapped her from her thoughts. She held her breath in a desperate attempt to stop crying and to be brave, though she felt she might fall over if someone looked at her too strongly. "I love you both," she whispered and kissed her mother's cheek before she ran to the bedroom.

The pounding on the door grew louder, accompanied by the shouts of men outside. She struggled with the heavy glass pane and flinched as she heard the splintering crack of a shotgun blowing the handle of their door off. Elena turned back despite her mother's warning, freezing with horror as she saw the wood splinter off their door.

Anya had grabbed a kitchen knife at some point, though Elena could not place when, and as soon as the door swung open, she charged the men. She bared her teeth like a wild animal protecting her young and screamed what Elena could only imagine a war cry sounded like. Before she could even manage to land a scratch on them, though, her throat exploded with the sound of a rifle. A low guttural noise came from her mother before her body collapsed to the ground in one big heap—blood, sinew, and flesh covering her once pale blue dress.

One of the men looked unsure at the way her mother's body crumpled and began oozing red, but the man who shot her simply said, "It was in defense. Her body will burn all of the same."

Elena wanted to scream, but she could not bring her body to make any sound. She wanted to run back to her mother, but she knew even from this far that her mother was gone. Time slowed, and she felt like she was moving through mud, gliding her eyes to look at her grandmother, who still sat in the rocking chair.

Her grandmother sat calmly, a threat to no one, as the men walked over to her. She had her eyes closed, looking as though she was mourning or praying as one of them struck a match. Elena felt the wind sucked from her lungs as they dropped it onto her lap, setting her shawl on fire as the fire spread and consumed her body. Her grandmother did not once move or cry out in pain, but Elena finally made a strangled noise as she frantically turned back towards the window, shoving her shoulder against it as hard as she could until it finally burst free. She crawled from the window with the light of her grandmother's flames and the smell of burning hair and flesh behind her. Distantly, she heard her grandmother's empty cup shatter as it fell to the floor, the only sound aside from growing flames.

Elena held her breath as her feet hit the ground, and she scrambled into a run, pushing her legs to move faster than they ever had despite her unused muscles protesting. Her heart was seized with panic, too much adrenaline to feel the sting of grief that she knew was looming at the corners of her mind. Her lungs burned, and she realized she had been holding her breath the entire time to avoid the smoke and fumes. She gasped in air, running as far as she could away from her house, which had now begun to take on more flames.

Thick black smoke billowed in the air and threatened to suffocate her, but she persisted. Her shins ached from running so hard, and her dress added resistance as she ran, threatening to trip her as she gathered her skirts in fists and held them until her knuckles turned white. She heard the shouting, aware that they were shouts of people looking for her.

As she rounded the corner, she collided with the baker, whose strong arms engulfed her and crushed her. "I got her!" he screamed. It was not long before three other men came, struggling to pin down Elena as she kicked and thrashed. They wrestled to get a grasp on her as she finally released the pent-up scream that had been building in her lungs.

She was outnumbered and overpowered as they shoved her face into the ground. Elena inhaled a cloud of dust and coughed violently as the men managed to tie ropes around her wrists, then around her arms and chest just to be secure. Elena's hair fell loosely around her shoulders and over her face as she remembered her mother's pleas never to admit what she was. She was caught, but perhaps all hope would not be lost.

"Please! I am not a witch!"

"Then why did you run?" one of the men sneered in a mocking tone, clearly not believing Elena as he and the other men dragged her toward the middle of town. A crowd had begun to gather, though none of them particularly looked surprised at the events unfolding.

"You just killed my family! You did not even hold a trial where they could defend themselves. I thought you would kill me without a second thought, too!" she reasoned quickly, her mind racing to think of excuses through her panic.

"Your mother attacked us with a knife, and your grandmother was dangerous."

"She was old and could barely move without help most days! And mother was just trying to protect me. You shot our door down!"

"She was protecting a witch. She earned her fate," he snapped, unclear to which woman he was referring. He threw Elena forward, and she landed face down in front of the crowd.

"Please! A trial! That's all I ask!" Her voice was shrill now, higher-pitched with desperation. A helpless feeling had consumed her and threatened to cloud her mind. She had not noticed that the crowd had paused in murmur to consider her plea. Her lungs heaved, trying to catch up with herself as her throat tightened. Her mind raced with short choppy thoughts.

I can't breathe. I'm going to die. They are all going to kill me. I can't do this.

One man finally broke the silence. "We owe it to her father, who died at the hands of this witch's curse, to make sure she suffers. He was a good man who saw the good in everyone, much to his downfall. No true daughter of his would reduce herself so pathetically. This... this changeling, this *witch*, will stand to serve as a warning in the middle of our town to anyone who dares think about following down her dark paths. She will be left to know death looms over her, and she cannot escape it. Then let it be said that we are nothing if not merciful for granting her wish of trial while the people of the town seek a fitting punishment for such sorcery," he announced.

People around him nodded in agreement, but some murmured protests that killing her now would be the right choice of action. Elena hardly felt the relief, but she lowered her forehead to the dirt and closed her eyes in a silent thank you to the gods above.

E lena was tied to a metal pole in the center of town a short time after. The villagers took a post for tying horses and hammered it into the ground. They tied her hands behind it and tied her waist tightly to the post. She would not be able to try and make a run for it, but even if she could, she knew she would never make it out of the town alive. Her mind raced constantly, trying to think of some kind of solution to get herself out of this mess.

The first night was horrible. Crowds of people had gathered to look upon her, casting their judgmental stares. She made eye contact with as many of them as possible, as if she could stare into their souls. She spent the entire night and the next day begging, pleading, and screaming for any of them to simply just listen. She lied, telling them that she didn't know if her family were witches, but she certainly was not. The lie felt horrible and thick on her tongue, so she spoke it as little as possible. She begged and cried for them to see her and recognize her as their neighbor and friend.

Some people frowned, and for a moment, Elena thought that she might be making progress. If she could convince one person, maybe they could say something. They could convince the next person. Each time though, whoever was assigned to guard her actively worked against her. He or she would tell people about the man from the river who had seen her swim like a fish. Elena remembered being a piss-poor fish, but of course, she still tried to deny swimming in general. They would tell the townsfolk about how her mother attacked them or how her grandmother's gardens had poisonous flowers in them when they had sifted through the remnants of the house and found her garden out back. Suddenly, her grandmother's pale, quiet posture before being consumed by flames seemed to make much more sense. Elena couldn't explain the poisons to the villagers but hoped the genuine shock on her face conveyed that she truly knew nothing about it.

Of course, it did not work.

The second night was far worse than the first. Elena's body ached from being tied and unable to move, and she was starting to watch the sun's position in the sky to try and reason how much time she had left. Her throat was raw and dry from all of her screaming, and she had not eaten or drunk water since the morning before when her mother had baked bread. The sun had set far beyond the mountains, and the moon was now full and bright in the sky when Elena heard people approaching.

As she lifted her head, relief washed over her ever so slightly. A small group of women had made their way toward her. Elena recognized them as some of her schoolmates, neighbors, and even nannies. A faint smile curled on her lips, and she felt like weeping at seeing them, familiar and looking around as if they were worried about being seen talking to her. It made Elena think that maybe she did have people who believed her after all.

"Oh, thank goodness. I am so happy to see all of you." A tense moment of silence passed, and Elena felt a sudden unease turn in her stomach.

"Is it true? Are you a witch, Elena?" a young girl named Mara asked. Elena had gone to classes with her.

"No! Gods, no! I have been trying to tell them this is all some kind of big mistake. They won't listen to me. They said they would offer a trial, but they aren't really. They have already made their decision on my fate," she said quickly, rambling a bit. She saw the uncertain looks on the girls' faces and knew she was losing them, so she kept talking. "It's me! You all know me! I would never hurt anyone, and I have never done something like what they are accusing me of."

The silence remained, and only then did Elena realize that the women were holding a pot with oven mitts, and she could smell something slightly bitter. Elena's first reaction was to wonder if these kind women had brought her food to show mercy to her, but as she saw the way that they scowled and looked at her with disdain, she began to feel visceral fear. She shifted a bit, and her heart began racing. Something was not right.

The women moved suddenly, and Elena found herself flinching away from them. Two came over and stood at the side, and one of them forced her head back. Elena panicked and began screaming, but of course, no one would come to her rescue. The man who was guarding her turned his back to them. Then Elena smelled the hot vinegar. Her chest rose and fell quickly as the woman holding her face forced her to look up.

The smell of vinegar was eye-watering, and Elena blinked the tears away. She stopped trying to figure out what was happening, stopped watching the women move quickly around her, and turned her eyes to the sky. She looked at the thousands of stars that the thick black blanket of the night sky held and tried to focus on every single one of them. She saw the moon and how bright it was, even with the smoky air. She looked at the stars and inhaled sharply, taking in how beautiful it was.

"Witches can't have a third eye if we blind the two," one of them sneered. Elena did not know who spoke and never would.

Suddenly, one of them scooped a ladle full of the boiling hot vinegar and poured it over Elena's eyes. Elena shrieked louder than she ever had, her lungs aching with the force of it. Her throat felt like it ripped open, and she could taste the coppery taste of blood on her tongue. She tried to thrash her head away, but they held her down tighter. Their nails dug into her skin and pulled at her hair roughly to keep her head back. One of them pried her eyes open when she tried to squeeze them shut. The pain was unbearable, slow ladles of hot burning vinegar being poured over her eyes again and again.

"Please... no more!" Elena pleaded with them. "Please! I'll do anything. Just stop!" She had sobbed and wailed, her pleas going unanswered before the pain became too much to bear, and she fell unconscious.

When she woke up, Elena was horrified to realize that she could no longer see. She rubbed her eyes against the fabric of her dress on her shoulder to make sure nothing was covering her eyes. The action caused her to recoil and wince in pain. Nothingness engulfed her, sending her spiraling into a suffocating void. She had no idea how long her torment had lasted. She had no idea when they had decided that Elena had finally had enough. Her eyes ached and burned, and she had the terrible urge to want to rub or itch them, but she could do nothing of the sort with the way her hands were bound. A scream rose from her raw throat once more, pure hatred and agony coursing through her.

The worst part for Elena was not knowing how much time she had left. She could no longer watch the sun and keep track of them. She could no longer look in the faces of people from her village, begging them to reconsider. Sinking into hopelessness, she slumped against the post, resigned and ready for death. At that moment, she had considered confessing if it would end things faster. But three days was not long to wait, and she would not break her last promise to her mother by telling the townsfolk that she was a witch. They would not get the satisfaction of knowing they were justified in killing her. She thought about how useless it was to be a witch if she still would die in the end. What good could magic bring if it always ended like this in the stories?

Then came the memories. With a lack of sight, Elena was forced to imagine things in her silence. She could not stare at something and study the texture of it like she once might have done to distract herself from thoughts that loomed too close to things she did not want to think about. Instead, her mind plunged her forward through the void as she relived the last moments of her grandmother's and mother's lives. She thought about the sound that her mother made when she died. She thought of the way her grandmother smelled when she burned. Elena cried harder until no tears would come, and then she sank into her misery. If there was a hell, Elena was sure that it was this.

CHAPTER SIX

DUALITY

Herrick sat alone at the kitchen table, listening to the muffled voices of his parents talking in the other room. Neither one of them had ever been as quiet as they thought that they were, but Herrick would never tell. More often than not, he found himself listening to people, gathering information from those who did not assume he could hear them. He listened more to those who spilled their secrets to him, knowing that he would never tell. Information, to him, was more valuable than any currency. So he gathered it on everyone and everything he could, and this would be no different.

There had been a coven of witches in their small little village, it seemed, and their attempts to eliminate the coven had resulted in the death of two, but they were hesitating on the third. He had heard his father whisper to his mother before about how some had even considered simply banishing her from the village and hoping that she succumbed to the elements. His father had led the group who advocated against this, though, arguing that to let her live would be risking her vengeance later on. The sacred teachings were clear; magic was the disease, and mankind was meant to eradicate it.

His father spoke to his mother in the room, giving her the update on the last town meeting. He knew that a decision had finally been made about the witch tied to the post in the middle of town, and Herrick could feel the anxiousness of the town, brimming to know how to rid themselves of her. Herrick was of the opinion that they should just stab her through the heart and then burn the body—offering a quick death to those who felt she deserved mercy and satisfying the need to see her truly die to ensure the prosperity of their village. Herrick could not immediately tell if the news had been good or bad when his father came home, and even now, as he listened to the muffled voices and tried to decode them, he could not tell which direction the meeting had gone.

Finally, the door creaked open, and his father walked out from the bedroom, perhaps a little surprised to see Herrick still awake and sitting at the kitchen table. Herrick could not allow himself to be more patient, though. He needed answers.

"Well? What did they decide?" he blurted out, rising from the table as his eyes lit up with fervency. "Tell me they did not declare leniency on that... that *witch*," he seethed, unable to think of an insult past her true nature.

His father chuckled, regaining his composure from the slight startle at seeing his son waiting for him as he walked over to the kitchen table. He pulled out a chair for himself and motioned for Herrick to sit, which he reluctantly obliged.

"They did not decide on leniency."

Herrick's shoulders relaxed ever so slightly, but he felt as though that was not the end of it. If it had been that simple, his father would not have felt the need to explain things privately to his mother. Herrick was now a man, though, and it was time for men to talk honestly amongst each other. So, he did what he did best and sat silently in waiting, listening for what came next.

"It has been decided that two men will walk the witch deep into the Northern woods before killing and disposing of the body. The witch is weak, blind, and too new to its craft to pose any real threat currently. Even so, there will still be two men so that one may serve as a witness and so that the men can keep each other from falling prey to the witch's tongue. We simply cannot risk another fire. As it stands, the fires from its damned house nearly blew to the neighbors' roof when the winds picked up—no doubt as a final act of vengeance."

Herrick frowned. "But the *Northern* forest? Isn't that where magic is said to reside and flow freely? Is that not a risk of making her stronger?"

His father leaned into the chair, stretching as he folded his arms behind his head and sighed. "Some people say it is to keep its soul from escaping somehow and coming back since the forest likes to keep things. Others say it will be good to kill a magical thing in a magical forest so as not to taint the land anymore and serve as a warning to any other magical being. This abomination had been living amongst us in secret for its entire life. My friend lost his life because he had not known better. They are sneaky and conniving things, but while they speak of nice things to your face, they are surreptitiously pulling the strings to stab you in the back. The Northern forest is the best place for the death to occur."

His father paused, looking at Herrick with eyes that spoke of something underlying the information that he had just told him. Herrick took a moment, searching his eyes before a new realization crawled into his mind like a spider.

"Two men... you and who else?"

Herrick's father chuckled a bit and smirked, letting Herrick know that he had done well. "Too clever for your own good you are. It will be Goddard and I."

"Why does it have to be you?

His father's smile disappeared as he lowered his hands to place his palms flat on the table, staring at his son with a new intensity. He spoke slowly, his voice deep and severe. "It is an honor to go and deliver us from this evil, my boy. I volunteered for it, but even if I had been told, I would have done it proudly. Do you not know your teachings? Have we not taught you the ways of the true gods?"

Herrick felt the heat in the room, unable to look away from his father's eyes as something akin to disappointment radiated from him, and Herrick knew he had asked the wrong question. His heart began to pick up in speed instantly, and his tongue felt dry. Then he did what he despised others doing and began to fumble, needing approval. "I just—"

"Hush," his father said and sighed with exasperation. Herrick snapped his jaw shut, kicking himself and yet struggling not to try again before his father continued.

"Do you know why we must eradicate this disease that has plagued us?"

Herrick nodded, not trusting himself to speak, but as his father stared at him in waiting, he took a deep breath. "The old gods were said to encourage chaos amongst humans, planting the seeds of destruction and allowing us to sow the results. They encouraged magic, preaching that anyone could have a fraction of their power. They created creatures to awe people and distract them from the truth of their nature. They claimed that magic was everywhere in the world and that anyone could dip their toes into it. They hoped that we would get drunk off of the feeling.

"Then the prophets of the new gods came—the *true* gods—and explained the truth behind their deception. They explained how the blood of magic users had become tainted, condemning the user to damnation and how no being could ever truly harness the power of the gods without causing destruction to everything that they touched. They explained that magic had become a disease and that the new gods were the only ones who could ever hold such power. By not worshiping and idolizing them, mankind had become complacent to the evil that had begun to root itself in our world."

Herrick stopped, thinking that was enough of the story, but his father began speaking, continuing the history of their religious teachings.

"Yes, and the true gods blessed us with the knowledge, removing the blindfold from our eyes. They touched the souls of the clean and told them that they could save themselves and their loved ones still. Magic users... they are nothing but invasive weeds for the crop. The new gods gave us the fortitude in our minds needed to remember the truth. They could have eliminated all of the evil in the world, but then what will mankind have learned? We would be doomed to repeat our history. So they equipped us and gave us the tools needed, and we are to walk in their path, cleansing the world of impurities. Magic is synonymous with corruption; committing heresy by feigning the power of gods for their own ego."

Herrick nodded in bashful agreement, and his father gave him a stern look, passionately and quietly speaking now. "To be one of the ones to cleanse the world of their evil, and to be the one who makes the disease that much smaller, is an honor. What better way to prove your worth to the gods? Do you wish that I ought not take this chance just to live a slightly more comfortable life?"

"No, sir. I did not mean it like that."

"There will always be risk when there are high rewards, my boy. But this witch? It is nothing. It is pathetic and a mockery even to its own kind. To be frank, its death will be nothing more than a detour from my daily routine. And Goddard is a good man. With the two of us, it will be fine, so you needn't worry."

Feeling the tension drain from the room, Herrick allowed himself a small smile. His father was brave and passionate, all things Herrick aspired to be. The way his father spoke made him truly believe that he should fear no evil. Whatever hubris these witches had could not hold a candle to radiant truth. How foolish could they be to think that they could hold a fraction of the power of the gods? They were nothing more than disgusting imposters meant to sway good men to indulge in their own destruction. They were heathens.

In truth, Herrick was not too much older than the witch. In fact, there had been a time when he considered asking for her hand in marriage. She was not particularly pretty to him—too many freckles littering her plain face, and eyes that always looked like they were in contemplation of something—but her father was a skilled hunter. He was almost as good as his own father, and those genes could have proven to provide strong children. Besides, there were not many eligible women in the village. However, before he could ever truly consider her, she had lost her father. She had *killed* her father, most likely. So Herrick did what he did best, and he waited. He listened to the whispers. The gods had rewarded his patience in looking for a wife by sparing him a witch's wrath.

Now? Now Herrick relished knowing her death crept closer. He had been the guard for the witch on the night the women in the village conspired to take her eyes. One woman had even asked for his approval. He considered the punishment and saw it fitting, so he allowed it but gave them some tips to ensure Elena was truly blinded. Then he simply sat back and watched them take back their dignity as true pure women. Now he would get the privilege of knowing his own father would be the one to wipe her existence away like the stain she was.

"She is just an extension of evil, and it is our duty to cure the world of her plague. I understand the honor behind the choice," Herrick concluded.

His father nodded and smiled again in approval which was a relief Herrick did not know he had badly needed.

"You're right about almost everything," he said.

"Almost?"

He nodded again solemnly and leaned back in his chair once more. "Don't call it a 'her.' That is a creature with hell in its veins and nothing more. An impostor. An *it*, at best."

Herrick did not know why but this idea made his grin widen ever so slightly. "Well, then *it* doesn't stand a chance."

"You're damn right about that."

CHAPTER SEVEN

A GRAVE SITUATION

"**G**et up."

Elena stirred, unaware of when she had fallen asleep or for how long. Time crawled by, and what was supposed to have only been three days could very well have been a week for all she had known. She woke up to the same sensation of not being able to see anything—no total darkness, no shapes, or bright white light, but simply *nothing*. She had hoped that it might be a temporary injury, but as time went on, Elena began to feel the very real dread that she might indeed be permanently impaired for the rest of her short life.

The irony of it all was when the girls from her village, former friends of hers, had done this to her. They talked about blinding her so that she might not be able to access her "third eye". The third eye was common in myths about witches, more of a symbolic thing rather than another eyeball placed somewhere on the body. The third eye was supposed to help witches delve deep into their intuition and enlighten them to become more powerful. Elena had never thought much of that part of the myths, but ever since she had been blinded, she could not deny that her sense of the world seemed to become a little more crisp inside of her mind.

Her sense of the world did not come to her like it used to. She could not tell what things were or where she was. However, her sense of simply knowing came to her much stronger. All of her intrinsic feelings of certainty that she could not explain felt nearly overwhelming. It felt *powerful*. This, unfortunately, also included the knowing feeling that if she did not change something quickly, she would be killed.

"Get up!" the voice shouted again, and Elena remembered sluggishly that someone or something had woken her up. She lifted her head just in time to feel someone's boot slam into her rib cage. She did not cry out, not even having the energy for that anymore, and simply took a shuddering breath as she lifted her head and tried to blink out of habit.

"I think we may have finally found a punishment deserving of a heathen like yourself," he said, his voice rather mocking.

Elena frowned a bit and spoke for the first time since she had been blinded. "I'm not a witch," she said almost automatically, realizing how raw her voice sounded even to her. The words earned her another sharp kick to the ribs and Elena swore, feeling her ribs crack with a terrifying ache that made it hard to breathe for a few moments.

Her swears seemed to have appeased the man as he chuckled a bit. Elena wondered if a crowd was watching her or if they were alone. She wondered which man of the village was looming over her and torturing her. She had never been good at discerning voices, but she was determined to memorize his. If there was a hell, she would make sure that when his time was up, she would be the one to personally drag his soul down.

"You are to be taken into the Northern Forest this evening to be burned. Your soul will be forfeit to the horrors there," he said, sounding utterly proud of the decision.

Something inside Elena snapped to attention, and she felt her heart restart which must have looked like anxiety or fear to the man. He didn't know it was hope. She fought the trudging way that her mind tried to process the information and knew she could not show them hope in her eyes. She frowned deeply and shook her head.

"No, no, please! It is haunted there!" Her voice scraped against her throat as she screamed. She tried to widen her eyes to look horrified as best as she could and pulled weakly against the ropes that held her there, wincing from the sudden sharp, stabbing pain in her ribs again.

"It is a good thing you will be a ghost soon too. You should fit right in." His footsteps receded, but Elena did not dare to relax or show any signs of relief. She pretended to fret over the news, occasionally whimpering until she eventually fell into silence, taking care not to let her face reveal something by accident. She embraced the horrifying memories for once, knowing that they would be impossible to smile through until she was shaking against the post with silent tears. The memories still crushed her, but this time she focused on the smaller details, like her mother baring her teeth or her grandmother taking her death into her own hands. She thought of those details, and as painful as they were, she tried her hardest to channel the same strength it took for them to do these things. Elena would face whatever came next with her head held high, just as they did.

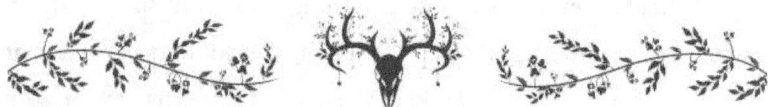

A short time after, the ropes around Elena's waist were cut without much of a warning. They cut the binding on her wrists next and she flexed her hands carefully, nursing the ache in her joints before she was grabbed and shoved to her feet. Her legs shook beneath her weight, stiff from disuse and weak from lack of energy. They grabbed her wrists, shoving them behind her back again and binding her. They tied the ropes so hard that they burned, and for a moment, Elena could barely feel her fingertips. She subtly adjusted her hands despite the pain and felt the blood rush back into her fingers, much to her relief.

They shoved her forward and Elena walked barefoot through the town slowly, dirt caking the soles of her feet as pebbles occasionally bit into her flesh. She listened to the murmurs of people as she passed through the crowds that had gathered to see her off. Fingernails swiped at her arms and face as she passed, causing her to flinch as she was unable to shield herself from them. Some threw things at her that she barely managed not to trip over, but she kept pushing herself forward. She heard the mix of familiar and unfamiliar voices blend together as they shouted things at her, and she gritted her teeth.

"Demon! Back to hell with you!"

"Burn the heathen out!"

"Save our families! Cast her away!"

Elena felt like she was walking out of a nightmare as the surrealness of it finally settled into her bones. These were people who she had grown up with and who she had loved and cared for. These were people whom she had laughed with and wished great things for. Now, they acted as if she had never met them before. They hissed and spat at her. They killed her family, and for what? As far as they knew, they believed one man who was ready to drown her mother—who was certainly not a witch—just because she refused to remarry after her loving husband had died. Because she refused to send her daughter away and force her to readjust to even more changes. Because they were slightly too different for their liking; too independent.

Elena was busy trying to look scared—which was not hard since she truly had no plan and still did not know what would happen—or else she would have scowled at them. Or she might have cursed them, pretending to be the witch from their stories so that they would live for a day in fear that they had angered the wrong witch. But that would mean revealing she was a witch. It may also mean they might burn her in front of the townsfolk just to prove a point, and at least by them taking her to the forest, she had a chance.

Eventually, their leers and taunts faded away, replaced by the slow swaying of leaves and creaking of ancient wood as the two men and Elena approached the Northern forest. It was known to be unforgiving to those who disturbed it, according to the legends that terrified her village. She wondered now if her hope might have been misplaced when she found out that they were taking her here. Even if she had managed to escape, she could sense something in the air that felt off to her. There was a tension throughout the whole forest as though it had sensed them entering and now waited to deliver its judgment. She felt eyes watching her and knew it was not the two men who guided her. Gooseflesh crept over her pale skin at the sensation and she held her breath as they walked and as they tormented her, seemingly unaware of the presence in these woods.

Elena stayed silent, listening to the men's hushed conversation as they walked her deeper into the forest. Eventually, she was able to piece together some information about why they had chosen this place for her death. Not only would her soul be trapped by the forest according to their superstitions, but apparently, when the men had tried to set her house on fire, it had nearly spread to the neighboring houses and had caused quite the uproar in town as people said that the witch spirits' were trying to exact their revenge. Elena wanted to snort when she heard this, wishing it were true but also knowing that the winds of the rainy season had been blowing through their village for the last week, and that was far more likely.

Elena could not see the sky, but she could tell that it had darkened early with clouds tonight due to the smell of rain in the wind that blew through the leaves. She listened as the bark of the trees creaked, remaining firmly rooted despite nature's feeble attempts to sway it. She also listened to the birds as they fluttered to their nests that were hidden amongst the branches, and the crickets began to chirp with the evening sun. *It would have been a lovely evening had it not been for the unfortunate circumstance of my death*, she thought to herself.

In the distance, a hollow scream echoed, sounding eerily familiar to the noise her mother had made as she had charged the men who dared to enter their home. Elena stopped dead in her tracks, her heart beginning to race. *Was that her?* She moved her head around as if she was looking, trying to gauge where the sound came from despite not being able to see. She knew deep down that it was not her mother, but her heart raced anyways with the childish hope. Somewhere distantly in her mind, she knew that the lack of food and the pain were beginning to affect her mind, but it didn't stop her from hoping.

One of the men grabbed her hair roughly and shoved his face close to hers.

"It is a fox, you stupid witch. If you do not keep walking, we will just leave you here and watch them eat you alive," the man she recognized as Poe spat angrily, the faint scent of cheap whiskey and burnt bacon on his lips on his breath causing her to grimace. That action alone had nearly instantly pulled her back to the reality of the situation. She knew two things for certain again; her mother was gone, and this man needed to bathe.

Elena scrunched up her nose and tensed her shoulders to try and move away from the stench of his breath. "Surely being eaten alive by a fox is a better punishment than whatever you fools have planned," she said in a quick and sharp tone that surprised even herself.

She could not see the dumbfounded man's eyes widen nor his face turn red in embarrassment at being talked to in this way. Elena could, however, feel the full strength of his fist hitting her jaw, knocking her to the ground. He kicked his boots into her ribs, causing a sharp pain to radiate throughout her entire body. She gasped but did not scream, and this only angered him further.

He prowled over to her, clenching his jaw as he stood over her frail form sprawled on the forest floor. He paused for a moment and she wondered foolishly if maybe he truly had decided to leave her for the foxes to eat. She hoped he did. She hoped as desperately as one could hope.

She held her breath in anticipation. Once Poe had stopped staring at her, making a decision, he took another step towards her, lifting to put his foot onto her throat. A sharp gasp sucked air into her lungs as he eased the weight of his body down on her neck. Kicking and arching her back, she desperately attempted to wiggle her body out from underneath him before he could crush her windpipe. She could not breathe, and her face began to turn deep shades of red and then purple before the other man shoved him off of her.

Elena gasped for air that burned her lungs as she tried to inhale as much as her body would allow. This was not an act of mercy, she knew this, but his next words only confirmed it for her. "If they find out you killed her, they will think that her magic infected you, and you will be next. Or her spirit will latch onto you and follow us back to the village," he reminded him. Poe grunted but conceded, turning away for just a brief moment to try and cool down.

She tried to catch her breath as best as she could and then gritted her teeth. Elena awkwardly pushed herself to her feet, hands still tied behind her back, and felt disoriented from the foreign environment. She tried moving away from their voices, a desperate attempt to flee her captors while avoiding unseen obstacles. They noticed her immediately, and she did not get more than a few feet before one of them tackled her face-first into the ground this time. Elena could tell it was not Poe as this man did not weigh nearly as much as him. He grabbed a fist full of her hair and ripped her head back so he exposed her neck.

A wry laugh left his lips as he pushed her face into the dirt. She inhaled the wet soil and squeezed her eyes shut tightly. "You can't run away from us. You know that, little girl," he scowled into her ear.

"Am I a girl now or a witch?" she spat, her voice raspy from being choked and inhaling the soil. Not giving him a chance to answer, she threw her head back as soon as he had let go of her hair, smashing into his nose and breaking it. She tried to crawl away, wiggling along the earth like a worm of the forest.

The man whose nose she had broken had cried out in pain, but Elena did not get far. Suddenly a shot from a gun— sounding eerily similar to the kind that had killed her mother—echoed throughout the entire forest, causing birds to wake, screeching and flying from their nests. Elena froze as she felt the earth beside her change, and she knew that the shot had come extremely close to hitting her face. She thought of her mother, gurgling as she choked on her blood with her body contorted on the ground.

"I have had just about enough of this. We are far enough into the woods. She dies here," Poe said, his voice shaking with anger. There was no protest from the other man. Elena closed her eyes, preparing for another sound of a shot that would echo the last moments in her body throughout the forest, but it did not come. Instead, something solid fell to the ground in front of her with a dull *thud*.

"Dig," the man growled, his voice deep and low. The fear and superstition of witches and this forest seemed to slip away entirely, replaced with annoyance. Elena had demonstrated more fight in her than he assumed she had left, but his patience had clearly worn thin as his breath rasped with exasperation in short, shallow pants.

Elena kept her face near the ground, terrified to move. "D-Dig?" she stammered innocently, not quite understanding the new task laid before her.

Poe kicked her again in the hip, and the other man untied her hands with a knife, holding it tightly in his fists in case she tried to run again. The knife sawed into her hands, leaving them bleeding in its wake as she shakily tried to breathe through the pain. He kicked something hard at her, and she shakily reached her hands down, trying to feel out what object she was holding, following the sharp curves of it and trying to imagine its shape. Then it came to her. She was holding the spade of a shovel that had its stick removed, most likely to prevent her from using it as a weapon.

"Dig your grave," the man hissed as if she should have known that this was coming. "If you try to run, then I will shoot you in your leg, so you bleed out much slower than your harlot mother," he spat.

Anger rose in her as her hands gripped the shovel spade tighter after hearing him call her mother such a horrible name, finally remembering where she recognized his voice from; he had been one of the men who failed to court her mother. He had screamed the same obscenity to her while in their kitchen before he stormed out.

Slowly, her grip on the spade eased. Her chest rose and fell, breathing becoming a chore. She was weak, and she didn't think that she had any more fight left in her. Nor could her legs carry her any further. This was it, and Elena had no more strength in her to try and fight them.

Her mother had told her to be brave, but Elena felt the furthest thing from it. She did not feel like a fighter. Elena was not her mother or her grandmother, and she felt much weaker for that. She thought about how fierce the women in her life had been, even down to the bitter end. She thought about her petite mother desperately trying to attack the men who easily outnumbered her, just to try and give Elena more of a chance. She thought about how that chance had been wasted, and her mother had died in vain because here she was, about to dig her own grave.

The hopelessness of it all overwhelmed her. As a final blow to their memory, Elena began to cry softly, the tears burning her eyes like the vinegar that stole her sight. She cried because her mother and grandmother had been killed, and she was not strong enough to honor them with 'teeth and claws.' The only thing that she had left were her tears, and she wanted to be held by them again while they told her that she was merely having a bad dream. She wanted her mother to soothe her hair and sing softly to her.

Elena clenched her teeth and bitterly began to thrust the shovel into the earth, scraping into it. Thunder rolled, bellowing a deep echo throughout the entire forest and valley, and the wind seemed to shake a little more vigorously at that moment. The rusted and jagged edges of the spade tore at the small gash on her hands as she gripped it. She yelped at the sudden searing pain, and the forest quieted beneath her bleeding hands. Panting softly to regain her breath, she gripped the spade tighter and forced herself to continue, ready to end this quicker. Each movement tore flesh away from her palms, making the wound deeper as the blood made her hands slick. A low, shaky groan rumbled through her chest with the next wave of thunder, and Elena could not stop the tears from turning into soft sobs.

After a few minutes, rain began to pour. It came as just a few drops at first against her skin, but then it came down in sheets. The rain made it harder for Elena to dig—the ground turning to mush and filling her small amounts of progress with water—but she did not care. She dug hard, any final thoughts of escaping slipping from her mind. She sobbed into the earth, drowned out by the rain around her. Her body was shaking as she inhaled deeply, a sharp pain suddenly radiating from her ribs.

She paused to catch her breath from the pain before opening her eyes out of habit, remembering once again the lullaby her mother and father used to sing to her. Softly at first, she began to sing to the earth beneath her hands. As she sang, her voice found itself once again, and she began to sing the familiar lullaby once again.

"Down deep in the forest
The crickets sing their haunting chorus
Darling sing your sweet lullaby
And know that I will protect you tonight.
Here may you never truly be alone,
The forest life is felt through your bones,
Sing sweet melody;
I love you, and you love me
Hear my call through the trees,
Just simply say:
Guardian, protect me, please."

"See, I told you all witches had lost their minds. No sane person acts like this," one of them murmured, though Elena could not discern who over the sound of the rain pelting against her now.

"Hush, I don't trust this. The forest is too quiet..." he trailed off, lowering his voice. Elena stopped trying to listen anyway.

The blood from her hands gradually mixed with the mud beneath her as she continued to sing. She whispered to the earth under the cover of rain so that the men could not hear her over the sound of their own voices. "I am so sorry to disturb this forest with my death. Please forgive me for causing such a mess here," she whispered, knowing that the forest would not respond to her, but if these men thought this forest was truly unforgiving to anyone who had disturbed it, then she wanted to at least make it known that this was not her intention. Her family had always respected this forest, and they had never quite been afraid of it before, but today, she was terrified. She was resigned to letting the terror consume her. It was almost over now.

She continued to dig and sing the haunting melody of her parents until her grave was now a shallow couple of feet deep—misshapen most likely, but enough for her to lay in. The sun had sunk into the horizon, and the moon lifted her figure to greet the earth by the time they had decided she was finished.

"Poe, the trees. I am telling you, my Nana used to tell me stories of them trees coming to life. Don't they look a little too still for how much rain is pouring? Something ain't right. Let's finish this."

"Alright, that is enough," Poe agreed, casting a weary glance around at their surroundings as his finger rested over the trigger of his shotgun.

Elena stopped digging into the earth and crawled into the grave as if it were a warm and welcoming bed. She had run out of tears now, feeling dizzy and drained of energy. A dark part of her was happy that she could finally rest now and be with her family once more.

Elena sat inside of her shallow grave and dropped the shovel spade, folding her muddied hands onto the skirt of her once white and red dress. Her fingers traced over the embroidery on them as her bottom lip quivered. Her mother had made this dress, red intricate stitching of traditional designs on the white part of her underskirt that brought out the red in the top layer. It made her happy to know that this was the dress that she would die in, even if she could never see it again. She closed her blind eyes slowly, remembering small glimpses of her family's smiles and the stars she saw on the night she lost her vision. A quote her grandmother had once murmured in prayer slithers its way into her mind now:

May the witches whose lives end in flames burn brightly amongst the stars.

Elena waited for the sound of the gun and wished it was not so loud, so it would not disturb the poor animals that lived in the forest more than her screaming already had. She held her breath and flinched as an equally loud noise came. She pushed her back against the edge of her grave in fear and instinct.

This was not a gunshot but sounded as if one of the tall trees looming above them had snapped completely in half, but she did not feel anything fall. Instead, she heard one of the men scream and the sound of something being dragged far away from her. There was another sound, this one a sickening crunch followed by a scream cut far too short. Everything was happening quickly, and Elena's sluggish mind was barely able to process the new turn of events.

She opened her eyes, her heart pounding in her ears, as she wondered what was happening. She wondered why the men were screaming, as it should be her screaming instead. She wondered if perhaps the forest had come alive just as it did in the legends to kill them all for disturbing it. Or maybe some of the wolves or bears of these woods had come and ambushed them. She waited to feel the feeling of teeth piercing her skin, tearing her apart.

"Are you okay?" an unfamiliar male voice whispered, somehow completely clear even through the rain. He had an accent unlike anyone else from their village that was distinctive, and she was sure that she would have remembered him—even if she was terrible at remembering voices. Not to mention that she did not believe that anyone from her village could show enough mercy to utter those words to her.

Elena did not answer, deciding that it must be a hallucination of her mind from all of the blood that she had lost from her hands. However, the voice came again, a little more urgent this time.

"Please tell me that I am not too late," he said, closer to her face now.

"Who are...?" Elena started to say but no longer had the strength to try and understand. The air from her lungs squeezed out, and everything around her went quiet. Her ears were ringing like warning sirens, and she felt overwhelmed with a disorienting sense of vertigo as her body finally gave out. Her small frame collapsed to the ground, and the last thing that she felt was something catch her before she fell into unconsciousness.

PART TWO:
THE COTTAGE

CHAPTER EIGHT

REELING

F og crept in from the North on the night the brave men had walked the witch of Innorin into the woods. Herrick had been waiting along with a few others in the town square, warmed only by the alcohol that burned their throats when the fog rolled in from the forest. The fog was not inherently uncommon in the spring evenings or early mornings in the village. Still, something about the ominous nature of it had immediately sent an uneasy feeling reeling through Herrick's veins. His eyes strained as he watched the treeline, waiting for any sign of the men that did not come.

Once dawn rose over the horizon, the men looked at each other with unspoken dread. What had been set up as a small gathering of booze to celebrate the men's bravery now felt awkward and out of place amongst the square. No one left immediately, waiting for someone else to make the first move. They didn't want to acknowledge the possibility that something had gone awry.

As the smell of fresh bread from the bakery began to waft in the air, two of the men looked at each other with a nod and stood up to leave. Herrick tightened his fingers around the neck of his bottle but did not tear his eyes away from the forest. Eventually, the other men left too. Some might have muttered sympathetic encouragement to Herrick, but he could not hear them over the ringing in his ears. Something was wrong. Where were they?

A younger girl, who Herrick had not bothered to learn the name of yet, was walking by on her way to her to no doubt run errands for her mother when she stopped and noticed him. She frowned as he met her eye, blinking away the dryness of his eyes.

"Is your papa late?" she asked, undoubtedly knowing the excitement that had rocked their village. The fire from the witches' house had barely settled to ash.

Herrick nodded and rose to his feet. There was no point in waiting here and drawing more attention to it. He began to clean up the beer bottles that lay scattered in the dirt, hoping the little girl would go away now. She did not.

"What happens if he doesn't come back?"

He wanted to snap that his father would come back, but he knew better than to bet on uncertainties. He swallowed the words despite his own protest. "Then we find his remains," he said bluntly. There was no need to sugarcoat the truth.

"Will the witch hurt us?"

He paused his collection of bottles and glanced at the little girl. He was tired, bags under his eyes from the long night, but she was as fresh as the morning with a familiar fear in her eyes that he hated himself for recognizing. He took a deep breath, taking a moment to collect his thoughts as he stared down at her small stature. She could not have been more than seven years of age.

"No. I won't let it hurt us."

"But what if she comes back?"

"Then I will kill it myself, but it won't come back. You are safe here, I promise. This village won't let anything happen to you."

Her relief was palpable as she ran to Herrick, throwing her arms around his hips in a hug. "I hope he is just late coming home. My mama said he helped our family last winter when my papa broke his leg by falling on some ice. Surely the gods would help guide him home."He set one of the bottles down and ruffled her hair with a grunt as he feigned being disgruntled by the act of hugging him while she rambled on. Truthfully, however, it felt good to feel appreciated. To know that he would protect their village at all costs, just as his father had taught him. He placed a hand on the girl's shoulder, casting his gaze back to the tree line. He knew what he had to do to put the rest of his village's fears at rest with this wretched witch, but there was a chance to start small—starting with this girl.

"Do you want to hear the story of when I encountered my first witch?" he asked, breaking the silence as he pulled away from her small arms and moved to lean against the pole that their own witch had been recently tied to.

The small girl nodded enthusiastically, and he took a deep breath, recalling the memory as if it had happened just a short time ago.

"Well, I couldn't have been much older than you are now. My father used to take me to the large cities in order to sell off some of the pelts to more wealthy merchants. There was this one time when we arrived in the city and could see everyone on their toes a little more than usual. The entire town seemed to just be buzzin' with some kind of nervous excitement or tension. My father sold the pelts as usual, but we didn't leave right away. Instead, he took me to the middle of town, saying he wanted to show me something important. As a young kiddo myself, that felt like an awfully big responsibility to be privy to something he deemed important.

"Before we even got to the center of that city, we could hear the witch howlin' with anger. It was screaming this and that, cursing the town up and down for what they were doing. The locals there told us it had been pleading for most of the day, but desperation was beginning to set in, and its true nature was revealed. The witch was vile and feral, like a creature that had merely the mask of a plump woman. The eyes were the worst part. The whites had turned nearly bloodshot, buggin' out of their sockets like they were about to pop.

"Not long after that, they set fire to the straw beneath its pyre. The witch's screams turned to shrieks. Its pleas turned to unintelligible babble. The fire licked at its feet, but before its skirts truly caught the flame, the body had gone slack. See, that is the power of those cleansing fires. Of prayers to the new gods to repel the demonic ways of the false gods from the body. The sight was horrifying, honestly, and I felt like I might wretch from the smell of burnt hair and flesh."

The girl scrunched her nose. "Why did your papa make you watch it then?"

"Because it was *important,*" he emphasized. "See, my father explained as we rode back to Innorin. Witches are a disease—a plague, if you will—and if you let it spread, you risk losing everything you love. When old Oro caught the frost a couple of winters ago, and the healer's treatment did not work, did you see his foot? It turned black with decay and rot. He was still very much alive, but if he had waited, his foot would have killed him. So, what did they do?"

"They... chopped it off?"

"They chopped it off. They rid him of the plagued, diseased part of his body so he might continue to live his life. The same is true for witches. It hurts to cut off those diseased things that we might have even been fond of, but it is for the health of the village. If they are allowed to live, they will only spread their wickedness. It is never an overly pleasant process, but the people of that city celebrated once the witch was well and truly reduced to ash because they were free to live. They were free from its sins."

The girl nodded as she seemed to understand, smiling a little wider. "And they all lived happily ever after once the witch was gone?"

Herrick nodded and smiled a bit as she seemed to understand. "Exactly. So, I am going to make sure she is well and truly gone because you and your mama and every other person in this village deserve that happy ending. We will find her body in those woods. And if we don't, then I will find her and bring peace to Innorin once again by running my sword straight through her and setting her to ash—just as we should have done in the first place."

"Promise?"

"You have my word."

CHAPTER NINE

DISORIENTATION

E lena became vaguely aware of small details intermittently, not knowing how much time passed between each morsel of information. Time seemed to be anything but linear, coming in small snippets of information with no beginning or end.

~

Her body felt too heavy to move, and she had the horrifying thought that she had become paralyzed. Unconsciousness overtook her almost immediately after that.

~

Her fingertips slowly traced the small precise stitching of a quilt. *A bed?* She could feel the care that went into each and every stitch and wondered who made it.

~

She inhaled deeply through her nose, and a sharp blinding pain pierced her ribs at the action of expanding her lungs. The smells of dust, mildew, and aging wood filled her nose before the void drowned her once more. She wondered if the afterlife smelled ancient because it was.

~

I'm all that is left of my family, she thought distantly. Something inside of her broke all over again.

~

She was sitting up, her lips parting as warm salty broth slid down her throat. She swallowed and shuddered from the warmth, gooseflesh rising on her arms.

~

A damp rag carefully moved along her arms, and a cool breeze kissed her freshly wet skin.

~

Weight shifting on the bed, *someone sitting next to me?*

~

Her fingers traced the palm of her hand where she had been cut by the spade of the shovel. There was pain there when she touched it, but she found comfort in the sensation feeling real, so she did it again. *Why did the night feel so long ago? Who wrapped my wound?*

~

"You are safe now," a man murmured, the deep timbre of his voice filling the room. *How can I ever be safe again? I am a witch. According to my village, I must be in purgatory or hell, awaiting worse. Regardless, I cannot be safe from myself.*

She thought she might have made a sound similar to a short laugh or a snort before her world faded once more.

~

"I'm not a witch," she murmured quietly, repeating her mantra for her mother's sake. A still silence passed for many heartbeats, and her shoulders slumped, though she was unsure if it was relief or disappointment that motivated the action.

"That's a shame. I rather like witches," a voice remarked as it cut through the silence.

Elena sucked a breath into her lungs and held it there. His voice sounded almost amused or playful but not mocking. She vaguely recognized it from earlier and wondered what accent he had but tried to keep her thoughts centered on the conversation. She did not want it to end so quickly, realizing that it felt nice to have a conversation in which she was not begging or screaming and where the other person was not cursing her existence.

"Don't leave," she managed to croak softly, her heart racing inside of her chest. Her mind felt like a muddied mess, but when he spoke, it became a little more clear.

"I don't plan to. Rest now. You are still plenty weak."

And with the knowledge that he would not leave her, she finally obeyed and let the darkness consume her once more.

CHAPTER TEN

AWAKENING

D mitri sat in a chair on the opposite side of the room from the girl, wondering, not for the first time, exactly what he was doing there. It had been a long time since he had cared for anyone, and even then, he did not remember ever having to nurse someone this far gone back to health. Looking at her now, he marveled that she was alive at all with the condition in which he had found her in.

The night that he had brought her back to this cottage, he had addressed the major wounds and tried to keep her as warm and as dry as he could. The monsoons were upon them now, and she had been soaking wet when he found her. Her skin was cold to the touch, and had he not known better, he would have assumed she was already dead. Hell, she slept like the dead too. As soon as he had done all that he could do for her for the time being, he simply sat in the same chair he resided in now and was left to wait and simmer in his thoughts.

Dmitri pondered the way the forest had shifted as soon as the girl had entered it. He couldn't place what had changed at first, but he could hear the way the trees had held their whispers back, listening for once instead of their normal bristling gossip. Their roots stretched beneath the soil ever so slightly as if readying themselves in preparation for a race. Even he could feel the subtle anticipation of change thick in the air, simply waiting to be seized.

Something pulled him, causing him to wander idly in a certain direction. He was not particularly feeling rushed, but he also knew he would not want to miss whatever seemed to have the forest reacting in such a way. As he had gotten closer, he had heard the screams of frustration and despair of a woman that shook him down to his core. He had stopped dead in his tracks, panic nearly seizing him. He had never particularly cared before if people had managed to find trouble in this forest, but this was different.

Then he felt the magic.

It was a magic so volatile and powerful, reeking of desperation and despair, and he recognized the kind almost immediately. A sour taste filled his mouth at a memory that had collected dust in some forgotten corner of his mind. This was blood magic, one that he was now compelled to obey. However, even if the call of magic had not burned at his feet, he would have still run to her. He couldn't quite place why the pull was so strong, but he would not question the intuition that burned inside of him.

When he had finally found her, he took in the situation quickly. He did not know the details, and he did not need to. What he had seen filled him with a rage so pure and sacrosanct that, frankly, they were lucky she was in the condition she was in, and he was rushing to her aid, or else he might've dragged out their fate just for his own amusement. That was a darker side of himself that was rarely touched upon anymore, but, at that moment, it felt almost unsurpassable. He wanted them to suffer and knew nearly nothing outside of that fact. Nearly. Thankfully, the girl was still his primary focus.

When she had not awoken after that first night, he had panicked. She had fallen unconscious into his arms as he found her more fragile than a newly hatched bird. He was horrified at the thought of breaking her by accident. He took her to the only place he knew of that would be safe and hoped for the best outcome, but her not waking made him dread the possibility that she might not make it through this. It had been so long since he had seen a new creature of magic in this forest and something about this woman awoke a memory inside of him that he thought had long been forgotten.

He waited patiently, feeling the moments tick by as he watched the rise and fall of her chest under the blankets. Most of the time, it was slow and steady. But every now and then, she would breathe a little shakier or more erratic, and in those moments, he felt like his own lungs had ceased to work. He would become more alert, hoping it would pass on its own, which it usually did, before he could allow himself to relax once more.

He noticed that there had been moments when her head lulled to the side or when her fingers crept along the quilts as if she was searching for something with shaky movements. Her eyes never opened, but he found himself watching her with an intense curiosity to see what she would do next. He wished that he could help her more, but the human body was not his specialty. She would have to work to heal herself, and he would have to do what little he knew how to and hope it was enough.

There had even been moments when she had spoken to him or when she had murmured in her sleep, though he doubted that she was lucid for any of them. At one point, he had tried to coax her name out of her, but she had simply replied with the fact that she was not a witch. It had been an interesting response, but as much as it had provoked questions, he had to bite his tongue not to push her progress beyond what she was ready for.

Eventually, she finally groaned a soft low noise, and Dmitri rose to his feet. He stalked cautiously over to her but stopped a few feet away from the bed, not daring to get too close to avoid scaring her. She turned her head to the side, and her eyelashes fluttered open. At first, it was a lazy movement, but then she seemed to gasp awake as if remembering something important. She tried to sit up quickly, and her face instantly twisted with regret, her hand going to her side as she dug her nails into the skin as if to claw out the source of pain. Dmitri grimaced, feeling a pang of sympathy for her.

"You're okay. You're safe," he said again, repeating it like a mantra for her whenever she woke up. He had hoped that she might be able to stay awake longer, and the fact that she was sitting up on her own—even if it was a painful movement—was still a sign of progress that he could not ignore. He made sure to keep his voice calm and slow around her, just as if she was a wounded animal of the forest. Though the forest and its inhabitants at least listened to him, this woman seemed far too stubborn to consider it. He thought he might have rather liked that fire in her if she had not been injured and nearly dying days ago.

She lifted her head quickly to the sound of his voice, her attention drawn away from the pain in her ribs. "Who are you?" she asked, her voice slow and tentative but not quite afraid. Her shoulders were tensed like an animal ready to run or attack at any hint of danger.

He regretted drawing attention to himself now that she was more awake. Speaking had never been a strong quality for him, and he was not used to interacting with people, much less like this.

She turned her head around the room, the action odd and searching. Though, as her eyes seemingly landed on him despite him not making a sound, he understood why. Her eyes were a milky opaque white, the ghost of green irises staring into him with an unfocused glance. His heart sank a little deeper into his stomach. *She is blind. Well, that explains why she did not scream when we first met. That also explains the strange scarring around her eyes.*

"I know you are there. Who are you? And where am I?" she asked again, and Dmitri realized he had been too absorbed in looking into her eyes to answer the question.

He shook his head a bit to pull himself from the trance. "My name is Dmitri. You're—" he paused, seemingly realizing where she was and what it meant that he brought her here. "You're in my home," he said deliberately, tasting each word's truth as he spoke it.

She considered this information for a moment while her fingers slid over the stitching on the quilt, almost as an anxious habit. "Am I dead?" Her voice was so quiet that it was nearly a whisper.

To this, Dmitri laughed. It was a rusty sound, one that he himself had not heard for a long time. Her statement wasn't really funny, and he should be a little more sensitive to her situation. She probably did feel like she had died for a while there, after all. Still, he was merely relieved that she seemed to have come back to her senses enough to at least ask the question. It was a laugh of relief.

She had bristled at hearing his laugh, and he realized that she probably thought that he was laughing *at* her. Her hands tightened over the stitching of the quilt, and her eyes narrowed, her gaze looking past him and to the right a little bit—though it was close enough.

"No, I can't say that you are, thankfully. Does that upset you?"

She paused and looked surprised. She genuinely considered the question before giving her answer. "I suppose that depends. What is going to happen to me?"

"That is up to you. You are welcome to stay here as long as you please, or I could give you safe passage to one of the nearby villages once you are healed enough. I simply ask that you try to get better first before you go running off if you choose the latter," he said calmly. *I would prefer you no longer bleed over my forest,* he thought, though he did not say that part out loud.

"I thought... I dreamt of a creature mistaking me for a sacrifice. Do you not fear the monsters that live in this forest?"

"They aren't so bad when you get to know them," he said easily, as though it was completely normal. When she stayed quiet, frowning at his words, he decided to add, "What is your name?"

Her shoulders tensed, and he could tell that she was debating lying to him. He wondered what she had gone through to make her so distrusting that even giving her name seemed to give her pause. Gradually, however, she forced herself to relax.

"Elena."

His lips curled into a slow smile at the fitting name. He noticed that he was more relaxed than he had suspected to be around her and chalked it up to knowing that she could not actually see him. He decided to check if she had full vision loss by taking the risk of looking like a fool and extended one of his arms out wide, shaking it wildly. She did not move or react, didn't even blink at the movement. Her eyes were still calm and unfocused on him as she waited for him to speak next. He lowered his arm to his side, not quite knowing what to say, so she decided to speak again to fill the silence.

"What happened to the men who were with me?" she asked. Confusion was written across her face as he watched her try to trace her memory back to that night.

Dmitri's smile vanished, and his jaw clenched as he remembered the night clearly. "They can't hurt you anymore." He did not want to elaborate and suddenly wished that she would stop asking questions.

She frowned at his vague and cryptic answer. "What happened?" she asked again. He knew that she deserved answers, but he could not bring himself to give her a detailed account of that night, especially when she had only just begun to speak again.

Dmitri walked over and poured some water from a pitcher into a cup to keep himself busy as he spoke. "I found you. Is that not enough? I heard you, and I came. I saw what they were forcing you to do, what they were planning on doing, and I put a stop to it," he said, forcing his voice to remain calm and even. He walked the glass of water over and nudged the cup against her hand. He waited for her hands to grasp it firmly before he slowly let go of it. "Please, you need rest. We can discuss all of these things, and I promise I will tell you everything you wish to know once you get a little bit better, alright?" He kicked himself for the promise, knowing damn well he wanted to never speak of it at all, so he could not fathom why he had given her a reason to ask him again later.

Elena held the cup tightly in her hands, and he looked at how small she was. Her hands were thin and frail, and he knew she would need real food soon instead of merely broth. She cast her gaze downward, and he wondered how long she had been blind. She acted as if she was still trying to look and search for things.

"Okay," she said softly, her voice smaller as if he had yelled at her. He had almost begun to feel bad before she added, with a stubborn tone, "Later, then."

He scowled at that but did not argue. He had given his word, unfortunately. A slip of the tongue he would be sure to regret later on.

She brought the cup to her face, sniffing it as though she was making sure it did not contain anything nefarious in it. She tested the water with her tongue, ever so cautiously, before she finally brought the cup to her lips. She took a sip, and when she had decided that it was not dangerous, he watched as she began to drink graciously. She emptied the glass quickly, and he took it from her to refill it. However, by the time he walked back over to her, she had nestled her body back deeper under the blankets. He set the cup down beside the bed with a soft clink and then moved to walk away to give her time to rest.

"Thank you," she whispered from her cocoon of blankets.

"Just rest, Elena. I promised I would stay, remember?" he replied, softening his tone in hopes of getting her to relax.

She seemed to remember enough as she nodded and then closed her eyes, drifting off to sleep once more. Dmitri watched her from the corner of his eye out of habit and noticed how quickly her breathing seemed to even back out into slow deep breaths.

What have I gotten us into?

CHAPTER ELEVEN

HEALING

Two more days passed before Elena thought she could finally eat something solid instead of merely broth or small pieces of bread. She was still too weak to do much of anything, but her ribs had begun healing. She simply felt the dull ache if she moved the wrong way or moved too quickly. If she sat up for too long, sometimes it would feel as though her lungs were trying to collapse on her, but it began to simply take shifting positions or waiting out the pain before she could calm down once more. Now that she was beginning to heal, her body was beginning to demand more sustenance—both in terms of nutrition as well as answers.

Her first attempt to gain answers from Dmitri about what happened when he rescued her had been unsuccessful. She did not need her eyes to realize he had clammed up and got frustrated with her stubborn curiosity. So, she insisted her mind quiet the pressing questions until she was stronger. He had given her no reason to fear him yet, but she was not content to simply lay about and wait until that changed, and she was certainly not content to completely ignore the concerns her mind was raising.

One of which was how he managed to live in this forest alone for so long. Elena's village was not the only one surrounding these woods, and each village had its own superstitions surrounding what loomed in the forest. Treacherous uncharted terrain, monsters, malevolent ghosts, rabid beasts—no matter what it was, the consensus was clear about the danger. Even her own father did not dare wander too far. Yet, Dmitri lived in a cabin built seemingly in the middle of the supposed chaos. Where had he come from? Had he always been here, or did he decide to flee here and somehow managed to survive this long? And while she had an idea of what happened to the men who walked her to her fate, it was the details that eluded her as she tried to imagine him taking on the two alone and swiftly.

Despite these questions, which kept her up at night, Elena would much rather let her mind dwell on them rather than let her thoughts wander elsewhere. In the quiet moments, which were frequent and deafening inside this cabin, Elena reflected on what had happened. She often would cry—uncaring of who heard or saw—until her body gave out from the exhaustion of it. Everything and everyone was lost, leaving her completely alone in the world with no purpose or sense of direction.

Then again, there was Dmitri. She knew he cared for her health, though she did not know why and any attempts to dissuade him from doing so were in vain. The questions kept her from completely trusting him, but she found his presence to be comforting when she knew he was there. He had not been the best conversational partner in her time here. More often than not, she could not even hear him moving around or any sign of him truly existing, even when she tried her hardest to listen for those small tell-tale signs. When she had almost been certain that he was missing or that he had left her, she would call his name in a small voice. He would reply as if he was waiting for her to ask, simply saying, "I'm here," as if he knew that was all of the reassurance that she needed to hear before she could relax once more.

The need to know that she was not alone made Elena crave Dmitri's presence, even if she still did not know much about him. She could not explain why she wanted him specifically, though she reasoned it was because of how calm he remained. It was a sharp contrast to the loudness of her mind. He was often stoic and tentative, but he was kind to her. He rubbed salve around her eyes until the pain numbed away. He changed the bandages on her hands and around her ribs. Elena still displayed caution with him, smelling and testing any food or drink that he brought her before she would relax and ingest it. She knew it was silly in a sense because she reasoned that he would not save her just to poison her. Still, she did not think that her friends would blind her or try to burn her alive, and she had been plenty wrong about that.

She wondered how the men had planned to burn her in the rain that night, which led to more and more questions that she still had no answers for. She promised herself that she would get those answers in time somehow. She was not particularly looking forward to reliving that day again and found her mind trying to skirt around the memory when she did try to think of it. However, she needed to know how dangerous Dmitri was and why he had saved her. He had told her she called out to him, but she could remember doing no such thing. She had screamed, sure, but it had been just a sound burning inside of her. There were no names called. She did not even say 'help me'—though she wondered now if she should have tried that sooner.

Dmitri did not seem overjoyed at having company, but he did not seem upset by her presence either. He was simply here, even in the times she could not be sure of his presence. And while he had not yet tried to poison her, she could feel how uneasy he got if their idle conversation ventured too close to those questions. For his part, he would still talk to her in idle conversation and humor her, and she would oblige him by ceasing her barrage of questions to the poor man who was indeed helping her. At least for now.

A part of her wanted to be angry at him though she knew she did not have any reason to be. He may have been secretive over certain things, but she had her own secrets, and she would not like to divulge them either. She was thankful he had not asked her questions about her past. His focus remained solely on her in the present. He would ask occasional questions awkwardly, like if she was comfortable enough or if she needed anything. She didn't, and she found his questions to be kind and not overbearing, which made her more frustrated for not giving her a reason to be frustrated. She did not believe she deserved this kindness. Still, she could not bring herself to truly be angry at him beyond withholding information that involved her. She was primarily angry at herself, and she knew that deep down.

When he had asked if she was willing to try eating real food, she had hesitantly agreed to try, which he was audibly relieved at.

"I can go hunt for some meat. I shouldn't be gone for too long, and there are some herbs and vegetables in the garden on the side of the cottage," he said thoughtfully.

Elena stiffened as he mentioned going out on a hunt. "I don't want you to go out on a hunt on my behalf. Besides, wouldn't you have to be gone for a couple of days at least? What if something happened to me in the meantime? What if something happened to *you*?"

Anxiety churned inside her stomach, and her ribs warned her of pain as she began to breathe a little deeper and quicker. She looked around the room for his voice, wishing she could see him properly. Memories of her father kissing her mother goodbye festered inside of her, and she wanted to shove them away. She didn't want to remember anymore. She did not want it to happen again.

"I would be gone for an hour at most, Elena. Nothing bad will happen to you in that time, I can swear to you. You are safe here. I give you my word."

At this, she paused, and confusion overwrote the panic in her white eyes. "Only an hour?" she whispered.

"Yes, just an hour. These woods are plentiful since no hunters dare to step into them. It truly isn't any trouble."

"What if you get hurt? Animals could still attack you or... or there could be dangerous terrain, and you could get injured." Her hands began to fidget.

"I know these woods like the back of my hand. I know the terrain, and I have lived here for most of my life, but I have never had the animals here attack me. I know your experiences may have been different if your village used to hunt in other forests, but this one is mine. I will be safe. I will come back to you, Elena. You have my word."

The words settled too close to home as she remembered a similar promise, and despite not entirely trusting him, Elena thought that being without him would be entirely worse. "Do you have to?" she asked childishly.

"No, I do not have to. Though I do think it is necessary for you to have some meat if you think you can keep it down. You have barely eaten the broth and bread, and we are almost out of bread. A stew would help you heal," he said.

Elena frowned but considered this for a long moment before she spoke again, sitting up in the bed a little straighter. "What if you don't come back? What will I do? I'm blind and can't exactly navigate an entire forest to civilization."

"You don't even have to consider it because I gave you my word. I will come back to you. No beast, terrain, or force of earth could keep me from fulfilling that promise."

There was a small pause, and then, "One hour?"

"One hour tops."

Elena took a deep breath and nodded, conceding to him. She could nearly feel the weight of his promise stir inside of her chest. She knew he could not prevent accidents but something about the way he had said it made her almost think that, for a moment, he could. Slowly her body sank back into the blankets, and she pulled them up just barely past her lips.

"If you break your promise, I am going to curse your spirit," she mumbled begrudgingly.

Dmitri chuckled softly. "And here I thought you weren't a witch," he mused as he walked away from her toward the door.

"I've heard plenty of religious people curse the dead," she said easily, though she did not outright deny it this time.

"Isn't that the truth." Then Dmitri was gone, and the door clicked shut quietly, leaving Elena alone with her thoughts for the first time since she had woken up.

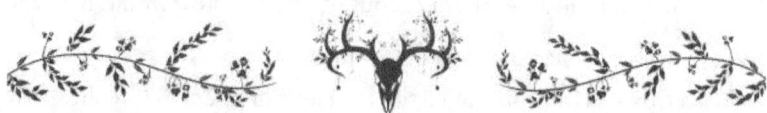

D mitri stepped out of the cottage and walked amongst the overgrown wildflowers of the field to the edge of the forest. As soon as he stepped into the forest once more, he could feel the way it welcomed him, unusually alive and vibrant. He raised an eyebrow at this reaction, resisting the urge to glance back over his shoulder to the cottage where Elena resided. *Was this because of her?* It was as if the forest was excited about her. More so, it was as though the forest was excited that he was helping her.

"She is healing," he said to no one and everyone at the same time. A breeze bristled past him, warm for the spring, as it ran along his cheek. The trees seemed to lean ever so slightly closer as if wanting more of an explanation, but he scowled at them. *Gossipy little things.*

He took a deep breath and began to walk deeper into the woods. His connection to the forest once again strengthened. He closed his eyes and inhaled as he took in the flooding sensation of information as the forest filled him in on what he had missed. Nothing exciting truly happened in these woods anymore. He had made sure of it. Besides, too many villages nearby were terrified of these woods to risk entering and causing problems. Though, occasionally, they decided to do something particularly stupid, such as bring a girl here to kill her.

When Dmitri had mentioned going on the hunt, he had seen how her face suddenly changed. He knew he needed to help soothe her before she found herself in a full-blown panic attack, but comforting others had never really been his strong suit. He wondered why this, of all things, was causing her to react this way. If he knew her past, it would be easier to console her, but he could never bring himself to ask those questions. If she had wanted to tell him, she would've. Still, at least she had seemed to calm down once he had promised her his safe return. If only she knew just how much these woods were not a threat to him.

Once he got deeper into the woods, and after he had made sure there had been no other disturbances, he did what he had come here to do. He opened his eyes, running his hands along the bark of one of the trees, admiring the growth of moss on it.

"She needs meat. Her body needs nutrients, and I promised her that I would get back to her quickly," he explained to the air. He did not need to make the request, but having her around him reminded him of something he thought he might be losing sight of.

The forest, hearing his request, answered without hesitation. Within a few minutes, a deer approached him tentatively. As Dmitri looked at the creature, information seeped into his veins as the world began to whisper about what had happened to it. The deer had fallen and had a broken leg that had not quite healed throughout the winter, causing it a permanent limp. It was a surprise that wolves or bears had not already devoured the creature, but it seemed he was volunteering for a quicker and painless death. Once the deer was close enough, it bowed its head to him out of respect and honor.

Dmitri ran his hand along the fur of the animal. "Thank you," he said softly and closed his eyes. The body of the deer fell to Dmitri's feet with a soft thump, and he opened his eyes. He felt the spirit of the animal run through him and pass on to wherever it returned to after this life, and Dmitri shuddered at the feeling, gooseflesh rising over his skin. He wondered if he would ever get used to that.

He wrapped a rope that he had brought tightly around the antlers of the deer and dragged it back towards the cottage. Once he was right at the edge but still sheltered by trees, he began the process of skinning and gutting the deer. He made quick work of it, setting aside the skins to keep them from going to waste before dicing the meat. He hung some to come back and season to make jerky for her later tonight, knowing no other creatures of the forest would touch his kill, and then put the chunks of meat into a burlap sack.

Once he had finished, he tied off the sack and walked back to the cottage with it. His hands and arms were covered in the deer's blood, but he could clean them later. If she could see him, he thought that she might be terrified by how much blood the animal had produced and how careless he was about letting the blood cover his skin. Blood seldom bothered him, though, and he knew that since she could not see him, cleaning and wasting more time would be unnecessary. His clothes remained nearly pristine throughout it all, as he made sure to make quick cuts and keep his sleeves tightly rolled. All in all, he estimated the work took about forty-five minutes, and he grinned to himself for his punctuality.

He opened the door to the cottage and then abruptly paused. Elena was sitting in the middle of the floor in the living area, right before the door.

"What in the gods are you doing?" he asked, not moving from the doorway. He was too struck with curiosity and a little concern, despite how her face seemed more bashful than troubled.

"I wanted to explore and see if I could walk around on my own." Her voice held equal parts innocence and stubbornness that left him more flustered than he wanted to let on. He was thankful that she could not see the dumbstruck look on his face.

"And have you reached a conclusion?" he managed to ask, arching an eyebrow.

"I have," she said and then paused. Her cheeks were tinted pink, and she bowed her head shyly. "I have concluded that I cannot find my way back to the bed. I am... not skilled in navigation. Less so now that I have no eyes to see with."

He chuckled now, shaking his head as he set the burlap sack down on the floor. "Do you want me to help you, Elena?"

"Yes. Or at least direct me so I can find my way back if you do not wish to."

"Why would I not wish to?"

She looked as if she was about to say something—*admit* some-thing—but she closed her mouth tightly and shrugged softly instead.

"Give me just a moment to wash my hands off, then." Dmitri walked to the kitchen, washing the water over his arms and scrubbing away the blood. He dried himself off and then walked over to her small frame in the middle of the floor.

"Would you like me to help you walk, or would you prefer I carried you?" he asked, not wanting to touch her too much or make assump-tions.

She seemed to hesitate at this. "I can walk, I think. I might just need a little bit of help."

He was thankful for her honesty in admitting that she might need help. Truthfully, he thought she would be better off having him carry her and save her the energy, but he was glad to simply be able to assist. "Alright. I'm going to help you up. Then I will slip an arm around your waist to steady you. You wrap your arm around my torso as well, and we will walk in slow steps," he explained, not wanting to surprise her with any of his movements.

She nodded in response, and he bent down, wrapping an arm around her small figure and carefully lifting her to her feet. He kept his arm around her and held her close to his side to steady her as she slipped her arm around his own waist. He waited until she was standing well enough and then slowly took a step, guiding her back to the bedroom a step at a time.

Her fingers gripped tightly onto his shirt, holding onto him as if he might slip away through her fingers. She clung to him so tightly that Dmitri tugged her a little closer, just to try and bring her peace of mind that he would not let her fall. As soon as he eased her down onto the bed, her fingers went to the familiar stitching of the quilts for comfort as she forced herself to let go of him though he could see the hesitation in doing so.

"I have to admit, when I first saw you sitting there, I thought you were trying to leave," Dmitri said, chuckling again to himself.

"No. Though... I admit the thought had indeed occurred to me," she confessed quietly as she slipped under the blankets. He picked up a glass of water, thinking she must be parched, and handed it to her carefully once she was settled.

"I admit I am rather glad you didn't. However, I meant it when I said you are free to leave whenever you wish. If you decide that you wish to do so, though, please allow me to help you get somewhere safely. These woods can be unforgiving to some, and it is also terribly easy to get lost here."

"Did you catch anything?" she asked curiously.

"I did," he said, and then thought it was too short of an answer, so he added, "A deer. I am going to make you a stew, and there should be plenty of meat afterward to do other things with. The stew might be the easiest for you to keep down, though, so I figured we could start there."

Elena lifted her head to look in his general direction quickly, her eyes wide and confused. "You caught a *deer*? Is... Is the forest truly that plentiful?" she asked with a voice filled with something that might have been awe or disbelief.

"I would not say it is more plentiful than any other forest, though there is a significantly less amount of people hunting here in these woods. The forest will always provide, though. And I will always keep my promise. It was about forty-five minutes that I was gone," he said, wanting to emphasize that he had kept his promise.

Elena looked a bit flustered. "I-I know. I believed that you would keep your promise, but that is why I thought you would be going to check some traps for rabbits or something. I did not expect you to hunt and kill a *deer*."

He could see the beginnings of questions begin to form in her mind and hesitated. "I suppose I just got lucky."

She furrowed her eyebrows but no longer asked any more questions. Instead, she shuffled a little further under the blankets in quiet contemplation.

Dmitri took this as his sign to leave, so he made his way out of the bedroom to begin preparing the stew. He walked outside to the garden on the side of the house and plucked some of the vegetables that had been planted. He had maintained the field and the garden around this cottage for a while now, thankful for having done so. He brought his small harvest inside and picked up the leaking burlap sack full of juicy red venison meat before walking it to the kitchen and getting lost in his thoughts.

Elena was quite intriguing to him. She carried magic in her veins and yet did not seem to know how to use any of it to assist in her healing. At first, he thought that she was simply too weak to do so, but as the past couple of days crawled by, he realized she might not be able to. She had gone through trauma, more than he had witnessed, he presumed, and her emotions often seemed to suffocate her. Dmitri tried to mitigate the wounds as much as he could, using a unique salve to help the burns and scarring diminish—though he did not know if they would ever truly disappear. He knew even less about her mental scars. He had never been good at consoling others or lying to tell them it would be alright. The truth was, he didn't know. Until her appetite had finally made an appearance, he didn't even truly know if she would pull through.

It had only been two days, and while, at first, it had been his curiosity keeping her here, his intentions rapidly began to shift into something new entirely. He began to remember what it was like to have others around; to simply have another presence nearby. She was most likely terrified of him, and yet she still spoke to him idly and treated him with kindness. Part of him simply enjoyed her company. Another part of him felt something crack and crumble every time he heard her cry herself to sleep each night. He didn't know what to say in those moments, but he knew there was a part of him that wanted to help, even if that was simply by making stew.

Dmitri cut and sliced the meat into smaller chunks now with a finer knife, making them into more conveniently bite-sized pieces. He skinned and chopped vegetables, moving perhaps a bit slowly as cooking stews had never been his strong suit. He had found the process fascinating when others did it, but he himself could scarcely ever make one that was as tasteful as others. Though considering how long it had been since Elena had eaten, he hoped she would not mind his lack of culinary skills.

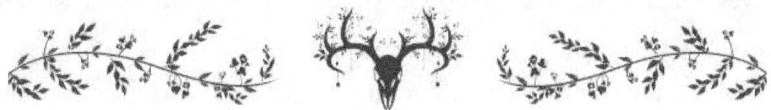

A short time later, a delectable smell wafted into the bedroom and filled Elena's nostrils, making her stomach growl. Despite the smell being clear evidence of the stew brewing, Elena could not hear any sound of him cooking. She had heard the soft creak of the door opening and closing when he went out to the garden he spoke of earlier and then again as he came back inside, but after that, it was almost complete and utter silence. She marveled at how someone could make such little noise when doing things, especially things like chopping meat and vegetables for a stew or working with pots, presumably.

Elena missed the bustling sounds that her mother would make when she made her way around the kitchen. Her mother used to hum as she cooked, chopping away at things loudly and making her presence known to everyone. Elena missed hearing her curse in a manner not quite befitting of a lady when she would burn her fingers or spill something over her counters that she had just cleaned. The memories of her mother squeezed at her chest, and she felt nearly suffocated by them. Just when she thought that she could not take it any longer, Dmitri came in to announce that dinner was ready.

After a short conversation about how she would manage to eat, they decided that he would help guide her to the dining room table. Then after dinner, they would trace the path of the house in a formal tour. She knew she would need to do that a couple of times before the pathways stuck in her mind, especially seeing as this was a foreign environment to her altogether and not one that she had been used to before the loss of her eyes. Though, she was thankful for him offering it to her so she would not have to ask herself.

She sat down at the dining room table, and he handed her a spoon. She fumbled a few times before managing to scoop the hot stew and then bring it to her lips. She ate in silence with him for a short time until she could hardly stand the silence any longer.

"Tell me about this house. Did you build it when you decided to live in the forest?" she practically blurted out. Embarrassed at her slight outburst and not used to making small talk, she quickly shoveled another bite of the stew into her mouth to keep from making a fool of herself any further.

Dmitri did not seem to mind the outburst or find it abnormal in the slightest. "Well, to be honest with you, this is not exactly my house," he answered casually as though it was common information.

Elena nearly choked on her stew, coughing as she covered her mouth. Her eyes widened, and she sputtered a bit. "What do you mean this is not your house? What happened to the people who lived here? Are they going to be back soon?" She listed off questions quickly, panic rising in her chest.

"No, Elena, please. I'm sorry. I phrased that poorly. I grew up in this house. There used to be an elderly couple who lived here that adopted me. Unfortunately, both of them have since passed on. I... I have not stayed here very often since their deaths, though I cannot bear the place to fall into too much disrepair. So, I tend to the garden that she used to have, and I try to keep the place relatively clean—though I admit to that never being a strong quality of mine. They were good people, and this was my home for a very important period of my life. It is the closest thing I have to a home, but I hesitate to call it my own since it was more inherited rather than built," he explained.

Elena had not realized how tense her shoulders had gotten until the muscles started to relax. She frowned softly at his explanation and slowly set down the spoon that she had been holding in a tight fist. "I am sorry to hear that you have lost them," she said quietly, realizing they were both alike in having lost their families. "Were you close to them?"

"Yes," he answered, his voice quieter now in a more somber tone. "I never called them mother or father, though they may as well have been. The woman's name was June, and her husband's name was Silas. They were different in many ways, but sometimes it was as though they had been cut from the same cloth with how well they worked through life together."

"How long ago did they die?" she asked quietly, her voice tentative as she wondered if perhaps it was too personal of a question to ask. She could seldom rein in her curiosity, though, once it had been piqued. Besides, this was a chance to answer one of her burning questions as long as she tread carefully.

"A long time ago. I... I do not remember how long. The days have begun to blend together for me. I just know it has been quite a long time," he admitted softly.

Elena nodded in understanding and picked up her spoon once more, scooping up a bite as her mind wandered momentarily. She swallowed before she took a deep breath and then decided to speak once more.

"I have lost all that was left of my family within the year. My father, then my grandmother, and lastly, my mother. I am the last of my family now." Speaking the words into existence left a bitter taste on her tongue, and she regretted the acknowledgment as soon as she had said it. She shook her head as her throat began to feel tighter. She had meant to say it as a way to comfort him and acknowledge that she understood what it had meant to lose people, but now it felt as if she was about to be crushed by it.

She could hear the frown in his voice when he spoke next. "I am sorry that they are gone, Elena. I know that it will not bring them back, but I am sorry that you are suffering the grief of their absence."

Elena shrugged, spooning stew into her mouth idly. She had the feeling she was being watched and wished that she could shrink away from him. She wished that she knew for certain whether or not he truly was looking at her. That way, she could snap at him if he was. If he wasn't, however, she did not want to look foolish. Instead, she forced the suffocating feeling down and ate her soup as if they had just had a perfectly average conversation. Her fingers were shaking, though, and she knew it was only a matter of time before her soul cracked under the weight of her acknowledgment, and she would break.

When she finished her stew, she stood up from the table. "I think I am too tired for that tour of the house. If you do not mind, I would very much like to go back to bed now."

"Of course, Elena."

"Thank you, and thank you for the stew. It was delicious."

He chuckled as he wrapped his arm around her waist to guide her back. "Really? Cooking has never been a talent of mine."

Despite the sadness creeping into her mind, she smiled a bit at that. He gave her shoulder a small squeeze before she thanked him once more. She crawled under the blankets, and when she thought she might have heard him make a tiny sound in the other room, she finally pulled the blankets over her face and cried in silence until she fell asleep.

CHAPTER TWELVE

GHOSTS

"Elena, what have you done?"

Her father's voice screamed out to her, echoing around the room as flames engulfed their house. Elena was more surprised at being able to see again than she was at seeing her father alive still, but her surprise quickly melted under the heat of the flame and dissolved into horror. Her father sat in the middle of their living area, cradling her mother's body in his arms. Blood had soaked her dress, half of her neck was missing, and what remained of it was a shredded mess of flesh.

"Me?" Elena asked dumbly, barely aware that she was answering at all. She was too busy staring at the look of pain and defeat in her mother's dead eyes. Elena whimpered at the sight, wondering if her mother thought that she had failed before she died.

"What have you done?!" Her father's voice, now a wail, snapped her from her thoughts, and she looked at the man cradling her mother. Her father's body was crawling with worms and bugs as he cradled her, but that was hardly the most upsetting part. Elena saw that her father was sobbing—the man who she had only ever seen cry a small handful of times—now weeping over his wife's body.

Elena choked on her sob, and she tried to take a step toward them, but he sheltered her mother's body protectively with his own, and Elena realized that she was on fire. The panic inside of her chest was now nearly *unbearable, and she fell to her knees in front of them, flames flaring and exploding around them.*

"Papa, I promise I didn't mean to do any of this! Please, you must believe me!" she screamed over the sound of the flames engulfing her. Her father wept over her mother, and Elena screamed as the pain from the fire fully consumed her.

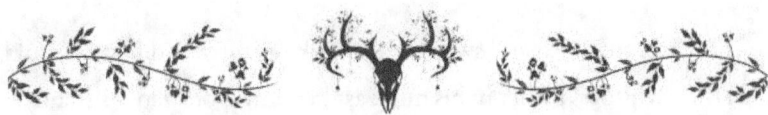

D mitri measured the days with the progress that Elena made in her recovery. Her body was getting stronger now, and soon her injuries should be healed enough that she would no longer need his constant and lingering presence to care for her. He wondered idly what would happen when that point came, but he was prepared for the reality that she could eventually leave, even if that was not what he particularly wanted. It was hard for him to admit, even to himself, he wanted her company. He had decided to take a walk out in the forest to clear his mind and focus more on the obligations that he was bound to in order to distract himself from this possibility. After Elena had fallen into a deep sleep, he left the small cottage—making sure to stay nearby in case she needed him.

He walked through the forest, mud sinking ever so slightly beneath his weight as his footprints began to fill with water and disappear almost as soon as he had made them. It had been raining almost constantly for the past week—sometimes soft drizzles of rain and other times thunderstorms that threatened to wreak havoc amongst the trees. Tonight was one of the latter kinds of nights.

He had been walking around the forest for around an hour, maybe even two, when the wind picked up suddenly. He had only a moment to prepare himself before a gust of it shoved him back, knocking the air from his lungs before another one came and swirled around him. He grunted a bit, eyes dangerously glaring at the shifting trees and wisping wind of his environment.

"What in the gods is your problem—" he began but then stopped short.

The trees trembled and swayed their bark urgently, and Dmitri could feel their whispers gather in his mind as their leaves bristled insistently.

Elena

   Elena

      Elena

         Elena!

Dmitri wasted no time, running as fast as his legs could carry him, his own magic flooding through his veins. His mind raced faster than his legs as he thought about what could be happening to have the trees worked up like this. His heart thumped wildly inside of his chest with adrenaline and fear as all of the worst-case scenarios flooded his thoughts, scarcely aware of the rain pelting against him. If anything or anyone was hurting her inside of *his* home, no less, he would tear their limbs apart. An unearthly rage filled his soul, and he growled, struggling to keep it at bay until he finally got close enough to understand; Elena was screaming.

All of the anger melted into a pure sense of dread and panic that made him nauseous. The last remaining distance felt too far, even as he barreled through the door of the cottage. His chest rose and fell quickly, his senses on high alert as he readied himself to fight, but as his eyes scanned the cottage, he found nothing out of place. His body dripped mud and water onto the floor as his chest heaved, furrowing his eyebrows in confusion.

Elena screamed again from the bedroom, and his concern quickly changed to wondering if something had happened to her injuries. He ran to her and saw her writhing beneath the blankets. His eyes were wide, unsure of what to do, when he realized she was having a nightmare.

"Elena!" He called her name in an attempt to wake her up, his voice projecting so it filled the entire room.

Elena flinched away from him and awoke with a gasp, practically hyperventilating. Dmitri wanted to touch and console her but was unsure if she would like that, so he forced his hands to remain at his side. Not to mention he was still soaking wet from the rain.

"Elena, hey shh, it's just me. I'm here. It was only a nightmare, okay?" He tried to coax her with his voice, but his own hands were shaking as the magic within him settled beneath his skin.

Tears flooded down her face, and she made a strangled sound as she wrapped her small arms around her waist to hold herself. "I killed them. I killed everyone. It's all my fault," she managed to gasp out the words between her breaths. Her body was wracked with sobs, shaking like a leaf under the weight of her statements.

Dmitri frowned at the state that she was in. He did not know what she had gone through and did not want to feign as though he did by offering her hollow words of condolence. Though, something told him that it was not truly her fault that her family had died. Still, he did not know how to help her without knowing.

"Elena, was it your hand that killed them?" he asked softly.

"Well, n-no, but—"

He pushed forward and cut her off, not wanting to allow her the opportunity to create more excuses. "Did you tell someone else to kill them?"

"No, Dmitri, but if it weren't for me—"

"Elena, you did not kill your family then. Your existence and presence are not a death sentence. Do you understand me? Whatever you dreamt of was just a dream. Whatever led to their deaths was tragic, but you cannot shoulder that blame."

Elena gasped for air between her sobs, looking defeated before she covered her face. She folded in on herself and cried into her lap, her shoulders trembling with sobs. Her long chestnut-colored hair fell loosely around her like the roots of a tree splayed out. Dmitri decided to risk walking closer to her when her head jerked up a moment later.

"Are you even real?" she asked breathlessly, her voice strained from the tears and laced with an exasperated panic.

Dmitri was taken aback by the question, freezing in his place as he furrowed his eyebrows together in confusion. "Am I real?" he echoed, wondering if he had heard her correctly.

Elena swallowed as she nodded, a gasping noise escaping her throat as tears cascaded down her cheeks. "I never hear you," she stated, her voice small and fragile as if she was admitting some kind of great secret. She continued mercilessly before Dmitri could even begin to process the statement.

"I never hear you. I do not hear you walk, breathe, or move. I don't hear you cooking or snoring or *anything!* It is like you don't even exist except when I ask or need you to. So what is it? Am I dying in that grave and hallucinating all of this in some kind of sick way for my soul to cope with everything before I die? Did I imagine you just so that I might have a moment of kindness in a world that had turned its back on me? I thought I knew you were real when you touched me earlier, but perhaps I conjured that too. Am I dying, Dmitri?" Her voice rose with each question, becoming increasingly more distressed with each one.

Dmitri listened to her and frowned deeply. Something inside of him ached for her, so unsure of the world around her and how to navigate it. He also realized his own part he had played in making her come to this conclusion and mentally kicked himself for it. His feet were moving before they knew how to stop, and he crouched by her bedside, wiping the water away from his arms with the blanket before he took her hand within his own. She flinched at first but then held him tightly. Her hand felt smooth and a little clammy in his own as he gave her a firm squeeze.

"You are *not* dying. I am right here, and you can feel my hand squeezing yours, can't you?"

Elena's lungs took in short labored breaths as she tried to stop herself from crying so hard. She weakly curled her fingers around his hand and nodded but could not bring herself to talk anymore through the sobs that shook her shoulders.

Dmitri kept a hold of her hand carefully, running his thumb over her knuckles carefully as his other hand gently brushed some of the tears away from her face. "Listen to my voice now, okay? Just try and focus on it. You have been through so much—things I don't even know about yet—but you are here because you are strong. I know things seem a little confusing and terrifying right now as you adjust to things, but it will get easier."

Elena looked a little uncertain of him, but she did not try to argue. She sniffled, trying to breathe a little steadier as her tears dripped down onto his skin where their hands met.

Dmitri took this as slight progress, so he decided to continue on as he attempted to comfort her. It had been so long since he had spoken to someone like this, and even then, he had not done it often in his past. Her presence provoked something inside of him, though. He knew that the entire forest could sense it as well and seeing as they were so adamantly excited about the change. So, he had decided to embrace it with her now by trying to do his best to console her—even if he was terribly awkward or uncertain in his attempts to do so.

"Do you want to tell me about the nightmare, Elena?" he asked quietly. He decided he would not push the matter if she were to show any kind of hesitation or negative reaction to the question, but he wanted her to know that he was willing to listen if she needed to tell someone.

Elena did not say anything for a long moment, and Dmitri thought about changing the topic away or reassuring her again, but then she surprised him. She began to tell the story of what she had dreamt about, her fingers shaking a little harder when she told him about the part where she realized she was the fire that was spreading and hurting her family.

"Would your father truly ever say those things to you?" Dmitri asked, wondering if that was truly his character or if that was her anxiety speaking through him in her dreams.

She sniffled a bit louder and shrugged half-heartedly. "I don't think so, but I realize that there was much that I did not know of him already," she said and then lowered her voice to a whisper that she spoke mostly to herself. "I did not know he was a witch. If I had understood... maybe I could have done something to help, you know? Instead, I was a witch who was clueless about my own magic, and my family was killed while my village hunted me. I don't even know if they truly knew or were too blinded by their superstitions, but it didn't matter because, in the end, they were right, and my family still paid for it while I am still here."

The admission that she was a witch had not surprised him as it was something he already intrinsically knew. This was a side of her that he had immediately accepted. Dmitri wiped another one of her tears with his free hand, watching her face carefully as she spoke. He realized that she was telling him things that she had previously been guarded about, and he did not want to take advantage of the situation by trying to get more information out of her. Already she had explained a lot, and he could fill in the rest of the blanks.

"He might have hidden that part of his life around you, but it is much harder to hide a person's character. Your father would never blame you for what has happened, and I think you know that. It doesn't make it easier. In fact, it may even make it harder to not be able to blame yourself."

At this, Elena looked confused as she scrunched her nose and twisted her mouth to the side slightly. Dmitri chuckled at her look and squeezed her hand as he continued.

"I mean it. Sometimes it is easier to simply blame ourselves for things outside of our control. It makes it feel more tangible or as though it was a mistake that we could learn from and maybe prevent in the future. Sometimes it is easier to cling to that bitterness or anger towards ourselves than it is to face the grief of knowing that things will always happen to us that are out of our control to some extent. What happened to you was awful, but it wasn't your fault, and blaming yourself like this so wholly will only ever prevent you from being able to move forward from this. It will take time, but the process begins with the acceptance that the world does not operate based on the decisions of one person."

"It feels... it feels like I am still digging my grave," Elena said quietly. "It feels like I am standing in it, clawing to try and get out, only to make it deeper."

Dmitri was quiet for a long moment, searching for the right words to say. He wondered what June or Silas might say in a moment like this, and he hesitantly took a deep breath. "Maybe you need to stop trying to get out on your own then. If that was the case, and you were standing in your grave and only making it deeper, maybe it is time for you to simply let someone reach down and pull you out," he murmured, looking into her opaque eyes and admiring the faintest ghostly shade of jade green that used to be there. He squeezed her hand gently to emphasize his point, letting her know that he was here and he would pull her from any grave if she simply let him reach for her.

Elena had stopped crying, her breaths still shaky occasionally as she inhaled, but she simply looked in his direction as though she was desperately trying to see him.

"Dmitri? I... I need to know what happened that night."

He dreaded the implied question, but he gently nudged her shoulder to tell her to lean back in the bed with his free hand. He did not let go of her other hand as she still held onto him tightly—scared that he might slip through her fingers if she were to let go of him. She obeyed his nudge and leaned back into the bed, and he pulled the blankets over her before he sat down in a chair by her bedside.

"The truth?"

"Yes, please."

There was no easy way to say what he was about to say. He thought about how poor the timing was in telling her this, imagining that the information would not help with her fears. Still, he knew that if he put this off any longer that she would begin to lose her trust in him. It would never get easier to say, so he simply forced his tongue to work the words out of his mouth.

"I killed them," he admitted quietly. His voice was calm as he spoke to her, but he frowned. "I saw what was happening, and I wanted to make sure that they could never even consider doing something like that again. So, I killed them. I don't regret my decision to save you. I don't regret my decision to kill them. The truth, Elena, is that I would kill anyone who ever touched you like that again. Whoever touched anyone like that but especially you, since you did not deserve that treatment for something as simple as your heritage. They made their decision to enter my forest, and I made my decision to take their lives. It is something that I will live with, but it is not something that I would have done differently. I guess monsters just come in all different shapes and sizes. I am sorry if that is not what you wanted to hear."

Elena stayed quiet for a moment, and he studied her face, waiting to see the signs of fear or disgust. Instead, she simply nodded slowly. "You won't let them hurt me again?" her voice whispered.

Dmitri, surprised at the relief that washed over him, nodded out of habit but then forced out words, sounding a bit shaken and breathless. "I won't."

She nodded and inhaled a shaky breath as she settled into the blankets. "You won't hurt me?"

"Never. I swear to you," he said fervently. Never having been one for comforting others, he latched onto this tangible thing that he knew he could promise. Something burned inside of him, needing her to understand this, even if he did not.

There was a pause as she seemed to consider whether or not she was making the right decision in trusting him. He knew that she still would want the details of that night, but she seemed to accept the simple truth for the time being.

She held onto his hand as though it was her only lifeline and took a deep breath. "Will you stay until I fall back asleep?" she asked softly, a shyness creeping up on her.

"I will stay as long as you want me to."

She nodded her head once more as her eyelashes fluttered closed. Her breathing evened out as she gradually drifted to sleep—even with a self-proclaimed 'monster' holding her hand.

Chapter Thirteen

GROUNDING

Dmitri watched as Elena fluttered her eyes open—birds chirping away outside of the glass window pane by the bed. The rain that pelted against the window last night felt far away and distant. She stretched in the warmth from the sun as it shone against her skin, opening her eyes unhurriedly. Dmitri could see the exhaustion in the form of bags under her eyes.

Dmitri had stayed in the chair by her bedside all night, not moving his hand away from hers. His clothes had been soaking wet from the rain, but they were mostly dried by now. He had no intention of letting go of her hand to go change his clothes, though, so he had been content to remain like this throughout the night. At least it gave him some time to sort out his thoughts.

She must have realized her fingers were still wrapped around his as she flexed and carefully adjusted her fingers. His hand was much larger than hers, easily engulfing hers. He had held it gently as though he was scared of breaking her—giving a small squeeze only occasionally throughout the night to let her know it was still okay when he noticed her breathing begin to falter. He wanted to remind her that she did not imagine him. If anything, Dmitri thought her hand might break his with how tightly she had held on. Now, as the morning had come and the worst of the night had passed, her grip finally relaxed.

Dmitri cleared his throat, a deep sound that made Elena become more alert as she lulled her head to look in his direction. She blushed, her movements still clearly influenced by how sleepy she was.

"Good morning," his voice creaked softly, stretching his muscles and straining before relaxing once again into the chair.

"Good morning, Dmitri," she whispered as if she was trying not to wake the earth.

Dmitri smiled a bit at the way she made no move to immediately rise from the bed or pull her hand away from his. She was lazy in the mornings, he had noticed, taking her time to savor the warmth of the blankets before her mind had fully begun to work. He had watched her wake quite a few times over the duration of her stay here, and almost always, it was warm, languid movements as she welcomed her senses back to life gradually. It was a hypnotic process most days when he could see her out of the corner of his eye from the other room.

"I've been thinking... I'd like to take you out of the cottage today and show you something. Only if you are comfortable with it, though," he said, his voice hesitant as he broached the idea with her. He had been awake for quite a while, in contrast. In that time, his mind had wandered, wondering idly what he might be able to do for Elena to help pull her out of this metaphorical grave she felt stuck in. He figured some fresh air was a good place to start.

"Outside? Is it... safe?" she asked tentatively, though he could see how the idea had gripped her already as she lifted her head. He grinned at that.

"Yes, it's perfectly safe. It isn't far either, so you don't have to walk too far, and I will be there by your side to guide you. I could pack some food for us as well so we can make a picnic out of it. The sun is shining bright today, and the rain from last night seems to have left everything feeling a little fresher. I could run a bath for you, and some of June's old clothes should fit you."

Elena blushed softly at this. She had mostly been washing with a rag and basin he had brought for her. But now that she was stronger and healing, Dmitri saw no reason why she shouldn't enjoy a soothing bath. She had been wearing June's old nightgowns he had left for her after they agreed that she shouldn't be wearing something too tight with the way her ribs were injured. At first, Elena had been mortified he had expected her to wear nightgowns around him, but the circumstances gave way to necessity, and she conceded. Now she should also be healed enough to get into proper clothes as well, which he was sure she would appreciate.

"All of that sounds lovely, Dmitri. Thank you. Could... Could you help me to the bath? I can do everything on my own, of course. I just still don't know my way around quite yet," she said, her cheeks burning pink as she flustered.

Dmitri chuckled and gave her hand another small squeeze, once again letting her know that he was still here out of habit that he had built throughout the night.

"Of course, just let me know when you are ready."

Elena took another minute or so, soaking in the sunlight through the window as Dmitri ran his thumbs over her knuckles absentmindedly. He could get used to the easy and relaxed look written on her face like this. He looked at her face in truth now, taking in all of the small features about her. This woman was becoming the closest thing he had to a friend—another soul to simply interact with—and while he would not overstep boundaries after such trauma she had experienced, he would be a fool to deny her beauty and the effects that it had on him.

She had long brown hair that reminded him of the earth in the best way. It was often kept braided off to the side when she was awake, but currently, it hung in thick loose waves down her shoulders. She was rather thin, but he could still see the curves of her hips even with the unflattering nightgowns. Scars, still pink and prevalent, stood out against the pale skin of her wrists from where she had been bound. But just like everything else, those, too, were healing.

Freckles splattered along her cheeks and nose, and her eyes—which she had voiced being so unsure of since her incident—were beautiful to him. The green that hid behind the white of her eyes reminded him of the spring grass waiting underneath the snow. Another memory came to him as he stared at her, and he remembered Silas.

"What are you painting?" a young Dmitri, only about fourteen years old at the time, had asked as he meandered on over to where Silas sat. His voice had cracked, and he hated it, but Silas did not poke fun at him. For that, he was thankful.

Silas had stretched dry deer hides to make his own canvases and crushed flowers, berries, and other things into pigments for the last week. Now, after all of his preparations, he finally sat cross-legged in the field outside of their cottage and faced the garden in which June worked feverishly to pull weeds. Silas looked up at Dmitri as he approached and smiled with a devilish grin.

"A surprise. Be quiet now," he said as he lowered the painting medium for Dmitri to get a better look at.

Dmitri was surprised to see a fraction of a woman's face focused in on her eye as wisps of hair fell over her face. There was sunlight reflected in her eye. It almost looked as though it was a puzzle piece taken away from a woman's face, incomplete and yet telling enough. Dmitri looked a little closer as a hint of recognition crossed his face, and he rose quickly to look at June in the garden. She had the same shade of eye color as the woman in his painting—a beautiful and rich hazel.

"It's...June's eye?" Dmitri asked quietly, uncertain as to why Silas would paint such a thing.

As if Silas could read his thoughts, he chuckled a bit to himself and nodded in confirmation. "Indeed. They say that eyes are the window to the soul, Dmitri. It is my belief that a woman's eyes can hold the secrets of the universe, and you and I would never even realize it," Silas said in a conspiratorial voice that hinted there was more that he was not saying.

"Why not?"

"Because if we look long enough, we are bound to fall in love with the soul behind them. The secrets of the universe hardly seem to shine a light in comparison to that. Don't you think?"

Dmitri had made a face and waved off Silas and his inclinations, leaving him to paint June's eye in peace.

He had thought no more of what Silas had said, too preoccupied in his own world at the time to realize the truth of his statement. It wasn't until later that night, when Silas had given June the painting as a gift and saw the way her eyes lit up with joy at the gesture, that Dmitri had the faintest idea that Silas might actually know what he was talking about. But it wasn't until this morning, staring into Elena's eyes idly as she took in the morning, that he began to truly understand the weight of it.

Elena sighed softly, pulling him from his trance as she propped herself up and then nodded. "Alright, I'm ready," she said softly as she gently swung her legs over the edge of the bed. She pulled one of the blankets over her shoulders to cover herself from view.

Dmitri shook his head from his thoughts, thankful she could not see the blush that tinted his cheeks as he helped her stand. "Right," he acknowledged quietly. Despite what Silas had once said, it did not change the fact that sometimes people did not deserve those things, even if it would be terribly easy to drown in her eyes. He realized that he was simply happy that she was here—someone to fill the cottage he had outgrown and someone to fill the silence he was accustomed to. But as she carefully let go of his hand to allow him to move, he already selfishly missed the weight of it.

Dmitri left her to go heat up water for her bath, managing to do it relatively quickly before he came back to her. He had been a little more deliberate about making sound when he was in the other room, though it was a work in progress. He made sure to bump against something every now and then or to pour the water quickly to make the sound of splashing water. It wasn't much, though he was not used to making his presence known, so it did take a couple of tries before he started to think of more natural ways to make sounds in order to comfort her.

As he came back to her, he explained what he was doing before he helped her to stand again, slipping an arm around her carefully as they walked in tandem to the bath. Elena waited, per his instructions, for him to come back and hang up a dress over the cracked door. He guided her fingers to it so she would know how to find it when she was done and gave her something to dry off with as well. Once he made sure she also knew where the soap was and answered any questions she had, he left her alone in the washroom to go tend to the kitchen and begin to pack some food for them.

He could see how nervous she was to be doing the task alone for the first time, but he also saw the way that she craved independence. As much as he wanted to be there for her and help her, there were some things she simply would have to do on her own. That, too, was a part of healing he knew all too well. It would be good for her to simply have some alone time as well so she would feel like he was not hovering over her. He was not used to having someone else around, and while he was usually very content to be solitary, he found her presence to be intoxicating and had to be careful not to cross that border of being overbearing.

Dmitri had changed out of his old clothes, washing himself off as well. He wore some slacks and a black button-up shirt of Silas's, sleeves rolled to his elbows and suspenders holding up his slacks. Dmitri's black hair was kept mostly faded short, with the top of his hair longer and a little messier. His hand slid over his face slowly, feeling the beard that he had kept cropped close to his face as he looked himself over in the mirror earlier this morning. He did not often pay attention to his appearance, even when he was younger, but the facial hair was something that he did focus on upkeep. Some days it had been his only indication of the passing of time when he would feel it grow too long and then religiously cut or trim it back down to length. It was the style that Silas had worn his in, and Dmitri had always liked the way it was cleanly cut and not in the way, yet framed his face.

After some time had passed, he could hear Elena bumping around inside the washroom as she got dressed, mumbling soft curses to herself. He struggled not to chuckle before he made his way over to the door, knocking on it lightly.

"Elena?"

"I'm ready," she said, voice muffled by the door.

Dmitri opened the door carefully so as not to hit her by accident as its old hinges creaked. A part of him wanted to compliment her somehow, but he could not bring himself to torture himself like that. He had no right to yearn for her. Still, it did not feel right not to say anything.

"I am, uh, glad that it fits you well," he said, stumbling slightly over his words.

June had been a little taller than her, but other than that, the dress had fit her perfectly well. The dress had a pale pastel shade of yellow for the skirt and a white top with sleeves that went to her elbows. The dress had no tight lacing or form-fitting curves—June did not tend to like dresses that were restraining like that—and the fabric flowed easily around her. Her cheeks had regained some color to them from the warm water as well as his awkward compliment, and her eyes looked a little brighter with life. She smelled like lemongrass as the scent still wafted strongly in the air.

"Are you ready?" he asked, holding out an arm for her as he gently nudged her so she would know.

"One moment," she said. Her fingers began to twist her long wet hair, weaving it into a braid. She closed her eyes, her focus on the simple action that Dmitri could tell she had memorized long ago. Her hands were automatic, finishing as the braid fell over her shoulders.

She took a deep breath and nodded in confirmation that she was ready now, a little nervous or shy perhaps, but slipped her arm easily through his. He guided her out of the washroom slowly, helped her put on her shoes, and then grabbed the small wicker basket that held the food that he had packed. They walked outside together, moving down the steps of the cottage carefully as they began the day.

They walked in silence for a moment and listened to the nature around them as he silently guided her. He had not told her exactly where they were going, but he thought a surprise might be nice. The grass of the field wisped by their ankles as they walked. They heard birds, squirrels, and other critters going about their day as a gentle warm breeze caressed her cheek like a mother's touch. Dmitri could see the way she nearly leaned into it.

Dmitri tried his best not to think of the trees or how everything was reacting to finally seeing her once again. There was a genuine happiness and joy at seeing Elena healthier and walking on her own. Moreover, they also took notice of him and the way his arm was hooked around her. His eyes held a protectiveness to them, warning the forest to go easy on her with a glance. Everything bristled at that but reluctantly obeyed in the end.

"Will you describe it to me?" Elena asked suddenly, her voice nearly a whisper.

Dmitri turned his attention away from the tree line to look down at her, realizing he had been silent with the distractions. She was nearly a head shorter than him, if not just slightly more. "Describe what?" he asked, his own voice softer than he had expected it to be.

"Everything. I want to know what you see," she said softly and squeezed his arm just slightly.

Dmitri continued to look at her for a long moment, simply taking her in before he pulled his eyes away and let them scan everything.

"Well, we are walking through a field. There—" he began, but she cut him off.

"Tell me more about the field, please."

Dmitri swallowed and hesitated as he forced himself to look a little closer at all of the details. Once again, he thought of Silas and how he seemed to see the world as poetry and proverbs. Dmitri had never been great at being able to express the things inside his mind—less so since their deaths. He could tell her that, use it as some kind of flimsy excuse, but he heard the timidness in her voice when she had asked. This was harder for her than it was for him. The least that he could do was try.

He cleared his throat before he began again. "The clearing is shaped almost like a spoon, and we are walking along the part that would be the handle," he began. "The cottage is back in the scoop. Trees surround us, outlining the clearing. They are tall and vary in what kind they are. They are all exceptionally green today from the rain, and if you look through the expansive maze of their bark, you can see where the sun filters through, casting rays on the soil of the ground. The field we are walking through is green and—" He paused to look around him at the flowers that bloomed brightly at their feet. "And it is absolutely covered in wildflowers. They are small flowers, and they range in color."

"What colors are there?" Elena prompted him gently.

"An entire rainbow, it seems. There is yellow, white, purple, pink, and even a little bit of red here and there. My favorite ones are the daisies," he said, murmuring the last part bashfully. He watched as the flowers all seemed to brighten around them as if trying to be seen by him next, and he had to bite back a chuckle.

Dmitri watched as the ghost of a smile painted her soft pink lips, and his heartbeat ceased to beat in that moment. It had been the first time that she had smiled since he met her, and while it was not big or full of joy, it was still warm and happy. He understood now why someone might want to be a poet if it meant that there was a chance of seeing a smile like hers. He felt flustered at that, clearing his throat as his own smile spread across his face.

He began to explain everything to her one thing at a time. He still did not feel very articulate when he described things, but she didn't seem to mind his odd analogies or the simplistic way he spoke of colors. He was on a mission to paint a picture of the world for her, even if nothing he could describe would be as beautiful as her smile.

Dmitri had to keep telling himself that he should not be thinking like this. He knew the consequences of his decisions and knew he would not want to drag her down with him in the end, but it did not stop his foolish heart from holding onto her. He admired her like a painting, knowing he could never truly have what he saw but getting lost in the idea all the same. She was beautiful, and he would be a fool to deny it. She was strong, and anyone could see it.

He could never have her, and he knew it.

Instead, he told her about the sky and the shapes of fluffy white clouds that rolled through. He told her about some of the animals he could see, such as squirrels or birds or even a rabbit that dashed away from their path. Her smile grew slowly but steadily, like a blooming flower of its own. He wanted to water it and nurture that growth.

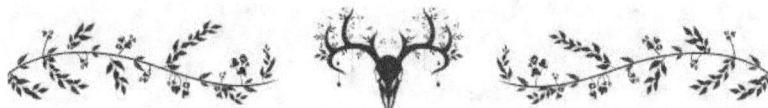

PART THREE: SKIN

CHAPTER FOURTEEN

NEW BEGINNINGS

D mitri sat awake at night by the fireplace that crackled softly, dwindling down to mere embers now. Elena slept peacefully in the other room, the day's events and adventures having taken their toll on her. Dmitri was tired too, but his mind was too active as it raced and thought of how he was going to go about teaching her magic. While not a witch himself, he did possess magic and had a deep understanding of how a witch's magic worked, thanks to June's teachings.

He sat there as he distantly stared at the low light in the fireplace, torn between getting consumed by memories and then coming back to the present only to mildly fret. He worried that this teaching would come to reveal more about himself than he had intended to. Truly, it felt nearly impossible to say no to her. Telling her about him, however, and what exactly he was almost guaranteed the end of something.

The end of their time together is what he feared most. He worried that she would understand what it meant to be around him or realize that monsters of myth truly do exist. He didn't want her to leave and then doubt or second-guess people in the future with the knowledge that monsters could hide amongst humans. Selfishly, he simply did not want her to think differently of him.

He looked down at the palm of one of his hands as a new foolish hope festered inside of him like a parasite. *What if she wants to stay?*

He scowled at the thought as if he could scare it away, but it persisted stubbornly.

If he looked at his situation realistically, he knew there was truly no way he could be saved. What remained of his humanity had been fading gradually throughout the years and soon would be gone completely due to decisions he had made. Decisions he did not completely regret. He would suffer the consequences of them just as he had been doing every single day since that day. And she would be foolish for wanting to stick around that kind of damage after everything she had been through.

Still, as he looked at his hand in the dim firelight, he thought about how easily her hand filled the space there. How she had been the first one to curl her fingers around his as they laid together by the river, and how tightly she had held onto him throughout the night even after she found out he had murdered people. She had asked him if he would ever hurt her, but she believed him instantly when he had said he would never. He wondered if he could truly promise that with where his life was heading, but then quickly shook his head. He would tear himself apart before he ever laid a hand on her.

He thought about her eyes again and the determination behind them when she had asked him if he would teach her magic. Perhaps... this would not be the end after all. Maybe this was merely the beginning of something new. Life would change with or without him. He decided he would tell her the truth, but only after he had taught her enough to be able to defend herself. That way, if she chose to leave, it would not be in vain, and he would know she still had a chance.

Deep inside his chest, his heart kicked to life fervently. Hope was a terribly contagious thing.

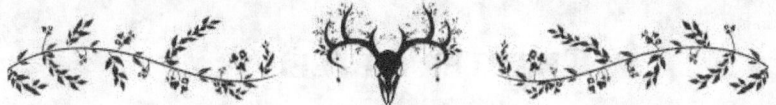

CHAPTER FIFTEEN

LESSON ONE: CONTROL

Elena woke the next day feeling refreshed and ready. She still had nightmares and knew there was no magic that would simply make them disappear, but they did seem less volatile than they previously had been. She slept throughout the night, waking only in the morning with a tiny gasp as she came back to reality. *Dmitri is going to teach me magic today*, she thought to herself.

Rubbing her eyes, she sat up slightly. Taking a moment to listen for him, she was not immediately surprised when she did not hear any sounds in the house. She wondered if he had perhaps gone outside or maybe he was just moving silently again. Sliding from the blankets, she swung her legs over the side of her bed. She had slept in her clothes last night, too tired to attempt the long process of changing out of them by the time they had gotten back to the cottage in the evening, made dinner, and eaten. She was thankful for it now as she was slightly less self-conscious about walking around. She was also thankful that June did not like the tightly laced dresses that Elena had grown used to in the village, as it made for a much more comfortable sleep this way.

Elena placed her hand on the wall and slowly walked as she listened for any sign of him. She still did not quite know her way around the cottage, but Dmitri had also officially given her a tour of the rooms last night. Two bedrooms, one washroom, a kitchen and dining room, and a small living area with comfortable rocking chairs and a fireplace. She checked the other bedroom first, hearing no sign of him, and decided to explore other areas of the house.

She walked carefully, struggling for a moment to remember which direction to go in before she forced her feet to simply trust her instincts and move forward. She walked to the living area quietly, and for the first time since she had been here, she was surprised to hear that he was still asleep. He did not snore like her father used to—able to shake mountains sometimes with how loud he used to snore—but Elena could hear the faint sound of slow deep breathing. She smiled at being able to hear the soft breathing, and as much as she wanted to move closer to him, she hesitated to remove her hand from the wall. She did not want to risk getting disoriented again or, worse, end up tripping over him and giving him a rude awakening.

Instead, she inched her way along the wall until she managed to make her way to the kitchen with newfound determination. She had managed to find the pantry and sniff all of the spices and herbs, happily recognizing some of them and making mental notes to ask about the ones she did not. Her grandmother had taught her plenty about herbs, and Elena was confident in her ability to decipher them well enough.

She quietly put a pot of water on the stove and was able to light it without burning herself—a miracle on its own with her lack of sight. She kept her ear close as she focused, trying not to be distracted by the soft sleepy breaths coming from a short distance away. Once she heard it properly boiling, she blew out the fire on the stove and then waited patiently until it was cool enough. She managed to find cups, which was trickier than she expected it to be, and then carefully poured tea into them.

At the sound of the liquid pouring, or perhaps Elena's soft, delighted giggle at being able to accomplish the task on her own, Dmitri finally stirred. His breathing was silent once again, no longer slow and audible.

"Elena?" His voice was thicker, and she noticed the difference in how deep it was immediately after he had woken up.

Dmitri sat up from the rocking chair—the sound scraped against the floor in a teetering pendulum motion before falling silent—and he groggily groaned as his breath hissed with a stretch.

"That chair is far less comfortable to—" Dmitri stopped himself from finishing the sentence as he looked into the kitchen to see Elena grinning from ear to ear as if he had just caught her in some great mischievous thing. Then he realized she *was in the kitchen.*

"What have you been up to?" His voice was relaxed, with a lazy grin spreading across his lips.

"I think... I just made tea," Elena said, still smiling brightly in his direction.

"Did you now?" he intoned, his deep voice causing goosebumps once again to cover Elena's arms beneath the sleeves of her dress.

She nodded, and Dmitri came over, placing a hand gently on her hip as he slid past her into the small kitchen space. He saw the tea and chuckled in pleasant delight. "You did amazing. I am surprised you managed to find everything. I have lived here for many years, and I still have not deciphered June's way of organizing things."

Elena turned to face him, his hand still resting lightly on her waist. She was blushing from a mix of the compliment as well as the touch. "It was very difficult indeed, though I assumed that was just me," she chuckled.

There was a small pause as Dmitri realized where his hand still rested, but he did not pull away. Instead, he doubled down on the action, lightly tracing his thumb over her waist. Elena blushed but made no move to pull away from him. It did not feel as though he was trying to imply anything from the small gesture but merely felt like he enjoyed the small domestic ways in which he could touch her. And she certainly did not mind the touch. It was another gentle reminder that he was here—*real*—and she welcomed that easily.

"Do you want any honey or sugar with your tea, Elena?" he asked, his voice quiet with how close their faces were together.

"Yes, please," she replied softly, barely even trusting herself to speak.

A chuckle fell from his lips, and she could practically feel his breath. "I figured you would lean toward sweet things," he said. If there had not been a smirk on his lips before, Elena was certain there was one now with the way he playfully teased her. He finally forced himself to pull his hand away from her begrudgingly, walking the short distance to grab some honey and sugar. He began to scoop one spoonful each into her tea when Elena spoke up again.

"You have to drink some, too!" she practically blurted out. She mentally kicked herself for how urgent she sounded.

Dmitri paused from scooping the spoonful of honey at her excitement as if he'd only just noticed that there were two cups.

"You are very kind to me, Elena. I will gladly have some with you." He finished scooping the honey into her cup and then decided to keep with the theme of sweetness this morning by adding a spoonful to his own cup. Elena heard the soft clink of the spoon into each cup as he did so. "Think you can walk to the table? I will carry our cups there and grab us some food."

Elena nodded with excitement before she found the wall again and carefully made her way to the area she guessed was the living room. He watched her for a moment before she carefully bumped into the table and then pulled a chair out for herself. She was making progress, even with small steps. He grabbed the cups of tea, perfectly warm, before he grabbed some bread and cheese in his other hand. Carefully so as not to spill, he made his own way to the table before setting everything down.

He took his cup and blew on it slightly to be safe before he sipped it, humming in delight. "This is wonderful. Thank you again, Elena."

If it was possible for her to be consumed with pride and delight in herself, Elena thought she would have drowned in it then. The simple task had taken her a little over an hour to make tea, but she had done it by herself nonetheless. They ate their bread and cheese and drank their tea, happily sharing the morning together.

When they finished, both of them changed into new outfits for the day since neither one of them had bothered to change from the day prior. Elena wore a pastel blue dress with white sleeves that had small white daisies embroidered on it from the waist up. She wore her hair braided in her usual fashion off to the side.

As for Dmitri, he disappeared into the other room before coming back out a few minutes later, stating that he was clean and changed. When Elena asked him what color his shirt was out of curiosity, he told her it was a simple pale green button-down shirt. Elena found herself asking Dmitri for small details about their surroundings or about the day-to-day life that she could no longer see from time to time in order to better visualize things in her mind. He always obliged her, never making her feel like she was a bother from the sometimes silly questions.

Dmitri explained they were going to go back to their spot on the river for their first lesson together in magic. He also explained that if at any time she wished to stop, she simply had to let him know, and he would oblige or slow down. As for their self-defense lessons, those would be in the evening, either before or after dinner, when the sun was beginning to set and temperatures would be cooler. He said that the last thing they needed was for her to get heat sickness from too much sunlight.

As soon as they stepped outside, Elena hooked her arm around his in a familiar way, and he instinctively tugged her a little closer to his side. She smiled at this and then closed her eyes as she basked in the sunlight, trusting him to guide her.

"Are you nervous at all, or are you excited?" Dmitri asked her as they walked.

She thought about her answer for a moment before chuckling. "Is it possible to be an equal measure of both?" she asked, and he gently squeezed her arm for reassurance, not quite knowing what to say to her.

Dmitri stayed silent after that, and Elena could not tell if she had touched upon something personal or if he was simply resuming his comfortable silence. Her mind whispered to her that it was the former.

"I want to know more about you, too, if you will tell me." Her voice was soft, and he almost did not hear her, but he had been watching the way she moved ever since he left the cottage.

He considered this, an idea creeping into his mind. *"That could work..."* he murmured to himself, which Elena just barely heard. Before she could ask what he meant, he spoke again. "Alright then, I will make you a deal," Dmitri started and then saw how Elena's curiosity latched onto him then. He had a hard time not smiling at how subtle she had tried to be before letting her true curiosity show. "I will teach you your magic lesson, and at the end of each night of the lessons, you can ask me something important about myself. Smaller or random questions can be asked at any time."

Elena grinned, her mind swarming like angry bees as she tried to think of what questions she might want to ask, nodding in agreement. "Deal. How many lessons are there going to be?" she asked curiously, wondering how many big questions she would get the opportunity to ask.

"There are three major lessons of magic to be learned. Everything after that is of little consequence."

Elena huffed. "Three is hardly enough questions."

"Well then, you better think carefully about what you want to ask." Dmitri's tone was easy and playful, but Elena could feel his pulse speed up as her hand rested over his wrist. She could tell that three questions felt like far too many for him.

Elena thought over the proposal before giving a dramatic sigh. "Fine, three major questions," she said—as if she would ever say no to satiating her curiosity.

"There is one more part of the deal. You have to tell me something about yourself too. Preferably stories. I find I learn the most about people from their stories." He grinned at his own cunning, hoping to know more about the little witch wrapped around his arm.

Elena made a face when he mentioned she would have to answer the same questions but sighed as she conceded and nodded. "Alright then. Three major questions. You said that I could ask you smaller questions though anytime, right?" she prodded him, her eagerness and curiosity shining through unabashedly now.

He chuckled softly. "Yes, those you can ask anytime."

"What's your favorite color then?" she asked as if testing to see if he would actually answer her questions.

"Green," he answered without missing a beat. "What about yours?"

"Yellow. It always seemed like a happy color," she answered.

They took turns asking each other a couple of smaller questions as they walked to the river. Once they got there, Dmitri took a deep breath, and Elena felt the mood in the air change as he began to get a little more serious. He explained to Elena that they were going to sit by the edge of the river together, and instantly she could feel her own heart begin to race. It was one thing to hear it and yet know she was far enough away from it, but now her mind raced with 'what ifs' and negative possibilities.

What if I slip and fall in?

What if Dmitri falls in?

Can I really trust him?

Elena swallowed softly, but she let Dmitri guide her to the edge, her legs beginning to feel weaker beneath her as the sound got louder. He finally stopped, and then his hand slid down hers as he sat down. She frowned but slowly followed suit and sat beside him. Memories of her mother flooded back to her as soon as she knelt on the ground. Small glimpses of that day screaming in her ears over the sound of the running water.

"You are going to kill me! Please, think of Elena! She can't lose both of us!" her mother's voice screamed in echoes of her memory.

"I'm doing this town a favor."

The feeling of cold water that had shocked her system and her mother's eyes, dreading Elena's decision. Would she have gone quietly if she knew Elena was watching, just to prevent her from putting a target on her back for the village?

The fear in the man's eyes as he stared at Elena and how she stared back, ready to claw his eyes out if he came closer to her mother at that moment. Where had that fight gone when they had killed her family in front of her? Elena was a coward. She had run. She should have burned with her family that night.

"Elena."

The soft but stern sound of Dmitri's voice cut through her memories, and she could hear the concern. She was suddenly aware of the tears that burned down her cheeks and quickly wiped them away, embarrassed that she was already losing composure and they had not even begun. She sniffed softly and took a deep, shaky breath.

"I'm okay," she said quietly.

"It's okay if you aren't."

Elena gripped the fabric of her skirt until her knuckles turned white, feeling like she might shatter at a moment's notice, but she forced herself to nod.

"I know what I would like my question to be then," Dmitri said softly.

Elena felt like she was suffocating. "Dmitri..."

"Elena, your past cannot hurt you anymore. What has happened to you was terrible, and nothing I can say will change that. But for today's lesson, you must take the first step in simply admitting that it *has* happened. It will not make it hurt any less, but it will be necessary. You cannot work with magic if your mind is too busy giving control to other things."

Elena could not stop the tears now, and she hated this moment. She did not want to feel weak and vulnerable in front of him. A part of her wanted to get up, go back to the cottage, and forget that she had ever asked him to teach her. She wanted to crawl under the blankets and cry. She wanted to selfishly hoard the memories away so wouldn't see that everything that had happened was her fault because she had to swim. Dread bubbled up inside of her at the words that she knew were coming.

"Elena? Will you tell me what led those men to bring you to my forest?"

And just like that, the last of Elena's strength came undone. She began to sob, her shoulders shaking as she covered her face and folded in on herself. Time ticked by until Elena was sure that Dmitri would simply get sick of hearing her cries and force them to go back home. She cried harder at that idea, not wanting to ruin her opportunity to learn and yet unable to console herself. She cried deeply until she was simply too tired to cry again. Eventually, she teetered off into quiet sniffling and occasional hiccups. She couldn't bring herself to look in his direction, but he had not left her side or teased her for her tears. Then she surprised herself by nodding.

Elena took a deep, shaky breath and hesitantly loosened her grip on her skirt. Dmitri was right about one thing; her mind was far too busy giving control over this memory. It was exhausting to hold in her past, exhausting to be the last living person to know what had occurred. Exhausting to have the guilt on her shoulders. She would tell him, and if he thought badly of her, then she would at least have the courtesy of knowing that she had been right.

So, finally, Elena began to tell him her story. She could not bring herself to go into too much detail with him—not nearly having the strength to do so and simply not wanting to, but she still told him everything. She told him how her father had died, and that led to the village shunning her family for not offering themselves to be married off. They called her family unnatural, and a family of unnatural females must simply be the beginnings of a coven of witches. She told him about how she saved her mother and how scared she had been to do so, but not entirely regretting it—even if they died that day anyway. If she had done nothing, she thought that might have been worse, and that admission was enough to start the tears again. She forced herself to continue on, though.

She told him of losing her sight after her family had died and the last thing she had seen. At this, she could feel him tense next to her, and she could swear she heard him grit his teeth, biting back anger at her situation. Lastly, she told him of their decision to take her into the forest.

"I didn't know what would happen if they took me to this forest, but something inside of me told me that at least I would have a chance. I pretended to be terrified of it even, just so they would not change their minds. My family has always taught me that there was never anything to be scared of in this forest—at least not things that weren't everywhere else as well—and I grew up with a healthy respect for it. By the time they had made me begin digging my grave, I just kept thinking about how badly I felt about disturbing it. I had tried to run or escape, but... I was starting to give up hope."

Dmitri nodded to himself. "But you didn't give up hope, at least not all of the way. In the end, you survived, and you are honoring your family by living and breathing. Sometimes that is the most courageous thing that one can do. You are honoring your father by trying to learn magic now. Your mom wanted you to be brave, but bravery is not the total absence of fear. The bravest warriors can still be shaking as they hold their weapons, but they push forward regardless. You suffered greatly, but you have kept moving forward, and in the end, that is all that matters."

Elena sniffed and wiped the last remaining tears from her eyes. Suddenly, she heard Dmitri shuffling and the sounds of his shoes being tossed to the side. Elena widened her eyes with confusion written all over her face.

"What are you..?" she started to ask but then heard a soft splash. "Dmitri!" she shrieked.

"Relax. The water is not deep, nor is the current strong here. It barely comes up past my waist. Thank you for telling me your story, Elena. Now, it is time to learn the first lesson of magic. First, do you trust me?"

She hesitated but nodded, her heart still racing in her chest.

"Usually, I might say you should be more careful who you trust then, but, for today at least, it's a good thing. Care to join me?"

"Dmitri, I am in a dress, and I *assumed* that you were dressed too," she said, giving a now skeptical look at him.

He laughed at that and came over to the edge of the water, placing his wet hands on her knees. Water began to soak into the fabric of her dress where his hands laid, and she gave him a small glare, but there was no real anger behind it.

"I *am* dressed, just like you. Trust me when I say that this is necessary for the lesson, though. I won't let anything happen to you, okay? Now take off your shoes, and I will help you in. You can even keep your clothes on," He smirked cheekily, talking casually and lightly as if this was perfectly normal.

Elena thought he had gone mad. She gave him an incredulous look for a moment before murmuring to herself, "What a gentleman." She thought of the memory of her mother nearly drowning, but before it could sink its claws too deep into her mind, she thought of magic. She thought about the reason she had asked him to teach her to begin with; she was sick and tired of being scared all of the time. Suddenly, she understood why this might be necessary after all, and her face softened.

She sighed and obliged by unlacing her boots and setting them off to the side neatly. "Alright," she said quietly and held out her hand for him.

Dmitri grinned at her and took her hand carefully before he gently tugged her closer into the water. Her legs slid in, and she gave him a small shriek, but his hand was instantly on her waist to steady her—just like it had in the kitchen. The current of the river slithered around her waist, pushing her slightly, and she clung tighter to him, feeling like her feet might slip from under her.

"Dmitri! You said it wasn't strong here!"

Dmitri wrapped his arms around her waist and held her to his chest so she would not be swept away. Her hands gripped his wet shirt tightly. *At least I know he is dressed now,* she thought to herself indignantly.

"I did say you should be careful with whom you trust," he said playfully.

Elena felt her cheeks heat up, and she glared in his direction. "Is the lesson here not to trust you then?" she bit back sharply.

His grip suddenly tightened a little bit on her waist. "Not at all," he said in a suddenly serious tone that nearly gave Elena whiplash. She blushed again, at a loss for words, as her body pressed against him. She was torn between wanting to strangle him and wanting him to hold her closer.

"Then what is it?" she asked, her voice calmer and a little quieter. She could feel the vibrations in his chest when he spoke, and she tried not to find it too terribly distracting but definitely wanted it to continue.

"Magic and fear have more in common than you think." His voice rumbled by her ear, and gooseflesh pricked her skin as her heart raced. There was an unspoken question accompanied by his statement. It was as though he was asking her, *"And are you scared now? Are you scared of me?"*

He continued, not pulling away from her. "Both of them are impossible to ever truly be rid of. They will both simmer under your skin, waiting for the chance to devour you if you let it. As I said, bravery is not the complete absence of fear. You, here and now, are not without your magic. It waits for you to call to it, whether you know that you are doing it or not. We are standing in the river right now together, and the current was strong for you when you faced your fear and jumped in, but what about now?"

Elena blinked and realized the water around them had completely stilled. She could hear the water rushing around them, but she only felt the still stagnant water. Dmitri kept one arm tightly around her waist and took one of her hands in his own as he guided it over the water. She felt the surface tension change from still to quickly flowing once again as it got further away, as if there was merely an invisible barrier around them to keep away the current.

"Magic will only ever hurt you if you let it. When you do magic, you focus it into existence to turn tangible. Today's lesson, Elena, is about channeling your energy. It is letting the emotions exist inside of you—even fear—but not fueling them. Close your eyes and focus on the magic inside of you. Call it to you to do your bidding and show it that you are the one in control here."

Dmitri paused, and Elena realized that he was waiting for her to do something. "I don't know how," she admitted quietly, still not quite understanding.

"That's okay. Magic is... well, it is turning a very intangible thing into something real. It is calling the world to bend and distort to fill your intentions. When you channel your magic to do work for you, you are creating. You are focusing on your intent as you surrender yourself to magic while still remaining in control of your mind. You are still thinking of what you want it to do for you. Some things require more clarity and precision, other things, you just simply have to feel and accept the magic into the world through yourself.

"I brought you into the river because you were terrified of it, but it was something that I knew you could get past. If you let fear drive your magic, you will never be able to truly control it. You came into the water, and you faced your fear because you were focused more on your determination to learn. Those two healthy emotions trumped the fear and allowed you to regain control of yourself in order to do something that scared you, right?" he asked.

Elena nodded, understanding starting to unfold in her mind as he continued.

"When you first went into the river back in your village, you had used your magic then, too, even if you had not realized it. Your intent was clear; saving your mother. You had a determination that caused you to forget your fear of the man or the fear of consequences, and you let the magic guide your body through the water to your mother despite never having been taught how to swim. Your magic is within you right now. Focus on what you want it to do for you, something small to start with, like bringing back the water current. Acknowledge the presence of magic, and then simply allow it to come into existence as much as you will allow it to. Feel inside of yourself that you want the current to come back, and it will. You control your magic—your life even—and you decide what to do with it."

Elena nodded again and took a deep breath. Closing her eyes—despite it not making much of a difference—she tried to focus on the task. She remembered all of the small ways that her magic had nudged her throughout her life, whispering that it had been there all along and waiting for her to acknowledge it. Her thoughts circled around her intuition, her connection to the earth, her knowledge of impossible possibilities, and then lastly, she thought about the night in the rain. She had felt sorrow and hopelessness, yes, but she had also remembered singing in one last defiant act. She remembered the words as if they were some kind of prayer, her intent being to beg the world to save her, and she felt the way magic tasted on her tongue before it had answered her.

The world had sent Dmitri to save her.

She felt the air pulled from her lungs and her hands gripped his shirt a little tighter at the realization. Slowly, coming back to her senses, she could feel the magic bristling underneath her skin. The feeling felt like static for a moment, as if it was saying, *'Finally! You are awake!'* and Elena laughed breathlessly. She pictured the voice talking to her as her father, and she smiled as another tear rolled down her cheek. This time, not from fear or sorrow, but finally glimpsing the edges of hope and healing.

Dmitri's wet hand came up to wipe the tear away, making more of her face wet than before, and then they both chuckled at that before she opened her eyes. He didn't remove his hand immediately, and she smiled.

I want the current to come back. I will not be swept away.

Elena felt the magic answer her instantly, removing what invisible barrier had been blocking her and Dmitri as the current came back strongly. She wavered at the sudden feeling, but he held her tighter and laughed before picking her up and spinning her around in the water, causing her to shriek a bit but laugh. He set her down quickly.

"Beautiful!" he announced.

Elena grinned proudly, the feeling almost exhilarating. "Can we do more?"

"Of course, it wouldn't be much practice if you just did it once. Besides," he said as a hint of playfulness crept into his voice, "You still have to prove it wasn't just beginners' luck."

Elena could imagine the smirk on his face, and so she matched it with her own, a challenging gleam in her eye. Dmitri carefully set her down into the water, and she missed feeling the strong way that he had held her so effortlessly and made her feel safe. Now she felt exposed and vulnerable, but she readied herself for the water this time. She would not fall. And this time, she would stand firm on her own.

The two spent the next half hour practicing with the current of the water until Elena could do it easily, not thinking the words so much as simply calling to it. Then they practiced other things, like controlling the heat of the water, which took a little more concentration. Elena felt as though she was stretching muscles that she never knew she had before today, but it felt *good*.

"Wait a second! Is that how you got the bathwater to be warm so quickly?" she asked suddenly after he had shown her how to gradually raise the temperature.

"I wondered when you would guess that." His voice was amused.

She huffed dramatically but shook her head in amusement. "Show me again."

Eventually, they pulled themselves from the water of the river. They laid in the warm grass under the sun as they relaxed for a bit, drying off slightly and continuing to ask each other questions here and there about small things about themselves. The process of discovering things about each other and about themselves left them both feeling elated. It was a successful lesson, and Dmitri even gave her work to do once they got back home—small things that she could do to practice with her intent. He explained that magic was not the answer to everything and, like all things, using too much of it could leave you feeling exhausted, so she had agreed not to overdo it.

After they had spent hours together by the river, Elena realized that she was not as afraid of the river as she once was. In fact, she looked forward to the next time that they could come out here together. She even considered asking Dmitri to teach her to swim better. After all, there was no longer a reason why she should not indulge that part of herself.

They walked back to the cottage together idly, sometimes silent, though it felt more comfortable and far less suffocating now. Once they got back, Dmitri announced that he would cook them something for dinner, and Elena realized that they had spent the entire day out there. Time had flown by, and she had not even considered that they had not eaten anything for the entire time out there. As if he had summoned it, though, she suddenly realized that her hunger was gnawing at her.

"That sounds lovely. Today has been wonderful. Thank you, Dmitri." Elena smiled brightly.

"Oh, we aren't done yet," he chuckled.

Elena raised an eyebrow. "We aren't?"

"Nope." He smirked a bit, and she could hear the cockiness in his voice that made her want to roll her eyes. "After dinner, we will start the real exercise."

A feeling of excitement and dread toiled inside of her stomach, but she would not allow him to see the satisfaction of the latter, so she merely grinned.

"Looking forward to it then."

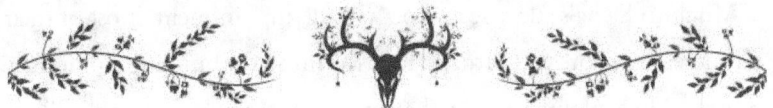

Chapter Sixteen

Dmitri's Mother

E lena had come to the conclusion that Dmitri was a sadist.

Her chest rose and fell quickly, completely out of breath as loose strands of hair fell over her face and her hands gripped onto her knees as she doubled over. Her skin was slick with sweat, and her ribs ached from their old injuries, but Dmitri was relentless.

"Stand up and place your arms over your head if you are struggling to breathe, Elena." His voice was stern, but he never once got angry or frustrated with her. He was calm as he directed and commanded her to work her muscles.

Much to Elena's surprise and perhaps disappointment, most of their self-defense lesson was actually focused more on building up healthy muscle. He explained to her that while fighting was a useful skill, it would mean nothing if she did not learn to leverage her body, and if it came down to it, she would need to be strong enough to run away to fight another day. Elena had grimaced at this, pointing out that the whole reason that she was learning these things was so that she could stop running away, but Dmitri had an answer for that too.

"Survival is your goal, or else you will never live to see another fight. No matter what, a fight is not worth losing your life over. Do you understand me? Pride can be a nasty thing, my little witch."

The nickname startled her, as she was not used to people outside of her family acting so familiar to her. His voice was a mix of endearing and playful, but she could not tell if he was teasing her or if it was perhaps something else. Instead of responding, she shot him a quick glare—even though her shy smile had given her away as not meaning it.

Elena now lifted her arms above her head as he had instructed, forcing her body to stand upright as she took air into her lungs. She had been running, stretching, and working out for the last two hours after dinner. They had eased into the workout, teaching her about the proper breathing exercises to do while exerting herself and warming up before they could truly begin. When she had begun to complain a little under an hour in, he had laughed and told her to keep going. The entire time he did the moves alongside her, not letting her suffer alone at least.

Sadist, Elena thought for the hundredth time.

Once she had finally caught her breath, Dmitri came over to her and gently placed his hand on her shoulder. "Alright, we should call it a night. Tomorrow we will take a break from strengthening to actually learn a couple of moves to help you leverage your opponent. We can switch off days so your body has time to rest," he explained.

Elena turned so that her body faced him a little more. "My body is going to need a year to rest after that." She pouted up at him, and he chuckled again.

"It won't always be this intense," he promised her softly.

She sighed in acceptance and nodded a little bit. "Regardless, would you mind leading me inside to the washroom and starting a bath?"

"Of course. Would you like me to heat the water for you?"

Elena nodded, nearly whimpering when she thought about using more focus and concentration to try and heat the bath water. "Yes, please." She was thoroughly exhausted and took a deep breath as his arm hooked around hers to begin leading her inside the cottage.

A short time later, Elena had stripped down and sank into the hot bathwater. Her muscles screamed in protest at any kind of movement, but the warmth helped to eventually coax them into relaxing. She smiled at the feeling of a productive day and sank lower into the bathtub. The smell of lemongrass soap filled her nose again, and she realized how tired she was. She had battled through harsh emotions that she had wanted to bury. Still, even now, she felt the familiar ache of guilt settle down onto her chest as she thought of it, but it no longer felt quite as final. She had practiced magic today and learned how to channel her intentions to create tangible magic. She had found new muscles that she never even knew that she had.

All in all, she was very pleased with the day's events, but there was still one thing left to do before she could be truly satisfied with it; Elena still had to ask Dmitri her question. She wondered if he thought that she had forgotten. She wondered if he would have let her forget or if he had been hoping for that. But she had been thinking of it whenever her mind had not been otherwise occupied with training.

Three important questions were hardly enough to truly get to know someone. She wanted to know everything about him. Could that be one of her questions? *What is your life story, Dmitri?* No. Elena knew that he most likely would allow her to ask more questions after the three, but something about this felt like he was leading her to something. It felt as though this was another test, and he wanted—no, *needed*—her to ask something specific. Now it was up to her to simply figure out what exactly it was.

Elena took her time before she finally pulled herself from the bathwater, which had managed to retain the same warmth since the moment she had stepped in. She smiled a little bit at that before she dried the water from her skin and slipped into one of the nightgowns that he had grabbed for her. It was beginning to get easier to dress herself, but she still struggled with understanding which side was the front and which was the back. This one was easier since she could feel that it had buttons along the chest of it.

Once she had gotten dressed again, she cautiously opened the door and could hear the sound of the fireplace crackling softly. "Dmitri?" she called, wondering which room he was in.

"I'm here." His deep voice was closer to her than she had expected, and she nearly jumped out of her skin. Dmitri smiled sheepishly and chuckled. "Sorry, didn't mean to frighten you. I had just been coming to check on you."

Elena's heart calmed down, and she chuckled. "I won't drown in the bath."

"You can never be too certain. For a moment there, I wondered if I had overworked you, and you couldn't even push yourself out of the bath."

"Wait, you truly thought I had drowned?"

Dmitri chuckled again, and she could practically hear the embarrassment in it. "You were quiet. I was worried."

Elena relaxed her shoulders and smiled in his direction. "Well, I am fine. I was just enjoying the warm water." She paused for a moment before adding, "I was also trying to think of what question I was going to ask you tonight." Elena felt like she was holding her breath as she waited for his response, nervous that he may have changed his mind already or perhaps she was wrong, and he did not really want her to remember about their deal. Instead, he simply took a deep breath.

"I was wondering when you'd ask. Have you thought of your first question?"

She nodded. "Would... you like to sit down first?"

"You should lay in your bed and relax your muscles. I can sit by your bedside while we talk, and when we are done, you can just try to get some rest."

When she agreed, he offered his arm to her before leading her to the bedroom. She probably could have taken the time to fumble her own way there but was indeed tired from the day, and she was fond of the way he tugged her closer as they walked together. Besides, she knew he would not let her stumble or fall.

Slipping under the blankets, she pulled them up and over her shoulders as she laid on her side and faced his direction. She could hear the subtle creak of the chair as he sat down as well and smiled, knowing he had been trying his hardest to make more sounds for her since her little breakdown. She appreciated the effort that he had been putting into it, even if there had still been long periods of silence here and there. Slowly, she took a deep breath and nodded, nervous for some reason.

This was the first night in which she would get a glimpse into the life of the man she had been spending her time with.

Dmitri had finally settled into acceptance that she was going to be asking him personal questions about himself. During her bath, he had begun to get anxious over it, pacing along the kitchen and wondering if there was a way to get out of this. He could answer vaguely. He could *lie*. No, he couldn't, not to her. He wondered if he could bargain with her then, convince her not to ask. Distract her maybe until she forgot about it altogether. He thought he was panicking before but then realized how quiet she had been.

Thoughts of her drowning in the bath and it being his fault ran through his mind. He swore, then strode towards the washroom and promised himself that if she was okay, he would answer anything for her. Then the door had practically flown open. His heart nearly ceased in his chest, and by the time he had recovered, he nearly cursed the world for tricking him into the promise, especially when he found out that she had been already thinking of the question.

The only thing left to do was to surrender himself to her, for better or for worse.

"You told me that you were not related to June and Silas before. You also mentioned that they used to talk of a time before they lived out in the forest, but you spoke about it as if you had not been around at that point. So, how did you come to live with them?" Elena asked, speaking carefully as though she was trying to find the right way to phrase her question.

Dmitri smiled softly at her, pleased and resigned to know she was on the right track.

"Alright," he said quietly. "I'll tell you the beginning of my story."

"When I was born, for one reason or another, the woman who gave birth to me had thought me to be cursed. I don't know what she saw when she looked at me as a small child, but whatever it was must have terrified her. Maybe she saw my future, maybe she saw a reflection of herself or the man who had bedded her, but whatever it was caused a loathing to build in her. I was young, barely able to walk well enough on my own, when she walked me out to this forest. I was so young that I don't remember much of her, only the way that she looked at me with hatred and perhaps a little regret.

"She walked me deep into the woods, constantly tugging me to keep going even as I protested. Once we were deep enough, she finally allowed us to rest. Overcome with exhaustion, I had fallen asleep with my head on her lap, only to awaken sometime later to find I was alone. I vaguely remember panicking, running as fast as I could in a direction I thought was the way back to our village.

"At some point, it had gotten dark and then light again. I do not know the exact amount of time that passed while I was out there wandering the forest. By some miracle, wild animals had avoided me. Perhaps I was too scrawny to even be considered to be a meal, or maybe they, too, thought I was cursed. Regardless, by the time June found me, I was nearly dead.

"I thought she was my mother at first, finally coming back to me. She carried me in her arms to the cottage, where she and Silas discussed what to do with me. They had always wanted a child, and they were loath to think that someone had just abandoned me there. For a very long time after they saved me, I refused to speak altogether. It took nearly a year of June and Silas gently coaxing me back into the world and out from the inside of my mind before I finally began to speak once more.

"June and Silas raised me like their own. Silas was... well, he was different from most men that you are probably used to. He was poetic, and some days he acted like he could pluck the invisible strings of the world to make them sing for him. He was wild and creative, constantly driving June wildly mad with frustration and happiness. June was a little bit more on the quiet side, though she was certainly not timid. I think she understood during my first year there that I simply needed time. She understood far more than she would ever let on, though I think that her being a witch had a lot to do with that.

"June was what you would call a 'Green Witch.' Basically, it means that a lot of her power came from nature, and she was strongest when working alongside the earth. For such a quiet woman, she had a terribly loud laugh. I could hear her laughing all the way from the river some days. Silas loved to bring out that laugh in her as often as they could. She was not afraid to tell me when I was brooding too much or scold me.

"They weren't my parents, but they were better. They were people who had chosen me, and I had chosen them. When I got older, June would take me once a year to a town further to the east where we would pretend to be travelers in order to get some supplies like fabric, paints, or books for Silas, shoes, or other things. She harvested all of their food, and until I was older and could hunt, they rarely ate meat. On one of our trips, June had sat me down and told me that if I wanted to stay in these villages, then she would find a home for me. She was sure she could find someone to take me in if I wanted a more 'normal' life, but the idea had appalled me. They were my chosen family. I would have no one else.

"I never liked the idea of family being people who were required to love you. I loved June and Silas because they were good, not because my blood tied me to them. I liked the way they lived with freedom. This forest... became my home. I traveled all edges of it as I got older, learning all of the nooks and crannies of it that I could. On our travels, I met people in villages, even people my age, but most of them simply treated me differently. Maybe they could see the wild Silas rubbed off on me or the unnatural June. Or maybe I was perfectly unnatural all on my own. Regardless, all of it felt just as foreign to me as I was to them.

"They taught me all kinds of things about the world. I taught myself others. June especially told me about the forest and how it would always provide for them as long as they cared for it in return. She was protective of it, and she would always make sure I knew how important it was to care for the world. I think, looking back on it, that she was a big influence as to why I have made some of the choices that I have."

Dmitri finally paused his story for a long moment as Elena held the blankets tightly to her chest in suspense. She realized she had been holding her breath, captivated by every word as he wove his story. She forced herself to bite back questions as she felt a lingering silence. It was as if he was debating adding something, and she did not want to risk interrupting.

"When June died, Silas lost a really large part of his life. He remained poetic and creative, but it seemed like the eternal light in his eyes had finally begun to dim. I stayed with him until he passed away about two years later and then buried him beside June in the forest under a particularly large tree that they had liked to spend time under. With both of them gone, it felt like my time with them was all some kind of surreal dream sometimes. It is hard to think of them and remember all of the happiness and ease that I had with them. I think for a long time, I had simply decided that I wouldn't think of them at all because then the pain would feel further away. Now I have realized it was a foolish notion. The pain was always there, but by not thinking of them, I had simply removed the happiness. Eventually, the pain faded, but by choosing not to remember them, I had prevented myself from moving on and truly being happy, I think."

"What made you change your mind?" she asked quietly. Her heart ached with empathy. He had gone through so much, and he had answered far more of her question than she had been expecting.

Dmitri stood from his chair as Elena could hear the creaking. Her heart raced as she wondered where he was going. Too many questions flooded her mind, but mostly, she simply did not want him to go yet. She wondered if she had upset or offended him by her question. She heard him walk to the doorway and then pause, so she scrambled to open her mouth to speak—to say anything to apologize. Instead, his voice was calm and warm as it filled the entire room.

"You did." He paused for a moment, looking at the way she looked confused, but he made no move to try and explain himself. "Goodnight, Elena."

And with that, the door clicked shut.

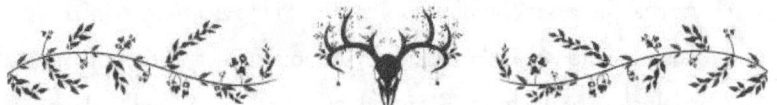

CHAPTER SEVENTEEN

FOREBODING

After Dmitri left Elena's room, he wandered his way to the kitchen and poured himself a glass of water before he leaned against the counter. His mind felt carefully blank, trying hard not to think of the information he had just spilled. He drank the water, focusing with more intensity than necessary on how cool the liquid felt against his dry tongue and throat. He did not feel particularly anxious, upset, or even happy. In fact, he felt close to nothing. His mind protected him from the thoughts that threatened to seep in, instead providing him with a feeling of existing just outside the edge of something.

Once he finished his water, he made his way silently into the living room, making himself comfortable in the chair by the fireplace that simmered in its fading embers. He thought that he should probably start the fire again, but he could not will his legs to move. His body felt heavy and weary, made of stone. He stretched to try and loosen his muscles before he sighed heavily, sinking deeper into the chair. He could move to the other bedroom of the cottage and fully stretch out there, but more often than not, he found himself coming back out here in the middle of the night anyways. He was unable to stay in that room for too long, with the memories threatening to drown him.

He was unsure of how much time had passed or when precisely he had fallen asleep, but when his eyes reopened, he would awaken within a dream.

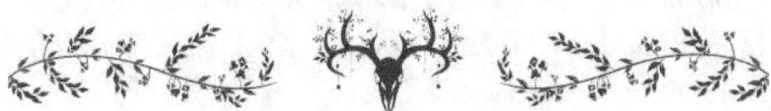

*D*mitri *opened his eyes to see that he was still sitting in the same rocking chair inside the cottage, but something was different. He felt himself become more aware of his surroundings, looking for the source of the change as he rose from the chair. His gaze was investigative and suspicious as he looked for the tell-tale signs of a glamour. It would not have been the first time he had run into a magical creature who had tried to pull their mischief on him, but this felt different, and the other magical creatures had long since disappeared from his forest. He glanced around again when it suddenly dawned on him; the room was the same, but everything had lost its fine detail. What once had been an assortment of various details or flaws now simply resembled bland, hazy shapes and outlines. At a glance, everything looked to be in place, but if he focused his eyes on any one thing that he might have overlooked in his day-to-day life, he would see that it was as if it was an unfinished drawing.*

He recognized the feeling immediately and let his shoulders relax. He was simply dreaming.

He sighed softly and rubbed his face, beginning to walk to the door of Elena's bedroom before he paused with his hand on the handle.

"Come here," an androgynous creaking voice whispered to him inside his mind, echoing around the space.

Dmitri frowned. Why did that voice seem so familiar?

He hesitated, knowing it was just a dream and that the real Elena was safely asleep, before he cautiously pulled his hand away from the handle and turned to go towards the front door. His curiosity had gotten the better of him, but something inside of his chest felt like it was seizing with horror. He should not be looking for whatever called out to him, and he knew this. He should go back to the rocking chair, close his eyes, and hope to wake up. So why did his feet keep moving?

His heart raced as he pushed open the door and walked outside. Fog encapsulated the meadow, hiding and muting all color from the once vibrant field. He frowned, eyes scanning the scene.

"Well, I am here. Where are you?" he announced loudly.

Silence followed, and Dmitri felt his annoyance overpower his hesitation. His mind had conjured the voice. The least it could do was not waste his time trying to fret over why it was so familiar. Dmitri stared, waiting for a few moments before he shook his head and turned to face the cabin.

"So... impatient," the voice droned slowly, drawing out each and every syllable.

Dmitri froze, his blood running cold as recognition finally dawned on him. He did not turn around this time, simply closing his eyes and resting his forehead against the door of the cottage.

"Please, no," Dmitri pleaded quietly, his voice barely audible, and yet he knew the creature would have no issues with hearing him.

"Do you fear this?"

Dmitri frowned a little deeper. "Yes."

"It is what you have chosen. You should embrace your choices. Is this... because of the human?" The voice was slow, taking its time as if each word was a struggle to utter.

"Yes," he admitted. "Is there nothing I can do to stop it?"

"I am afraid that I do not know of any way to cease what has been put into motion."

Dmitri squeezed his eyes shut tighter. "This is a nightmare," he groaned.

"If only it were that easy."

Dmitri took a deep breath as he readied himself for what he knew came next. He would be brave. This part was only a dream—a nightmare. He opened his eyes and turned just in time to see the creature lunge at him, opening its unhinged jaw before consuming him and drowning his mind in a voided darkness.

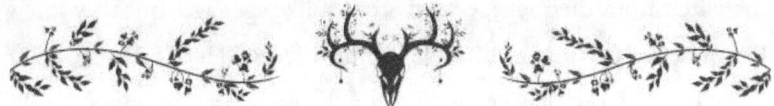

CHAPTER EIGHTEEN

INNORIN

The villagers of Innorin gathered quickly to receive news of the latest scouting mission within the cursed woods. They had purged the witch from their village what seemed like ages ago, but they knew her presence still lingered in that damned forest. Her body had never been retrieved, but they knew the forest did not let go of things so easily. Her existence stood as an act of defiance, one that the villagers would no longer tolerate. Her life went against everything that they had stood for, everything that they had built, and they would not sit back and continue to let her spread her plague while good men had died in her stead.

After Poe and Goddard had not come home from their deliverance of the witch, a search party was sent into the woods after some convincing from Herrick, Poe's only son. The two men had strict orders to go northeast into the forest towards an area where—according to old maps of the terrain—the mountain curved like a wave, providing a dry enough area to burn the witch in, so that is where the search party was led. What they found had been a partially dug grave halfway to the ledge, guns and a shovel spade laying about in the dirt, and blood that coated the surrounding trees like an explosion of paint. After another day of searching in the daylight, they found Goddard with his throat torn to ribbons and mouth opened wide in a silent scream. His eyes were glazed over, and his body had already begun to bloat and decay as a symptom of the forest. A short time after that, the only remains that they had found of Poe were two teeth, his clothes, and one eyeball.

The search party brought back the news to Innorin with heavy hearts that had begun filling with rage. Herrick, knowing that this was a possibility when they had not come home that first night, wasted no time in rallying the townsfolk together. He spoke of what an honorable man his father was and how Goddard had been the town's finest blacksmith. He spoke about what the witch had stolen from them: their peace of mind, their friends, and their family. He raged on, spitting with anger as he addressed the town. The only solution here was to find the witch and truly put her to death for her crimes. They would drag her back to the village if need be, but she would suffer for her crimes, just as their village now suffered from their own loss.

Many people had come together and agreed with Herrick. He offered to lead the scouting missions personally, saying he would go alone if need be to prevent anyone else from risking themselves. This ended up not being necessary as other villagers readily volunteered to assist. Herrick had traveled in and around the forest as well, going to other villages and speaking to them about the witch of the woods. He convinced many that she needed to become an example to many, or else many would fall victim to her misdeeds later on. Alone, they might not have stood a chance, but together they would burn the entire forest down if they needed to.

Navigating the terrain of the northern forest was trickier than he might have expected, constantly getting lost within the woods. Herrick was a strong hunter, though, and he had survived much harsher climates and terrain. He was determined to see the light drain from the witch's eyes, even if it took his own last breath. They wore shoes with iron slates on the bottom so that the magical entity of the forest would not be able to sense their movements. They wore hats made of leaves and covered themselves in mud in order to hide in plain sight from whatever monstrous eyes leered at them. All of their hard work had paid off. Finally, he returned to the village on this night with good news.

He addressed the gathered villagers, noticing surprisingly more women than in the previous meeting. "We have found it," he spoke firmly.

A chorus of gasps and cheers of delight echoed throughout the building. He nodded, trying to remain stoic and not smile too widely. The hard part had yet to come after all.

"In the morning, I will leave to inform our allies. I suggest you rest well. When I return, we will gather all of the torches, weapons, and bravest souls. You have but a few weeks to prepare. It will take a solid day of traversing the forest to reach the witch's cottage once we begin, but there is no room for error. Men, it is time to rid ourselves of the Innorin witch."

CHAPTER NINETEEN

LESSON TWO: COMMUNICATING

Dmitri had woken up the next morning, moving around silently so as not to wake Elena. He knew that yesterday had been a lot of information and work for her, and he knew she would need to sleep. He, too, felt tired from the day. Dmitri had never been known for being the most talkative of people, and last night he had spoken more than he had since Silas died so long ago. Not to mention the nightmare that had plagued him last night, warning him of the inevitability of his fate. He shook away that thought.

When he had left Elena last night, it had not been because she had upset him or because he had not wanted to spend more time with her. It was because once he had started talking, he could not trust himself to stop. His words spilled from him as he recounted his time spent with June and Silas. Even though he had been very young when his birth mother abandoned him in the forest, what little memory he had of the woman was still strong. He had thought about the look in her eyes often throughout his life, always wondering 'why.'

He had long since accepted that, for one reason or another, she had not wanted him. More so than that, she did not want him to go to another family in the village, but she wanted him dead. She had left him out in those woods to die, and whether it was from slow starvation or being ripped apart by animals, she didn't care as long as the job had gotten done. He had accepted it, but he still hated to think of it.

After June and Silas were both gone, Dmitri had convinced himself that his birth mother must have looked at him and seen what kind of future awaited him. She had seen the monster that he would become and had wanted to kill it. Truly, he would not blame her if this had been her reasoning, though he always knew deep down that it was not. Even the most powerful witches could not predict the future so fully.

Whenever Dmitri had brought up this idea before they had died, June was adamant that even if his birth mother had been a witch, the future was never truly set in stone, and witches could only ever see general or vague feelings. June would also remind him that her own village had thought her to be completely unnatural and would see her burned for living. They would have seen Silas hanged for his ideas. Some people's ideas of monsters were simply anything they did not understand. To add to this, if she had been a witch, then Dmitri would have had the blood of a witch flowing through his veins, and he simply did not.

So, this left Dmitri to keep guessing. Had his birth mother simply been that cruel to kill her son for no reason? Had he been born to be a sacrifice for the woods? Silas had mentioned that idea, saying that sometimes women were impregnated in order to birth a child meant to be given up as a sacrifice to keep the gods appeased. Dmitri never paid this idea much mind but would later laugh at the irony that the idea had been brought. If he was meant to be a sacrifice to this forest to appease some kind of god, he laughed at how poorly it had backfired on them.

Elena was too smart for her own good. She could have asked him anything last night, like what is his biggest fear or asked him to tell her about the best moment of his life. Those were indeed personal questions that make a person who they are, but no. She had seen through his game, and she was working her way toward the end by starting at the beginning. She was clever, and it terrified him. It now meant that there would be no way to simply avoid telling her the truth now. He had made his decision to tell her already, but to have it be set in stone like this was something else entirely.

Last night, after he had told her his story, he needed to walk away before he told her everything. Before he told her the circumstances around June's death, what happened after, and before he told her about what was inevitably coming. Dmitri had felt bad about leaving, especially after seeing how concerned she looked when he walked to the door, but he simply could not stay any longer. Perhaps there was a reason that he had not spoken much throughout his life. So why, then, was her presence enough to make the floodgates of his mind open so wildly?

He had never had a friend before—much less one who made him feel alive again or whose name made his thoughts nearly irrational with the desire to be around her. While losing her was becoming increasingly terrifying, he still found it to be quite the learning curve to open himself up for dissection. His mind was a mess of contradictions; wanting to be there for her and his determination to do so conflicted with the knowledge that he may not have a choice one day. Not wanting to let her get close and yet wanting to allow her that freedom of choice that he felt he was losing. He wanted to imagine what life by her side might look like in whatever capacity she allowed him to be there, letting her guide the time they had together, and yet wondered if it was simply too selfish to want such things.

Today, however, was a new day, and Dmitri was trying not to think of the night prior by instead focusing on the magic lesson. He was readying himself by trying to figure out exactly how to explain it. He had never thought that he would be teaching someone magic like this. He had been struggling to figure out exactly how to explain this next lesson since it had been something that he had always just felt since he was younger—even without the blood of a witch inside of him.

The bedroom door finally creaked open, and Dmitri paused, looking up to see Elena slowly tracing her hand along the wall until she paused near the living area. "Dmitri?"

"Good morning, Elena."

"You're being quiet again. I listened for you before I came out here, and I thought you might have left. Now I wonder if perhaps you have left me in other ways," she said quietly, frowning a little bit.

Dmitri frowned as well. He had indeed been quiet, but it was simply to allow her time to sleep in this morning. Though now, of course, he could see why she thought that he was closing himself off to her again. *Was he?*

"I'm sorry for last night," Elena continued. "If you do not wish to answer any more questions, then I will not ask them, and you can simply tell me what you are comfortable with. Please, just don't leave me alone again. I cannot bear that." Her voice wavered as tears threatened to spill from her eyes, but she squared her shoulders back stubbornly, refusing to let them fall.

Dmitri was moving as soon as he remembered that his legs could work. "No, no, Elena, that is not it at all. I was just trying to let you sleep," he explained quickly, stopping as he stood in front of her. Elena's face remained even and calm, but Dmitri could see the hurt in her eyes. His stomach flipped at that.

"Last night, you just left."

Dmitri cursed himself inside of his mind. He was never good with people, and it truly showed right now. He tried to think of how to explain himself and yet could not think of the words nor make them form on his lips, so instead, Elena frowned deeper like his silence was confirmation of something. She looked down, and Dmitri could feel his heart racing at the thought of making her upset this quickly in the morning. He took one more step closer to her and finally spoke.

"Gods, Elena—" he began, her name feeling strained on his tongue. He forced himself to swallow the lump in his throat, and he tried to start again. "Last night, I left, but it was not because I was upset, I promise. I just... I am not used to talking to people, alright? It felt good to answer your question, but it is not something that I am used to doing. I left because I just needed time to process how telling you everything made me feel."

Elena looked back up at him, still frowning and looking skeptical. "And how did it make you feel?"

Dmitri lifted his hand to touch her cheek but stopped and then forced himself to lower it, unsure if he should be touching her like that, especially right now. "It made me feel scared but excited. I don't want you to stop asking questions, but I have never told another soul some of the things that I am going to be telling you. It is new to me, so I ask you to be patient with me. I have been alone for far too long of a time. I do not wish to be alone again. Though I do not wish to make *you* feel alone again either."

Elena's shoulders seemed to relax a little bit. "You don't regret telling me, then? And... you aren't shutting me out?"

"No, my little witch. I don't regret a single moment with you, except maybe the ones where I made you think this way. I am not shutting you out either, just simply learning how to let you in."

Elena's frown melted away into a soft, tentative smile. "Before you left last night, I wanted to tell you something. May I tell you now before we move forward from this?" she asked, sounding a little more emboldened.

Dmitri chuckled softly, nearly breathless with relief. "Of course."

"I had wanted to tell you that I was not unfortunate enough to have met the woman who abandoned you in this forest, but I have met plenty of cruel people who wore masks of pleasantness for a long time. Whatever her reasoning might have been, it was misguided at best. You had a rough beginning to your life, but perhaps we need those terrible things in order to realize that there are better things out there waiting to find us, just as June found you."

She took a deep breath, and then she held out her hand as an invitation for him to take, stunning him as he obliged. He was careful not to grab her too quickly or roughly, but he held her hand with a firmness that he hoped conveyed that he was not going to let her go that easily. Her fingers wrapped around his, squeezing equally as tight.

"I am happy that you had two people who continued to choose you over and over again. I am glad that they got to experience you do the same for them. I am sorry that they are gone, but I am glad that you are still here," Elena concluded softly.

Dmitri had not realized how desperately he needed to hear those words coming from her lips until she had said them. His heart was racing inside of his chest, and he could think of no words that could match hers. Instead of staying quiet, though, and risking letting her think that he was potentially upset again, he did the only other thing that came to mind at the moment.

Dmitri gently pulled Elena's hand so that her body gently stumbled forward. There was not far to go since the distance between them was small, but she still gasped softly as his large arms engulfed her small frame in an embrace. He wrapped his arms around her, having to stoop slightly to keep from sweeping her off of her feet completely, and he held her close to him, burying his face in her hair that had come loose from her braid.

He closed his eyes, breathing her in as his mind raced with conflicting thoughts that ranged from anxiety at his actions to relief at finally doing this.

Elena's eyes widened as he wrapped his arms around her waist. He could feel the subtle thumping of her heart—or maybe it was his own? He was so close to her that he could no longer tell the difference. Her cheeks reddened slightly, clearly not expecting this reaction from him but she did not act upset by it. Once she had recovered from her shock, her arms slid around his torso as well, and she stood on her tiptoes to keep him from having to stoop so low for her. She held him tightly back, smiling as her own face buried into his shoulder.

How long has it been since someone held me like this? Dmitri wondered, smelling the faint lemongrass in her hair as a feeling of nostalgia overcame him.

"Thank you," Dmitri murmured into her hair, and Elena blushed harder.

She shook her head slightly. "There's no need for that. I haven't done anything. I am sorry for not saying good morning to you today."

Dmitri laughed softly beside her ear as he had not even thought of that, and he was surprised that she was still apologizing. He held her a little tighter in response. "Don't worry. I am glad you didn't waste time and told me what was on your mind. I don't want to scare you."

"Still, good morning, Dmitri." Her voice was smooth and nearly gave him chills at how soft it was. In truth, everything about her was far softer than he had expected.

"Good morning, my little witch."

Elena smiled, and he could feel the curve of her lips against his shoulder. Finally, he forced himself to pull away from her. They were both left feeling slightly colder without the other's embrace, but they smiled shyly at each other.

"I think you helped me finally figure out how to explain today's lesson. Are you ready for it?"

She nodded, and her smile brightened a little bit. "I am now."

D mitri and Elena ate breakfast together, sitting perhaps a little closer to each other than they had previously. The air between them was far more relaxed than it had been earlier. They had survived the first day of lessons and questions together, and the trust between them was far more tangible.

After they ate breakfast, they both got dressed in clothes for the day and then left the small cottage once more with linked arms. As they began to walk, Elena could feel the subtle ways the ground shifted beneath her feet, from the soft wisping grass of the wildflower field around the cottage to familiar soil. Dmitri had once again not explained where they were going, and a familiar dread settled into her stomach.

"Are we going into the forest?" she asked cautiously.

"We are, but nothing bad is going to happen to you. I am right here. Remember our lesson yesterday?"

Elena did, and it was the sole reason why she was not teetering on the edge of a panic attack at the idea of being here. She held his arm a little closer as they walked, her mind trying to rationalize her fears.

"What about wild animals?" she asked.

"They won't hurt you. Truthfully, they are probably more scared of you than you are of them, as a general rule of thumb." Dimitri's own body relaxed as he placed his hand over hers. "Trust me. The forest won't hurt you. In fact, it has been dying to see you again," he said matter-of-factly.

Elena's eyebrows knitted together, his tone making it hard to distinguish if he was joking or not. His comment about animals being more afraid of her seemed highly improbable, but his reassurance that the forest would not hurt her made her feel a little better, so she did not argue.

"How far are we going?" she asked instead.

"Not terribly far since I know that you are still sore from yesterday. Just far enough to where we can see the forest in all directions and no sign of the cottage."

She nodded, though it only raised more questions. Why did they need to be far enough away from the cottage that they could not see it? That could be now for all she knew. They walked in silence for a short time after that, and Elena could feel the way his body seemed to loosen and relax the further they got. Her own grip on him loosened as the anxiety began to be replaced with mere curiosity. She listened to their surroundings, taking in the familiar and alien sounds of the forest that she had never been allowed to explore whilst living in Innorin.

While her body was definitely still sore, all Elena could think of was the way she felt like melting into his arms earlier this morning. She thought about the way the muscles of his arms tightened around her. Or how she had still been in her nightgown, and yet he made her feel safe and sheltered.

Finally, just as she thought the burning in her cheeks might start a forest fire, he stopped walking. He led her to sit down on a tree that had fallen from one of the last storms of the season. She folded her hands over her lap and felt like a small child taking lessons once more as she waited patiently for him to begin. He did not sit down with her immediately, and she could tell he was anxious by the way he could not stand still. He took a deep breath.

"Yesterday, we talked about how you are in control of your mind and act as a gateway for the magic to pass into this world in order to become something more tangible," he reiterated. "While opening yourself up and acknowledging the presence of magic is important and the first step, the real magic comes when you learn how to communicate with the world around you. Magic is sort of like a conversation, and when you begin to do more complex things, the conversation begins to change. It is the difference between talking to a child and a scholar. You can go on to command your magic to do small things for you, but without building a relationship with the world and your magic, you will find it to be very limiting.

"Actually, this morning was the perfect example of what I am talking about," he said, beginning to get a little excited over the analogy. Elena blushed at the mention of this morning, feeling bad about the miscommunication and wondering if she had overreacted too quickly, but Dmitri continued on as if he had read her mind.

"If you had not told me that my actions were beginning to worry you, the chances are that I would have continued to do them. I would not have learned. And if I had pushed you away, even indirectly, then I would have been worse for it. You started the conversation, though, and by the end, we had a deeper understanding of what the other was feeling, didn't we?"

Elena nodded. "Well, yes, but what does this have to do with magic?"

"Everything," he said and grinned like a fool. The wind wisped around the two of them, almost a soft buzz as if his excitement was contagious.

"The world around you is alive, Elena," he declared. "It thrives around us even right now. Things are living, dying, and talking right now at this very second. As a witch, if you were to focus on them, you could hear them. As you ask the world to bend to you, you are initiating a conversation of understanding, just like you did with me this morning, only this time on a much more intuitive scale. Sometimes, it answers back by saying that it cannot do what you are asking of it. Other times it might surprise you and say that it could help you in ways that you had not previously thought of.

"As your magic grows, so will your connection with the world. There are many different kinds of witches in the world. I told you before that June was what you would call a Green witch, but many kinds of witches specialize in different things. There are blood and bone witches, river and sea witches, divination witches, star witches, and more. Frankly, there are probably some that I don't even know about. Their studies are the foundations of most of the scholarly teachings and sciences of the world, even if they do not want to admit that.

"You never have to officially become aligned with one kind of witch over another either. You can be an amalgamation of all of them if you want to be. Sometimes though, realizing a specific affinity can lead to you honing in on utilizing those skills more often than not. Your relationship with the world in regard to those skills becomes sharper, and the world becomes more likely to answer to you. It doesn't mean that you cannot do the other types of magic, but it just means you tend to be less likely to gravitate to using them simply because you may feel more powerful using another one.

"Anyways, once you open yourself up to magic and become a gateway to letting it through in order to bend the world, you may need to begin a conversation with your surroundings. So, Elena, today I want you to have a conversation with the world. You may initiate it by opening yourself up to the magic inside of you, but then I want you to listen, truly listen, and hear the magic that the universe holds all around you. Feel the energy that flows through the trees and listen to what it is trying to tell you. Or feel the health and wisdom of the moss that grows on the log that you are sitting on right now. Just open yourself up to your magic, to the environment and its magic, and surrender yourself to the conversation as it flows.

"It also may be important to let you know that the world does not speak as you and I do, and you must understand it and not try to force it to speak in our tongue. If you met someone from another nation, you would not expect them to speak as you do. It is another language entirely to listen to the world. It is one you will have to learn and practice, but it is also something that you will understand intrinsically to some extent. So pick one thing to listen to, and open yourself up to the understanding that you hold inside of you."

Elena felt startled to know that everything around her was truly alive. She had heard her father describe the forest as this many times when she was younger. He explained how it thrived around them or changes, but to hold a conversation with it felt like a different level of life that she had not expected. Elena took a deep breath and looked up in the direction of his voice.

"I have questions," she stated firmly.

Dmitri paused, grinning a little bit as he had not expected anything different from her. "Ask then," he encouraged.

"Does it... does the world get angry when you ask things of it? Does it ever say no to you when you are asking it for something simply because it does not like you?" she asked curiously.

"Yes, and no. The world may shift in discomfort at some of the things you are asking of it, and you will feel that tension. You might interpret that as anger. However, it will never say no to you for reasons that a human might say no. The world sometimes simply needs to understand what or why you are asking it to do something before it agrees, and if you truly want it, then it will be an easy conversation to explain. It will only ever truly say no if you are asking it to do something that is completely out of its ability. You cannot force a fish to climb a tree and expect it to live there happily.

"Sometimes, the world is able to perform small miracles. For example, June used to enchant her cookbooks to float near her while she cooked. What she was actually doing was conversing with the world and simply shifting the gravity away from the book to something else, like a jar that she was not currently using. It was a transfer of energy. So while the book could never float on its own ability and asking it to would be beyond its control, shifting or compromising with the world may be a little easier to accomplish. So if the world understands you and what you are trying to do, it may answer your original request with no but then give you an alternative that works better."

Elena considered this, and she gently ran her hand along the moss beside her on the log, her palm pressing into the spongy texture carefully. "Does it hurt the world to change?"

Dmitri looked at Elena with a new appreciation. He walked over to sit down beside her. "Why don't you ask it?" he prompted gently.

Elena looked a little bit unsure, but she knew that he was nudging her to begin the lesson. She nodded, clearing her mind as she felt the familiar static feeling of her magic awakening inside of her. She kept her eyes open, and she thought about the trees that surrounded them, listening and biting her bottom lip gently in concentration as she focused on not making any sound.

She sat in silence for a long minute, trying to hear how the world might be trying to talk to her. She heard only the simple things that one typically hears in the forest but could not decipher them in earnest. She huffed in mild frustration but would not let it deter her so easily. Magic was still new to her, and this would take time.

After another few minutes, Dmitri decided to give another gentle prompt. "Remember, it will not sound like words exactly. It will be an entirely new thing hidden between each sound that the world makes. It is like finding a gem under the mud."

Elena realized that she had been focusing on listening for individual and familiar sounds the entire time as if the knowledge that there was something deeper would have prompted her to understand immediately. She sighed softly, nodding and clearing her mind before she focused once more.

Instead of listening for sound, Elena ran her hand along an upright tree beside her, thinking of each ring of life inside of it. She thought of the years that it took to grow, the energy that it received from the sun, and the shade it provided to the creatures. Elena focused on these energies and could feel the connection between them that reached all the way up to the leaves. They bristled in what she had assumed was wind, but then she paused. No, that wasn't it, was it?

They were bristling a *hello* to her.

Elena smiled as she could understand the greeting, imagining leaves vigorously shaking above them as if waving frantically to have her see them.

"Hello," Elena replied to them softly.

The air had been still, for the most part, blocked by the trees of the forest, but now a warm breeze wrapped around her in excitement. It swirled, blowing her hair wildly around her in encouragement, and Dmitri laughed with glee.

"It is lovely to meet you too. Have... have you been waiting for me?" Elena asked suddenly as she felt like she could hear them bristling a soft and happy '*Finally!*'

Dmitri brushed some of her windswept hair away from her shoulder gently. "They have been talking about you ever since you arrived. Now they are even more excited since they have not had anyone else aside from me to talk to in quite some time. Now, go on and ask your question," he said, and Elena could hear the smile in his voice.

Elena blushed at him and giggled before she looked up toward the trees. To imagine that the forest had not only a voice, but also sentience that had been waiting for her to come back after healing from her injuries, made Elena feel small in the grand scheme of a universe that had barely opened up to her. "Does it hurt when witches ask things of you? When they ask the world to bend or change?" she asked in a polite but timid voice, trying to focus on the lesson for now. She sat there listening to the trees bristling as if all were trying to talk over one another. Dmitri was right in a sense when he said that it was another language completely. She giggled at the attention that the trees were giving her question and tried to decipher what they were trying to tell her.

After a moment, Elena got the general idea of '*No, it does not hurt*'. Some of them had ignored her question entirely to ask simply about *her*.

"The trees like to gossip. Most things in nature are easier to talk to, I promise. They are very old, though, and they like to fill their time with idle chatter. If you find yourself feeling in need of conversation or information, they are perfect for that and will gladly indulge you," Dmitri explained. "I know that is a lot of information to process."

"I think they are lovely. I would love to talk to them once I know more about how they communicate," Elena said softly.

"That's what this lesson is all about. Life is all about learning how to communicate properly with things, just like you and I do every day. We are learning from each other, just as you are learning how to talk to the trees and the world around us." His voice was soft next to her ear.

"It feels good. It feels less lonely," she mused softly.

Dmitri nodded a little bit. "As I said, I have been alone for quite some time. I think if it had not been the world talking back to me in its own way, I would have gone crazy, even if it wasn't quite the same as having real people around."

Elena chuckled and leaned her head against his shoulder. "I meant it felt less lonely with you, Dmitri."

Dmitri's cheeks turned a bashful shade of pink. He smiled softly down at her resting against him and decided to risk draping an arm loosely around her shoulders. "You make me feel less lonely too, Elena. I am grateful to have you here."

Elena blushed and smiled as she kept her eyes downcast. The leaves above them were still bristling excitedly, so she turned her focus back to them as she tried to decipher their messages.

"Why don't you try to speak with something other than the trees?" Dmitri suggested softly after a few minutes.

"Like what?"

"Anything really. There's the wind, moss, stones, animals, seeds, flowers, water," he rattled off before pausing since he knew he could probably list far too many things and risk overwhelming her. "Now that you know you can talk to it, why don't you try applying your conversations to your magic a little bit? Keep in mind that larger things will take a larger concentration."

Elena thought about what she could ask for as she hummed softly. Finally, a small idea formed. Elena slowly moved her boot back and forth against the soil until a small hole appeared.

"Would it be possible to please fill this hole?" she asked softly.

The forest waited a moment before she listened and seemed to hear it respond. '*The dirt cannot move on its own,*' it said as if it was challenging her decision.

"True... but I was thinking the wind could perhaps blow the dirt that I had just disturbed back into the hole to fill it," Elena explained back out loud. She realized that she had seen Dmitri communicate with the world without spoken words, but for her, it felt easier to say her intentions out loud.

As if in answer, a breeze picked up around them, and the dirt that she had moved with her boot now filled the small hole once more. Elena could taste her own magic on her tongue as it influenced the world to do this task. She smiled once the breeze had died down and bent down from the log, feeling the soil with her fingers to feel the hole filled once more.

"That was excellent," Dmitri complimented.

Elena nodded and smiled a bit before she stood up and brushed her hands off on her skirt. "I know what I would like to ask next," she announced, and Dmitri looked at her curiously, waiting to hear what she was planning.

"I want you to take me to where you found me."

Dmitri's shoulders tensed, his jaw clenching a bit at even the mention of going that close to her old village. "Why would you want—" he began and then stopped himself as he glanced down at the now filled hole at her feet, understanding dawning on him. "Elena, there is no reason to go back there just to fill a hole," he said softly as he stood up.

"A grave," she corrected him gently. "To fill a *grave*."

Dmitri's frown deepened. "It's not a grave anymore. They did not kill you, and they will never get the chance to."

"You taught me yesterday that intentions are important. They intended to bury me in that hole, that grave, and I was forced to dig it. I did not want to disturb the forest when I did, and I intend to erase what I have done. I do not want to go back and know that there is a hole my size out there waiting to be filled, Dmitri." Her voice was pleading, as though she was begging him to understand.

The wind picked up ever so slightly amongst the trees as if they agreed with her too. Dmitri held a hand up to the forest, and begrudgingly, the trees quieted down again.

"Alright, we will fill the grave, but we do it my way," he said slowly.

Elena raised an eyebrow curiously at him. "And what exactly is your way?"

"The way that doesn't involve you going back there. Just... trust me."

Dmitri came over and grabbed her hands as he carefully guided her to sit on her knees as he did as well in front of her. He held both of her hands and slowly placed her palms on the earth, keeping his hands held over hers firmly.

"Close your eyes, and think of the intent to fill that hole. You will have to be specific and remember everything that you can of it. Remember the memory and command your magic to fill it."

"How will I know if it is actually being done if I cannot see it?" she asked curiously.

"You will know. Just focus on your intent and trust me."

Elena closed her eyes and bowed her head slightly to the earth as she reawakened the magic inside of her. She thought that it might be more difficult to focus on the memory, but as soon as she felt the soil beneath her fingertips, it was like she was back in the memory. She dug her nails into the dirt, and Dmitri's hands gripped hers tighter, pushing her hands into the earth firmly.

"I want that grave to no longer exist. I want the wind to fill it with the soil that I removed. Please, assist me."

Elena suddenly felt something like burning throughout her veins through her hands—through the point in which Dmitri held onto her tightly—though the burning did not hurt. Wind picked up around them, causing Elena's hair to whip around her, but she focused on the memory of the grave. A new taste of magic washed over her tongue, this one similar to some kind of spice, and she knew it was Dmitri's doing. It tasted like maple and vanilla, and it was so strong that she could nearly smell it.

Suddenly Elena sensed the earth shifting beneath her grasp. She could not see anything, but it was as though she felt the roots beneath the ground touching and interconnected as she traced a line toward a destination she already knew. She breathed a bit heavier, and Dmitri murmured something that she could not quite hear, though she knew he was speaking to the world and not to her ears.

With a certainty inside of her, she felt the soil shifting around that gravesite, rushing to be filled, and she gasped softly at the feeling. She could not see it, but she could feel the way the earth bent to him at that moment. She could feel the grave being covered with fresh soil and packed tightly back into the earth. Within a few moments, she knew it had been filled with more certainty than she would have had she been standing right there in front of it.

Once it was done, Dmitri pulled her hands back to the earth, holding them within his own. The wind died down, still once more, as it seemed to be waiting for the both of them to give their next command. The taste of maple and vanilla vanished as if it had never been there to begin with, and Elena felt breathless.

"That was your magic?" she asked softly. Her fingers were trembling from the experience, with adrenaline coursing through her.

Dmitri's voice was calm, though more serious. "It was the both of us."

"I felt it be filled. It... it's just gone. The world just listened to you without any hesitation. You are so powerful," she said softly in awe and held his hands.

Dmitri shifted uncomfortably at hearing himself be called powerful and gave her own hands a small squeeze. "I am glad that it excites you."

Elena paused, her mind still reeling a little bit, but she forced herself to focus on him. "Are you okay?" she asked softly. "I didn't mean to ask you to do that if it had bothered you."

"No, that is not it. It was not a bother at all to do it. I just have never shown someone my magic like that. I have never used it to enhance someone else's."

"Even June's?" she asked curiously.

"Even hers."

"How did you know it would work then?"

"I just knew. I can't explain it that much, but it was like when the world suggests an alternative to you when you ask it to do something. You mentioned filling the grave, and I dreaded having you go near it. So my magic gave me an alternative, and I simply trusted it."

"So, if it isn't that, then what's wrong?"

Dmitri paused for a moment and sighed. "I don't like how powerful it feels sometimes, that's all. Come on. I want you to practice a little more before it gets too dark. Then we can head back home, and I will show you some of those self-defense moves that I mentioned." He smiled, relaxing now that it was over.

Elena echoed his smile back at him, even though she could not see him. "I'd love that."

CHAPTER TWENTY

GUILT

E lena and Dmitri walked back home to the cottage together, taking their time to enjoy the shade that the trees provided for them on the warm summer day. This lesson had been far less exhausting for Elena since it was mostly just focusing on listening to the world around her. She had begun to sift through the various personalities that things had seemed to take on.

Dmitri had explained to her that they did not have individual personalities like humans seemed to, but rather the trees in this forest had one collective one. The wildflowers in the field around their cottage had one. The wind in this region had one, and so on. Dmitri also explained that while the river that they had her first lesson in was indeed different from the river that she had rescued her mother from since they were not connected physically, the river still knew of her.

"The world has billions of invisible interconnecting strings that tie everything together. While the rivers were different, they had a string that tied them together, and it knew of you before you ever stepped foot inside of it because of that reason. It remembered you and knew you. It formed its own opinion of you that day, but it had a general idea of you already from its connection to the other river. The world is vast and varied, and yet it is the same. It is all connected and to care for one part of it is to nurture a part of a bigger whole.

"Something as small as watering the wildflowers around the cottage is just as important as caring for an entire forest in the end. It is another reason why witches who choose a specific affinity for something, like Green Witches, are still able to work with other parts of the world if they choose to. The other connecting strings are aware that they nurture their specialty, and that is just as important as doing a little bit of everything, so they respect the witch all the same," Dmitri had explained.

Elena had thought of the way she had felt when Dmitri used his magic to amplify her own as they filled her grave. She could not see those strings, but she had felt each one as they traced one of them to the area focused on by her intent. It had happened quickly, but Elena had felt the way that those strings pulled taut against the world, and she could feel how easily Dmitri had manipulated them. She knew that he did not like being called powerful, but she could not ignore how strong the magic had been. Idly she remembered her first lesson when he had told her that magic, like fear, could be consuming at times if you let it take too much control, and she wondered if using magic that powerful made him feel like he might lose control.

Elena had also begun to wonder what kind of witch she would gravitate towards or if she might never align herself at all. She had been hesitant about the idea of Blood and Bone witches at first, but Dmitri had reassured her that it was not as scary as it had sounded.

There were certain things that were frowned upon in witchcraft, and in every kind of affinity, there were witches who did those things anyway, but Blood and Bone witches were no different than Green witches in the end. Their focus was on the anatomy and physiology of things, and oftentimes they had felt their connections deepen with the earth as they formed deeper understandings of it. A lot of them become healers, which felt like it went against everything that Elena had been told by her village and yet made much more sense. She wondered if her village had simply been misinformed or if they had chosen to ignore that fact as their fears and superstitions had guided them.

Elena did not want to think of her village anymore, though. It was no longer hers anyways; it was simply the village that had turned its back on her. It was the village that killed her family and had its first witch hunt since before Elena was even born. It was her past, but it was not her present or her future. The last string connecting her to that village had been cut when the grave had been filled, and now she had only the memories as evidence that she had existed within their lives. That thought left her feeling far freer than before. It was no longer *her* village. It was simply a village called Innorin.

Dmitri led her back to the cottage, helping her so that she would not stumble over the occasional uneven terrain. She had gotten better at navigating. She no longer felt like a newborn foal as she tried to feel her way around and no longer felt so disoriented in simple open spaces. She had been beginning to get accustomed to no longer having her eyesight, even if the process was still rather slow and had many hiccups. She was thankful to have Dmitri there to help her through those moments as well as celebrate the progress.

Once they were back, they decided to do the self-defense lesson first so that Elena could spend the rest of the evening relaxing and recovering. Her body still ached from yesterday, so Dmitri taught her some new stretches to help loosen her muscles. They hurt to do at first, but by the time she had finished them, she could feel the relief that had flooded through them. Dmitri asked which parts of her body were the most sore, and after Elena listed them off, he surprised her by showing stretches for each and every one. She had never known that there were so many different ways to stretch her body.

"A lot of self-defense is about anticipating your opponent's moves," he began as they finished stretching and got ready for the actual lesson. "It is impossible to know their moves entirely, even with a witch's intuition and even with eyesight, but we are practicing without both of those things. Once we can anticipate what someone might do, it gives us the advantage of being able to deflect or counter their moves."

"I know you would like to teach me self-defense without the use of magic, but do you think once I get a little bit better about channeling my magic and listening to the world, you could teach me self-defense with magic too?" she asked curiously.

"Of course. There is no such thing as knowing too many defense skills. Like I said before, your goal in the fight is always to survive to fight another day. Sometimes, that does mean knowing when to get away and putting as much distance between you and your opponent as possible. Sometimes it means incapacitating your opponent. The more skills you have at your disposal, the better. These woods are safe, but there is always the stray hunter or traveler that might cross your path. Even without knowing who or what you are, sometimes people can just be cruel. So it would be better to know more rather than not.

"I am going to teach you basic self-defense skills first. Then once you get a good grasp on those moves, we will focus on listening to your opponent and predicting. Sound alright?"

"Sounds perfect," she said and grinned at him.

From there, Dmitri taught Elena move after move. The moves were slow, and they went through them repeatedly until Elena could do them swiftly, and then picked up the pace from there to practice the moves in real-time. Some of the moves required Dmitri to grab her or wrap his arms around her. He always made sure to let her know how he would be grabbing her and always made sure to reiterate that if he hurt her or if she did not want him to touch her, he would stop.

Elena had to constantly reassure him that she was okay with him touching her to correct her motions. She knew that his grabbing her like this was for a reason. She also knew that if she ever found herself in a position where she had to use these moves, it would most likely mean that the other person would be far less considerate about hurting her. She also knew that for practice, his gentle movements would be okay. But if they were to truly practice, he would have to be okay with holding her tighter and even potentially hurting her so she could practice with real strength. When she had told him as much, she could hear the frown in his voice.

"I know," he said quietly, regret in his voice.

For now, the slow and ritualistic movements of the self-defense poses reminded Elena of a dance. In the past, she had watched her father spin her mother around their home and into his arms. They had been laughing and joyous together, and the memory made Elena's heart ache. The way Dmitri moved alongside her was almost a completely different kind of dance. Each move they made against each other was slow and calculated. He slid his hands along her arm slowly, so she had time to remember the way in which to properly grab his. They would spin around each other, parrying each other's movements intently. There was no music to their dance, only the soft exhale of each other's breath against the other person's skin as they moved close against each other, only to pull away once more.

Step, pull, block, grab. Closer, then further, only to be pulled back to his grasp once more.

Even with the slow movements, Elena still managed to find herself breathless. Dmitri snaked his fingers through her hair, grabbed her at the base of the scalp, and tilted her neck back, and Elena was relieved to know she was not the only breathless one. She grabbed his other hand, the movement a little softer than it had been, and she could feel the pink of her cheeks. She had forgotten what move came next, her mind fuzzy and flustered.

"I surrender," she breathed out in a whisper and chuckled softly as her chest rose and fell slightly quicker.

Dmitri seemed to pause, and she desperately wished that she could see his face to know what he was thinking. Elena felt the vulnerability of the position with her neck exposed to him, like a dog turning its belly over to his master in submission. His fingers carefully untangled from her hair, smoothing out the long brown hair until his hand was free of her. She held on still to his other hand as she stood straighter once more.

"We should end here for the day. It is starting to get dark outside," he murmured, a slight rasp to his voice before he cleared his throat.

Elena, still blushing, managed to nod. "Can I help cook with you tonight?" she asked quietly. She did not quite want to leave his side yet.

He chuckled at this, any tension in his voice gone. "Of course, Elena. I would like that."

They walked back inside the cottage together, and Elena and Dmitri stood in the all-too-small kitchen. Elena stayed in her spot near the stove as Dmitri showed her how to cut the vegetables from the garden without hurting herself and then stirred their porridge to keep it from burning after that. Dmitri handled the meat—rabbit this time—and the two worked together in tandem as they cooked. It was a slow process, mostly quiet at first, until Dmitri spoke up.

"I still want you to ask me a question tonight," he said softly.

Elena lifted her head in shock and paused her stirring. "You do?"

"Yes. I meant it when I told you that you had not upset me by asking your questions. I would very much like it if you asked me another one if you would still like to know me."

"Of course I do," she said softly and smiled. She had been hoping to be able to ask him another question, but she did not intend to press the matter. She felt relief at him being the one to broach the subject tonight. Her mind began to wander with what question she might ask him when she paused. "Do you still want to know about me?" she asked curiously, not wanting this to be one-sided if he had not wished to know her as well.

"I would. I even have my question prepared if you would like me to ask it now while we wait?"

"Ask me, Dmitri."

Dmitri smiled a little bit and continued the slow process of preparing their food beside her. "Before your father died and before everything happened, what did you want in life? What did you hope for?"

Elena considered his question for a few long minutes in silence, during which Dmitri waited patiently for her. That time had felt so far away from her now that it was hard for her to actually remember what her hopes had been.

"Well," she began softly. "I suppose there was a small part of me that wanted to find a love like my mother and father one day and get married like most of the girls my age hoped for, but it was hard to think of that most days. Most of the men in my village that were eligible were not people that I could have ever seen myself with. My father hated most of the men for me as well and had refused to give his blessing to any of them before his passing. He often used to joke that many of them couldn't even tie their own shoes. So, while I had hoped to find someone one day that would care for me like my mother and father cared for each other, it had never been something that I was actively seeking.

"Most of my life I had simply spent existing for the moment. I did not think of the future beyond a few weeks at a time. Life just always felt like it was too unpredictable for more than that, and I suppose I ended up being right in that regard. My mother taught me stitching, even though I was bad at it, and my grandmother taught me about herbs and gardening. My father taught me how to tie knots and how to skin a rabbit once. I loved to learn things, so my hopes were simply to learn and understand more. I guess I just wanted the ability to do so without being judged for it. Love sounded nice and all, but it felt too far away or not meant for me.

"I was considered a little weird and quiet by some of the village children growing up. I was quiet and had a curiosity that was hard to satiate. Kids would play games, and I would play them too sometimes, but other times I would be far more interested in trying to get the town drunkard to tell me more stories when he was too far gone to remember my face. Even if they had been slurred, I found he spoke more truths than most. Before my father passed away, I was perfectly fine with existing within the moment and accepting things as they came to me. I had no aspirations beyond what I could feasibly achieve, but that was okay because I had my family who supported me, and there was never an absence of that love and acceptance."

At some point during her story, Dmitri had stopped moving in order to simply just listen to her. "And now? What do you hope for Elena?"

Elena stirred the porridge again. "Now, I think it is hard to ignore the future. Whereas before, I could pretend it would not exist for me until I was ready to face it, now it is here, and it will come again. Now, I hope for safety. I hope not to be alone. And yet... I still hope for that insatiable curiosity—the curiosity to learn of the old gods, magic, and how things work—to lead me to things I may not have found before. He is gone, and my life has changed in some ways, but I think in other ways, it has stayed the same. Life will change again, and this time I will welcome the changes. I only hope that I do not have to suffer that loneliness ever again."

"You won't," Dmitri said in a soft yet resolute tone.

"You cannot be certain of that, Dmitri."

"I can. Elena, for as long as you want me around, I will be here. You will never have to be alone like that again. And if you decide that you do not wish to stay here, then I know that you will be able to move forward. You have a determination that I have rarely seen in people. If you want something that badly, I know you will find it. You are stubborn like that," he said, a hint of playfulness in his voice at the end though she could hear the sincerity there too.

Elena smiled warmly in his direction at that, her heart swelling with gratefulness at his faith in her and his adamancy that he would stay with her for as long as she wanted him to. "Thank you," she said gently.

They finished cooking together and sat down to eat, savoring each and every bite of the meal that they had made together. Elena told Dmitri jokes to try and get him to chuckle more as she found the sound to be entirely fulfilling to her. Dmitri told her a story of one of his trips into a village to the east with June when he was younger, in which he had tricked a baker into giving June an extra sack of flour.

Once they finished eating, they both washed up, and Elena slipped into a nightgown. She was beginning to feel less self-conscious around him and no longer constantly tried to shelter herself with blankets as extra coverings. They walked into the bedroom where Elena could settle down for the night after their conversations, though this time, he promised to simply not walk away. She had promised to let him leave if he needed time. Together they had smiled at each other in mutual understanding.

D mitri sat in the chair by her bedside and sighed in contentment as he stretched his torso. "Have you thought of your question?"

Elena nodded and relaxed her head into the pillow. "Why do you think you do not deserve happiness?" she asked softly.

Dmitri froze at her question, his mouth curling downward in surprise at the question. "Wh-What do you mean?"

"You have never actually said so, and I might be wrong, but you act as though you do not deserve the good things in your life that have happened to you. The way you talk about yourself sometimes... It's how I think about myself sometimes too. Yesterday, you told me that you considered your birth mother thought that you were cursed," she explained. "Maybe I should rephrase my question. *Do you* think you deserve happiness, Dmitri?"

Dmitri sat in stunned silence for a moment, too dumbfounded to speak. Did he deserve happiness? "No," he whispered numbly.

She nodded knowingly. "So, why don't you?"

Dmitri swallowed and took a deep breath. She definitely had a knack for asking the right questions. He took a calming breath as he thought about his answer. Every answer that came to mind immediately felt too quick and vague.

Because I'm a monster, his mind kept circling back to.

"I have... done a lot of terrible things, Elena." He paused, and she seemed to be waiting for him to continue on. His leg began to bounce as he spoke. "I guess I blame myself for June's death the most, and after Silas died too, I could feel myself slipping further and further away from who I had once been."

"Why do you blame yourself for June's death?"

Dmitri inhaled shakily, and she reached out, gently taking his hand within her own and giving him a small reassuring squeeze. He looked down at how small and fragile her hand felt in his own, and he squeezed her hand back as he nodded to himself. This was necessary.

"The village that I came from was called Damarel. It was originally a small village that had begun to truly grow into itself and expand as time went on. Eventually, some of their hunters got lost here in the woods. It is terribly easy to do so if you do not know your way around and even worse if you have no connection to the world like witches do. They got so turned around that they had wandered for days before finally stumbling upon this cottage.

"They found me first, and one of them grabbed my arm and began asking me questions about navigating the woods, completely unconcerned with the fact that I was out there to begin with. Most of the men were tired and starving. I had told them that June most likely had some spare food for them since they were in need, and they had questioned me as to why I called my mother by her name. I told them simply she was not my real mother, and I rather liked her name. They were suspicious of that, but as I led them back to the cottage to speak to her, I realized we had all been walking rather silently. June had not heard us approach, and the men had witnessed her use her magic.

"They called her a witch and horrible names. We were greatly outnumbered by them, but they were tired and starving, so they decided to bargain. They reassured June and Silas that if someone showed them the way back, they would leave us to live our lives in peace as long as we stayed away from the village. Tentatively, June and Silas agreed.

"Unfortunately, they did not hold up their end of the deal. They had been hearing rumors of the Baba Yaga living amongst the forests, stealing children away from villages to eat them. She was a real witch who sold her humanity for more power, but she had never stepped foot in these woods. The hunters, however, would have no way of knowing that. They saw her power and equated her to the gods, making her omnipresent in all of the shadows to scare children into behaving or feed the superstition spurred on by whatever religion had taken root at the time.

"The Baba Yaga's story had truly begun to gain traction in these villages. Her acts were heinous, and whatever sins they claimed she had committed, most likely had done those and worse. Unfortunately, this spelled trouble for any witch seeking safety and refuge in the forests, as they would all then be guilty by association. By my admission that June was not my mother, they had assumed that she had already committed mortal sins, and a price was placed on her head. Some time had passed as it had taken the hunters a while to gather a plan and enough men, and even longer for them to eventually find their way back to our cottage, but when they came, they attacked us with the intent to kill everyone.

"Silas, who had never held a weapon in his life, had attacked those men with garden hoes in order to buy June more time and to save me. I had been severely injured by one of the men and was focusing my energy on holding him off from killing me. June saw this and used her magic and called upon the world to save her home and family. It drained her to call on so much magic, and her senses were dulled to the rest of the world as she cast her spell on the house, Silas, and me. She did not hear the man with an axe sneak up behind her before she could cast the spell on herself as well. I called out her name, seeing it a moment too late. She fell, and then her protection spell fell with her. She died trying to save us—*me*—from those men who would have never been there to begin with had I not led them to us and given them a reason to attack.

"Later, when Silas would eventually die as well, I simply snapped from the grief. Elena, I hurt people, and I killed many more. I became the reason why this forest gained its reputation for being so unforgiving. I let my magic consume me and eat away at me for a long time, just as my grief did. I would have burnt the world to the ground to get rid of that feeling. Eventually, when time began to heal even that wound as well, it was too late. The damage had been done. I have done many, *many* terrible things. I do not think the world allows happiness for someone like me, and I have accepted that for the most part," he finished quietly.

Elena squeezed his hand a little tighter. "I don't think you have."

Dmitri let out a wry chuckle. "Haven't I?"

"No, because you and I were laughing during dinner together tonight. Did I make you feel happy?" she asked softly.

He glanced down at her, and his expression lightened a bit. "Yes..."

"Well, the world allowed that, didn't it? We were not struck down together. Dmitri, did you kill June with your own hand? Did you ask someone else to kill her?" she asked, repeating words he had once said to her.

"No," he conceded softly. "Though I have killed plenty of others with my own hands, Elena."

"Perhaps. I do not know all of your sins, and I do not know that I wish to. I do know that you saved me, and that you had tried to be kind to those men to bring them to your home and try to help them before they turned on you. I know you care about this forest deeply, and June taught you to protect and honor it. I know that you are kind, and monsters do not change the bandages on girls' hands or feed them broth. You could have killed those men and still left me to find my own way. You could have left me any day since then, now that I can walk on my own, and yet you have not. Whatever you have done in the past, even terrible things, does not mean that you are beyond saving. It does not mean that you are not deserving of happiness as well. I cannot see your face, but I see you, Dmitri. You are simply not without hope, and I will not allow you to be."

Dmitri looked at her and felt his chest tighten. His heart was racing against his ribs as she spoke with such certainty that he wondered for a moment if she might have learned to enchant her words to make him believe her. But no, that was simply her. He squeezed her hand and slowly brought it to his lips to give her knuckles a soft kiss, barely pressing his lips against her skin.

"Thank you," he whispered sincerely.

Elena smiled softly and laced their fingers together. "Stay with me tonight? Just for a while longer?"

"Of course. As long as you want me here," he said softly. He watched as she relaxed into the blankets. They spoke of lighter things for a while longer, never leaving each other's hands, before she finally began to drift off to sleep.

If anyone can save me, it is you, Elena.

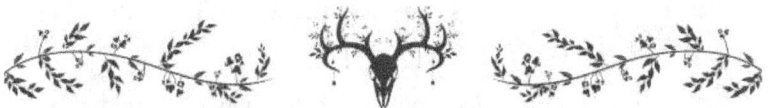

CHAPTER TWENTY-ONE

LESSON THREE: COST

D mitri was the first to wake up. He had not remembered falling asleep exactly as his eyes drowsily blinked awake. He remembered talking with Elena and holding her hand as they continued to talk for a while after that. He remembered the way her eyelids began to grow heavy until they closed. She had tried to stay awake as long as she could, but in the end, sleep had consumed her. He had stayed there by her side, tracing his thumb lightly over the knuckles of her hand as he reflected on the night. At some point, he must have dozed off, though, as he woke up with the sunlight just barely beginning to stream in through the window into his eyes.

He had not intended to fall asleep next to her once again, but he was not upset by the fact that he had. Truly he would never get tired of the sleepy surprise he experienced when waking up next to her. He would never get over the surprise he felt when he turned the corner into the room and saw her just there, existing beautifully. The feeling was almost domestic, and it had always surprised him just to know that she had stayed.

Perhaps she had been right the night before when she told him that he deserved happiness. Perhaps his sins did not define him if he worked towards repenting them. He could see why people would get drunk on the idea of religion if it offered such promises. He could see himself falling to her feet and begging for a fraction of her grace. That thought was indeed a dangerous one. Because the thought of begging on his knees then led him to think of other things he could do while he was down there. He pushed the thoughts away quickly, adjusting himself in the chair quietly to ease the strain against his slacks.

To remove the thought from his mind, he simply reminded himself that the gods do not busy themselves with offering grace. No, he knew what the gods were like. They were cruel jokes that religion made a mockery of. Do the gods themselves not sin by abandoning their followers to silence and ruin? They did not answer pleading prayers except with their silent laughter. They did not provide miracles or dish out salvation.

Yet, Elena was here, and was that not a miracle in and of itself? Perhaps her and salvation were one and the same.

Elena stirred, and her hand tightened ever so slightly on his own as her eyes fluttered open. He smiled softly down at her as she instantly captivated his attention.

"Good morning," she murmured sleepily and then stretched her body, making a small squeak before relaxing with a contented sigh.

"Good morning," he chuckled softly at the small sound she had made.

She gave a little grin up at him. "Today is the last major lesson, right?" she asked quietly.

Dmitri nodded out of habit and then said out loud, "Yes. There are always smaller lessons to be learned as you go on, but those come with experience, practice, and your own search for knowledge. These are just the big three that you have to have a basic understanding of before you can pursue magic more seriously."

"What is today's lesson about?" she asked, her voice still sleepy from the morning.

"Cost," Dmitri answered without hesitation.

Elena looked curious but nodded and asked no more questions, for which he was grateful. Dmitri knew that today was edging closer to the point where he could no longer turn back. Whether Elena asked the right question or not, by the end of the lesson, he knew he would tell her the truth. She had tried to be reassuring to him last night when they spoke about deserving happiness. He wondered if her ideas of what people deserve would change when she found out the truth. He wondered if it made him more of a monster if it did.

Would he ruin her optimistic way of thinking? Would she curse him for hiding the truth from her? He had never lied and had been careful about that, but was hiding the truth not the same thing in the end? The idea of him leaving without a say in the matter, especially after her determination last night to prove that he deserved this reprieve of happiness that he had been gifted, nearly gutted him.

They spent the morning lazily together, and Dmitri realized a part of him was dragging his feet. He was stalling, hoping for just a little more time. It was a dream he did not want to end. Whereas before, when the time had blurred so seamlessly by himself—losing track of himself in it—Dmitri was hyper-aware of each and every second they had spent together. Not all of them had been happy, some terrifying even, but he would not trade a single one of them. And now he felt as though those grains of moments were beginning to slip between the cracks in his fingers.

Today's lesson was about cost. What did this happiness cost him? Had he unwittingly traded something else for this? Was this a testament to what he was losing? His mind tortured him relentlessly.

Elena slipped her hand over his shoulder as he sat at the kitchen table. She had gotten up to use the washroom and had come back, and he had barely noticed. *More seconds lost.* He flinched when her delicate fingers brought him back to reality, but then he instantly relaxed beneath her touch.

"Elena," he said her name like it was a reassurance. "I'm sorry, I didn't hear you."

"I know. I could hear your breathing start to get quicker from across the room. At first, I thought you were sleeping, but then I recognized it. What are you worried about?" she asked softly, her voice coaxing him gently.

He reached up to rub his hand over her own, rubbing her wrist carefully. She had scars there from the men he had rescued her from. He knew she was not a dream, simply because if she were, she would have never been hurt like this to begin with. He would have gotten there sooner.

"Truth?" he murmured.

"Always the truth, Dmitri."

Dmitri nodded, taking her hand gently and kissing her knuckles before he let go and stood up to face her.

"I simply do not want this to end," he said softly.

"Why would it end?" she asked, her voice gentle and withholding any judgment.

"Maybe... the cost of staying would be too great for you."

"This is about today's lesson?"

"Yes... and no. It's just about everything," he said, feeling like he might begin rambling at any point.

Elena looked up at him and gave him a small reassuring smile. "Do you want more time? We don't have to have a lesson today," she offered quietly.

Dmitri shook his head. She was offering more time, and he should be jumping at the opportunity. He should be holding onto her so tight that his hands ached. He should beg her more and more, but it would never be enough, and she would not truly be happy with that. He knew she could tell that something was about to change too, and maybe she didn't want it to either. Maybe that was why she had offered to begin with. In the end, though, they would both be holding their breath, and the lack of truth would be the same as lying to her. She deserved more than that.

"No, I think I am ready. Though we should go before I change my mind again," he muttered.

She did not wrap her arm around his, but instead, she gently traced her hand along his arm until she found his hand again. She took his hand, lacing their fingers together. "Whatever happens, it's going to be alright," she promised him softly.

"I hope so," he said, looking at the way that their hands fit so nicely together. The gods were cruel indeed.

"It will be. And whatever the lesson is, it can wait just a few more hours," she said, her voice soothing and warm like honey.

Dmitri raised an eyebrow, his throat feeling tight with the desire to simply spend time with her before she knew the truth of things. It was funny to him how a few extra hours felt like it could be a lifetime in the best possible way. It felt like a reprieve or an escape. He knew he should say no, but he felt selfish, and she was offering him a temporary fix. How could he say no?

"Okay," he said in a voice barely above a whisper. "What will we do then?"

"You, Dmitri, are going to take a lesson in learning how to relax." She had a devilish grin on her lips as she held his hand, and he gave a small snort as he shook his head.

"I know how to relax," he protested.

Elena rolled her eyes at this. "Fine, then show me how you relax."

He chuckled, and her easy smile returned as he conceded. They walked outside together, and Dmitri led her to the forest once more. Dmitri was the one unable to handle the silence this time, so he filled his time by asking her quiet questions as they walked. Elena humored him by answering them all and then asking some of her own in the pursuit of knowing each other better. Dmitri loathed how final it felt, but he savored each piece of information as best as he could, committing them each to memory just in case.

They walked through the quiet, shaded trails the forest had laid out for them, silent chaperones for their stroll. He showed her the quiet nooks and crannies of the forest that he would walk through and the tall trees he climbed when he was a kid. Elena had insisted they try to climb one together now, but they had both fallen from the first branch. They fell together, landing with heavy thuds before they broke out into a fit of laughter. The walk was easier after that but eventually came to an end as he led them back to the cottage. They practiced a few workouts before the lesson this time, and as the sun began to set, Dmitri sighed as he knew what loomed for him.

He was foolish to think a lifetime would ever be enough time with her.

She washed herself off, and they ate dinner together before they decided to have their lesson in the field of wildflowers just outside of the house. They sat in the overgrown grass together, sitting with their legs crossed. The sun was barely still visible, disappearing over the clearing as the sky melted into orange with soft specks of blue still poking through.

"Are you ready?" he asked.

"Yes. Are you?" Elena countered softly.

Dmitri smiled weakly. "As I will ever be."

He took a deep breath before he began. "Recite the lessons for me that you have learned so far, Elena."

She smiled indulgently. "The first lesson was about acknowledging that your magic is inside of you always, just like your emotions. You need to have control over both of those so that they do not control you. You acknowledge your magic, channel your intentions, and guide it into the world through yourself as a gate. The second lesson was about being able to listen and understand the world around you. You have to understand the flow of the world that you are attempting to change, and sometimes that means that you need to rephrase your intentions in order to make it work for you. You also told me about caring for the world, even in small ways, and how that influences your power in positive ways since everything is connected," she said softly as she remembered the past two days.

Dmitri relaxed ever so slightly to know that she had been grasping what he was trying to tell her with these lessons. She had summarized everything that he had rambled on about in a few quick sentences. He hoped that she took this next lesson and committed it to memory just as easily, as this held the potential to be the most crucial one that she ever learned.

"Very good," he complimented gently and then rubbed his face, feeling the soft brush of his beard against his palm. "It is important for you to understand that, in some ways, your magic and your emotions are very similar—maybe even tied together. That is why it is important to acknowledge that both of them exist when performing magic and yet not give either of them control over you and your mind.

"Practicing magic when you are experiencing stronger emotions is not a bad thing. Both magic and your emotions, in general, are not bad things. However, when you experience extremely strong emotions that influence your decisions, your magic will try to capitalize on that to give you more power. Fear, anger, lust, anything. If your emotions are strong enough, it will be as though your magic is drunk off of them, and your mind will be inhibited. This will be when your magic becomes the most potent and raw.

"There will come times when you ask something of the world and, in return, it will ask for something of you. Things that matter, of life or death, or things that simply require your magic to bend the world too much for you, all will require a cost. Nothing truly worth having is ever going to be free, and at the moment, the deal will always seem too sweet to turn up. It will seem like a necessary evil, or it might seem like the world is going easy on you. It isn't. Your magic will burn in you, and it will seek out a deal with the world that will try to give it the most amount of power. That cost, in the end, could end up being far more than you could bear."

The way Dmitri spoke made Elena shift uncomfortably. "What costs are there?"

Dmitri let out a wry chuckle, despite not finding the conversation funny in the slightest. "It can ask anything, Elena." He paused as he tried to think of a proper example and then snapped his fingers as he thought of one.

"Do you remember me telling you the story of the Baba Yaga?"

"Yes. I never knew she was real before last night. I had always assumed she was just a story conjured by people to try and warn others of the dangers of witches."

"Do not be mistaken. Her story is indeed a cautionary tale, though not against witches as a whole. It is a warning of what can happen when you do not heed this rule. When she was still a young witch, she suffered greatly, and she grew to hold a bitter resentment toward people in her heart. That feeling grew more and more volatile inside of her, and eventually, she was blinded by that hatred. So, she made a bargain with the world. She traded away her humanity, something that had seemed so small to her in the grand scheme of things, in order to take more power for herself. Her name alone became powerful enough to scare some people into submission.

"Originally, her reasoning for this decision was to simply make the world think twice about hunting those blessed with magic. As time went on, though, and once she had sacrificed that part of herself, none of it mattered. She ended up feeding into their fear, making their suspicions stronger and confirming their bias toward us. Then she simply surrendered to her magic. If they were going to see her as a demon, she would become the devil. She didn't wait for humanity to fade with time. She simply gave it away. It was easy for her to do so, like casting away chains that held her down. She was free from any moral conflicts. So she decided to hit humans where it counted. She stole their children away, sometimes in broad daylight, and she brought them back to the woods, where she proceeded to kill and eat them.

"Her magic grew so potent and powerful, feeding off of these emotions that she could not control, and in the end, she is weaker for that. She would slaughter me for suggesting that, but Elena, your humanity is what makes you a gateway to the realm of magic. It is what separates us from the trees or the river. It is what separates us from the unruly fae and other creatures. We have control and to sacrifice that control for power makes us weaker in the end. The world is not black and white, good or evil. Our world is covered in grey, and to forget that is to never grow with it. We are not mindless and should never strive to be."

Dmitri had begun to feel impassioned as he spoke, emphasizing to her the horrors that could befall someone so easily. He spoke of the Baba Yaga, but in truth, he knew he also spoke for himself in some ways. Never before had he made the comparison that he had been similar to that witch, and the realization was chilling, making gooseflesh crawl up his spine to his ears like a spider.

"If your mind is drunk on emotions, how do you prevent yourself from doing something to bargain with the world?" she asked quietly, taking each bit of new information in as she tried to process what he was telling her.

"You have to be careful. A coven of people around you who can notice these things is always best, but if you don't have one, then it's important to simply check with yourself. If you are feeling a certain emotion particularly strongly, just wait a few minutes to calm down and focus on your breathing before getting into the mind space of magic. Ask yourself what exactly your intention is and why you are doing it. And if the world starts asking things of you, no matter what happens, say no."

Elena nodded and took a deep breath. "It sounds dangerous."

"It is. Like I said before, your emotions and your magic are not bad things, though, Elena. They should not be feared or repressed. As you grow stronger, things will become easier to control as well. Some witches go their entire lives with the world, never asking anything of them. It is important to understand that there is a possibility it will happen and what the consequences of that will be."

"Do most witches practice their magic from a young age to gain better control of it?"

"It depends on the family or coven or even region. Everyone is different. Some swear that practicing when you are young will leave you with better control. Other people swear that introducing magic at that young of an age, where *everything* seems to be a powerful emotion, is simply too dangerous."

"What about you?"

"What do I believe? Well—" he began, but she shook her head quickly.

"No, I mean, did June let you practice magic at a young age, then? Or did you wait until later on?"

Dmitri paused, a calmness washing over him. Was it resignation? Acceptance? "I didn't have magic when I was younger, Elena."

She furrowed her eyebrows a bit at this. "I thought you said that you did not have the blood of a witch in you before, but I *felt* your magic yesterday."

"Magic is hereditary, passed through the blood. Sometimes, though, it simply appears in someone who has no magical ties before them, and then they become the first of their line."

She paused. "So that is what happened to you?"

There was another slight pause as Dmitri hesitated before answering. "No."

"Then, how did you get your magic?"

"I took it," he said simply, his voice as soft as a confession could be. He forced himself to continue before she could ask him any more questions. "I had... well, I had always been able to feel the invisible strings of the universe. They were like individual veins that I could pick out. I could follow them if I closed my eyes and sat in silence for long enough, and I saw things I shouldn't have been able to without magic. They were dull and sometimes hard to follow, but I could if I tried. June noticed the difference in me first, and it is why she tried to teach me to begin with. When she died, the world called to me, and I answered. I took what I needed then, but I was not, nor have I ever been, a witch."

Elena remained quiet for a long moment, and Dmitri desperately wanted to see what was going on inside her mind. He decided he would break the silence at last. "Have you figured out your last question, Elena?" he asked softly, hoping to nudge her in the right direction.

She nodded, staying silent for another tense minute before she looked up at him. If he had not known that she was blind, he would have sworn that she could see him at that moment. He would have sworn that he could see straight through his skin and into his soul. As she finally asked her last question, Dmitri felt a small smile creep onto his face as he finally placed the feeling he had been feeling; it had been relief.

"What exactly are you, Dmitri?"

CHAPTER TWENTY-TWO

SKIN

E lena sat on a soft blanket in the grass, listening to Dmitri start a fire in a small pit for them. She had a separate blanket wrapped around her shoulders despite the summer evening, her face carefully calm and collected. There was a part of her that had felt silly for asking her final question, and yet when she had asked, he had not answered her immediately. In fact, he had simply chuckled and said that they should start a fire since it was getting dark outside. The light outside made no difference to Elena, though, and the silence felt unnerving.

She had put her arms around him, felt his hands, and touched him. She had done all of these things, and he had seemed perfectly human, though that meant little. There were plenty of magical beings that resembled humans and yet were not. There were the fae, nymphs, spirits, or any number of things that immediately came to mind. Something about his silence made her think it was none of these things, however.

Finally, she felt the warmth of the fire as it sparked to life and grew to size. Dmitri came over and sat beside her on the blanket, bending his legs slowly as he draped his arms loosely over his knees and stared at his creation. Despite the anxiety rising inside of Elena's stomach, there was a stoic way in which he took his time with each movement or gesture of starting the fire. The same languid acceptance was felt as he waited to ease into the conversation, and it was all Elena could do not to repeat her question in order to prompt him to answer her sooner. They sat there together in silence for a moment before Dmitri finally spoke.

"I want to tell you a story," he murmured, his voice rumbling softly.

Elena glanced over in his direction, her voice quiet and calm. "You are starting to scare me, Dmitri."

"I might very well scare you more before the night is over," he admitted remorsefully.

She frowned—the situation making her uneasy with concern for him—but took a deep breath and then conceded by nodding. A few strands of her brown hair had come loose from her braid, and they now hung at the sides, framing her face. Dmitri felt the strong urge to brush some of those strands away, but he forced himself to resist and instead do what he promised by telling her a story that he knew all too well.

"Once, in a time very long ago, there was a boy," he began quietly, forcing himself to look away from her. He stared into the fire as he wove the tale, similar to what she had heard before in pieces but now completed. "His mother, for reasons unbeknownst to him, abandoned him in this forest and left him to die. On the eve of what should have been his death, he saw things that he told no one of, not even the people who would eventually save him from such a demise. What he had seen had shocked him into silence for a little over a year, simply trying to unravel the strings that the world had laid before his eyes.

"His adoptive mother and father, an older man and woman, noticed the difference in him. Despite no magic in his bloodline and no magical ability, he could see things that only those inclined to magic could. Perhaps that had been the universe gifting him for such a horrible beginning, or, the more likely reason, it was giving him the tools for what was yet to come. So, he continued his life. He learned the lessons of magic through the old woman, committing them to memory out of fascination rather than necessity. He grew, he learned, and he was even loved. However, all good things must eventually come to an end, and they certainly did for this boy. At least, they did for a while, but we will get back to that.

"Hunters came, lost and starving, and found the boy. The boy, who had been taught such kindness and knew the horrors of being lost in these woods, took pity on them. He brought them back to his home, unaware that the hunters had planned on making them their next hunt. Unaware that hunters preyed on weakness, no matter what their intended hunt was. Unaware that he had suffered his family to now be lost in their sights.

"Time passed, and they came back. They stalked and hunted the boy and his family like they were nothing more than rabbits. The old woman, brave 'till the very end, was the first to die as she tried to protect her family. The old man, once peaceful and harmless, became a wild thing as he cut the hunters down one by one. But he, too, was overpowered.

"The boy, having killed his own share in defense, was wounded terribly. He bled from a wound in his side where his entrails had begun to spill onto the soil. He had tied his shirt around his waist to hold himself together like a doll losing stuffing. He refused to give up, but he was scared. He was terrified. He had never seen bloodshed. He had never seen the way a man's body fell to the earth or the groan it made as it died. He had killed animals in the forest for food, but this was far different, and it made him sick.

"But he saw the old woman fall to the ground with an axe sticking out between her shoulder blades. He heard the whimpering sound she made as she tried to crawl, only for the man who hurt her to rip the axe out and drop it on her neck before she could even scream. He saw it, and then he did not care about anything. He did not care how scared he was because all he felt was blinding rage and agony. His hands were bloodied and shaking as most of the hunters targeted the old man, knowing the scrawny boy would bleed out soon enough. The boy did not want to be helpless anymore, so as he bled into the earth, he traced a symbol that he had seen only in hazy moments out of the corner of his eye throughout his life, and he prayed to the gods he didn't believe in.

"He begged the world for the power needed to protect what remained of his family. He said that he would give anything, and when the world demanded too much, he did not hear it. He heard a chance, and he took it. He gripped onto it tighter than he had ever held anything before, and for the first time in his life, he felt something like magic through his veins. It was potent and made him feel nauseous at how volatile it was as time seemed to cease around him. That was when the creature arrived.

"The creature was tall, made of wood and moss in what could vaguely be a human-like shape. His face, however, was not human. It was the skull of a deer with antlers that spread wide, worn with age and looking fearsome. It was huge, especially compared to the boy. The figure emerged from the treeline of the forest unhurriedly. Time bent to him, and he was not pressured to be rushed with it as it approached the boy. It spoke in a language that he didn't know he could understand before that moment. Its voice droned slowly, and yet information flooded the boy's mind so fast that it ached. This was a Leshy—the Guardian of this forest—and he had grown old and weary over the years. Now, it was the boy's turn to take on the mantle. This was the power that he had summoned, and this was the payment for his trade.

"The power seared into him and weighed his body down like he was made of the heaviest stone. The world opened up, swallowing him whole as he swallowed the world, choking on mud, bones, and stones. His injuries disappeared as his body shifted into something not made of flesh.

"When the boy, who was no longer a boy, could no longer breathe, he clawed his way from the ground with arms that felt foreign to him. He wondered if he had been too late to save the old man, wondered what exactly he had truly agreed to, and wondered why his hands could suddenly cut through and part the earth like warm butter. When he emerged, time had continued to stay still as he gasped air into his lungs and vomited. He stood finally, eyes blinded with rage as he remembered what he was there to do.

"Time flowed back into the correct tempo, but the boy—the creature—was faster now. He moved with speed, ripping weapons away from the hunters and breaking them. They screamed, begged, cried, and pissed themselves. It did not stop, though. It didn't until everyone around him was dead. The old man was weak and did not understand what had happened to his adopted son. Even bleeding and nearly dead himself, he tried to fight the monster that his adopted son had become. He demanded it regurgitate the boy, as he could not see the boy's body laying anywhere in the carnage. The creature, finally understanding he was not recognizable and not hurt by the makeshift weapons that were taken against him, finally seemed to remember something.

"The shift happened gradually, like wood popping and groaning under the weight of the fire, but he managed to bring himself back into his human body. The boy had only been nineteen when his bargain had been struck. He explained to the man what had happened and what choice he had made. The old man was confused, relieved, and scared all at once for the boy he raised. There was still work to be done, so they put this problem aside and focused on the tasks at hand. They carried the pieces of the old woman and buried her beneath her favorite tree. Then, while the old man rested and tended to his wounds, the boy stretched his new muscles and disposed of the rest of the bodies. He burned most, buried others, and he felt *nothing*."

Dmitri hissed the last word through his teeth, bitterness sinking into his voice as he spoke the story—his story—out loud for the first time. He took a slow breath to calm himself and could not bring himself to look at Elena. He stared at the flames as though they might consume him if he were to blink. He focused on it intensely and then pushed through to continue.

"He felt nothing," he said, clearing his voice of any of the emotion or bitterness that came with it. "The boy was no longer a boy. He was a monster of his own creation, with no one to blame except himself. Time moved on, but he didn't. The old man withered shortly after but the creature... it lasted. So much time passed that the creature thought that he had sacrificed himself to suffer in a place somewhere between true life or death. The bitterness that had created him festered, and it nearly consumed him as he forgot the first rule of magic.

"He became deadly, killing almost anything that entered his forest and becoming the nightmare that humans of the surrounding villages told their children of at night. He tore humans to shreds and, worse, let some of them live with what they had seen. He let the rumors spread. Ghosts, curses, murderous creatures, or malevolent beings—all of them the same, and none of them truly a lie. He made it to where no one would dare to be foolish enough to cross him ever again, and he lived with the isolation and burden.

"Just like the story of the Baba Yaga I told you about earlier, he, too, nearly surrendered himself to it. It would have been easy. With each and every kill, his humanity slipped further and further away. For someone who had never seen bloodshed before, it became the main focus of his life for a long time. Besides, what was humanity, really? He didn't even notice it fading from him at first. It was like losing one strand of hair at a time. Then he started noticing patches missing and panicked. He remembered what the old man and woman would have wanted for him, and it was not this. So he tried to bargain again. After all, what greater emotion is there than desperation?

"The world, however, could see his heart. The panic was not his own but rather of the humans he had once known. Already, he had lost too much and become complacent. He tried to bargain for them, but in truth, he was a monster. Did he not deserve to suffer the life of one? So, it refused him. The Leshy—nothing more than a creature made of earth and bone—found he could barely muster any strong emotions of his own anymore, except maybe rage. A symptom of the rot, perhaps. Or maybe it was simply his own form of punishment to numb himself to the world. The rot of his soul was slow, eating him and saving the best parts for last so that the creature could suffer until the last moment. Time passed by with agonizing slowness. First a year, then ten, twenty, then nearly a hundred. It—"

Elena snapped herself from the stupor of listening to his story as she blinked. "A hundred?" she asked suddenly, her voice too quiet. The man who had wrapped his arms around her did not feel like he was over a hundred years old.

"Almost a hundred," he corrected gently. "The time is coming soon when the creature will be only that; a creature. It will not remember the man he once was. It will not know the man he could have become. It will not remember the family he had or... or you."

Dmitri took a deep breath and rubbed his face. "See, you want to know the kicker, Elena? A hundred years pass, and the monster accepts himself for what he is. He knows his fate, and he doesn't rush to it, but he doesn't run from it either. Then you want to know what happens?" he asked, his voice raising slightly in almost a deranged way.

"What?" she asked quietly, her voice gentle and small.

"You," he said firmly, his tone sharper than she had expected. "Nearly a hundred years, and the rot has consumed almost every part of his humanity. It has faded his soul. The last thing is the heart that continues trying to pump its human blood through his veins like it is running out of time; because it is. Nearly surrendered to it, and then a girl stumbles into his forest, and the forest awakens. It can feel the change that you have brought, and it holds its breath. I hold my breath. Then, you summon me," he said, deciding to stop referring to himself as a character in a fairytale. Not that he thought he was fooling her anyways, but it made the story feel suddenly much more realistic.

"Your blood contains some of the most volatile magic that I have ever experienced since the day when I gave myself away and became a monster. You bled into the earth, and you summoned me. I could taste your desperation in my mouth as if I had tasted your tongue for myself, and it made me sick. So, I move, and I answer your call."

"I... I didn't summon anything," Elena says quietly, shaking her head. From the pregnant silence that followed, she could tell he was not convinced. He continued relentlessly.

"You did," he said firmly. "You bled into the world and then summoned the Guardian. The Guardian of this forest is me, Elena. Do you understand? I am a Leshy. I am no longer as human as you might think."

Recognition burned in her blind eyes as she gasped softly. "The lullaby," she whispered in shock.

Now, it was Dmitri's turn to furrow his eyebrows. "Lullaby?"

"My father taught me a lullaby when I was younger. Both he and my mother made sure I knew the words and would sing them to me when

I was scared. I was digging my grave, bleeding from the spade, and I sang. The song calls for the Guardian to protect me. I always... I always thought it was one of the gods that our village worshiped."

Dmitri chuckled, the sound deep and edging on darkness. "Don't you wish it was?"

Elena frowned at that but ignored the comment and pressed on. "What did my summoning you have to do with the rot of your humanity?" she asked softly, urging him to continue as a desire to know the truth of that night consumed her.

"Right," he murmured, remembering where he was. "You came into my forest after nearly a hundred years, and you summoned me. I could have chosen any way to answer you, but I saw those men and realized what they were about to do to you through my connection to the forest that I guard. My memories at the time of June and Silas had been dusty, nearly forgotten, but something inside of me registered the situation, and rage boiled inside of me. I had to act quickly, so as the taller one cocked his gun, I made my decision.

"Faster than any human can blink their eyes, I was there. I had bent the world and made it contort to kneel before me. At that moment, I was more than just the Guardian; I *was* the god of this forest. I killed them violently but quickly because you were my main concern. I tore one of them in half and snapped his bones up to his neck in an instant before the trees dragged him away. They may be gossipy little things, but that night they craved blood just as much as I. For the other one who screamed, I simply ripped his throat out with my teeth and snapped his neck for good measure. I would have torn each sinew and vein from their body if I had the time. Killing had become a part of the job, but these humans personally offended me.

"But then I saw you, how small and still you were, and I thought I was too late. I thought maybe they had gotten a shot off, or the one that had screamed had gotten to you. The only human that I could bring myself to care for beyond just answering a summoning. You were bleeding and pale, but you were shaking and alive. I thought you would scream to see me in my Leshy form just before I shifted back and ran to you, but you didn't even flinch at me. I realized later it was because you simply couldn't see me. You fell into my arms, and the panic in my chest was so visceral that I could have moved mountains if I had needed to in order to get you to safety.

"I brought you back to the cottage without thinking. It was like muscle memory. I barely realized where I even was at first until I spent more time with you. I dusted off the memories. I waited for you to wake up and then leave. If you had asked, I would have arranged to take you to any village of your choosing that borders the forest, but you never asked to leave. As I spent more time with you, I remembered what it was like to have skin. I remembered what it was like to live and breathe as a human.

"And now? Now I am terrified to lose you. I am terrified to even lose the memories of you. I am searching every corner of my mind for a way out, even if you were to leave tonight, just so I could remember you. I am terrified of this complacency that I have subjected myself to. I remember what I was fighting for all of those years ago. I remember what it meant to care for someone. You being here is simultaneously the best and worst thing that could have ever happened to me."

Elena frowned at Dmitri's last sentence, furrowing her eyebrows together. Her expression looked as though he had physically wounded her. Slowly she pulled the blanket tighter around her shoulders as thoughts filled her mind. Here Dmitri was, a self-proclaimed 'monster,' and even he thought she was the worst thing that could happen to him. *Am I truly that evil? That unwanted?* she thought to herself.

Dmitri could see the shift behind her eyes, and he cursed under his breath, but the dam had burst, and he could not stop himself from barreling forward. She was the first person to know his story, for better or for worse.

"You being here..." he continued, pausing for a moment as he shook his head to try and will the right words to his tongue. "It is like the world has shoved hope down my throat, only to choke me with it. Every day you are here and smiling, it reminds me of what I am losing or what one could argue that I have already lost. Every day that I see you and look into your eyes, I am reminded that there will come a day that I do not appreciate them as I should. You being here, after surviving what you have gone through and refusing to let life bury you, makes me think that, just for a moment, I could stand to face my fate. Having met you, I wonder for a moment if I would have made the decision all over again just for the chance to meet you. You are an insufferably wonderful reprieve from my darkness. You are delightfully intoxicating, and do not think for one moment that I would not willingly drown myself in your light.

"I know what comes next. I know the sins of my past and the inevitability of my future. I do not know if it will happen next week, next year, or maybe even five years from now, but I am truly a monster because I know it will happen regardless of what happens tonight, and yet I still want to beg you to stay. I am selfish. I am a Leshy. And yet you make me feel a little less of all of those things and a little bit more like... just plain Dmitri. I loathe myself for how much I want you over what I know is best for you. Despite all of this, if you wish to leave, I will still provide safe passage to you. It will not change. You have never been, nor will you ever be my prisoner, and that is the one small promise that I can give you in this lifetime. I do not believe you could ever save me from my fate, but I believe that my time spent with you has saved me from myself. That alone is something I do not think I will ever be able to repay you for."

Elena was trying to piece together all of the information that crashed in her mind like waves. It felt surreal, like she was dreaming. She might have called him insane for him suggesting that he was a Leshy—she thought it sounded like a story that her grandmother might have told her—but if this last year had taught her anything, it was that this world was bigger than she had known. Magic had been real and buried under her skin the whole time. What's more, things had begun to start making sense as soon as he started speaking. The night she was rescued, she had heard things that she could not explain. He had already admitted to killing the men before, but these sounds made more sense. It made sense why so many different villages had different theories about why these woods were forbidden to go into. It made sense that the cottage behind them was so dusty and old, abandoned in the middle of these woods like a relic to honor the life he once had.

She was, however, conflicted in her feelings. It was relieving to finally know the truth, and while it hadn't changed how she felt about him, it was hard to come to grips with it all. Her grandmother had once told her magic was very seldom given to humans who did not have a bloodline, so hearing it spoken about in this manner felt like a rarity. A part of her also felt betrayed. He hadn't lied to her, but he had kept so many secrets from her as she came to him and opened up about her past. He made her play a game of questions just to get to the truth instead of talking to her. Even as the thought occurred, it was hard not to consider the other circumstances. He had been alone for the majority of his long life. She could, perhaps, grant him some grace that speaking to her had not come easily, and he was at least trying.

"Can I not hear you because you are a Leshy?" she asked, speaking her thoughts out loud as she tried to piece together the information.

Dmitri swallowed and looked at his hands shamefully. "Yes," he admitted quietly. "I never meant to make you think that you were crazy. I have never heard anyone else complain about it, so I had simply not been aware of the lack of sound that I made. It makes sense, though. In the forest, there are times when there is pure silence. I am a Guardian. I am meant not to interfere unless things disrupt the balance of these woods. Some Guardians choose to root themselves into the ground and sleep dormant within trees, where their roots spread amongst the entire forest to provide their vision. Others wander amongst the blades of grass, silent as the wind and out of sight from the harm. I have simply learned how to make myself invisible in other ways, it seems, simply by learning to tread silently and become... well, as much of a ghost as I can be while still technically breathing."

"Will you show me?"

Dmitri froze, and it was his turn to knit his eyebrows together in mild confusion. "Show you?" he asked, not understanding.

"You told me in your story that you could shift between your Leshy form and your human form. I have felt your skin as a human, and I wish to know the other side of you before I make my decision. I may not be able to see you, but I refuse to turn my cheek to what you are and live as though it does not exist."

Dmitri felt his face warm as he stuttered with confusion. "W-Why would you even want to know it? It is terrifying. It is an execrable, hellish thing."

"Then prove it," she challenged, undeterred from his warnings. She believed his story, but the logical side of her mind still demanded her curiosity be satiated. If he was truly as terrible as he described, then she would like to know beyond his skewed bias.

He stared at her for a long moment, conflict written across his features. Resigning, he sighed. "Alright... Alright, give me a moment."

Dmitri carefully shifted himself back from the fire as it still danced with life. He inhaled deeply, holding it within his lungs, and felt the way his bones shifted, thickening into wood as it melded with his skin. His body groaned like a tree creaking before it fell; slow and ominous as his size stretched out. His face contorted into the skeleton of a deer, antlers sprouting and spiraling out. Moss fell from his antlers and scattered along his body, along with vines and soil. His hands stretched, resembling pointed claws more than they did fingers now. As he finished, he exhaled the breath through the hollow fractures of the skull, nothing more than a breeze as a reminder of his human form.

Elena's eyes widened as she heard the transformation take place, loosening her grip on the blankets around her as she felt the other blanket beneath her shifting slightly. The reality of the situation truly set in then. He was a Leshy. He was the guardian of this forest.

Dmitri sat still beside her.

Elena let the blanket pool around her sides. "Dmitri?" she asked quietly, checking to make sure that he was still there, though she knew he was. There was no way he could not be.

"I'm still here," he said, his voice slightly scratchier.

"Can... Can I touch you?" she asked quietly.

Dmitri felt like he was choking on his words. If he had flesh, it would have risen with goosebumps at the innocence of her question. At a loss for words, he tentatively reached a shaking hand out for hers, curling his fingers around her carefully as though he was scared of breaking her with this touch alone. She let out a small breath of surprise, feeling wood where she had expected skin, and her eyes widened further. She was not scared but felt awe as she let him touch her.

He guided her hand to the bark of his chest, carefully gliding her hand along it, and was careful not to scrape her hand too roughly. He stopped her hand to rest over his still-beating heart, pounding too quickly to count the beats.

"The last of my humanity, resting beneath your fingertips," he mused. Shaking his head, he continued. "I am not a creature that one stops to marvel at. I am something rough and made of splinters and thorns. I am something that people see out of the corner of their eyes as they stumble through my forest if I feel generous enough to let them survive. I am a bedtime story told to scare little children. I am the life and death of this forest, creating and destroying in a constant ebb and flow. It is the latter that people tend to fear the most, and I have given them good reasons to. I ache and weep with the forest as it burns throughout the dry seasons. I soak in the rain with relief as it stops. I have feelings, I do, but I am not made of the same thing that you are. I am made of broken branches and skeletons of animals that have passed now. I can never be fully human ever again," Dmitri explained quietly to her.

Elena listened to him talk and carefully slid her hand away from his own, tracing the grooves in the bark over his chest in idle designs. She flattened her palm against him, moving her body a little closer to his own. She moved her hand upward, tracing the side of his neck slowly, sliding it up along the smooth bleached bone of the skull where his face should be. Dmitri shuddered beneath her investigating touch, and she paused her hand, caressing his face as she concluded the study of his skin.

"I think you are beautiful," she murmured. "You are the Guardian of this forest, Dmitri. You protect it and have made difficult decisions in the past—and some of them were probably the wrong decisions. But are you not made of the same material as the trees of this forest? If they can grow, overcoming obstacles of nature in their attempts to touch the clouds, then what is to say that you cannot grow as well? You get to choose who you are right now before the curse takes that choice away from you. Why do you choose to call yourself a monster?"

"I feel as though it is what I deserve," he answered honestly.

Elena shook her head and gently grazed her thumb over the bone as her other hand came to rest on a soft mossy patch on the middle of his chest. "Who you are is not defined by what kind of creature you are. I am a witch, and some would say that alone makes me a monster. I have met humans who make the word monster feel tame and domesticated. Right now, you get to choose who you want to be. Instead of a monster, be a protector. Instead of a Leshy, simply be Dmitri, the Guardian of the forest. You give power to the names you assign yourself. So give power to this one; you are powerful. You are strong. You are dedicated and loyal. You are beautiful in any form you decide to wear. You are my Dmitri, and I am not going anywhere. We will face what comes next. Together."

Gradually Dmitri's Leshy form began to melt away beneath her touch. Her breathing hitched in her throat at feeling the change from rough to smooth as she now caressed his cheek. She could feel his body shrink back into its normal size beside her as the fire crackled behind them. She felt something wet drop gently upon her skin and wondered for a brief moment if it was going to rain again before she realized that it was his tears. She brushed the tear away with her thumb and felt her heart ache for him. His hand came up, sliding along her own hand that caressed his cheek. His fingers slid between the cracks of her own, bringing her hand away from his skin only to guide it to his lips as he placed a slow, lingering kiss against her knuckles.

Slowly she felt his other hand come over, sliding around the curve of her hips as he gently pulled her body towards him. She obliged, moving closer as they embraced each other. He buried his face in the crook of her neck, and for the first time, she could feel the shape of his face. She felt the softness of his lips as they grazed her skin and the feeling of his short-cropped beard. Gooseflesh rose on her skin as she wrapped her arms tighter around him, emboldened enough to run her fingers languidly through his hair as she caressed him gently, holding him against her as a few extra tears dripped down onto her own skin.

"You aren't leaving," he murmured, his lips brushing barely against her flesh as he tightened his hold on her waist. He had meant it more as a question, but it had come out as a statement of disbelief.

"No, you cannot be rid of me so easily," she confirmed, her own voice like silk beside his ear.

Dmitri let out a breathless chuckle of relief before he pulled back a fraction of an inch, wiping his tears away with the back of his hand. He kept one hand tightly around her waist as he pressed her body against his chest. His other hand came up to caress her cheek. She was so small compared to him, even in his human form. He brushed away those loose strands of hair that had framed her face and tucked them carefully behind her ear.

"Tell me something that you like about yourself," Elena whispered in the small space between their faces. She could feel his breath against her lips, the distance feeling too far, but she needed to know that he still did not think of himself entirely as a monster. A Leshy, yes, but never a monster.

Dmitri paused, admiring the way her eyelids fluttered a bit when his thumb idly stroked the skin of her cheek. "Something that I like about myself?" he echoed quietly, barely focusing on the question, despite his efforts to do so.

Elena nodded, her own heart racing as she felt his touch. She wondered for a moment if he had ever touched someone like this before. He moved as though he had some kind of intrinsic knowledge of all of the spots along her skin that would cause her to react, but his hands were slow and hesitant, as if he, too, was discovering her skin for the first time.

He hummed softly for a moment in thought as his eyes struggled to remain on hers, glancing down at the soft pink shade of her lips against her pale skin. "I like that I am yours."

"Mine?" she asked, innocence lacing her voice though she did not act surprised at this comment. It made Dmitri grin as he chuckled softly to himself. Elena felt the deep rumble of his chest as he did so and found her hand gently sliding to his chest out of instinct. She could feel the way his eyes grazed along her, though she did not know exactly where his eyes had decided to land.

"A few moments ago, you said that we give power to the names we assign ourselves, only to then list off a few very lovely adjectives. Including... 'your Dmitri,'" he said softly, a grin pulling at his lips. "I happen to like that about myself."

Elena's cheeks blushed at this realization, but she smiled affectionately at him. "You have been calling me your 'little witch' for quite a while now," she pointed out.

Dmitri tightened his grip on her waist. "I know."

Elena felt the slight blush of her cheeks redden further. She had never been touched like this before by anyone. She had never been held so closely or intimately and had never imagined that someone would ever make her feel as though she was simultaneously as light as the breeze as well as grounded like the roots of a tree. She knew that she should show some discretion, pull back now and tread carefully to maintain the illusion of her propriety. She knew that there were technically ways that a person was supposed to be courted. So then, she could not understand why her hand gently grabbed the fabric of his shirt. She could not fathom why, despite knowing how things were supposed to be done, she guided his lips to hers and closed the little space that remained between them.

Dmitri, humming with surprise, wasted no time before closing his eyes and getting lost in the softness of her touch. His eyebrows scrunched together, sliding his hand to the back of her neck to caress her and deepen the kiss. Her lips were cool against his own, and he made sure to hold her gently as she melted against him. Her breathing shifted slightly, surprised that he would kiss her back so easily, and his mouth curled into a languid smile against her lips, her own smile following shortly after.

After a long minute, Elena pulled back hesitantly, her breaths short quiet pants as she rested her forehead against his. She blushed, smiling as her eyes remained closed. She had not expected to feel so breathless with her first kiss. Dmitri caressed her face, keeping her face close to his own as his own breath was slightly more ragged.

There was a moment of pause between the two as they took in each other's breath quietly, a decision creeping between the two of them. Their lips brushed slowly, the question dancing silently along with the gesture. Elena nodded first, a bare and gentle movement as her heart thrummed inside of her chest. Dmitri slid a hand along her waist, feeling the curve of her hips as he possessively tugged her closer to him as if to be sure of her answer. A small breath of surprise fell from her lips, but she smiled, and he obliged her.

"Do you still think I am not real, my little witch?" Dmitri's voice murmured against her lips, moving from her as he moved down her jaw and neck, leaving a soft wet trail of kisses against her flesh in his wake.

The movement made Elena's breathing hitch inside of her throat as she struggled to focus on his words when his lips moved along her skin. "If you keep touching me, I will never have to wonder," her voice whispered beside his ear. Her comment was rewarded with his hands tensing on her hips, and she grinned playfully.

"You will be the death of me," His voice came out strained and tense as his breath trailed over the trail of kisses he made on her skin.

She opened her mouth to reply, but his mouth was on hers before she could utter a single word. She hummed in pleasant surprise, the sound nearly a moan, as his hands gripped the fabric of her dress tighter.

She slid her hand up along his chest, draping both of her arms loosely around his neck as her fingers tangled in his hair. He shifted his body closer to her, easing her back down against the blanket. She pulled him closer as she laid back against the ground, pressing their bodies together once more and leaving no space between them. She could feel the strength of his hands as they slid under her dress and against her skin. She shivered at the feeling of being so vulnerable to this man and yet pulled him closer, a fervent plea to be devoured entirely by his touch.

Dmitri savored each slow touch, taking his time with her and relishing all of the soft noises that she made in response. Even he, a normally silent creature by nature, had trouble keeping himself muffled against her skin.

All Elena knew was that the way her body took his, was a perfect design, as though they had been carved of the same material. The way that their bodies moved in tandem together forged their bond deeper, and she knew that he was truly irrevocably hers, and she was his. Their bodies came together until they were no longer two separate things but rather one being, whole in completion.

The fire had tempered down into soft glowing embers, revealing a blanket of stars above them. Even the forest, normally watching at all times, seemed to turn its gaze away from the pair, leaving them to their intimate privacy. Many decisions had been made, ones that they could never come back from, but both Elena and Dmitri welcomed the change with ease, ready to step into the next chapter of their lives in the only way they knew how anymore; together.

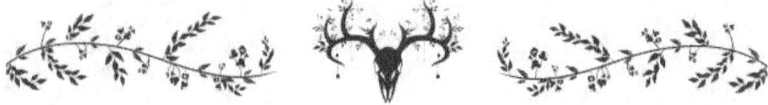

PART FOUR:
INTO THE WOODS

Chapter Twenty-Three

SANCTUARY

The days had begun to blend together once again for Dmitri. This time, however, he found himself welcoming it. For Dmitri, there had been two solid linear directions of time in his life; that which was before Elena and that which was now. He never wanted there to be an *after*. He shoved the thought away so vehemently that his mind reeled. At times, the truth of his situation threatened to drown him.

The thing that made him 'Dmitri' was beginning to fall apart.

His humanity was fading a little more with each passing day, and yet still, he fought to hold on. He fought to keep her here with him. He would never be able to permanently put off his fate, but he would take this reprieve of fresh air, and he would take it all into his lungs until they burst. He didn't even know how long he had left in truth. It could be a day or a month, or even ten years, depending on how the rot took to his humanity. For now, however, he would live for the moment, this moment, right here by her side. And when the weight of his decisions threatened to weigh in on him once more, Elena's smile grounded him right back down beside her.

Her smile... It was the sunlight just before the night. It was warmth encapsulated by soft pink curves. He could bask in the afterglow of her smile and never know another cold sleepless night. He could wake beside her and never know another day of violence in a perfect world. He caught himself thinking of her, even in the moments they were not together. She made him want to be better. She made him want to live the remainder of his days with humanity to the fullest. He was dying, but she made him feel more alive than he had ever had the pleasure of feeling.

The witch's magic that flowed through her veins had truly begun to shine as the days went by. Her intrinsic ability to simply know things had grown stronger. She had begun to truly grasp and understand the world around her through her conversations with it. Her intuition grew each and every day, and she never failed to remind him of that in subtle ways, like the way her hand found his knee when he began to retreat back into his mind or the way her lips found his skin in quiet moments of his fretting. Anytime that he thought too far ahead or behind him, she was there, roping him back to the present with her beautiful knowing smile.

They spent the days together in warm, quiet bliss. They had tried to brainstorm ways to slow the process, but it had proven to be fruitless and grim. Eventually, a decision was made to simply spend the time they had together and face reality when it came. Elena was beginning to prosper and fully come to terms with her lack of sight. She navigated things easier now, fully memorizing the space of the cottage and the garden. She challenged herself daily, wanting to become stronger and sturdier on her own, but there were still days when she leaned on Dmitri. He was happy to be there to support her in those moments, softly encouraging her that there would always be tomorrow.

How true that was, he could not be sure. He knew the promise of tomorrow could never truly be guaranteed, much less a tomorrow in which they were together. Still, he coaxed her to be more gentle with herself with her progress. The truth of the matter was that she was healing exceptionally well. He had even awoken to her cooking breakfast on her own some days. They had spent an entire day rearranging June's kitchen to something that was a little more accessible and easier to navigate for the both of them after he had noticed how peaceful she became when she began to cook.

Dmitri taught her more self-defense moves and techniques, and Elena became skilled in anticipating moves. At first, Dmitri had wondered if he was simply becoming too predictable, which would not help her should she actually ever need to use these moves, so he had begun to switch things up. To his surprise and delight, Elena was still able to anticipate well. This was something else he wondered was in part due to her own intuition of things. Elena seemed to be particularly skilled in seeking out her connection to the world and trusting her gut feelings on things. When Dmitri had mentioned that her intuition was abnormally strong for someone so new to magic, she had blushed and gotten a little shy. She had begun opening up to Dmitri more about her past, so she told him about how there had been times before she knew her heritage in which she had feelings that were overwhelmingly strong that she could not explain. Her father had begun to notice these, too, taking her abnormally seriously when she spoke of them. Dmitri had explained to her that it seemed as though she had the outlines of premonitions, and that is why her intuition on certain things was so strong. He also explained that, if he had to guess, time did not move as linearly for her as it did for others, and that is why her connection to future events felt so potent, as if they were currently happening.

Elena thrived on learning, and Dmitri adored watching her flourish as she took in new information, soaking it up like the earth taking to rain after a dry spell. Every knockdown in their practice only drove her to want to learn how to adjust and counter her next moves. In her training with magic, she pushed herself in ways Dmitri would not have thought of. Each day was filled with exploring the world, exploring themselves, and slowly but more confidently exploring each other as well.

Since the night that they shared by the fire with tangled limbs and breathless smiles, Elena had invited Dmitri to stay in bed beside her at night. His arms routinely wrapped easily around her small waist, holding her close to him protectively as she dozed to sleep. He often found himself playing with the ends of her hair once she had let it out of her braid or counting the freckles along her cheeks and nose. The first night, he had been too terrified to move and risk waking her. He had never held a woman through the night before and had never felt the desire to. Dmitri had never felt the way a woman's body fit so perfectly against his own. He never wanted to feel it with anyone aside from this woman beside him now.

The second night, her touch had lulled him into a sense of peace and comfort as her fingers idly traced smooth imaginary designs over his chest and her lips placed soft kisses on his skin. He thought he would fall apart with each gentle touch. Each night, it always ended the same, though. Her head would rest over his heart, the last aspect of his humanity that had yet to be infected by the rot of his decision, as if she was protecting it. She would fall asleep to the slow, steady beat against her ear, and he would will himself to stay awake just a little bit longer, just to memorize her features over and over again.

They had spent days learning the simplicity of each other's touch as well. Intimate moments were not scarce between the two, learning the other like the back of their hand. They were helplessly entwined with each other in body, mind, and heart now—nearly inseparable. The stakes of his life had changed. Elena was sacred to him now, and the idea of that terrified him. So long he had spent with the mentality of nothing to gain. Now, he felt as though he had everything to lose.

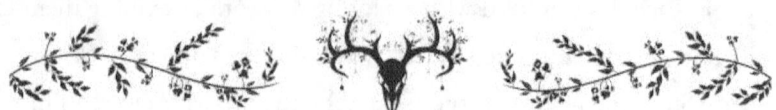

Chapter Twenty-Four

BINDING

E lena basked in the warm summer sun that shone down on her skin. The grass of the field tickled her skin, bristling against her as she breathed in the smell of soil and wildflowers that bloomed brightly around her. She listened carefully, picking apart the various noises that came to her and sorting them through her mind. It had become something of a mental practice to help her with recognition. Dmitri had taught her one of the most important lessons of magic was communicating with the world and her magic, and she found that the world often had much more to say to her than she originally thought. Her connection to it deepened further now that she and Dmitri had chosen each other.

She smiled idly to herself at that thought. Falling in love was something that other girls in her village often fantasized about, but this feeling she held felt so much more potent and powerful. They had not told each other that they loved one another yet, though Elena did not think this was due to a lack of feeling. Even without her intuition, Elena knew that this feeling inside of her chest was love. Though, she had not "fallen" into it. She had chosen it. She chose to love him with each passing day, knowing the consequences of doing so. She knew that their forever might not last, but she would choose to love him today. And when tomorrow would come, she would make the decision to love him then too.

Currently, Dmitri went to go collect some meat for the two of them. It could hardly be considered hunting, Elena had realized once Dmitri explained how he was able to get meat for them so quickly and easily. The forest bent to his will, and while he did not have to ask, he still did. Elena thought that was enough of a demonstration that his humanity still thrived inside of him, but Dmitri did not seem to agree. She asked for him to show her one day how he took the life of creatures without weapons, and even though he hesitated, he agreed, saying how it was probably important for her to see the darker sides of his role as well.

She was not as naive as Dmitri might think her to be. She had seen cruel men. She had seen death up close and personal. Most importantly, Elena was not afraid of Dmitri despite knowing that he, too, was capable of eliciting death. She knew that one day, he might not be the same man whom she chose to love today, but she refused to waste the days with him worrying about that. He would change, but she might change too. It would not make it easier. But today, she had chosen to love him—and that included the edges that had muddied with his darkness. It would not make losing him any easier if the time came during her lifetime, but everyone always lived in a similar way; loving despite the possibility of loss. They would not be exempt from this.

She inhaled once again, pushing away those thoughts once more as she lulled her head to the side and opened her eyes. She could hear the sparrows and the cicadas that hummed their bodies deep in the forest, indicating the day was beginning to shift toward the evening. She listened to their serenade with a smile, her hands resting on her stomach lightly. She loved listening to them in the evening, and it had become a pastime of hers now. At times, she imagined that they were all singing for her ears alone, humming their tune in a grand encore for her delight.

After a few minutes, her smile grew a little wider as she felt a shift. "You are doing it again," she said softly, sitting up a bit as small blades of grass fell from her hair.

Dmitri grinned to himself and chuckled, shaking his head as he walked closer to her. "Sorry, I just didn't want to disturb you. You looked so peaceful," he mused.

Elena rolled her eyes playfully, trying her best to look frustrated, but her smile gave her away. It felt like not that long ago that she thought she would never be able to smile again, and yet with him, it felt like a new permanent feature. She still had nightmares and terrible memories, panic attacks, and days where she simply just cried for no reason. That kind of pain did not simply disappear overnight after all, but he was always there to dry her tears. He was there to hold her through the nightmares. He was there, always, and he always managed to coax her smile back without even trying.

"Peaceful or not, you still promised you would not sneak up on me. And you promised to make more noise, so I can hear you coming."

"You have gotten better at knowing when I am here, even when I am silent. Maybe I am just testing your skills." Dmitri sat in the grass behind her and snaked his arms around her waist, pulling her onto his lap. His voice was playful and teasing, his grin stretching the corner of his mouth.

Elena sighed and tilted her face up, kissing his jaw sweetly before she leaned into his chest. "I am not going to be covered in blood, am I?" she murmured, relaxing once more.

"No, ma'am. I went to the river and washed off before making my way back. Besides, there wasn't too much blood to begin with. I just took some rabbits today."

She nodded and smiled as she leaned up and placed languid kisses along his neck up toward his cheek. He groaned in relaxation, exhaling softly beside her ear. "Dmitri?" she asked quietly.

He made a small hum of acknowledgement and opened one of his eyes to look down at her. "Yes?" he answered beside her ear, dragging his fingertips along her arm gently.

She shivered beneath his touch and placed her hand gently over his. "Listen to the cicadas with me? Just for a few minutes?" she asked him as if he would ever say no.

"You never have to ask."

Dmitri adjusted himself a bit so that his legs were spread and knees bent before pulling her back between them. He held her from behind, one arm securely around her waist and the other one idly picking small blades of grass away from her hair. She leaned back into him once more, resting her head against his shoulder as she closed her eyes and listened to the cicadas roar to life a little louder for their audience.

As the evening began to shift into nightfall, the cicadas tapered off into silence as the crickets and toads took up their turn for the encore. Elena sighed contentedly, and Dmitri grinned down at her. Elena's father had once explained to her that the cicadas were lullaby composers. She hadn't understood what he meant back then, but now as she listened to the cicadas lead the procession of their nightly symphony—followed by the crickets, frogs, and birds—she took the time to remember her father's smile fondly. The memory of him no longer ached so deeply, and she imagined his beloved worms dancing through the soil to the song that the cicadas led.

"Elena?" Dmitri murmured.

"Hmm?"

"What do you want right now? If the world could give you anything."

Elena smiled a little wider but did not open her eyes as she considered her answer for a few moments. "An eternity to spend with you. The ability to know you will always be mine, and I yours." Her answer was spoken in a softer tone as if whispering a confession.

A slight pause. "Would you not ask for your sight back?"

Elena shrugged. "I do not see my lack of sight as a flaw. I do miss being able to see things, but I am not a broken thing in need of being fixed. If I had to choose, it would be you, Dmitri. I will always choose you."

Her words felt heavier with her last sentence. Dmitri exhaled slowly as if he had been holding his breath unknowingly, and tucked a strand of hair behind her ear.

"Have I ever told you the story of the Sun and the Moon?"

She shook her head and opened her eyelids, tilting her head up to look in Dmitri's direction as she gave him her full attention now. Dmitri smiled as she focused on him, his heart beginning to pick up ever so slightly as she felt it thump against her back while leaning against him.

"Well, when June was young and still lived in her village, someone had once told her a story about the moon and the sun. It had varied, depending on who spoke the story to her. Sometimes the story went that the Moon loved the Sun so much that it would die every night just to let the Sun live. Sometimes it was told that the Moon had betrayed the Sun and that they were forced to never travel the skies together ever again. June had listened to these stories with fervency, but with each retelling, she found herself less content with the story, knowing within her mind that the tales being told were simply wrong.

"She told me about how she came out to the forest with Silas, and as they were building their home together, she would sit in this very field and stare at the moon and stars at night or stare at the sun through the clouds. She would listen to them, whispering to them to tell their story to her. It took years of coaxing, according to her, before she finally began to grasp the edges of their story. The story goes like this;

"The Moon and the Sun have loved each other for as long as the earth has existed. Before humans walked the world, they did not always move in sync with each other as we know them to now. The courtship between the two was slow and precise, made of compromise and understanding. Once the Moon and the Sun realized that their love was imperishable, they revealed their love to the universe. Their love was so undeniable and so potent that the universe could do nothing but accept their decision. It was stronger than any magic that the universe could ever hope to harness. So, in front of their audience of stars and planets, galaxies, and never-ending eternities, they pledged themself to one another, and their souls were combined into one.

"In celebration, the two entered into a timeless dance to display their love for one another. They dance through the stars, spinning each other around in their embrace. They orbit each other, parading throughout the galaxy and laughing with delight as they are eternally bound. There come points where they are closer, holding each other in an embrace before they continue their dance. They are together, dancing in tandem always, even when their dance leads them to drift apart physically. Always, they will make their cycle back to one another. No force in any world or in any universe could ever dream of separating the two—even death cannot destroy their love."

Elena's smile grew as he told the story, gliding her fingertips along the palm of his hand. When he finished talking, she brought his hand up to her lips and pressed a gentle kiss to his palm.

"I like that story a lot. Earlier, I was laying in this field before the cicadas began to sing to me. I was thinking about the concept of falling in love and how I didn't really like that phrase. It makes things seem so...

helpless. I would much rather choose whom I love and then proclaim it to the universe like the Sun and Moon did, daring the world to even try to intervene," Elena said, a hint of longing and yet determination in her voice.

"Did you mean what you said then... about always wanting to choose me?"

Elena's cheeks flushed pink as if she had just realized what she had admitted. Her smile was tentative and shy, but she did not deny his claim. Instead, she turned his hand over in her lap, sliding her fingers to interlock with his own. A silent promise to him.

"I am not a traditional man. I never grew up knowing customs or societal rules, and I have never cared to abide by ones set by selfish men who do nothing to try and understand the world. But I believe that there is truth in proclaiming your love in front of an audience, and if you let me, I want to choose you. Every day from now until the fraying edges of eternity. I have chosen to love you. And I will love you with the power of a thousand Suns if you only choose to be my Moon. I cannot promise that there will not be a time when circumstances may separate us, but I want to profess to the world and dare it to try and keep me away from you. I want to be seen as yours in every way and every tradition to leave no doubt in your mind that I love you. In this life or the next, my soul will always orbit yours. I want... I want to be bound to you."

Elena tensed for a moment, her eyes widening as she listened to his confession. She had thought of him in all of these ways that he now spoke out loud, but it had not sunk in that there was a possibility that he wanted all of the same things that she desired in secret. Her own heart raced in her chest, taken aback that he had spoken so smoothly as her mind raced.

"You want me?" she managed to breathe the words out. "Even if I am broken?"

"Broken?" he asked incredulously. "In what sense of the word? Because you have suffered immeasurable trauma and had the strength to endure? No, Elena. No, you are not broken, but even if you were, I would tear myself to pieces just to give you what you need. I love you."

"And bonding... it is like marriage?" she asked quietly.

Dmitri tilted his head from side to side for a moment as he considered the comparison. "In a way, yes, but binding is far more powerful. Marriage is a contract to appease humankind, and contracts can be broken—even if it is frowned upon. Binding is... it is proclaiming your love to the universe. It is forming an unbreakable bond that goes beyond words and vows. It is stronger. A binding can only be done for souls that are truly meant to be entwined. The ones with a love so strong and compatible that their souls merge to become one."

Elena blinked, and what he was asking her finally settled in her mind. She smiled, and her breath hitched inside her throat as she nodded, shifting her hips so that she faced him more. She placed a hand on his cheek, realizing her fingers were shaking now as she grazed her thumb along his beard. His hand came up, holding her hand gently but firmly against his face, and she giggled breathlessly.

"I love you, Dmitri. I meant it when I said I would always choose you. In whatever form you may come, I will always love you. I want to be bound to you."

Dmitri grinned wider, engulfing her in an embrace with both of his arms as he closed the space between them and kissed her. She giggled into his mouth, happiness overflowing from the both of them. He kissed her lovingly, relief in his smile as he relaxed with her and eventually pulled back.

"I want to tell the world. I am yours, and you are mine, and nothing can stop us," he murmured, pressing a few more soft kisses on her cheeks and jaw unhurriedly.

Elena was touched at the affection, blushing a deeper red under the moonlight. "Let the forest be our witness then. If the Sun and the Moon can have their binding ceremony as the universe and galaxies as their witness, then let us profess in front of the forest. Let the trees gossip amongst themselves, spreading our love like wildfire. Let the breeze and the river carry our commitment to the edge of the world. We have our witnesses. Let us not waste any more time."

"Tomorrow," he agreed. "That way, your cicadas will not miss a thing," he added with a small playful smirk.

Elena and Dmitri spent a few more minutes in the field, exchanging soft meaningful kisses before they finally went inside the cottage. Dmitri skinned the rabbit and prepared the meat, and then Elena instructed him on what to do to help her prepare dinner for the two of them.

Elena knew that eventually, there was going to be a time when he would have to guide her to a nearby village to get a few more supplies for them. He was unable to go himself as his body was bound to the forest, and he could only leave the boundaries of it for short periods of time. Even then, he had explained that it was an incredibly taxing thing to do. If he was not careful and fell unconscious outside of the forest boundaries, he would awaken inside of a hollowed tree—asleep within the wood for terribly long amounts of time. No, it would have to be Elena. He also explained that this was part of the reason that he had been so adamant about training her for self-defense as well.

Once they finished cooking and then ate their meal together, they spoke a little more of the binding ceremony before they retired to the bedroom for the night. Elena faced him, wrapping her arms around his torso as he played with her hair. After learning the true meaning of loss, Elena was glad to know that she would not have to worry about ever losing him. Even without the binding, she knew that they were bound in ways beyond their understanding.

She wished that her father would be there to see the ceremony tomorrow, but she knew within her bones that Dmitri was precisely the type of man that her father wanted her to end up with. Sure, her father would still have been worried about her. After all, Dmitri would not be himself one day and could not provide a life for Elena once that time came. However, Elena was more than capable of providing a life for herself. She did not want anyone else, and she would rather be happy for the short time that she could spend with Dmitri rather than submit to a husband out of conformity. Elena had fought to survive and nearly gave up once. She would continue to make the most of the life that she had been afforded. She would continue to learn and thrive. She was Elena, daughter of Mikhail and Anya. She could do anything. This was the life that she had chosen.

He placed a gentle kiss on her forehead before they drifted off to sleep, excited for the next step in their lives.

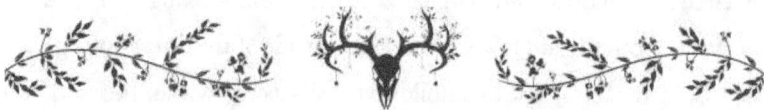

Dmitri held Elena's hand as they walked through the forest together, his heart thrumming inside of his chest. He never imagined that this would be the direction that his life would lead him. He did not think that love and binding was in the cards that he had been dealt. Abandoned and left for dead, choosing to become a monster, and brooding in the last of his days with his humanity are the only pillars of his life that he had known for so long. But now, with Elena giving his hand a soft encouraging squeeze as they walked side by side to the oldest tree in the forest, he could not be happier at how wrong he had been. She was a new beginning. She was the hope over the horizon. She made the pain bearable. He loved her and felt like a better man for having done so.

Together they finally approached the ancient tree, its bark wider and thicker than the two of them put together, and then some. Dmitri could smell the age of it, refined and dignified. It took strength to survive for as long as this tree had. It had weathered all elements and stood strong and firm. It had survived lightning strikes more times than Dmitri could count and yet continued to thrive. It had even survived a fire. Dmitri bowed his head out of respect for it, and to his surprise, Elena did the same without prompting. He smiled at her kindness to this forest.

Elena wore a black dress with white stitching designs all along the sleeves, skirt, and chest. They were intricate designs, each one neat and precise. She wore her hair braided and tucked up into a bun, loose strands framing the side of her face and wildflowers intertwined neatly throughout the braid. Dmitri wore a matching black tunic, white stitching only along the sleeves and neckline, and some slacks. Elena had picked bright wildflowers and wove them together as a sort of crown that she had placed on his head as well, matching her own flowers. He smiled brightly at the prominence of daisies and wondered if that had been a coincidence or something done on purpose. Knowing her, it was most likely the latter.

Black outfits had always been a customary color for witches in their binding ceremonies. On one hand, it was a contradiction to human weddings in which white was a primary color and their way of acknowledging that no one is ever truly 'pure.' The tradition stemmed back further than that, though, representing the death of one life apart and the celebration of a new life together as one. The wildflowers had been Elena's touch, and Dmitri could not help but smile at her excitement when he had told her yes.

The sun had begun to set on the day, and cicadas hummed to life. Dmitri wrapped a ceremonial cloth around their hands that held one another, a symbol of the bond that they were announcing to the world around them.

"Are you ready?" he asked softly.

Elena's smile outmatched the sun. "I am, are you?"

"I would not trade this moment for anything in the world."

They waited for the world to shift into place properly. Since the Sun and the Moon were the first ones to ever bind their souls together, Dmitri and Elena waited until the sun had just begun to set over one horizon and the moon rose over another. They wanted both to be present and grant their blessing on the binding. Their other witnesses were the entire forest, all moving in slightly closer to hear their Guardian bind himself to his witch. Dmitri squeezed her hand to indicate that they were ready and she nodded.

Together, they closed their eyes and let their magic flow through their veins. The breeze picked up naturally from Dmitri's magic, swirling around their feet but no higher. Elena could feel his magic against her own. She had grown more powerful in her own right since he had last displayed his magic. Now it was as though she could feel their magic blending together, creating something new entirely.

Dmitri was the first to speak, as he was the first one to ask her to be bound to him.

"Elena, my Moon, my little witch, my partner. I have chosen to love you, and I wish to choose to love you until beyond the end of days. My soul is no longer mine alone. In front of the audience of the universe, I bind myself to you. May death cower at our love for one another. May an eternity never be long enough to be by your side and continue to love you."

Both Dmitri and Elena blushed as they felt the universe shift. Dmitri knew it was surprised and delighted that the once isolated Guardian of the forest was now committing himself to another life of love and protection. He smiled a little wider, continuing to feel the magic in his veins. Elena had once told him that he was powerful and that it was not something to be ashamed of. Feeling the way his soul opened to her now, he knew his magic was indeed not something to be always feared. He could choose to be good right now in this moment. He could choose to be hers. What more could he want?

"Dmitri," Elena began. "Guardian of the forest, Leshy, my love. I have chosen to love you, and I wish to love you until the end of days. May my soul no longer be mine alone, intertwining with yours and becoming one. In front of our audience of the universe, I bind myself to you. May life revel in our love until the end of days. May an eternity never be long enough to be by your side and continue to love you. I am yours, you are mine, and we are one."

As she finished the binding, Dmitri took his other hand, which was not wrapped and intertwined with hers, and pulled her waist closer to his own. He kissed her lovingly as the trees swayed around them, almost as if dancing with excitement. The animals of the forest screamed in celebration from wherever they were. The moss around them grew brighter green, and the Sun and Moon, both witness to their display, coursed their blessing through the two of them. Elena gasped against Dmitri's mouth at the feeling, warmth, and coolness spreading throughout her in equal measures before tempering down once more.

The breeze at their feet ceased, and Dmitri gently slipped his hand away from the binding, using both of his hands now to cup her cheeks as he kissed her a little more firmly. Tears ran down both of their cheeks, and smiles curled their lips as they felt their souls merge into one. Elena's knees shook slightly, but he held her body firmly to his own, refusing to let her fall.

After a moment, she pulled away from his lips and laughed, wiping away her tears and sniffing. "I love you," she whispered.

"I love you too," he murmured, wiping his own tears and smiling down at her. His own hands were shaking as he felt the magic between them settle down. Carefully, he picked her up in his arms, causing a small gasp to fall from her lips. He chuckled softly. "Let's go home, my dear."

CHAPTER TWENTY-FIVE
THE APATHY OF NATURE

A few weeks had passed since the binding ceremony between Dmitri and Elena. The weight of her soul had changed slightly between the atoms of her body, the only indication that she had in which the world had blessed them and granted their request to merge their souls into one. It was a subtle thing that she often would not notice, but if she was in a quiet enough space, Elena swore that for the first time since she had been blinded that she could sense the edges of *color* when she focused her magic to reflect the aura of her soul. She had reflected on her aura once before the binding by accident, and she could sense a haze of feeling, but this was far different.

Upon seeing the first glimpse of shimmering gold, Elena audibly gasped. She began to weep as she found it once she had managed to regain her concentration again, happiness flooding through her at the revelation. It wasn't until Dmitri came into the room, hearing her weeping, that she looked up and noticed his own aura the same color. She wept harder at this, sinking to her knees on the floor of their home as she felt his strong arms sweep her up, muttering reassurances beside her ear until she had managed to laugh through the tears, throwing her arms around him in happiness.

When she finally explained the reasons behind her hysterics, he laughed in disbelief. As a Leshy, Dmitri did not have the magic to see the auras of people. In fact, even fewer witches had the ability in truth. But as Elena explained the sight to him, he could hardly suppress his grin, hugging her tightly to share in her happiness. While Dmitri had never been blind before, Elena had spoken of the things she dearly missed being able to see, and she knew that he understood what this meant for her. It would not be something she could utilize constantly, as seeing auras could be rather draining for witches, but this gave Elena something special. It had given her the gift of one color—one which held proof of their bond—that she would cherish for the rest of her life.

Seeing the color of their auras was not the only new thing that had changed between them. Dmitri had also explained that the creatures of this forest would not hurt Elena as her soul was now tied to their Guardian. This meant that Elena could now walk throughout the forest without any risk of harm coming to her. The forest was very hard to navigate, but Elena was determined to familiarize herself with her home.

So, they agreed that Elena would begin taking walks alone and attempt to use her magic to guide her way. If she ever got into trouble, Dmitri promised that he would come if she called. He had become rather protective of her and was hesitant about her going alone, but he agreed that she needed to learn this on her own. His connection to the forest would assure she never truly got lost, and that was enough to appease both of their worries—at least for the most part.

Elena wandered the forest, using her senses to guide her and remember certain landmarks in order for her to find her way back. She listened to the type of birds around, felt the warm areas of the forest where the sun filtered through the trees and cast sunlight onto her skin, and took note of how the earth shifted and changed with the terrain. She counted trees with her hands as she passed them, marking some with a temporary magic sigil that would alert her when she passed near them on her way back. It was something that she had been working on learning in the late evenings, so she was excited to officially try them out. She still tripped a couple of times, gasping as she managed to steady herself before she could reorient herself. Despite the challenge these woods presented, Elena would not let it deter her.

She had no idea how far she wanted to walk, still rather new to the completely foreign environment and still new to being completely alone, but Dmitri said that he had other business to attend to in the forest. So rather than sitting at home alone, she wanted to push herself a little bit.

She had been walking for what she had guessed was around two hours, enjoying the peaceful quietness until a distant scream ripped her out of her reverie. Elena froze in place, her heart seizing inside her chest. She had never heard Dmitri scream, but she could tell by the tone and pitch that this was not him. Relief and fear washed over her in equal measure. If it was not him, then it meant someone else was nearby.

Part of her wanted to run in the other direction to seek refuge and risk getting lost in order to ensure her own safety. Screams, no matter the cause, could never be a good omen when they come from deep within the forest. A thought rooted her to the ground and prevented her from doing just that. If Dmitri had not come when she had screamed and cried out, she would have died. What if someone else who was innocent was being hurt? She was not as helpless as she once was. She was not as cruel as the village she came from.

Without another moment of hesitation, Elena ran. She called her magic to her, helping to guide her feet to avoid falling as the man screamed once more. Her heart thrummed inside her chest, not knowing what to expect. After all, what could she truly do if this man was being attacked with guns? Though she reasoned that if his attacker had guns, his screams would not be continuing, or she would have heard a shot before the screams had started. This, of course, gave more questions than answers, but she hardly thought of it as she forced her legs to move faster.

As she got closer to the source of the screams, Elena realized a chilling truth as she slid to a halt. She heard the snarls of a beast and its teeth gnashing into the man as he cried out, pounding his fists against the beast's side as it relentlessly tore at his flesh. The blood drained from her face, horror crashing upon her. The man seemed to have noticed her or perhaps heard her running.

"Get out of here! Ahh!" he screamed, pain straining his voice.

Elena would do no such thing. After all, Dmitri had told her that the beasts of the forest would not hurt her. It was time to test the theory. She ran towards the man and the beast, falling between them quickly, bracing the man's body with her own.

"Stop!" she pleaded desperately.

The beast, which she could now recognize as a wolf, growled impatiently at the man behind her but took a step back away from the two of them.

Elena panted as she looked in the direction of the wolf. She closed her eyes, calling upon her magic to help her communicate with the world around her. She had never tried it with a beast before, but she was desperate.

"Please stop. He is not food," she said in a soft, breathless voice as her lungs tried to catch up with her.

"Are you insane?" the man asked incredulously but then gasped sharply in pain, shivering behind her with a groan.

Elena did not know how badly the man had been hurt, but she kept her eyes trained in the direction of the wolf. Part of her could not believe what she was doing. She knew nothing of which village this man came from or if he would hurt her like the others. She just knew she could not turn a blind eye like they had done to her. She was not *them*. The answer came to her inside of her mind, a language harder to understand, but the message was clear.

Humans should not hunt our woods.

"He will return to his village now. He will not take anymore," Elena tried to bargain with the creature.

He will not be pleased.

"Dmitri?" she asked, frowning a bit.

"No, that's not my name, it's—" The man croaked, still thinking that she was talking to him. She cut him off by shushing him. He huffed in indignation, mumbling something that she could not quite make out as she tried to focus on the wolf, knowing that where there was one, more were sure to be around.

Elena opened her mouth to say something but the sound of groaning and creaking wood made her stop short as she felt the familiar taste of maple and vanilla on her tongue.

"Oh fuck," the man behind her breathed out, grabbing Elena as he tried to shove her behind him. "Get back!" he shouted.

"Elena, what are you doing?" Dmitri asked, his voice devoid of any emotion.

Elena's relief faded as she heard the tone and the way his voice resembled hollowed wood. Her intuition flared inside of her, warning her of something. She tempered down the feeling before she rose to her feet slowly.

"I heard him screaming, and I think he is injured," she explained.

Dmitri made a humming noise as he glanced at the bloodied man behind her. The man's arm was covered with blood, bleeding as he dug his fingers into the puncture wounds to slow the bleeding. He had scratch marks over his face and chest as well, but those were not particularly life-threatening.

"So it seems," Dmitri replied.

"Yes... and I wanted to help him."

"Do the wolves not deserve their dinner?" Dmitri intoned, tilting his head to look at her curiously as his voice remained flat. He turned to look at the man whose eyes were wide with fear and confusion to see this girl speak to such a monster. Dmitri's bones of wood shifted slightly, causing him to creak again, and the man flinched once again.

Elena frowned at his answer. "The forest is plentiful without this man's life. I am confident that they can find dinner of their own volition without tearing more meat from his flesh."

"Everything serves a purpose. The sun provides nourishment for the grass. The grass provides for the deer. Humans are not exempt from this process, my dear. You eat the deer and the wolves? Well, sometimes, they find their teeth sunk in the flesh of man. Nature does not have sympathy for any creature. The hurricanes do not pity the house that holds a warm hearth. The winters do not pity an old man's bones. Why should I pity a fool who found himself in the path of a beast?"

"I will not just simply sit back and watch someone die, Dmitri."

"And why shouldn't we? Do you think he will not run back to his village and tell someone about you? Of me? He is nothing but a foolish human who came into my woods. It was his decision to enter and risk the consequences. Should he not learn the gravity of his decisions?" Dmitri asked, his voice nearly a growl.

Elena knew something was terribly wrong now. A horrifying feeling washed over her as she remembered his warnings; this was a symptom of his humanity fading. This was not her Dmitri, at least not entirely. Her body ached with fear, knowing her life could be in just as much danger as this man's now, but he had called her by name. He was not completely gone yet. Elena promised that she would stay by his side, and that is what she intended to do. If she had to drag him out kicking and screaming, she would try her hardest.

"My father died in a hunting accident," she reminded him quietly, her face firm and unmoving as she steadied herself. "I am helping this man to the nearest village. That is *my* decision, and you will either help me, or you will not interfere."

"Who are you to speak to me like that?" he growled, taking a step closer to her. The man cursed under his breath, flinching away. Elena did not move. She supposed there was one bright side to being blind; she could not see how terrifyingly Dmitri moved as he approached closer. His movements were animalistic with each step, and the calm before a storm when he stilled.

"I'm your little witch, or have you forgotten already?" she asked quietly. She knew there was no going back now. This man, if he had not already guessed from the way that she had spoken to the wolf, now would know for sure that she was a witch.

Her verbal jab worked as Dmitri paused, considering her for a moment. Emotions conflicted inside of him as he wondered if he should be impressed or enraged at her. In the end, he merely scowled and backed down. "If you insist on helping this mortal, then I shall assist. You have a terrible innocence, *little witch*. Let us hope that the consequences of your good deed do not come back to tear you to shreds as well."

"This isn't real..." the man murmured.

Dmitri chuckled, the sound dark and ominous as the wind bristled around them. "If she was not here, you would wish it was not. If you tell anyone of her, I will rip your limbs off and force them down your throat. That is a promise," he growled.

The man closed his mouth, managing a tight nod. Elena turned her back on Dmitri to face the man, offering her hand to help him up. He hesitated but took her hand, coating it in blood as he stood up and winced in pain.

"Do not get your vile blood on her," Dmitri growled, shifting down into his human form as he came over, grabbing the man's upper arm roughly to begin leading him toward the village. His eyes were blank and distant despite the rage in his voice.

The man grunted but did not argue. Instead, his eyes glanced at Elena as he stumbled forward, getting a good look at his savior's face for the first time. "You're blind?" he asked, his voice rusty and nearly croaking. "I'm sorry, it's just that... well, you're, uh, a girl and blind. And he's a Leshy but also... a man. Gods..."

Elena nodded at the man but did not acknowledge his rambling as she grabbed Dmitri's hand, pulling him to a stop. "He's bleeding. We need to stop it, or else he will not make it to the village." She did not know from where he was bleeding, but she had heard the sound of ripping flesh and knew it would be impossible not to be.

"That is merely nature taking its course."

"If we always let nature run its course, then I would have been buried in a shallow grave in your forest. Now, will you help him stop bleeding, or am I to rip my dress in front of this man?"

"Don't," he warned, sounding more pained than angry for a moment. He stared at her, and Elena prayed he would come back to himself. He didn't, not fully. Elena could tell he was still there, buried under the rot as he conflicted with himself. Elena stared ahead defiantly, raising one of her eyebrows as she kept her expression calm. She challenged him to doubt her.

When he did not move, she took a deep breath and bent over, grabbing the skirts of her dress. Dmitri growled, releasing the man and grabbing her hand firmly. "Alright!"

He grunted and let go of her, grabbing the man's shirt and ripping it roughly in a swift movement. He grabbed the man's arm, who was watching with confusion and amusement as this woman, this witch, made a Guardian of the forest bend to her whim by threatening to rip her dress. Dmitri tightened the fabric around the gashes of his arm tightly, making him groan loudly in pain as his attention snapped to the man.

"There," he said flatly, glaring at the man.

The man nodded. "Thanks," he murmured, sarcasm tinting his voice as he flexed his arm to regain some feeling there.

Dmitri curled his lip in a snarl but turned and began to lead the way. Even now, in this form, Elena noticed that Dmitri purposefully walked slow enough for her. She began to follow in his footsteps, and the man limped to walk beside her. They walked in silence together for a few minutes before the man began to speak.

"You are a witch?" he asked tentatively.

Elena did not move her head to look in his direction, and she tried to keep her expression even. Her voice was quiet, like a whisper, yet firm. "I am."

"But you saved me," he said slowly, trying to understand. The statement almost sounded like a question.

"I have. Is it truly so hard to believe that the things you have learned of witches might not be as true as you wish them to be?"

"I do not wish for cruel things to exist."

"Don't you? The world is far easier for you to explain and exist in when the fault of all evil lies beyond your reach. Yet it was humans who dragged me to the forest to die, and it is a witch who is dragging you from the forest to live."

The man was quiet for a long moment as they walked beside each other, but Elena could sense his tension. Despite the form Dmitri now took on, she knew there was nothing human about the way he seemed to prowl through the trees. His movements were stiff, like the bark from his skin had not truly gone away, and his joints creaked audibly. Elena was lost in her concerns when she suddenly tripped over an exposed root on the ground.

The man's arm extended quickly, catching her before she could fall face-first into the earth. She gasped, righting herself quickly as she shook her head. Dmitri stopped walking for a moment, and she carefully but quickly pulled her arm away from the man's grasp. She felt a shiver at the sensation of being touched by anyone else. It was not entirely unpleasant, but it brought the painful memories back to the surface now that her adrenaline had died down.

"I am capable of making up my own mind on things," the man murmured. Elena was unsure if he was trying to convince her or himself.

"Yes," Elena said, keeping her voice low.

The man looked at her and frowned a bit but nodded, seemingly content enough by her answer not to argue. The three began to walk again in mute silence. Once they reached a clearing, Dmitri grabbed both of their arms and bent the world, folding space in half like a piece of paper and dragging them through before they stepped into a separate clearing. They both tasted maple and vanilla, and Elena could faintly hear the chattering of a town. She turned to the man and nodded.

"We leave you here. I know I cannot ask this of you, but I must. Please do not speak of the circumstances of your rescue. Be a hero who fought off wolves, but do not be the man saved by a witch. For our sake, as well as your own," Elena said softly.

The man nodded, and while she did not see, there was nothing else that she could do. He walked a few more steps before pausing. "My name is Patryk. What are your names?"

"That does not concern you," Dmitri bit out.

"We are not figments of superstition." Her tone held defiance in it. She turned to face him and held her head confidently. "My name is Elena, and his name is Dmitri."

A low growl of protest left Dmitri's throat at her defiance, but he bit back his words.

The man nodded again. "Thank you, Elena, for saving my life." He said slowly and began his walk back to his village. Once he was far enough away that Elena could no longer hear him, she turned to Dmitri. "I know that he is a human, but you were once one too. It is important to remember that."

Dmitri looked down at her, frowning as if she spoke of nonsense. He did not react, and Elena feared the worst.

Elena sat by the fire, idly pushing needle and thread through a washcloth. She had felt a small hole in it earlier, so after washing it and letting it dry, she decided that once more, she would try stitching. Instead of weaving it through the cloth haphazardly, she truly took her time with it. Her stomach was sick with worry over Dmitri, and she needed the distraction.

After they returned to the cottage, Dmitri said he was going to go outside and chop some more wood for their fireplace tonight. Elena could hear the faint sound of an axe connecting down onto each solid chunk of wood outside and knew he had chopped far more wood than had been necessary but figured that it was better than him getting lost in the forest and perhaps even getting lost further inside of his mind.

Many thoughts had run through her mind as she wove the stitching. Had something happened that triggered this earlier when he attended to some business in the woods? Had she made it worse? And what would she do when the day came that he did not come back to her? For all she knew, that could very well be this day.

Elena knew the elation of the binding ceremony would not be permanent, but she still thought that they would have more time than this. Despite everything, Elena did not love him any less. She pitied him, knowing that these were not truly his thoughts and views. She had felt the conflict inside of him. She had convinced him to help the man, even if it had been begrudgingly. She knew that if he had fully succumbed to the creature inside of him, it would not have been possible. She tried to have as much hope and optimism as she could, but she could not ignore the trembling of her fingers as she thought of losing him so soon.

Elena paused, noticing that the chopping sound had stopped, and held her breath as she listened. After a few silent minutes, the door opened.

"Elena," Dmitri's voice cracked.

She continued to hold her breath, scared to hope too much. "Dmitri?"

He walked over and cautiously crouched before her in the rocking chair. He hesitated before taking her hands. "Elena, I am so sorry, I—" he started to say, but Elena threw her arms around him and buried her face in the crook of his neck. He ran his fingers through her hair, cradling her to him.

"I thought I lost you already," she said, tears building in her eyes.

Dmitri squeezed his eyes shut tightly and let out a sob. "Not yet," he breathed shakily. He pulled her closer to him, kneeling on his knees as she practically fell into his lap. Dmitri's body began to wrack with sobs. He tried to muffle himself by burying his face in her hair.

Elena sniffed as her own tears fell. She rubbed his back, moving her hands along his spine as she quietly shushed him. "It's okay, you're okay," she whispered beside his ear.

"I have so much blood on my hands. I was going to have more on them today. I would have watched him be torn apart, and I would have felt nothing. Do you see it now? Do you see what I am becoming? I am so sorry. I should have taken you somewhere far away from here—somewhere safe—but I was too selfish. I could have hurt you today," he rambled, his breathing becoming quicker.

Elena shook her head. "None of that. I have chosen to love you, and that includes all sides of you. The bad days and the days when you are not quite yourself are included. I cannot change your past, but I will not allow blood to be needlessly spilled. You could have torn him to shreds yourself or ordered the wolf to continue its attack, and yet you didn't. You restrained yourself. It's going to be okay."

"Next time, I might not. Don't you get it?"

"I'm not going anywhere, Dmitri. I still love you. I still choose you. I do not regret binding myself to you for a single moment. Today was not good, but tomorrow... tomorrow will be better. If it isn't, then we will work through that too."

"I am a monster," he choked on the word.

"No," she cooed softly. "You are my Dmitri."

"I think they are one of the same, my love."

Elena shook her head gently and pulled him closer to her, refusing to give up on him. "Not today," she whispered.

"Not today," he murmured—a resignation of an agreement but an agreement nonetheless.

Dmitri sobbed until his tears teetered off to quiet sniffles. She could feel the heaviness in his shoulders from carrying the weight of his guilt and internal conflict. Slowly she began to work her fingertips along his shoulders and muscles, whispering softly to him as he finally began to relax. They stayed like that for hours before she suggested they go to bed early. Dmitri, too tired to argue, nodded before sweeping her up into his arms and carrying her to the bedroom.

They laid in bed together, speaking quietly as they pressed against each other under the blankets. She could tell that he was both physically and mentally exhausted and yet did not want to sleep. So, he kept quietly prompting her to tell him stories about her past or stories of fiction that she could conjure. She obliged him, waiting for sleep to overtake him despite how he fought it.

"Thank you," he finally murmured, the words tumbling from his lips before his breathing finally evened out.

Elena stayed awake, lightly tracing her fingers along his skin. He had come back to her, but Elena knew it would not always be this easy. Still, she promised herself that she would not give up so easily. She would fight for both of them. Elena was not as helpless as she once was.

CHAPTER TWENTY-SIX

FOR WHOM THE BELL TOLLS

T he horse's hooves made muted thuds into the earth as Herrick made his way to the final town. He had been riding relentlessly, traveling to each town that had agreed to ally with them against the witch in order to tell them that its location had officially been found. Herrick had volunteered to take the journey to each village personally, claiming that he did not want anyone else to risk the treacherous uncharted forest that connected each village. While this was not entirely false, Herrick did have ulterior motives to travel alone. Simply put, he did not want anyone else to slow him down, and he did not want their allies to suddenly back out of their arrangement and cause further delays. As it was, it would take a few weeks to fully prepare and coordinate their attack now that they knew the surrounding terrain of its location. He did not trust others to be able to negotiate the severity of what needed to be done and the numbers they would need to do so. If they were going to kill the witch, Herrick wanted to make sure that they did it right this time and leave nothing up to chance.

The village of Pantauk had already voiced their hesitations now that they realized that finding the witch was no longer a theoretical scenario. Herrick was persistent, though, and he was finding that he could be convincing when the situation called for it. Where words failed, intimidation soared. Normally, he would have liked time to approach the conflict with more tact, but the time for that was narrowing along with his patience. If there was one thing that Herrick was coming to realize, it was that the bravery of men had grossly diminished in the presence of the disease that lingered in the Northern forest.

That wretched witch. Its presence made bile rise in Herrick's throat as he remembered its appearance. Had it always been so grotesque? Had the witch's demeanor always felt like knives were dangling above his head just at the mere thought of it? Certainly not, but this was the power of witches. They thrived off of fear, and he refused to feed them any longer. The true gods guided his soul now, pushing him forward in his crusade to cleanse this forest of the magic that plagued it.

Herrick had taken every precaution as he traveled through these forests, even down to fashioning iron horseshoes for his stallion to tread upon and avoid detection. Both he and his horse were covered in mud and leaves, charms to ward off spirits or third eyes seeking them out. He could not afford to take any chances as the end drew near. While it was slightly time-consuming to don such attire and prepare, he could not risk being impatient and ruining all of the progress that they had worked so hard for.

He was not the only one who was becoming anxious with anticipation either. With personal stakes of retribution for his father, it was easy to think that he was the only one who truly cared about the death of that witch. But as he had time to reflect while traveling to each town, he thought about the enthusiasm of his comrades. His friends and neighbors, and even some of their allies now, had all celebrated alongside him at the news of locating the witch. A fire was burning in each of them, ready to heal from all of the harm that it had caused or protect those that they cared for from having its harm reach them. It worried most people to think that the witch's power might eventually grow and become strong enough that it might even surpass the rumors of the infamous Baba Yaga. Herrick knew that would never happen, though; he would run his sword through its heart and burn the body before it ever had the chance.

His horse stopped as they came to a bog, looking too calm with fireflies dancing over it for him to believe it truly was as peaceful as it looked. It stretched too far to the sides to go around, and the distance across was not terrible. He clicked his tongue, easing the horse forward despite the hesitation he received from it. Pulled from his thoughts and fully alert now, he murmured a soft reassurance to the horse as it pressed on. The water came up to the horse's underbelly, but Herrick knew not to count on that depth. Bogs had a tendency to be unlevel terrain—shallow in some steps only to drop off at the next.

As they neared the embankment, a sharp crack of a branch to their right sent his already unnerved horse into a panic. Before Herrick could process what was happening, the horse was rearing up, neighing as he slipped off its back with a splash into the water. Inhaling the muddied waters, Herrick closed his eyes and coughed by instinct. His feet touched the mud at the bottom as he tried to push back up for air. Unfortunately, he had fallen into a deeper part of the bog, water coming up to his forehead, and the mud at the bottom acted as glue as it held his boots firmly planted.

He jerked his legs, thrashing against nature's hold on him as his own panic set in from the lack of oxygen already. Something brushed up against his legs, and his eyes opened beneath the water, unable to see even his own blurred hand in front of him in the dusk light. His mind went immediately to the other magical beings thought to inhabit this wretched forest, including the forest *Rusalka*.

Rusalka were vile feminine creatures that lingered near waters of the forest or rivers, luring men to watery deaths. Most of the time, it was said that they were once human women who had found their own graves beneath the waves for one reason or another. One thing was for certain, however, and that was that all Rusalka were malevolent maidens. If one were to be lurking in these waters, Herrick would have no doubt that they would kill him in a heartbeat.

Unwilling to become prey to magic, Herrick calmed his mind for a moment and said a quick, silent prayer to the true gods; *Guide me to salvation, my gods, and grant me the ability to carry out thy will.* Opening his eyes once more despite the stinging water, Herrick kicked at his ankles, knocking his boots off one at a time. By the time the second one came off, Herrick felt lightheaded, with his vision beginning to cloud. In the last moments, before he used his boots to stand on, he almost swore he saw a face lingering in front of his face.

Herrick gasped for air as his face finally breached the surface, shaking his hair out as his eyes scanned for his horse. The beast was waiting for him at the edge of the bog, prancing its hooves anxiously for him. Herrick pushed off from his boots, leaping through the water as he barely managed to catch the reins of the horse, which had fallen loose. Something brushed against his foot again—and whether it was a *rusalka* or merely the bog weeds, he did not know—and he heaved himself up as the horse pulled its weight back.

Grunting, he kicked away from the bog and looked at it frantically, searching for any sign of the vile magical beasts leering at him. He saw nothing as he sat there panting, shaken from the experience. These woods were dangerous for many reasons beyond those of magic. The terrain and weather within this forest were unforgiving, along with the average beasts who had been corrupted by the lingering magical effects. Despite this, Herrick would not be deterred from what had to be done.

Scowling at the small body of water, Herrick stood to his feet. The experience was unnerving, but his gods had spared his life and saved him from whatever disaster he had almost fallen victim to. Whatever the world threw at him, he knew that he would persevere. This was too important, and too many others were counting on him to pull through. Families were waiting in the villages, fear rattling through their bones each night as they wondered if that would be the day the witch came back to exact its revenge. He wanted to end it—he knew he *must*.

His gods knew his mission, and he had not been struck down. No true call to destiny had ever been without trials. Nothing worth wanting ever came easily. Whether or not this was the destiny that had been carved out before him, Herrick would not go down without a fight.

Climbing back on top of his horse, both of them now soaking wet, he sighed at the loss of his boots but was relieved to see his family sword still sheathed to the saddle. He patted the horse's haunches and clucked his tongue.

"Easy boy, we're almost there."

CHAPTER TWENTY-SEVEN

WAITING, WARNING, & WONDERING

Herrick fastened the sheath of his family's sword tightly to his body, making sure it was within ease of reach as it fit between his shoulder blades. The sword was a heavy weapon, long and sturdy as it had been within his family for generations. Herrick had to train for an entire year before he was able to properly wield the weapon and swing it with the precision needed for battle. His father once told him that the weapon had provided safety to its wearer for as long as they held it firmly within their grasp. It was a tool, made to be an extension of the body as he wielded it, used to slash through any evil which dared to threaten him or his family. Within the day, Herrick would be putting this weapon to the ultimate test of that ability.

The sun had not yet risen over the horizon as the sky remained dark. Even the stars knew better than to show themselves today. Herrick would have cut down every force of the earth in order to fulfill his task. It was smart of things to cower from his path. He sought the witch's blood, and he would not rest until his thirst had been satiated.

"You look so much like your father," his mother said softly as she stood in the doorway. Her face was tear-stained, and as much as he hated to see his mother looking as such, he would refuse to be swayed by her appearance.

So, instead, he merely nodded. He wasn't sure that he actually agreed with her statement, but he was proud of the compliment regardless. It would be an honor to be compared to the man.

"Must you go and do this?" she whispered, as if not truly expecting to be heard.

"I have already explained to you that I *must*, mother."

"I know what you have said, but—"

"I have to go. It is time," he interrupted, walking over and kissing her cheek before grabbing his bag and turning to the door without another word. He had heard her lectures and pleas. It did him no good to listen to them again, not when time was so valuable. They were on the cusp of something great, and he did not have a single second to waste. The longer he spent on this side of the forest boundary, the longer that witch continued to steal the valuable air.

The door to his home clicked softly shut behind him as he took in the atmosphere. A small crowd had begun to gather in the center square, listing off supplies and reading the replies of their allied villages as they went over the plan once again. Upon seeing Herrick walking towards them, some of them lifted their early breakfast rations to him in salute. He grinned at the camaraderie of his fellow men.

"How many more from our village are we waiting on?" Herrick asked, doing a quick tally in his mind.

"Just one more, I believe."

Herrick nodded. Good, he thought to himself. He did not want to linger here any longer. He was not foolish to enter these woods with the hubris that he would return unscathed, if at all, but this was his duty. Never before in his life did such purpose fuel him. He wanted to run to it with open arms. He wanted to waste no time and drive his sword into the heart of evil, just like the knights of kingdoms that his father once shared with him.

His father, who had been torn apart by the very evil which he was setting out to kill. Herrick, upon finding out that his father had died, had not felt much of anything at first. Numb to shock, he had been there when the search parties had found what little remains were left. He had wondered what kind of horrors his old man had been subjected to at its hands. Did the witch make his death quick? He had stared at the singular eyeball and teeth, the only remains of the mountain of a man who used to pick him up and swing him from his forearms. And now? Now he fits inside Herrick's pocket.

Indeed, Herrick had found an ornate case—something he supposed used to be his mother's jewelry box but now had been put to use for a far more noble cause—and delicately placed his father's decaying milky eye and yellowed teeth. His father's clothes he had given to his mother, letting her decide whether she should bury or burn them. He had not told her of what he now kept in his trouser pocket; A reminder of what the witch had taken. A refusal to let go. A promise to let the last of his father look upon the dead body of the witch who had killed him.

He would never admit this to another living soul, but he himself had committed a sin. He had not been in his right mind when doing so and told himself that the ends justified the means, but it did not change what he had done. He had gone to the old crone's house. The witch's grandmother had various poisons and herbs infused with magic out back of their home, unassuming to most. He had taken the eye immediately when finding it, brushing the dirt and maggots away, and took it to the garden surrounded by ash. He had heard the women of the village, who had been sent to investigate the old crone's garden, speaking earlier about how they had found enchanted herbs to preserve things for long periods of time. So he sought them out, brushing his father's eyeball in the dust before placing it in the ornate container it now resided in.

After all, she was dead. Perhaps her magic could do one good thing. To his delight and horror, his father's eye remained perfectly intact after that. It had been a miracle that animals had not devoured it, but he took this as a sign. His father's dying wish must have been to see the witch rot in hell. So Herrick would make sure of it and tell no one of his sin. He would repent later, he promised himself.

His hand instinctively checked to pat his side to make sure it was still there, just as he saw a man and a teenage boy walking toward them. He kept his face calm as he studied the man, but one of the villagers noticed the boy and grunted.

"This is no babysitting trip, Matthew," one of them chided.

Matthew stood up straighter, addressing the group as one. "This is my boy. He has been fearing for his family and is a good shot. He wants to help us kill the witch and bring his sisters some peace of mind. His mother agreed to it, and he says he is ready to become a man."

Herrick raised an eyebrow, standing up from the post he leaned against as he walked towards the boy. "You could die, you understand?"

The boy frowned deeply but managed a small nod. Herrick was not convinced that this boy would not up and run at the first sight of danger, but who was he to determine the strengths of one? Herrick was on the younger side as well, having just turned twenty-six, and was aware of how hard it was to make a name for yourself in a town that thrived on hunting rather than trade or wars. He nodded solemnly back at the boy.

"Alright, then he knows the risks. We need the numbers, and if his parents agree, then why shouldn't he? Boys younger than him fight in wars in times of need, and are we not in our own war, gentlemen?" he asked and looked at the others.

The crowd held their breaths, not daring to say a word. The last man who had dared to try and challenge Herrick to this decision had been found with his leg twisted backward at an odd angle. He had refused to say who had done it, but the townsfolk had a healthy suspicion. That was an argument between men, though, and if the man did not want to pursue a case with the townsfolk against Herrick, then they were content to believe that he had simply fallen off of his donkey in the fields. At the next town meeting, when he dared try to come once more, Herrick had calmly suggested that only the able-minded and able-bodied be a part of this discussion and that had been one thing that everyone else did agree on.

Herrick inhaled deeply. "Listen up because I am only going to say this to you all once. We cross that boundary into the forest, and no one is to make a sound. We wear mud, leaves, and iron. It is what the legends say protect against magic, and it is what has worked so far. So if it feels stupid, save it because I don't care. We do not know all of the magic or demonic things that reside in this forest. If you have to take a piss or stop, then tap someone. If you are tapped, make sure you tap someone until our entire group has stopped. I will not be stopping often, so if you can't keep up, then be prepared to be left behind. No fires until we get closer and you get the signal. We are moving on the element of surprise, and I intend to keep it that way as I do not want to lose one single man before we get there. Clear?"

Everyone murmured in agreement, and Herrick rubbed the hilt of his dagger on his side. He closed his eyes for a moment, pausing as he let the situation sink in. He opened his eyes, a new fire in them as he stared at them.

"How many of you attend worship services to the gods?"

The men around him all looked around at each other, wondering if it was a rhetorical question. When it became clear that Herrick would wait for their answers, some of them began to nod and murmur.

"I want you to ask yourself, would the gods be content to watch us sit idly by while this witch—this heathen—lays in wait in our forest? Can any single one of you attend a single service, knowing that you are enabling a murderess to breathe while our families take their last breaths? Can you stare upon the altars of the gods, knowing that you could be allowing more grief to come to your neighbors? The gods, when there was evil, struck it down. Their image is what we are meant to walk in. That is what the lessons teach, is it not?

"Now, if there are any doubts about what we are going to be doing here, let me spell it out for you. We are walking into a forest that we have allowed to become riddled and diseased with magic. It has haunted our thoughts for too long, and if we have to, we will indeed burn it down so that new healthy grounds may flourish. We are going there with the express intent to kill the witch, formerly known to us as Elena, and anything that stands in our way. It may have taken the skin of someone we might have once loved, but that girl is no longer. It has chosen its path of destruction, and if we allow it to continue down that path any longer, then we are no better than it in the end. It is time that we decide to act instead of becoming complacent to our fear.

"Its terror may not begin during our lifetime. We do not know how long witches live and how they choose to channel their magic. Do you want to risk it? Do you want to be old and helpless once our bodies begin to age naturally while its body remains strong, just to watch it terrorize our loved ones?"

Herrick paused, his eyes hardening as he looked into the eyes of the men who hung on every word he spoke. Herrick knew many of these men personally and was very involved in their lives. He had lived with them, drank with them, hunted with them, and today, he could very well die with them. Which is why he had to ensure that they knew that the reason they were fighting was something too important to give up on.

"Matthew, you and your son have women in your family, yes?" Herrick asked suddenly. The two nodded. Matthew clenched his jaw together a little tighter at the mention of the witch causing them harm.

"Your daughters and sisters will one day marry and bear children of their own. If the gods grant you grandchildren, nieces, or nephews, would you want to risk that the paths of their lives may cross with a witch that you allowed to live out of fear? Do you want this witch to steal your growing family from their cradles just to feed its belly? Do you want to risk the young children running off and entering the wrong forest out of curiosity or mistake, only to become lost in it until the witch's spindly fingers wrap around their throats? This witch thinks we killed its coven. Do you not think it would take her revenge on our families?"

Herrick glanced at another man from the crowd and lifted his chin. "And you? You may not have children yet, but you have a wife and sister, correct? The minds of women are fickle and unpredictable things. They may support and love you now, but that may not always last. What happens if you scold them for their misdoings in order to protect them, and they grow spite in their hearts for you? Out of resentment, they wander the forest and fall victim to the witch's silver tongue weaving lies of supposed freedom to them until they run away in order to join its new coven? Or become mindless slaves to its bidding once it finishes twisting their minds to pulp?"

Herrick had begun to raise his voice as he spoke, feeling more impassioned than ever. He could tell that their small village beyond this group of witch hunters had begun to listen to his speech, holding their breath in the silence of the background. *Good*, he thought, *let them all hear the truth and let it seep into their bones.*

He turned to another man. "Are you comfortable in your tiny house? Scrounging around for food before the hunts or trekking through the same forest to come up empty-handed by the end? Our village is expanding. Every single year it grows, and where do you suppose we go when we no longer fit within our borders? There is an entire forest of resources being hoarded at our fingertips that our forefathers had been too scared to tap into, but why shouldn't we? Why should we let the parasite of magic keep us from hunting a plentiful forest, keep us from cutting down trees, or mining resources from the earth to make our village larger and stronger? Are you content to live a life of 'good enough'? Because I am not! I am tired of just getting by year after year while this wretched forest prospers. We need not let it mock us any longer once the head of the witch is burnt to ash! Let her be the first of many if need be. We are stronger than them, even without magic, and it is time that they realize it.

"My father was a good man. Goddard was a good man. Mikhail was a good man, even before these witches cursed him and who knows how many others to fall. My father... he was a pioneer of greatness, and his death will sow the seeds for us to rise triumphantly to conquer this evil. He died, but we will not let his legacy be in vain. We will not let him down a second time." Herrick had to stop talking, choking on the last of his words. He swallowed them down, gritting his teeth as he tried to bury his emotion behind the hardness of his eyes.

One of the men stood, signaling the rest of them to follow. "We are with you until the end, Herrick. Let's go kill us a witch!"

The men cheered, lifting their weapons readily. Herrick nodded curtly, taking a deep breath. Once they calmed down, at last, the men proceeded to walk to the end of the woods, staring down at the ominous and foreboding darkness.

This is it, Herrick thought calmly. *This is my destiny.*

Elena grazed her hands through the soil, feeling for weeds or large stones in the garden on the side of the cottage. It was not the easiest task, but her magic guided her, making the weeds warmer to the touch than the plants that were supposed to be there. The sun had barely risen over the horizon, but Elena had found herself unable to fall back asleep this morning. Dmitri had begrudgingly let her leave his arms as he awoke, simply to make sure she was alright. Once she had reassured him, he nodded and promptly rolled over onto his back as he began the slow process of waking up.

From the moment Elena had opened her eyes, she had felt as though something in the forest was different. It was as though the forest was slightly on edge, but when she tried to inquire about it with her magic, it had given her no clear answer. So, instead, she tried to take her mind off of it by plucking the weeds and feeling the plants to check for any kind of harvest.

It was not until the cottage door slammed open that Elena gasped softly. She heard hasty steps and instantly sat up straighter, wiping some of the soil off on her skirt. "Dmitri?" she asked, concern filling her voice.

"Elena," his voice was filled with near relief, and she wondered for a brief moment if he simply could not find her and had panicked, but her wonders were soon answered. "I need you to get inside and lock the doors," he said quickly.

"What? What is happening? Is it in the forest?" she asked as she rose to her feet.

Elena could feel Dmitri's hands on her arms now, gripping them gently. She could imagine the concern or maybe confusion in his eyes at her guess. It was a look her father often gave her when she had managed to guess things as a child.

"Did you sense something? A premonition?" he asked softly, but his voice could not hide the urgency there.

She hesitated. "Sort of. I felt something different this morning, but I could not figure out what it was. I tried to talk to the trees, but they seemed to just be unnerved and could not place why."

Dmitri's grip tightened on her. "Go inside, please, my love."

"Not until you tell me what is happening, Dmitri," she said, making her own voice firm as she pulled away from his grasp. She frowned, knowing he would never be so rushed unless it was something important, which was all the more of a reason to slow down and explain to her what was happening.

He sighed in resignation. "I woke up and I could feel something different too. I was tired, and as I was waking up, I started to listen more closely to the trees. You are right that they do not know what was going on. I was foolish not to think of their tricks sooner, but it seems as though some villagers have sent people wielding weapons. I could not immediately sense their presence because they wear iron. It was only when I actively tried to look for something wrong through each little string of the universe around us that I felt it and could see what I had been blind to miss. They must be wearing some kind of leaves or earth disguise as well. The trees thought they were just moving bushes, so they did not think to warn me immediately. I... I think they are coming for you, Elena," Dmitri explained quickly. His voice held regret, especially following the events of yesterday.

"I should have begun taking measures to make sure that these things would not happen," he continued. "You had warned me of the extent of Innorin's superstitions. How could I be so foolish as not to sense the danger looming in my own forest? What kind of Guardian can I truly be if my ignorance had fallen so greatly?"

As he spoke, Elena fell into a neutral, wide-eyed expression at the news. She could hardly believe what she was hearing. It felt surreal to her that her village would still be trying to track her down and kill her, especially after everything. Had she not suffered enough at their hands? Memories of her mother's throat being shot away and her pale grandmother's empty teacup shattering to the floor flooded her mind. She remembered the stars as the final thing she would ever see and then the pain that had flooded through her until she had fallen unconscious. She felt dizzy at the idea that she might now watch Dmitri suffer the same fate as her family in order to try and protect her.

She shook her head vehemently. "No," she choked out.

"No?" Dmitri echoed, confusion plain in his voice as he scrunched his eyebrows together. "Please, there is no time. They are coming from different directions. As it is, I... I don't know if I can get to them all in time."

"No," Elena said again, this time more firmly. She took Dmitri's hand in her own and held it tightly. "Your soul and mine are bound together, right?"

"Yes, but—"

"Then we fight, *together*. Do you understand me? If you cannot beat them all at once, then you will let them come to us. This is our home, and they will not take it from us. You are my home Dmitri, and they will not take you from me either. I will be by your side, or I will not be there at all. I will not allow someone else to mindlessly charge off to die for my sake anymore. I cannot suffer that again. And you do not get to make a martyr of yourself to attempt to atone for whatever sins you have committed."

"I can't die, not really. I am an immortal being of these woods. Things can hurt me, yes, but my body heals faster than a human. I can handle this."

"It isn't your battle, and I will not wait and practice my stitching while a man fights my battles for me. I may not be an immortal, but I am a witch."

He hesitated, mind racing. "Elena, I cannot watch you get hurt either. I do not think I could live with myself if you were to get hurt. I promised that I would protect you."

"Then protect me here. You have taught me self-defense for melee combat, right? My magic can guide me elsewhere. I will not be alone, but neither will you. We know they are coming, so they no longer have the element of surprise. But if you attack them now, then who is to say what happens? You said they are coming in all directions. What if they come for me while you are gone in a different direction? Would you rather me be alone if that were to happen?"

He clenched his jaw tightly, and Elena knew from his silence that she had touched upon a truth that he could not ignore.

"Okay. We will fight them here, and we will fight together. We... we should prepare."

"When do you think they will arrive?" she asked softly, relaxing her shoulders as she tried to come to terms with the situation.

"If I had to guess," he paused for a moment in consideration. "Probably shortly before dawn."

Elena squeezed his hands gently in her own and then gave a short nod. "Then let's start making a plan."

"My beautiful wife, is there nothing I could do to convince you to stay safe somewhere and let me handle this?" he asked with an ounce of hope.

"Not a chance in hell."

He sighed, knowing that would be her answer regardless. "Figures. Alright then, let's go. There is much to be done if we are going to do this right."

The instructions from the other village had been clear; Do not speak once you enter the woods lest you awaken anything that you might have to fight. But Patryk knew better. He had never been the best hunter, and just a few days ago, when he risked entering these very woods, he had made plenty of noise. No malevolent beings of magic found him, trying to cause him harm. He had stumbled into a territorial pack of wolves, nearly causing his undoing, but it had been magic that had saved him. He still did not quite understand what had happened that day, spinning his beliefs into question.

Once he had arrived back to his village from the woods with ripped clothes and blood covering his dark skin, everyone in town had bombarded him with questions about his experience. Some had scolded him for being foolish enough to go alone. Some were relieved that he was alive. Others were curious or confused at how he had not succumbed to his wounds or managed to escape the maze of mostly uncharted land. So, as he was taken to be patched up, he told everyone that he would tell the story only once—so they had better listen closely. He claimed that he had wanted to forget about the experience altogether, but, in truth, he was more scared that he might get too tangled in his web of lies.

As the story he wove goes, he had taken to the woods to hunt—tired of fearing the unknown. No malevolent beings to speak of other than a hungry and territorial wolf. His bow and arrows had been broken in the altercation, but he had managed to grab a large stone while being attacked and, while pinned to the ground, struck the wolf repeatedly in the face until the beast had finally released him. He had caused a wound to the wolf's eye, convincing it to begrudgingly leave him be while he made enough noise and tried to make himself look bigger than he was. The wolf must've been separated from its pack, for nothing else attacked him. Once he was far enough out of sight, he began running until he was out of breath and then stopped to tie off his wounds. Then he somehow made his way back to his village, blessed by the gods it had seemed as he managed not to get lost.

There was no mention of witches or Leshys or any other magical creatures. The omitting of information and alterations had not tasted great on his tongue, but it was necessary. His village had never been overly cautious of magical things in the past—some of them even going as far as to give offerings to the elusive magical guardians of their homes called *Domovoy*—but they had been conversing with the neighboring villages in regards to the witch hunt that was about to happen. Patryk did not want to risk the disease of suspicion plaguing him next or risk a well-intentioned neighbor mentioning something of it to these other men who believed magic was a contagion and anything it touched needed to be destroyed.

Patryk wanted no part of the hunt, especially after the injuries to his arm and his ordeal with the magical beings which dwelled there. Patryk had never given much thought to the magical beings of the world before that day. Sure, he knew the horrifying stories of evil witches who ate children, unruly fae, ghouls, and a plethora of other stories. He knew some who believed and feared, others who believed and worshiped, and others who were like him, who lay somewhere in the middle of that spectrum. Most of the time, he had suspected that they were either untrue or that they were creatures that indeed may have once existed but no longer did. He had been proven wrong of the latter, but what of the first?

The way the witch—Elena—had spoken gave him pause. She was calm and collected, even in the face of something he had almost entirely considered evil. The way the Leshy—Dmitri—had spoken made him shudder with fear. Even while he wore the skin of a human, Dmitri's eyes had been as hollow as the sockets of the skull he adorned in his leshy form. He may have been what the stories were about, but she was certainly not. She had thrown herself down between himself and a wolf. The creature was bigger than her, and yet it had ceased, and she had actually spoken to it. No, she *conversed* with it. And Dmitri, all bitterness and apathy, had shown confliction as the fragile blind girl had stared him down. She had threatened to rip her own dress to help Patryk if Dmitri would not, and he had. Elena spoke of how men had tried to kill her once before, and after talking to the neighboring village of Innorin, he could easily see this to be true.

The people of Innorin had come to his village for assistance, speaking of a murderous being that had taken shelter in the woods. They spoke of how *she* had been the one to kill the two men inside the forest. Elena did say that men had attempted to kill her, obviously not succeeding, so where was the truth? Had Elena or Dmitri killed these men? And if so, had it been out of bloodlust, or had it been merely out of self-defense? She had agreed with Patryk when he said that he could make his own mind up about the individual, but what if he still chose to believe that she was the monster that this other village had spoken of? Patryk was unsure if he wanted to risk the chance of a bloodthirsty monster on the loose, but he was also not keen on hunting down the woman who had saved his life.

His village had agreed to help Innorin, along with another village to the West, because as much as they were lenient about magical beings, their human neighbors had begged them for help. Patryk's village had pledged to always help a neighbor in need long ago, and they had not forgotten. And as much as he did not wish to participate in the hunt for Elena's life, his village had all but insisted he be there to lead them through the forest. A horrific consequence of the lies that he had spoken already coming back to haunt him, it seemed.

"You have traveled these woods and made it out before without managing to get lost. We have the coordinates to get there, but who is to say we will not get lost still? We need you," they had told him.

Patryk loathed the idea of going back to the woods so soon, but his friends thought that they truly needed him, and the idea of letting them down was far worse. Still, as he now walked the woods with them, he could not stop his mind from wandering to Elena. His stomach twisted at the idea of hurting her and betraying the selfless act of saving him. He could not bring himself to watch someone from his village do it either, not without knowing that she might not truly be the monster that they had been told she was. So, if he was asked to go, then he would travel with them. But as soon as his feet crossed the threshold of the forest, something new burned inside of him. He needed to plant the same seeds of doubt in the people around him so that they may at least take pause and so that they could have the same chance that he did to make their own decisions for themselves.

His village had not taken the superstitious warnings of Innorin as seriously as that village hoped that they would. They agreed to wear the iron, leaves, and mud, but they would not walk in silence. They spoke quietly amongst themselves, chatting idly about random affairs of the village as they walked. There was a tension underlying them, knowing that what they were doing should not be taken lightly, but in their eyes, if this was to be their last day on earth to try and help this village eradicate a vicious monster, they deserved to at least enjoy the walk on the way to their fate.

Patryk had been silent until they had gotten a fair distance away from their village, thinking over what to say in his mind to his people. He was not a leader, despite what his village had labeled him as. He did not have the same silver tongue of the man who had ridden through their village and spoke like every word was a sermon of high stakes and damnation. He ran a hand through his short hair and walked up to another man, not making eye contact with him. He was a tall man with tanned skin from farming out in the sun with a burly black beard that covered half of his face.

"May I ask you something?"

The man, Sasha, nodded and glanced at Patryk, though Patryk kept his eyes directed at their walking path. "Of course."

"What if what we are doing here today is wrong?"

The others around him had stopped their idle conversations, listening to his conversation. They were surprised to hear this from him, but they did not immediately scold him for his doubts. The new audience had made Patryk feel tenser, and he could feel the warmth of the sun creeping up his neck.

The man glanced at Patryk for a moment longer and then turned his gaze away and hummed thoughtfully. "This village said the witch has started on a bloodlust. They lost three good men to her, apparently. What brings these doubts to your mind now?"

Patryk sucked air into his lungs. He would not lie to them, not anymore, but he did not want to come straight out with the truth either, so he chose his words carefully. "I think... that we afford the right of a trial to most, and we only truly know their side of the story. I am not saying that their men did not die, but how can we know that it was not from something such as self-defense? They have shown us how superstitious they are. Say she was a witch, but a harmless one. Do you still think that they would afford her any peace?"

The man weighed this thought in his mind for a moment, and a frown tugged at his lips. "The deaths of those men that were described to us seemed to be more than mere self-defense," he pointed out hesitantly.

Patryk nodded, though he did not think that the blind girl he met in the woods was necessarily capable of such carnage. *Her companion, however...*

"I know. I am not saying the witch is fully innocent, but I guess I am asking is, do we want her blood on our hands without knowing? Do we want to risk what other forces of the world may truly be out there just because some men came through and asked us to? I mean, we promised to help out our neighbors in need, but what if their need is an immoral one? I just think that gathering up the forces of three villages to see the death of one witch who has not caused most of us any harm or lack of sleep at night is a bit of a quick reaction."

"What if she is truly this powerful and this evil, though? What if she just has not made her way to our village to cause us harm yet but will in the future?" someone else in the group asked.

Patryk turned to look at them to see who had spoken, a thin pale man who was the blacksmith's son. "That could be true. I do not deny it. But would you risk killing someone innocent on the chance that they could do bad things in the future?"

The blacksmith's son frowned as well. The group had taken on a tense silence of consideration, so Patryk hesitated before deciding to prompt further, shoving his hands deep into his trouser pockets.

"There are a couple of families in our village who coexist with or even worship some magic. I never really believed them or paid them much mind before, but what if they did have the right ideas? For generations, we have been terrified to even step foot in this forest because our ancestors said it was haunted by malevolent spirits, and yet here we are, ready to hunt and kill a witch in this very same forest simply because someone asked us to. What if we had been wrong the whole time about these malevolent spirits and had simply been letting our fear dictate our decisions? Are we really going to let another fear—the fear of the unknown—continue to drive our choices? What if there was indeed magic in the forest, and we could talk to it in order to broker a peace so that we could coexist beside it, just like those families do? I ask because I am tired of having other people decide what I should and should not believe. I am confused and do not know what magic is real and what is myth. I do not know anything for certain anymore, and I believe those who claim to are delusional. My decisions are my own, though, and I must be honest. I do not want to kill this witch."

The silence extended beyond his words, and Patryk looked down, feeling more shameful than he had expected to be. This was his truth, though. He did not want to kill Elena. He wanted to thank her for saving him. His arm ached thinking about the wolf's teeth tearing into his flesh and the cold hollow stare of the Leshy. It also occurred to Patryk that some of those families who believed in magic would most likely see Dmitri as a god of this forest. He wished he had asked them what it would mean to anger one of the gods and what it might mean to kill one if it came down to it. Would his neighbors shun them? Would their souls be damned? More and more questions filled him.

Elena saw the good in that Leshy too. He could see the way she tried to coax that goodness out of him. He wanted her to teach him how to be so patient and so trusting with things she did not understand. He wanted to go home and knead bread as if it had offended him. He wanted his friends and brothers here to go home and be safe, not to die for someone else's cause.

"I have to admit," a man named Ivan spoke after a moment, "I don't know if I believe that the girl is innocent. That being said, I agree that this other village does not have the right to just ask us to kill their problem for them. Besides, what if our ancestors were right and ghosts do haunt this forest? What if they had taken this girl out to the woods to kill her because they thought she was a witch and a spirit possessed her? They would have created their own problem, and this girl... she could actually need rescuing instead of killing."

Someone else murmured in agreement. "Even if she is a powerful witch, a battle with her is sure to reap casualties. That is almost asking to make this forest haunted afterward. We could just be creating a new problem. I like what Patryk said about maybe being able to come to a peaceful agreement and avoid a fight."

"Not to mention that Herrick fellow was willing to burn the entire forest down in order to kill this supposed witch. What if the fire hurts our village more or even just the wildlife that lives here? For all we know, this could be his excuse to burn down some of the woods for expansion which could cause conflict between our villages," said another.

Their traveling group unanimously came to a stop as they all turned to look at one another. Patryk felt the beginning of hope blossoming inside of his chest. Others had doubts that had nothing to do with her character that he would not have thought of. Would they have just gone along with it if he had not spoken up? There was no going back now, though. Their doubts had begun to be voiced. They all spoke amongst themselves, the decision divided still, and yet, they were beginning to think for themselves now.

Patryk stood there dumbly, watching his family, friends, and neighbors talk to one another as they discussed what should happen now or their opinions. Though Patryk had known his village would be understanding of his doubts and not inherently judge him right away, he could not describe the relief of knowing that his concerns had not fallen on deaf ears.

"Alright, everyone, hush. There is no need to scare the birds away with our chatter," Sasha said in a calm but stern voice. Immediately the other villagers quieted down to look at him. He considered them all for a moment, rubbing his thick beard for a moment before turning his gaze back to Patryk. This time, Patryk did not shy away from his gaze.

"We promised these men that we would help them, and it is our duty to honor our word. However, helping them does not need to mean killing this girl," he said.

Patryk nodded and then looked at the group as well, holding his head higher than he felt he had the confidence for. "Sasha is right that we should not just turn our backs on our neighbors. I think we should go to show our support to them, but when we get there, I encourage everyone to take a look at this witch and watch this man Herrick interact with her. If you choose to fight on our neighbor's side, then I will not hold it against you, but I just think we should not be the first to draw our arrows. I encourage you to search your soul and ask yourself which side you want to be on in the end."

Everyone, including Sasha, agreed with Patryk and smiled with relief. Some mumbled some things about him being wise, but he ignored the flattery. They had to keep moving forward, but Patryk felt his decision solidify in his chest. Once they began walking once more, Sasha placed a hand on Patryk's shoulder and gave him a small reassuring grin.

"You did well, you know," he said quietly.

Patryk chuckled and shrugged, brushing the hand away from his shoulder. "I was just honest. I am not the most well-spoken of people," he said simply.

Sasha shrugged in return to the comment and took a deep breath. "You've met the witch, haven't you?" he asked quietly, not wanting the others to hear.

Patryk's smile faded a bit, but he had promised no more lies. A small amount of dread crept back into his chest. His tongue felt suddenly dry and far too heavy. "I have. She was the one who saved me the other day, but I was scared and did not know what to believe at the time."

Sasha nodded in gentle understanding, waiting another moment before adding, "And what do you believe now?"

Patryk looked up into Sasha's eyes, determination burning inside of him. "I believe that I want to know her long enough to make up my own mind. And I believe that she has been through terrible things already, so it is not hard to imagine that she might have been through worse at the hands of these people. I will not be fighting for Herrick. If I draw my arrows, it will be to defend. I will not kill another man or woman today."

Sasha's smile curled his lips ever so slightly beneath his facial hair, and he nodded in approval. "You are a good man Patryk. Let us hope some of these men learn something from you today."

"Let's just hope we survive long enough for that. Something tells me that these men would not take kindly to deciding against them."

Sasha nodded solemnly in agreement, and the two men fell into silence as they walked, lost in their own thoughts. The other villagers had begun to once again discuss other frivolous things to pass the time, but Patryk had noticed something in the moments of silence between the villagers; the woods were silent. There was no breeze to move the leaves of the trees, even the ones too high above them to feel. There were no birds or small creatures scurrying amongst the trees. No deer, no wolves, no bears, no sound. It felt as if the forest was holding its breath, waiting and watching with uncertainty of these new intruders within its boundaries.

Patryk prayed that this meant Elena and Dmitri had become aware of the danger slowly making its way toward them. He prayed that Elena did not throw herself in front of their jaws this time, at least not yet.

Hang on. We are coming. You are not alone in this fight any longer.

CHAPTER TWENTY-EIGHT

THE THICK OF IT

D mitri walked to the dining room and stopped in the doorway. Elena sat at the table, focusing on the last finishing touches of her magic spell for their home. The last time that this cottage witnessed a battle, June had tried to protect it, as well as her family, but in the end, was too caught off guard, and she suffered for it. Elena had explained to him that she had to be sure that they were prepared and not distracted by anything which might lead to their same fate. It was a simple enchantment, one to protect the cottage and the garden from burning and the windows from breaking. Knowing that the village of Innorin was on its way, Elena had said that she imagined that they would not hesitate to try and light her and her home on fire to burn away the magic.

Dmitri watched the way her face shifted as she concentrated. He waited a moment before her features seemed to relax as she finished the enchantment.

"Elena, they are close. We should go wait outside."

His inner voice was riddled with the fear and concern that he could not mask as hard as he had tried to. He was not happy about having her out on the battlefield beside him, but she had made her stance clear, and he would not force his preference onto her. She had made a point that if they had hidden from him inside of his own forest so far, then he could not be certain where she would be safe until this was over. While Dmitri was immortal and could not die in the traditional sense, his power was not infinite, and he did run the risk of over-exhausting himself and falling victim to them if they were persistent enough. More than that, though, this was personal to her, and he had no right to deny her the peace in knowing it would end today, in one way or another.

She opened her eyes slowly at the sound of his voice and inhaled deeply. "Alright," she whispered, rising from her chair gently.

Dmitri came over and gently wrapped an arm around her waist, leading her outside their home. They walked to the middle of the field, Dmitri staring harshly at the tree line, alert for any sign of them. He took something wrapped in a cloth and grabbed her hands, placing the bundle gently in her palms.

"I know you are going to use magic and combat, but it felt foolish to go into battle without some kind of weapon by your side. I made this dagger a long time ago for hunting, and I sharpened it today. I would rather you have this and not use it than be stuck and not have it."

A look of surprise flickered across Elena's face. She traced her fingers over the velvet cloth before sliding it away and revealing the sheath made of worn leather. She felt the hilt of the dagger and paused as she investigated the material carefully, furrowing her eyebrows a bit.

"Is this an antler?" she asked quietly as her eyes brightened with recognition.

Dmitri smiled despite the situation, his heart aching inside of his chest as he watched the love of his life light up with excitement at being able to identify something properly. There was an innocence in her eyes, despite all that she had seen and been through. He wished he could preserve that in time somewhere beyond the grasp of what was yet to happen still. He hoped that it would remain by the time they survived this if they even managed to do that.

"Yes, it is. The blade itself has some runes and symbols on it to help grant the wielder protection and efficiency. I spent months on it when I was younger, getting the handle and the blade right."

Elena adjusted the sheath around her waist carefully before hugging Dmitri, burying her face in his chest. "I love it. Thank you, Dmitri."

Dmitri hugged her back tightly, closing his eyes for a moment as he nestled his face in the top of her hair. She wore the dress that he had originally found her in. It had been washed, of course, but her blood still stained the edges of her white sleeves. Dmitri had offered to use magic to get it out, but Elena had insisted it remained for this battle. She wanted them to see that she had fought hard last time and that this time would be no different. The top skirt of her dress was a deep red, bringing out the stitching that her mother had embroidered on the white underskirt and on the white blouse of her dress. Dmitri breathed her in, feeling her heart racing against his own, and he did not want to let go but knew that their time was getting shorter.

"I love you, Elena," he whispered beside her ear.

"I love you too, Dmitri. We will get through this together, right?"

"Yes, together."

He was thankful that she was the one to pull away, as he did not know if he would be able to. She turned her head to the tree line, and as he followed her gaze, he saw the beginning of the end. They were here.

Men of various villages crept out from the tree line, hands on their weapons as they inched closer. Dmitri stared at them with dread, even his inner Leshy surprising him by not craving the usual bloodlust. Perhaps he was weary of the constant cycle of death. Perhaps he did not want Elena to see him like that ever again. Regardless, an overwhelming sense of pity washed over him as he saw the hardness in the villagers' eyes as they stared at her as if she might lunge out and attack them just by looking in their direction. He, better than anyone, knew how that kind of rage and apprehension took a toll on the body and spirit. Still, his priority was to protect Elena, and he would do that no matter the cost.

"That is far enough," Dmitri announced, his words bellowing around them and startling most of the men to a stop.

One man in particular—a blond man with a warrior's posture—took one last step out of defiance, and Dmitri knew that was the man leading this hunt.

"How did it know we were coming? You both do not seem particularly surprised to see so many surrounding you. Or has the witch simply made enough enemies that this comes as no surprise to you?" he called out.

At calling Elena an 'it', Dmitri's lip curled in disgust. "We will have no problem here if you and your hunting party turn around and leave. There does not need to be bloodshed today. We simply want to be left alone."

"It seems its magic has already affected you. I cannot reason with a man who is not in his right mind," he announced. "Step away, and let us end this. The witch is to face its crimes."

"And what exactly are my crimes?" Elena finally spoke, looking in the direction of the men as she frowned. "I was your friend and your neighbor, and I did not even know that I was a witch before the day you killed my family. And yes, I am a witch. It is not something that I am ashamed of anymore. I had no wish to harm anyone before knowing this, and I have no wish to harm anyone now, but I will do what is necessary to survive."

Now that the men were out in the open in front of Dmitri's eyes, his senses crept back to him—even though these men still wore the iron and leaves, which confused the trees and muddied his magic. His connection to the universe flared silently as his vision shifted for a moment, tracing the invisible lines to get an accurate count of the bodies in front of him. There were more than he expected, though, at Elena's proclamation, some turned to her and seemed to notice for the first time the way her opaque eyes could not quite focus. Dmitri could feel the uncertainty shift amongst them, even as their leader grew more impassioned.

"You claim that you had no wish to harm anyone, and yet you have killed people! Do you not recognize me, *witch*? My name is Herrick Atwood—son of Poe Atwood—and you murdered my father and another by the name of Goddard Risi!" he roared. "Your crimes? They are murder, heresy, the practice of magic, and *existing,* you vile, wretched thing!"

Dmitri released Elena's hand as his senses focused sharply once more onto this man—Herrick. Dmitri stood up taller in front of her, shielding her protectively. "I was the one who killed those men. They were going to kill her and nearly had when I got there." His voice was strained as the last of his humanity tried to plead with them one last time.

Herrick scoffed. "Do you expect me to believe a mere man could paint the forest red with their blood? No, only magic could have done that horror. Now get out of my way," he growled.

Dmitri opened his mouth to say something, to try and explain and defend Elena, but Herrick had grown tired of waiting. He drew his sword and began to close the distance between them. Other villagers drew their guns, bows, and other weapons, aiming them at Dmitri and Elena.

"Get out of my way or be cut down as well, the decision is yours in the end, but this is mine. The gods do not favor ignorance, so search yourself for the truth. This ends now."

Fine, Dmitri thought as he forced the Leshy inside of his soul to awaken from its groggy slumber, *Have it your way.*

CHAPTER TWENTY-NINE

SOUNDS OF WAR

D mitri stepped off of the porch with darkened eyes and apathy creeping into his veins. Talking to these men, especially the one deeming himself as their leader, was infuriating. It was as though he was talking to stone, though that would have been an insult to the stones that he knew personally. If they wished to fight against magic, then this was just as much his battle as it was hers.

They had entered *his* forest, threatened the love of his life, disturbed his peace, and threatened to consume what little time remained for him to spend with Elena by his side. If they refused to speak to him because they thought him to be merely a pawn, he had no problem with showing them exactly what they were dealing with now. There were consequences in nature, and if he had to learn this lesson a hundred years ago, he saw no reason to spare them from the brutality of it.

As he stepped away from their home, his bones exploded into wood and moss. His size grew, doubling that of his human form as his face shifted into the skull of a deer—moss and leaves hanging from his antlers. Everyone looked at the beast he had become in horror as the blood drained from their faces. Dmitri let out a bone-chilling roar from deep within his chest that echoed throughout the forest and chilled the blood of the men who now hesitated. Even their leader seemed to look at him wide-eyed for a brief moment before his gaze tore away and latched back onto Elena.

The only one who did not flinch was Patryk, who Dmitri recognized now by the scent guided amongst the trees. He stood there with a stoic look of recognition in his eyes as if to say, "*There is the monster I know.*" He looked at his fellow villagers, and Dmitri followed his gaze to see the men staring in shock at the creature in front of them where a man had once been. Dmitri noticed that none of them had notched their arrows, even now that Dmitri had shifted. Instead, they either stared in confusion at Elena's opaque eyes or watched the man leading this crusade anxiously. Dmitri was clearly not the creature that they had signed up to battle, and he could hear some of them uttering a small prayer inside of their mind to apologize to the Guardian for disturbing his forest.

Herrick shook his head, pushing past his moment of hesitation, and gripped the hilt of his handle tighter. His eyes remained locked on Elena even as he raised his voice to address the men behind him. "Do not let this witch's conjurings dissuade you from our purpose here today, men! We will send these demons back to hell where they belong!"

A rallying battle cry of men shouting in agreement rose and echoed throughout the small valley as Herrick doubled down on his determination to end her life and fulfill his duty to his father's spirit. Dmitri knew there would be no talking their way out of this mess. These men had made up their minds about her long ago, and Elena's pleas were now only seen as an admission. Hearing them now, screaming as they readied themself for the battle, Elena shrank slightly behind him.

Still, for the first time, Elena did not have to fight their persecution alone. Dmitri was by her side now, and he would do everything in his power to protect her. More than that, though, Elena had made sure that she would not be helpless anymore like she had once been. She may have been sheltered from her true heritage before, but now she was embracing it. She would face them today, and they would either die fighting—claws out and teeth bared as her mother taught her—or she would learn to never live in fear of these men again. Still, the day of judgment was here, signaling a change that no one would be able to step back from once the footsteps plunged forward. Elena unsheathed her dagger, and Dmitri could taste the soft shift of magic in the air as she readied herself.

Herrick lunged first, barreling toward Elena as the men behind him aimed their cocked guns at Dmitri. Dmitri felt a moment of hesitation, wanting to focus on protecting Elena, but knew he had to get rid of the guns, or else it would not matter. The Leshy part of his mind, now awakened, craved the blood of these men who dared to disturb his peace. Dmitri could feel the consuming nature of the beast within him begin to grab ahold of the corners of his mind, fighting for control. He growled a deep guttural noise before turning towards the guns in frustration. The wind picked up around him as the first shots were fired off.

Bullets pierced the bark of his skin, splintering it as his body absorbed the lead and gunpowder. He took a step towards the men who cowered behind the shelter of the tree line, rage muddying his vision. Gusts of wind sharply pushed them off balance, weaving around the trees to hit them effortlessly as Dmitri closed the distance between them. The trees themselves began to shake, a pleasant anxiousness creeping amongst them to be utilized as Dmitri's magic pulsated through their bark. Dmitri watched the lines of the universe, golden ties intricately woven together like roots as his magic latched onto them, pulling them like the strings of a marionette.

The trees shuddered, bark expanding unnaturally as branches protruded and reached out, wrapping around some of the men who cowered too close. Gasps and cries of horror erupted from the few while others ran towards the clearing, shouting commands to each other to get away from the grasp of the forest. Those who were unlucky enough to have engrossed the attention of the trees tried desperately to yank at their arms or other body parts that remained trapped by bark as a frantic dread pulled at them, but the trees were not done with them yet.

Dmitri could feel the darkness consuming him. *Suffer,* a voice inside of his mind croaked. *No death too quick for those who disturb.*

His magic flooded deeper into those strings as he took a step closer, ignoring the new wave of bullets that sent chunks of his skin flying before the earth filled and consumed the holes once more. The panic that ensued made the jaw of his skull creak open in what could be construed as a smirk to some, teeth falling out from that small movement as death and decay radiated from his mind before the teeth were promptly replaced with the life that persisted.

The trees grabbing the men pulled them in closer, grating their bark against human flesh like sandpaper as they cried out. It tore at them, contorting them at awkward angles as the trees began to absorb the men, bristling their leaves fiercely at the blood that dripped from them like renewed sap as bones crushed within their grasp.

One man grabbed a small hatchet that hung at his waist, beginning to hack at his wrist and the branches that grabbed him. His cries were shortened to agonized groans and wailing before he managed to pull himself free, his hand slipping from the rest of his body like the removal of a glove. The tree released his arm and wasted no time in consuming his weapon as penance. He looked around in a haze at the others still being overtaken, not registering the voices calling for him to run. He wavered, vomiting before falling unconscious in a pool of his own bodily fluids.

The trees did not bother with the man after that.

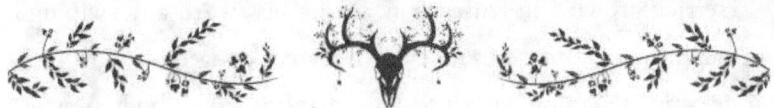

Herrick watched the witch standing still, calm despite the chaos, as its hand slipped to the dagger at its side. He scowled, knowing it did not need such things with its wicked magic. *It probably wants to distract me from its true nature*, he thought as he pushed his legs to close the distance between them.

As he got closer, his attention was torn from the witch as a blur of dark skin lunged at him, knocking him off of his feet in his pursuit and sending the two men tumbling into the wildflowers. Herrick grunted, scrambling for his family sword. His fingers grasped it, and he rolled to a defensive position, looking to see who or what had attacked him.

Patryk was already on his feet, hands in front of him as if trying to tame an animal. "Enough of this," he spat. Herrick recognized him from when he had gone to the village of Stapes to advocate for this battle. Originally, he had thought of the man as nothing more than a sheep. Now, he wondered if he had underestimated the man's resolve—even if it was foolish and misguided.

Herrick felt his face redden with rage at the audacity as his grip tightened, whitening the knuckles of his hand. "Get out of my way, you fool." His eyes trailed Patryk like a predator as he went to move past, but Patryk blocked his path once more.

"She is not your enemy, and if you pursue this, my village will not fight by your side. You will receive a fight if you wish to fight someone, though it will not be with that girl."

Herrick growled in frustration, lifting his sword and swiping it through the air to cut this man down. Patryk dodged his blow easily, anticipating the impulsive action as he maneuvered his body away in a nimble action. He wasted no time in countering, swiping his foot up and kicking Herrick's extended forearm. Herrick grunted, his grip on the sword loosening before Patryk tackled him, sending the sword flying out of reach.

"If you insist on dying today by the witch's side, then you will have your wish," Herrick hissed, lunging toward Patryk as the two began to grapple.

Elena felt the panic in her chest, able to sense movement all around her but having trouble deciphering where exactly it was coming from. Her senses were overwhelmed with stimulus, and she could feel the panic begin to claw its way from her chest as she desperately fought to keep her emotions in check. *Courage is not the absence of fear—*

Her thoughts were cut short as a man tackled her to the ground. She gasped as the air was knocked from her lungs, but she managed to hold tight onto the dagger that Dmitri had gifted her as she fell to the earth. The man slammed his knee into her gut as he pinned her, moving his hands to her throat. The wildflowers of the field instantly bent and contorted themselves to her, hiding her hand—or rather what was in her hand—and making her look unsuspecting. It was all they could do to help their friend.

Elena gasped and choked at the man's hands and the weight of him crushing her. For a horrifying moment, she forgot what she had been trained to do as he squeezed the life from her lungs. Struggling for air, she was desperate for relief until she felt the wildflowers tickle her hands frantically with their petals. She blinked, her mind working sluggishly as her body reacted. She did not remember moving her arm but felt the way the blade plunged through the man's neck under his chin smoothly, realizing that the blade would go in no further.

The man choked in surprise, spraying her with a slight mist of blood as his eyes widened. A dying groan fell from his lips as his grip slowly released her neck. She gasped air into her lungs frantically, her head spinning as the man's body slumped onto her, leaning against the hilt of her knife. The man's weight was heavier with the loss of life, and for a moment, Elena panicked at the thought that his limp body might suffocate her. With renewed energy, she shoved him off with bloodied hands, letting his body fall from her blade with a soft thud as she rolled away and moved to stand once more.

There was no time to process the fact that she had stolen his life. This was only going to be the beginning of the bloodshed. While Dmitri focused on keeping most people back and ridding them of long-distance weapons, Elena was left to her own devices. Small noises made her jump, reminding her of how wet the sounds were of a dying man as she feebly tried to hold her focus on the battle. She needed to be ready, and now, she felt the furthest thing from it. There was no glory in the killing. How men could speak so casually of it and their wars made her stomach lurch, and for a moment, she thought that she might be sick.

Her thoughts came to an abrupt halt as a sound from the East began to rumble throughout the trees. She forced her mind to focus on that noise instead, trying to piece together what it was as she gripped her knife tighter in preparation for the worst. As the sound got closer, however, her shoulders lowered. The flowers whispered excitedly to her to confirm her suspicions; *those are the sounds of animals running this way.*

"How?" she asked out loud to whatever would answer her. The flowers took the opportunity for conversation.

"This is our forest, he is our Guardian, and you are our friend." They chittered in unison.

Elena began laughing, softly at first, but then almost in hysterics as she felt the overwhelming sense of relief flooding through her. She hoped her laugh made the men around her nervous. The gesture of the woodland animals coming to their aid out of their own volition touched her, making her smile as the laughter died down. She remembered now what she was protecting. She wanted to survive, yes, but she also wanted to live. She cared for this forest deeply and wanted to spend more days knowing it, learning how the world worked and how to cherish it properly.

"Protect her!" Dmitri's voice rang out, raspy with desperation. Elena could imagine him looking at her, seeing the man's blood still freshly painted over her face and hands as she stood there with a grin plastered on her lips.

What a feral creature I must look like, she mused.

In the next moment, Elena heard the bear in her mind. His voice was akin to the feeling of thickness and weight as it trudged through the words that he spoke as if remembering how to speak all over again. He would remain by her side, and she spoke to him, telling him of her gratitude. He huffed through his nose, bellowing a roar of warning as a man got too close to her, clicking its jaw in agitation before the man pursuing her was soon caught up in a fight with another man—surprising Elena that someone other than Dmitri had been willing to fight on her behalf.

She took a deep breath and called her magic back to her. She was terrified, unsure of how she would cope with what still needed to be done, but ready. The terrible and ugly aspects of death were the only side when there was still a battle to be won, but she would face the consequences of it tomorrow. Because she *would* be alive come tomorrow.

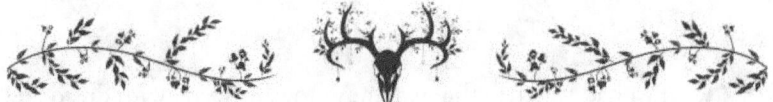

CHAPTER THIRTY

BATTLE CRIES

D mitri had watched the man move toward Elena with dread and anxiety built up inside him as he returned to himself in full. He was rooted to the ground, unable to move as the man had almost gotten to her. She was out of breath, tired from the fight, and covered in blood he hoped was not her own.

He had not expected the animals to charge onto the field on their own behalf. He had considered summoning them himself earlier, but he could not disrupt the balance of the forest like that. Slaughtering animals was not the way to win a battle. Still, they had come, and Dmitri had to admit that they were better off with the chaos surrounding them now. Deer, bears, wolves, and even some birds had rallied to their defense. It was not all of the animals of the forest, thankfully, but it was enough.

But there were still far too many men with weapons, even with Patryk and what Dmitri assumed were some of his villagers. Dmitri had no idea why Patryk had come back or how he even knew of what would be happening here today. He realized that it was very possible that Patryk had come here to help kill them after Dmitri had almost let the wolves eat him. Yet he now fought *for* them. Shifting his gaze to Elena again, he knew why. Yet despite all of the help that they received, Dmitri still saw the animals being cut down and their allies being wounded or killed.

He stared for a long moment, feeling as though his world was spinning violently around him.

"Dmitri!" Elena screamed, snapping him from his thoughts like a band pulling taut in his mind. He looked at her, dread flooding him as he realized he had wasted precious moments that could have been used to help her. The bear that he had sent to stay by her side roared in vicious cries of agony as fire lit its fur like kindling.

Dmitri moved quickly, his thoughts focused once more as a geyser of soil shot up beside the bear, startling it but then soothing its skin as mud coated the fire, suffocating the flames. It growled as it laid in the mud, exhausted and still pained. Dmitri grunted as the man with a torch grabbed Elena by her braid, and within an instant, he was behind the man, grabbing him roughly and throwing him aside like a doll. Dmitri snatched the torch from his hand before he hit the ground, crushing it in his hand and extinguishing the flame before he moved to Elena. He pulled her quickly to crouch behind the giant mass of the bear on the ground, still providing a brief reprieve of shelter.

Dmitri's size shrank to be closer in height to her as he placed his wooden hand against her cheek. She gasped and placed her hand over his instantly in recognition, her fingertips shaking as she glanced up in his direction. Despite everything, her lips curled into a faint smile of relief.

"Thank you," she breathed out. "That is the second time you saved me," she pointed out light-heartedly in what he recognized as her own attempt to relieve some of the tension—for herself or for him, he did not know.

As Dmitri looked at her in her ghostly green eyes, he said nothing for a moment. Something inside his mind clicked into place as he looked at her. For the first time since he had become the Guardian, he felt the true weight of the word. He was not just the Guardian of this forest. He was the Guardian of Elena and even of himself. And that meant that today the rot would not consume him. He would choose her, and he would choose his life with her. He was her Dmitri, in health and in war.

"Come on, let's end this."

She nodded as he pulled her to her feet and turned to face the men who had found their second wave of courage.

Dmitri did not hold back his power, but it was time to follow his own teaching. For a hundred years, his fear had consumed him. It had blinded him, making it seem as though the only option was to succumb to his fears. He was the Guardian, and this was his forest. If blood would be spilled, it would be quick. The goal was to survive, and this time, he was strong enough to ensure that they could make it out of this mess together. He was strong, powerful, and if this killed his humanity, then it would kill him tomorrow.

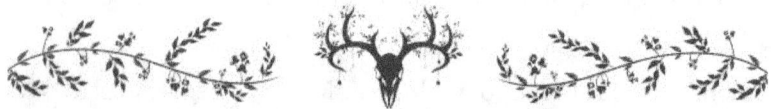

Herrick grunted as a blow from Patryk's fist rattled his jaw. The man fought honorably, Herrick had to admit, but he was getting tired of these games. He could see the wariness in his men's eyes as they watched the insufferable wildlife beckoning their master's call. He could see the renewed vigor in the monster's eyes as he spoke to his witch, no doubt borrowing more power from the heathen. Their allies of the western village of Pantauk and of his own village of Innorin were beginning to dwindle in their numbers rapidly. Herrick had to end this now.

Patryk went to land another blow on him, but Herrick seized his arm, yanking him to the ground. Herrick had noticed the way he favored his left arm and saw the hint of a bandage beneath his tunic. He struggled, ripping at the bandage until he saw puncture marks. Without hesitation, Herrick dove his fingers into the healing wounds, shoving his fingers deep within as blood oozed out of the reopened holes.

Patryk cried out in pain, screaming as he tried to pull his arm away, but Herrick was relentless as he hooked his fingers, pressing them in deeper. Once his grip was solid on this man's arm, he brought his other elbow up, slamming it roughly into his face over and over again until he swayed on his feet. Herrick withdrew his bloodied fingers from the wound, sending one last punch into the man's face as he was knocked to the ground. He spat on the man before panting and looking around as he found his sword in the grass.

To his horror, the villagers began to cry out to retreat. He watched as the cowards fled from the valley towards the river, careful to avoid the trees. Gritting his teeth, he looked around at what was left and made his decision. He had known there would be a chance that he would not survive this day, welcomed it even, but he would not fail. The fear of disappointing his father's spirit terrified him more than death ever had. *No*, he thought to himself as his free hand touched the bulge in his trouser pocket where his father's eye was. *I will not fail you again.*

The Leshy panted, looking exhausted from the magic and power he had demonstrated. His shoulders heaved with each panting breath. He smiled as he watched the men fleeing from them, relief written in his posture. When he turned to look at his witch, his body became rigid once more. His breath was robbed from his lungs as he choked on the shock.

There, his witch stood with a shocked expression as the blade protruding from its stomach dripped red. The red dress it donned was now soaked with a new shade as it looked forward blankly. The heathen made no sound as Herrick ripped the blade out from the witch. Originally, he had meant to stab it through the heart, but it sensed him somehow and moved at the last moment, causing his blade to miss its mark. He moved his arm to swing the blade down on it again, gratification in his eyes. He would hack his sword at its body as many times as it took in order to rid the world of this parasite.

"No!" the Leshy screamed, his voice filling the entire forest. Herrick watched as the creature's magic flared around him in a shockwave. Within the next breath, the creature was suddenly cradling the witch as its body sank into his arms. The creature cried out a scream of desperation, tearing at his throat as he grabbed the edge of Herrick's ornate sword, plunging it deep into Herrick's body.

Herrick looked down at his family's jagged broken sword sticking from his chest as his breathing began to feel more ragged and wet. Perhaps it was fitting that his family's sword broke with the end of his family line. He broke with the sword, collapsing to his knees. He felt the pain of death making his thoughts muddled, and yet, he couldn't help the smile on his lips as he looked down at the dying witch cradled on the ground. He chuckled, the sound gurgling on the blood that bubbled up in his throat, and yet he let out a soft sob of relief and not fear. His eyes were fixated on the blood pouring from its skin too quickly, and he felt giddy with the adrenaline of death—of the witch's or his own, he no longer knew.

"If I see you in hell, witch, it will have been worth it," he rasped before slumping into the mud, exhaling the last of his breath into the world.

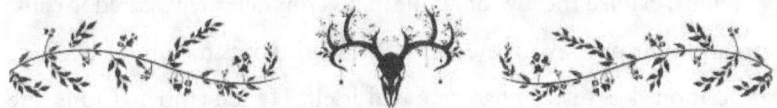

D mitri picked Elena up in his arms and moved her away from the dying man, cradling her body close to his own as he shifted back into his human form. His heart hammered inside of his chest as panic overtook every ounce of his being. Foolishly he had taken his eyes off of her, and now the sight of her surprised yet eerily calm expression would haunt him. He laid her amongst the wildflowers in a clean area with no carnage as he looked frantically at the wound. Tears poured down his cheeks.

"Elena, it's okay. It's me. I am right here. I am going to fix this. I can fix this, I—" he rambled but trailed off as he looked at the depth of the wound through the hole in her dress. He swallowed as his mouth felt like cotton, and he choked on his words.

Elena let a soft, shaky breath fall from her lips. Her skin was cold despite the summer heat, and she shivered in his arms, attempting to push herself closer into his embrace. He could see the pain searing through her body as she struggled not to cry out with each movement. She weakly reached her hand up, his own easily finding hers, so she did not have to search very long. She offered a weak smile up at him.

"It is going to be okay. I know I am dying," she whispered to him. "I know."

He felt all of the air escape him, and he choked on a sob, regretting his words from just moments before as he realized that this was not something he could help. "I do not want to lie to you, so please do not make me," he whispered pleadingly, unable to stop the tears that slid down his cheeks.

Dmitri cradled the love of his life in his arms delicately, scared to cause her any more pain. All of the memories flooded back to him in a crushing realization that history had repeated itself. He remembered June and how she died in a spot only a few steps from where they were now. He felt nearly inconsolable as the memory threatened to drown him. Instead of June's death, though, all he could see was Elena. Elena, and her blood spilling onto his hands.

Had history truly been so cruel as to repeat itself? The parallels of the situation made him nauseous as all of the emotions that he had buried now came clawing their way back to the surface. Dmitri was shaking now, trembling in fear. Everything he had sacrificed and given up had never been enough. He still could not save them. He was not worthy of the title of Guardian, and life, cruel and unforgiving, had punished him for this as it reminded him of what it was like to lose everything in a breath of a moment.

"Then don't lie to me, my love," Elena's quiet voice pulled him back ever so slightly.

He stared down at her and frowned, holding her body just slightly closer to him. "I can't lose you," he breathed out and placed a slow, lingering kiss against her cheek as he squeezed his eyes shut tightly to try and stop the tears from blurring his vision.

"Our..." Elena was beginning to struggle to speak, but she squeezed his hand slightly tighter, determined to push the words out. "Our souls are bound. I am with you, always, and... not even death can take that away from us."

Dmitri opened his eyes, widening as he looked down at her. He did not know what to say. He had never been good with words and had certainly never been good at showing his emotions to others. His mind raced as he tried to think of something—anything—to say to her to make this better. He should be the one comforting her, not the other way around. His mind felt like he was drowning, slowly and painfully. Frustration built up inside of him at his inability to even do this one simple thing for her.

"I failed you," he managed to say as his hands gripped the fabric of her dress gently. "Please, forgive me. I have failed you, and I am so sorry. I could not protect you."

Elena weakly shook her head. "You didn't fail me, Dmitri." He opened his mouth to speak again, but she cut him off with a shaky voice. "Tell me your certainties, and I will tell you mine."

Dmitri simultaneously felt nothing and everything at the same time. Numbness crept over him, and yet the agony threatened to overwhelm him. He swallowed his sob, forcing his tongue to work. He would do this for her.

"My name is Dmitri, and your name is Elena," he began quietly, wiping a stray tear that slid down her own cheek with his thumb.

"The f-flowers and the trees have become m-my friends, and I will never forget their kindness," she said, struggling to speak as her body shook in his arms a little harder. Time was fading quicker than either one of them were prepared for, but the smile on her pale lips was the only thing that convinced Dmitri to keep going.

"I had never felt alive before meeting you."

Elena weakly tugged at his hand, pulling him closer. As he was close enough, she placed a hand on his cheek. He tried to ignore how cold she was already as she guided his lips to hers. Silent tears slid down both of their cheeks as he kissed her gently for a few seconds before she tentatively pulled away.

"I love you, Dmitri."

Chapter Thirty-One

IN-BETWEEN

Elena knew that dying in this way would have been painful, but nothing she'd learned prepared her for the burning that coursed through her veins. She could feel the desperate and frantic attempts of her magic pulsating under her skin, screaming at her to attempt something—anything—to try and save herself. Her body fought nature, begging to slow the process and maybe give her just a few more moments. Indeed, what people have is never enough when the time comes for them to move past this world, it seems.

But Elena was tired. Her vocal cords refused to vibrate and work out any more words. Her tongue was too tired to even try to move. Her heart was racing too quickly, but Elena knew the real problem was when it started to slow down. She was unaware if her eyes were still open or if she had closed them, but for once, she welcomed that void of sensation as she fell into a feeling of suspension outside of her body. She was there, but not. She was alive, for now, and yet dying.

Dying had been painful until suddenly, it was not. Her body stopped feeling the cold unsettling sensation of her warm insides exposed to air. She stopped feeling all of her nerves come alive to scream in agony at the gaping wound in her stomach. Instead, her mind began to slow down, pacing itself for its final moments like someone who knew that they had won the race. The pain melted away into something familiar—and Elena felt as though she had been running exhaustedly for her entire life, only to now settle into a soft bed and warm blanket. Death was not peaceful in its entirety, but she was not alone, and in the end, that had always been what she had feared.

Distantly, she heard Dmitri still speaking to her. His voice muffled and absorbed the remaining sound around them until all she could hear was that beautiful distant sound. She fell into the timbre of his voice, letting the sound wrap around her like a blanket on an early winter morning before everyone had awoken. She found peace in it—in him.

He had always been her peace, and she had always enchanted him to a little chaos. Though she wondered if he might not say it was the opposite way around at times. Perhaps that balance was why they had worked so well together. The Sun and the Moon constantly swaying in a dance of ebb and flow around each other.

I have left my mark on this life, she thought to herself. *Innorin will never forget their monster, the trees will never forget my voice, and Dmitri... I pray that he will never forget his Elena. I know my soul will continue to live on with him forever. May it always remind him that he is loved and that death is taking care of me in his absence, but I will always be waiting somewhere in the after—not close, and yet never far. I have made my mark on this muddy life, even if only briefly. Now, I am ready to pull away and see my creation.*

Elena had not wanted to die, but now that the moment was here and as inevitable as the nature of things could be, she was ready. She had learned to live without fear, and she would die the same. Her body, still opposing the traitorous thoughts of acceptance, fought to hold on in contrast to her intentions. But in the end, her body could not fight forever. Eternity in a fraction of a second, consumed her as her heart slowed to a crawl.

Thump-Thump
  Thump-Thump
    Thump—

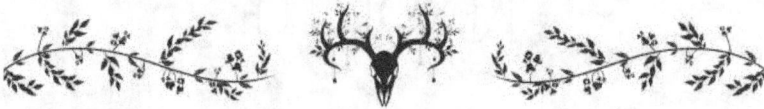

CHAPTER THIRTY-TWO

RESOLUTE

"Elena?" Dmitri's voice cracked as his throat felt like it was clos-ing. He needed to breathe. His heart was racing too fast. *No, this can't be the end.*

"Little witch... please, I need you. I love you." A moment passed by and then another. His heart raced far too fast, and not enough air was pulled into his lungs.

Dmitri forced his eyes away from her paling face, glancing down at the sticky red blood on his hands. He was quiet for a long moment as he stared at the bright contrast in color. His tongue was heavy in his mouth, and his cheeks too wet with grief. This was all wrong. Why did those he loved suffer the penance of his deeds? If he had not killed those men...

No. No, Dmitri did not regret his decisions. He wouldn't if he did not want to be crushed. If he had not killed those men, they would have killed her. If they had lived, there would have been two more men on this field today, for their minds could not be reckoned with. To allow magic to exist in the world so close to them would be to question their comfortable ideals.

They prayed to their gods, but if anything gets even remotely close to becoming a tangible god, a real thing that can tell them 'no', then they shut their eyes. The villagers worship a fiction of their bias. Some people would consider Dmitri to be a god of the woods, though he did not know the logistics of his title beyond Guardian. People worshiped his kind, though he did not know if they worshiped him or if he would even want them to if they did. But these people see power, see magic, and think of heresy. They think condemnation. It is fine to worship something so far away, but if it gets too close, then it seems everyone suddenly becomes blind and deaf. Their gods? They are nothing more than the ideals of man.

Elena did not deserve to die. Dmitri thought of all of the kindness that she had put out into the world. He thought of how her magic was still young, but her ambition was fearless. He was immortal and could not die, and yet she demanded to fight by his side because this was her battle too. And he knew the importance of taking a stand for oneself. He knew that there was indeed a sense of helplessness in safety. To have forced her to stay away from this battle in her name would have only been to force another cage around her. A fear of never knowing if she could have indeed handled it—and she had indeed handled it.

Elena had fought more bravely and at a disadvantage to most of these men. She was newly recovered, still learning defense, blind, and new to magic. She had not fought perfectly, but she had fought hard. She had known when to call for help, and all of this was for what? So that fool could stab her in the back once the battle had already dissipated?

He stared at the red—that horrible, awful color that was somewhere it did not belong—and he remembered June's blood spilled on this very field. He remembered the hollow thud that her head had made when it rolled. There had been no fear in her eyes, only regret that she could not have done more. Dmitri had never fully processed that grief. He had shoved it down deep into a hollow crevice of mind. When Silas died, he sealed off the memory. And Elena... she always did have a talent for making him remember.

This time would be different. He would not let it destroy him, and he would feel it in full when the time was right. He owed her that much, at least. He wished he could promise her that he would continue trying to grow, just like the trees, if only she would smile at him once more. Bargaining would get him nowhere, though, and he would honor her by continuing to try. He would adopt her tenacity and adaptability. He would try and make her proud, wherever she was in the beyond, once she left. Once she died.

He had never known of unconditional things before her. He had never loved someone so wholly. She was not perfect. She was anxious and presumptuous at times. She was traumatized and broken. But she was his. He wanted her in any way that she came, so long as she was there. She was smart and tied to the world in ways he didn't understand. Her magic was more volatile than he had ever seen, even from the fae that once roamed his woods. She was strong, funny, and wild. Losing her was breaking something so deep and potent inside of him that he felt he might be coming apart at the seams.

Dmitri could feel her heartbeat slowing as he held her hand, forcing his eyes to drag back up to her face. He squeezed her hand tightly, tears rolling slowly down his cheeks. He could not bring himself to scream, though his mind yearned to let the pent-up grief out. He sniffed, exhaling shakily as he kissed her hand and let his lips linger. He did not care who watched or if anyone was still there. He did not know if any animals or humans remained. He could not bring himself to look anywhere but at her.

"I'm right here. I am right here. It's okay," he whispered, knowing there was nothing else he could do but let nature take its course and—

No.

No.

Dmitri's eyes flashed with resolution as his mind kicked back to life. He glanced at her one last time with a renewed sense of urgency as the beginnings of an idea bloomed in his mind. The forest shifted around them, sensing yet another change clicking into place. They did not know the inner workings of his mind, and he had no time to explain them or try to reason with himself. No, Elena should not be the one lying here on the ground, and Dmitri was *not* that helpless boy who watched his life fall apart.

He had bargained with the world, stolen its magic. He had dissolved who he was and what he had known and become something else. Something that Elena had called powerful. He was not the monster he once thought he was. Dmitri *was* power. He was nature; life and death in endless cycles. He was the nature that took its course, and if he could have killed so many things—*people*—then he could do this and save her.

He took a deep breath. Dmitri was the Guardian of this forest. He was the Guardian of Elena and had promised her refuge. Hell, he would be a god this one time if it meant giving him the strength to do this next step. But one thing was clear: his bargain all of those years ago hadn't been a mistake. He did not regret it then, and he would not regret where it had led him now. Elena had told him that he could decide who he got to become, even with what he thought to be a curse looming over him. Perhaps that curse would be a blessing.

He made his decision.

Chapter Thirty-Three

CHANGE

E lena fluttered her eyes open. Her mind felt like the fog settling over a stagnant lake on an early twilight morning. Slow, peacefulness swam through her veins. She still could not see anything, but she became vaguely aware of the feeling of grass beneath her fingertips and the taste of maple and vanilla on her taste buds. The synapses of her mind began firing their electric signals once more, beckoning more senses of hers to life once more.

Friend! The flowers excitedly whispered as they nudged themselves against her hands. *Queen of the woods, you have returned to us once more!*

The air inflated her lungs again, expanding her chest with care as she breathed in the world. It smelled of iron in the air, and memories of the battle crept back into her mind. Her heart thumped against her ribs slowly at first, then more steadily as her blood flowed through her veins. She flexed her fingertips, sensations flooding through her once more as she blinked, surprised not to feel any pain. Her fingers trailed up her waist and found the dampened hole of her dress. She slipped her fingers into it carefully and was surprised to feel her skin solid and sealed.

Patryk lowered the tip of his knife from Dmitri's throat, and they both watched in awe as Elena sat up. Dmitri shoved him away, quickly crawling to Elena's side.

"Easy now," he murmured quietly, resting a trembling hand on her lower back.

"Dmitri?" Elena asked groggily, her head feeling lighter. "I don't understand. What happened?"

Dmitri cast a glance at Patryk before focusing his attention back on Elena. He lifted his hand and hesitated a brief moment before carefully brushing away the hair from her blood-stained face and tucking it behind her ear. "I thought I would never see you again," he whispered as an admission.

"I thought I died," she whispered back, remembering pieces as she sorted through the memories.

"Almost. You almost died. You were a breath away from something that not even I could return you from, my love. I... I don't know how to explain what I have done."

Elena frowned, a sudden anxiety creeping up her spine. "Dmitri, tell me you did not bargain with the world again to bring me back. Tell me. Please, tell me you did not bring me back just to make me lose you."

"I did not bargain."

Elena paused at this, relief and confusion flooding her in equal measures. "Then... what did you do exactly? Why do things feel *different*?"

Dmitri inhaled sharply as he held her hand, and Elena wondered if he realized that his fingers lightly pressed against her wrist to feel her pulse. His arm was covered in blood, both her own dark red as well as his black. Elena could feel the sticky wetness of the partially dried mess on his arms.

"I gave you my heart," he murmured.

She furrowed her eyebrows gently. "I gave you mine as well, but—"

"No darling, I gave you my actual heart."

She paused, wanting to question it, but then remembered the taste of his magic on her tongue. "How?" she whispered. "How are you still alive? How am I still alive?"

Dmitri squeezed her hand gently to comfort her, lifting it to his lips and pressing a quick gentle kiss to it. "I was losing you, and something inside of me just clicked. This whole time, I had been calling myself a monster for what I have done, but you had seen something better inside of me from the beginning. For once in my life, I didn't feel helpless to sit back and watch good people get dealt terrible endings. I felt the power inside of me just shift into something I don't know if I have ever truly felt. I might have tasted the edge once, but nothing like this. I opened myself to the universe, and I saw the strings pour from everything. It was... overwhelming.

"Things just started to make sense, and I guess I just sort of acted on this intrinsic primal instinct. I didn't have time to think about the consequences, though I knew they were there somewhere in the back of my mind. I ripped my chest open, and I pulled out my heart. I thought it might kill me after I let go of it, but I knew it would save you. It had been blessed with immortality, and it was the last thing still truly human about me, so I knew it would be compatible with you. Then the heart would turn your blood immortal to heal your wounds. You were so far gone, and I didn't want to hurt you, but like I said, I acted without thinking."

"He ripped your body open," Patryk said flatly. He finally sheathed his dagger into the strap on his thigh. "Herrick had knocked me out, but I came back around, only to see you dying and Dmitri tearing into you. I thought he had turned on you and killed you. My men and I were in the process of rushing to get him off of you. If nothing else than to give you a proper burial."

Elena turned her head at the new voice, her eyes opening a bit wider as she realized that they were not alone, though the voice did not frighten her. She took a moment, her mind still sluggishly processing it. "P-Patryk?" she asked, a bit bewildered as she had not even known that he was here, much less trying to save her from Dmitri.

He chuckled a bit and crossed his arms over his chest, not caring about the blood that still covered him. "In the flesh."

She smiled warmly in his direction and relaxed her shoulders. At the mention of flesh, though, she paused for a moment as she remembered something. Her hand slid to her chest and relaxed when she felt her dress and skin still intact. "How—" she began, but Dmitri cut her off gently.

"I rolled you onto your side. Don't worry. Nothing is exposed," he reassured her quietly.

She shook her head, touched that he cared about her dignity, but that was not something she cared about at the moment. There were burning questions in her mind still. "No, how are you still alive if I have your heart inside of me? And seeing as I have no wounds, does this mean I am immortal now? What about you?" She rattled off her questions quickly.

"Well, I managed to get my heart inside of you before Patryk tackled me to the ground. I didn't care because I thought I was going to die anyway, but then something snapped. All of the rot that I felt coursing through my veins over the last hundred years just seemed to stop. I could still feel it there, but even as I talk to you now, I can feel my humanity coming back. That being said, I have retained my magic. I am still the Guardian of these woods. Still a Leshy, and still immortal as well. But as my heart beats through you, it is as though the rot is being purified like a filter. As long as my heart remains inside of your chest, the rot will not consume me. At least, I think. There is not exactly a handbook for what happens when you shove your heart inside of your soulmate's body,"

Dmitri said, managing a sheepish smile as he tried to lighten the mood ever so slightly.

"It seems you two saved each other," Patryk mused.

Elena nodded numbly as she tried to process the information. She was an immortal now. The love of her life was safe from being stolen away from her. "We have many tomorrows then," she whispered in shock, almost to herself more than anything.

Dmitri smiled warmly at her then and pulled her into his arms as he had been aching to do since the moment she took air into her lungs once more. "We will have as many tomorrows as you wish, my little witch."

Elena hugged him back tightly, resting her chin on his shoulder. "I always knew you had it in you to make your own choices in life," she whispered beside his ear.

He gave her another small squeeze, smiling a little bit. "I promised I would always choose you."

She smiled, relaxing her shoulders again as she took another moment of savoring his arms around her. She breathed him in. She simply breathed. She had faced death and come back again for the second time in her life, though this time, it felt like a stable conclusion. She placed a kiss lovingly on Dmitri's cheek, grinning proudly to herself at the fear that he had faced. She felt glee at the confidence he held about himself. He knew this would work and that he would save her, even if he had not expected himself to survive the fallout. She knew how much resentment he had been holding for himself, but now it seemed just ever so slightly less. His heart pumped blood through her veins. Without her, he would cease to exist as the Leshy took over his mind. Without him, she would eventually fall to dust from injury or natural causes, just as any other mortal would.

Finally, Elena pulled back away from him, remembering that they still had an audience. She turned to face Patryk's direction before carefully pushing herself up and to her feet. Dmitri helped to steady her as she rose. She could feel his intense protectiveness, especially after coming so close to losing her, and knew he must be struggling not to gently scold her to take it easy.

"So, you are an immortal now, Miss?" Patryk asked softly.

She shrugged her shoulders as she stood facing him. She was proud of herself as well for being unafraid after all she had been through. She still felt an intense distrust for most people after what she had experienced, even Patryk, despite his help, but she was not afraid of him. And she would learn to trust again. This much she promised herself.

"It would seem so, though I am not exactly looking to test the theory."

"Good. Someone needs to make sure that the bloodlust of the Guardian does not return. I would say that you are more than suited for that task for a lifetime."

Elena inclined her head gently in a show of respect and gratitude. She did not think Dmitri would need to worry about that bloodlust—at least not to the extreme that he once had to live with. "I am happy to see that you have made your own decisions today as well. Are you hurt?"

"Not more than anyone else. Herrick there knocked me unconscious for a bit before he went to attack you. I am sorry that I could not hold him off any longer."

Elena smiled warmly at him, and even Dmitri relaxed his shoulders a bit, knowing that this man had fought so hard for her. "There is no need to apologize. You fought bravely, and your presence alone was more than we could have ever asked for. I don't know if you came here with the intent to help us, but the fact that you did remains. We will not forget your kindness."

Patryk shifted a bit, not used to the praise. He glanced back over his shoulder at Sasha and some of the other men watching him with pride as well. They were lucky to have not lost any of their men from their village of Stapes. Some of the men from Pantauk had survived as well, and while they remained at the edge of the clearing near the river, they had still heard and witnessed Dmitri's care of Elena and the way the dead had seemingly risen. Some of them were in awe of the two of them. Others feared them—but no longer as a witch and a Leshy. They looked at the two standing in the clearing, speaking to the man, and they feared the gods that they had become. They watched as the two in their human forms were covered and soaked with the blood of men, and the legends began their origin of the god and goddess inside of the woods.

Patryk looked back to Elena, opening his mouth to ask a new question, but Elena spoke as if reading his thoughts.

"Things are going to be different," Elena reassured him softly. Dmitri took her hand, lacing their fingers together as he let her speak for the both of them. "We haven't had much time to discuss things, but we promised each other that if we survived this, we would work towards change."

"Well, if there is to be a bridge between our kind, I can see no one better for it to be than you, Miss Elena," Patryk said quietly, and Dmitri dipped his head in silent agreement.

Elena lifted her chin. "Perhaps, though, I cannot say that I will be without my own share of mistakes."

"No great leader is."

"I am afraid that I must ask something of you in return."

"And that is?" Patryk asked, slightly surprised as he raised his eyebrows.

"Dmitri and I will allow people to once again hunt and travel through the forest. Unfortunately, we also know that we cannot expect people who have lived in fear for most of their lives to simply accept that there is indeed magic living in this forest beside them. I must ask you to return and to tell your villages whatever you must in order to keep those from seeking us out to hunt us once more. I will not tell you what to tell them, but I urge you to tell them anything that will prevent another hunt. We are willing to work for change, but we are not willing to become trophies for those who wish us harm," she said softly, and both Dmitri and Patryk glanced at Herrick's crumpled body on the ground, his smile still frozen on his lifeless lips as his eyes remained open.

"We will be taking our own precautions to make sure we are not disturbed, but I ask that you help us with this one last task. I believe there is much more to be discussed as well, but right now, I admit that dancing with death has taken its toll on me, and I wish to rest," she said, offering a small weak smile.

Patryk nodded briefly. "Of course," he said quietly. "Let us hope that upon our next meeting, there is far less bloodshed," he added with a soft grin at the two of them, his mind still spinning with how his life had changed so drastically in a matter of days.

He turned to walk away, making it only a few steps before Dmitri released Elena's hand and took a step forward. "Wait," he said in a firm but quiet voice.

Patryk stopped as if it had been a command and turned to look at them once more.

"I am sorry for the pain and the trouble that I have caused everyone. I wanted you to hear that from me. I cannot change what I have done, but... I know I can do better," Dmitri said.

Patryk gave a small half-smile. "As I said before, no great leader is without mistakes. I suppose that goes for the magical type as well. Me and my kind have done our own share of horrors, many of which you have seen firsthand as well."

"I would like to start now if you and your people will let me. It is a long and dangerous way to walk. I can make it easier," he said quietly.

Patryk, who had felt the magic of the Guardian and his traveling before, looked over his shoulder again at the others and hesitated before nodding. "I will speak to them first and explain what is to happen. Then I think everyone would very much appreciate the shorter journey back home."

Dmitri nodded, and Patryk walked back to the others. Dmitri turned to face Elena, coming over to her and caressing her cheek gently as he smiled down at her. "As for you," he murmured softly, placing a gentle kiss on her forehead. "Will you allow me to take you inside now to rest?"

Elena smiled lovingly at him, closing her eyes as she giggled. "I would appreciate it. I don't think I can walk another step," she admitted quietly.

He chuckled, shaking his head. "My little witch," he murmured affectionately, bending to scoop her small body into his arms.

She instinctively draped her arms around his neck, smiling wearily. "My brave Leshy," she whispered. She kissed his lips gently before resting her head against his shoulder, allowing him to walk her inside the cottage. Before, there had always been an ominous sense of what lay beyond the front door, but things had changed now. She felt safe and competent in her ability to protect herself, and this no longer felt like a home in which she was to temporarily reside. This was where she belonged—even with the dangers that they may face together. This was truly her home.

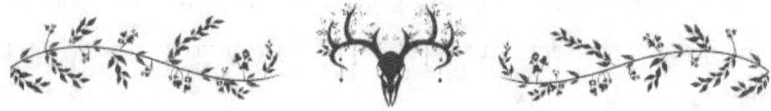

CHAPTER THIRTY-FOUR

HOME

O nce Dmitri had gotten Elena settled by the fireplace, he begrudgingly walked back outside. Shock had settled into his bones from the turn of events that the day had taken. All he wanted to do was to touch her skin and feel that she was indeed still alive. He wanted to remain by her side entirely, never leaving her for another moment. Which was precisely why he needed to pull himself away now, even if just only for a bit. He could not smother her as much as he wanted to protect her. He needed to prove to himself that this was not a dream and that she would still be there when he returned.

Power flowed inside of his veins, purer than he had ever felt it. He could feel the strength of it, and for the first time since he had taken this magic for himself, he truly did not feel like it was such a curse. In fact, he found himself idly wondering what other good things he could actually do. He lifted his eyes to the treeline of the forest that surrounded their home, wondering if perhaps he could have been doing better for them as well. Sure, the forest had been thriving without the humans around by his rules, but what if it could truly flourish with them here?

Glancing back at the cottage, Dmitri smiled to himself. Something told him that Elena would know or at least have some ideas. With a thousand lifetimes to learn magic should she choose, he knew that her power would be nearly unmatched. In fact, it truly already was. There were some witches who had gained immortality but lost themselves in the process before they could truly experience it. Elena was different in that regard, and he knew that she would not let this opportunity go to waste. Her insatiable curiosity would never have to worry about growing stagnant or not having enough time. And for him? He would never know another lonely day by her side.

Dmitri walked to Patryk and the other men, stopping a few feet away from the groups who eyed him tentatively. There would be a long road ahead of him for retribution, but it started here. It had been easy to let people see him as an evil untouchable thing of the forest. It had been easy to prey on their fear and use his own grief to block everyone out. It had been easy to blame the Leshy inside of his mind for the bloodlust and pain he had caused these villages. But none of that was him anymore, and he had the time to prove that. Still, Dmitri could not bring himself to trust any of these humans other than perhaps Patryk. He stared at them, keeping his expression neutral and calm as he looked at them. He would also not allow them to see fear in his eyes or weakness.

Patryk stepped forward to him as he looked up from his conversation with Sasha. "How many people can you travel with at once?"

Dmitri glanced down at his hands, not having thought about it before. He took a moment of thought before glancing around at some of the men. "I have never attempted to travel this way with more than two aside from myself. Though I think I can safely start with five at a time."

Patryk nodded in approval before Sasha turned to the groups of men, tired and bloodied. "Groups of five then," Sasha announced louder so that people could hear.

Dmitri took a deep breath as he began to fold the universe, walking between the space of a breath to new locations with each group. He took each one to the various villages of Pantauk, Stapes, and one man to Innorin—who had promptly sworn his faith to the Guardian. People had mixed reactions to the mode of travel, smacking their lips as the taste of spice surprised them, one person vomiting, others stumbling a bit and staring at him like he was a terrifying beast once more. Fear, awe, surprise—they went through each of the emotions and landed on a different one depending on each person.

As Dmitri came back to transport the last two—Sasha and Patryk—he stopped for a moment. "Patryk," Dmitri said and took a step closer to him. "I have allowed Elena to speak for me, but I will now speak for her. When discussions and terms are to be spoken about in the future, I am requesting that you are there. She does not trust people easily, and yet she has chosen to trust you. I trust you. Choose whoever you wish to come with you, have someone else speak for you, but please be there."

Patryk looked a bit unsure and glanced at Sasha, who stood there calmly, watching the interaction, before turning back to Dmitri. "I am not the most knowledgeable nor political."

"I can't say I am either, but that does not change the fact that we both trust you. And until trust is built further on both sides, this is my request for her. To be frank, you are the closest thing either one of us has to a friend. We would not be alive if it were not for you and your men either."

Sasha placed his hand on Patryk's shoulder as a gesture of reassurance and smiled. "I, for one, think it is a great idea. Though other villages may disagree."

"As I have said, you may bring others when we are to meet. Someone from each village, if you must."

Sasha nodded sagely and then gave Patryk's shoulder a small squeeze. "I could see no one else more fitting for our village."

Patryk turned and faced Sasha quickly, brows furrowed. "I can, and I am looking at him right now," he said indignantly.

Sasha chuckled softly. "I am getting older, and this travel will not suit me much longer. You are brave, if not a little reckless, Patryk. You are smarter than you allow yourself to be seen as. For now, at least, I truly do not think anyone is better suited than you."

Patryk studied his face for a long time before frowning ever so slightly, unable to argue with him as much as he wished to. He looked at Dmitri and then nodded firmly. "Alright, I will do it. Though you cannot say I did not warn you about me not being a diplomat."

Dmitri let a small half-smirk creep onto his face and dipped his head in approval and respect. "Elena mentioned that we will be taking our own steps to remain hidden from those who may still wish to seek us out to cause us harm. I have a brief idea of what she means, but it is something that is to still be discussed. As a show of my own gratitude for helping her, even if you thought it meant helping her from me, I wish to give you something as well."

He stepped closer to Patryk, ignoring the look of confusion on his face before he reached out, placing a hand on his cheek. Magic flooded through Patryk as he gasped, eyes widening before rolling back into his head. Sasha reached for his knife in alarm, ready to help his friend, but Dmitri held his hand up to stop him as the breeze swirled around Patryk's feet.

After another moment, Dmitri pulled his hand back, and the wind ceased as Patryk inhaled gulps of air into his lungs. "What the gods did you do to me?" he gasped out as Dmitri took a step back.

"These woods are very difficult to navigate, and something tells me that finding our home will no longer be as easy as it once was. I placed an enchantment in your mind. If you need to find us, the forest will guide your way. Alternatively, if you wish to reach us, you may write a letter and stick it into any tree within the forest boundaries. They will make sure that it is delivered to me."

"A warning next time," he rasped out.

Dmitri gave him a small grin and nodded. "My apologies. I did not mean to cause harm to you," he said sincerely.

"No, it did not hurt. It just felt... intense."

Dmitri nodded and then bowed his head to both of the men. "If you wish, I will take you home now, then. I do wish to spend some time with my wife."

The two men nodded as Sasha relaxed a little bit. Dmitri folded the universe for them, helping them to step through. Sasha looked in awe as they arrived at the border of their village, and Patryk turned to glance back at Dmitri, already seeing him disappear back to the cottage once more.

"Things are never going to be the same, you know," Patryk murmured.

"Change is not always a bad thing, son. Sometimes it is the only way to move forward. Without you, many of our men would have died today. That much is certain. After witnessing the Guardian's power with my own eyes, it is a miracle he did not wipe us all out much quicker."

Patryk considered this before beginning to walk towards his own home within the village. Despite everything, he no longer felt the fear and apprehension toward Dmitri that he had when they had first met. He did not know the details of the thing that had ailed him before, sensing that it had something to do with magic but knowing nothing else beyond that. He was not yet equipped to understand such things, but he had suspected that Elena had something to do with his motivation to improve. He had seen the intense care and heard the selflessness that this Guardian had demonstrated in order to try and protect her, and Patryk could understand and reason with someone like that.

"Regardless, our work here is not done. We still have to tell the villagers what has happened."

"What did you tell the other villages to say to their people?" Sasha asked as he stepped quickly to follow and walk beside him.

Patryk shrugged. "Different things. I told the injured man of Innorin to go home and say that they killed the witch, but there were scarce survivors. To spin a tale and go home a hero and then spend his days telling people the ends did not justify the means. Some of the villagers from Pantauk suggested that they tell their people that the evil of the forest was neutralized. I trust their judgment to know their people well enough. I do not think they expected what they had coming into this battle and are not looking to lose anyone else in a repeat scenario."

"And for our people? What will you tell them?"

"The truth. I think they are able to handle it, and if not, then I will take responsibility for what comes next."

Sasha grinned a bit to himself at the leader that Patryk had become and remained silent as they walked home, greeted by the other men who chose to wait for them. Smiles were exchanged as they all came to Patryk, finally celebrating their victory.

Maybe Sasha is right, Patryk thought to himself as he smiled at his friends. *Maybe change is a good thing. Maybe I have changed too, and that is okay.*

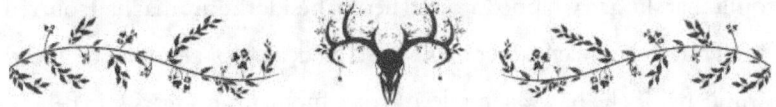

Dmitri stepped back into the still blood-coated field that held his home and smiled at the house in which she rested. He walked to the door, his eyes focused on it instead of the blood and bodies sprawled around the clearing. He told himself that he would care about the cleanup later, but right now, there were far more important things.

And now, the moment of truth was upon him as he stopped in front of the old wooden door. He brushed himself off, happy that the blood had dried, and he took a moment to try and shake off the anxious feeling inside of his chest. There was a sensation that he did not think he would get used to feeling—or rather, one that he would have trouble getting used to not feeling—and that was that his heart no longer remained inside his chest. Blood still flowed through his veins, but it was magic that now kept it flowing. He no longer felt his heart race in anxiety or fear, though the ghost of it remained. He was alive, but he was different. He was truly an immortal magical being now, and yet he had bent the rules of the universe to accommodate him. And truthfully, it almost felt as though the world was relieved that he had found this loophole.

He thought back to the lesson that he had taught Elena, where he explained how conversing with the world worked. Sometimes, you simply need to rephrase your question. Dmitri felt the parallels of it all, and though he wanted to kick himself for not realizing earlier on that he had gotten exactly what he wanted in his bargain, he was incredibly thankful to the world now for something he had once felt condemned to endure.

With one last deep breath, he opened the door to the cottage and walked inside. Elena remained where he had left her, curled into a thick quilt that she had wrapped around herself beside the fire that had spurred to life from her magic. Her eyes were closed, and for a moment, Dmitri wondered if she had fallen asleep. For a moment, his fears seized him. *What if she wasn't—*

His thoughts instantly stopped as he took another tentative step closer, and her head lifted. Her face was still splattered with blood, and her long brown hair had come loose from her braid as it hung in strands over her face. Sweat still clung lightly to her skin, but her chest slowly rising and falling was what Dmitri had focused on. He knew she would still have a scar there from the sword, but she was healed. She was *safe*.

"Dmitri?" she inquired with a soft voice that informed him that she must have dozed off to sleep.

Hearing her say his name made his breathing nearly stop altogether. He wanted to beg her to simply just say it again to reaffirm that she was really here. "Yes, it's me. Everyone is gone now."

She nodded her head approvingly. "Safe travels?"

His mouth quirked up into a small grin. "The safest."

She smiled lazily up at him and then begrudgingly rose from the rocking chair. Dmitri quickly stepped towards her, and she opened her arm with the blanket, offering him warmth as well. He hesitated, but when she shook her arm stubbornly, he chuckled and entered her cocoon of blankets, sweeping her up into his arms gently before settling back down into the chair with her draped on his lap.

Elena nestled her body closer to him, her cheek resting against his shoulder. He could feel each exhale of her lungs against his neck, causing the gooseflesh to rise over his skin. He tightened his hold on her protectively.

"I thought that I had lost you," he murmured softly as he kissed the top of her hair. "I admit to still not being certain that you are not a dream."

Elena giggled quietly. "Well, I am very much alive. Perhaps now you will understand how I have felt when being unable to hear you." She paused for a moment before gently pressing herself a little closer to him. "Dying felt different than I had expected it to. I just want you to know that I stopped being in pain after a time. And that I thought of you in those final moments."

Dmitri closed his eyes. "One day... One day I would very much wish for you to tell me about your experience if that suits you. For now, however, I just wish to hold you and be thankful that you are here with me. You are safe, my love."

Elena smiled and relaxed. "I know we are, for now at least. Though, I think I would feel safer if we did start to plan for our future. I think that lying in wait for the next hunt is not the right course of action. I do not wish for more bloodshed, Dmitri. And if we do open the borders of the forest to travelers and hunters, it stands to reason that someone will eventually stumble upon us if we do nothing. We cannot guarantee that their intentions will be that of peace."

"It sounded earlier as if you had an idea. You mentioned taking our own precautions. I am beside you each step of the way, so if there is something you have in mind, I am more than willing to listen to it. If not, then we will figure it out together."

"I... do have an idea. Though I have no idea if it would actually work."

"It could not hurt to try. Does it involve your magic?" Dmitri asked on a hunch.

Elena chuckled softly, and her cheeks blushed a soft pink against the darkened reddish-brown color of blood dried to her skin. "It does. I have felt my magic growing more curious, and sometimes, it is like ideas come to me in my dreams. And ever since your heart pushes blood through my veins, that has only strengthened it. I think it will take a while before I get it down just right, but I have an idea to put a protective border around our home. I could use your help, though, if you are willing, of course."

"Of course I am. Right now, however, you should rest."

"We are covered in grime. Should we not wash up? And what about the bodies on our front porch?" she asked quietly. "I still want you to tell me about the details that I missed during the fight. I also won't just let you clean up this mess on my own. But... Can it really be over just like that?"

Dmitri, sensing the building anxiety within her, gently ran his fingers through her hair and gently shushed her. "We will handle it together, but it does not need to be immediate. Getting back to normal will take some time, I know that, but I am going to be right here beside you for as long as you want me to be."

Elena was quiet for a long moment as she seemed to consider something. Dmitri wondered if he had touched upon a deeper truth, only confirmed by her next question.

"You still want to choose me? Even though I have brought this back to your doorstep? I... I know that today could not have been easy on you, either. I know you saved me, but I want you to know that it does not require you to continue to choose me if you have decided that it is too much work to do so. I would understand that."

Dmitri shook his head vehemently, pulling her small frame closer to him. "Elena, I will choose you every single day until the end of eternity. Even after that, I will still fight to hold onto you. I love you, even on days when it may not be easy. Even if it causes trouble to enter into my life. A chaotic life by your side is better than a calm one on my own by far. I love you, and that will not stop so easily. I... I have a lot of growth to do, but I will grow by your side if you let me. I want to continue to work and try and be better for you. It isn't always going to be the easy choice, but, for me, it is the right one. I love you, my beautiful moon, my goddess, my little witch. I love you, Elena. For who you are and who you have been. I love you for the woman you will become and the different variations of self that you will go through.

"And I will tell you this as often as is needed; this fight was not your fault. Those men chose to pursue you. They were given a warning as we tried to reason with them, and, in the end, you fought for yourself and for me. And I would fight a thousand wars for you. I have a thousand lives to live and refuse to squander another one without speaking my truth. You, Elena, are certainly not at fault for what has happened today. It is not a crime for you to exist. Today was awful for everyone, but there can be good that comes from this. Such as talking with Patryk about opening the borders. *You* thought of that, and it was a wonderful idea to start trying for change. To prevent this from happening again even. The world would be worse without you in it, my love. And I am just incredibly lucky to be allowed by your side."

Elena listened intently, and tears filled her eyes before slowly spilling down her face. Her hands gripped his shirt tightly, unwilling to let go. Dmitri, fully expecting the tears to come eventually, held her close as he rocked them together. She had to be strong for too long, and she could no longer hold on so tightly to her indifferent facade. He knew that the sounds of men dying and being torn apart would haunt her for some time yet, but he knew that seeing the carnage would have only made it worse. So in a way, he was thankful that she did not have her sight. She had gone through too much, though, in too short of a time. He admired her strength and adaptability, but he wanted to ease the burden on her. It was not fair that she had to endure all of these things, and that thought made the Leshy's judgment inside of his mind flare to life. He quickly tapered it down.

"I am scared," she whispered shakily.

Dmitri nodded in understanding, placing another slow, lingering kiss on the top of her hair. "I know, but we will be okay."

"You really aren't leaving? The part of being a Guardian that threatened to take you away from me, is it truly gone?"

"I wish I could say for sure, but unfortunately, I just don't know. I genuinely feel as though the rot inside of me is chipping away, but I don't know if that is just the Leshy inside of me being exhausted from so much use. What we have done... I don't think it has ever been done before. Becoming the Guardian of the forest comes with a deeper understanding and knowledge of certain things and of magic in ways that are hard for me to verbalize. I had never known of something like this. But Elena, I think it is not something we have to worry about. At the very least, not for a very long time now. I think you are simply stuck with me."

At that, Elena gave a short laugh through the tears and gently wiped her eyes with the back of her hand. "I think being stuck with you is something I can handle."

"Good, because I think those villagers are counting on it," Dmitri chuckled.

Elena relaxed comfortably in his arms and fluttered her eyelids closed as she took a few deep breaths, beginning to calm down. It would be a long process to heal, but Dmitri felt confident that she would be able to tackle it. And he could tackle his own burdens. He knew that she was not the answer to his problems, nor was he the answer to hers, but he felt like they provided good support for each other.

"You are stuck with me as well," she whispered.

"I would have it no other way."

Elena smiled to herself and kissed his cheek gently before hugging his torso. He breathed in deeply, praising the gods for another day with her, even if it had been tainted with bloodshed. Her body, thoroughly exhausted from the day's events, began to ease away from the tension that she had been holding onto as she bordered on the edge of sleep.

"Tomorrow, we will do what is needed, yes?" she whispered on the edge of sleep.

Dmitri idly played with the loose strands of hair as he wrapped them around his finger and smiled, his own eyes closing. "Yes. But for now, we simply enjoy this moment together."

Elena nodded her head and fell asleep with a small smile on her beautiful lips. After a while of holding of her, too scared to blink and miss a single moment, Dmitri finally allowed himself to rest as well, knowing that there would be many tomorrows in which she would be by his side.

THE FINALE

EPILOGUE

The crisp wind of the evening bristled along Elena's skin as a man from the village of Stapes escorted her over the threshold of the forest. Once upon a time, that was truly not so long ago, she had crossed the border of the forest with a foreboding sense of finality looming over her. She had been bound, weak, and injured by men who did not understand the world. They had been ruled by their fear, and so they had condemned her to death. And in a way, they had succeeded.

There was a part of Elena that those men had killed that rainy day as they forced her to dig her own grave, though it was certainly not the part that they had hoped. Instead of killing the witch, they merely erased the line that separated her from the heritage she had barely known. No longer two versions of herself, Elena was reborn into her identity. Her life was saved that day by a creature of the woods—a god of the forest and judgment—but Elena had spent each and every day since then saving herself.

She saved herself from letting the fear consume her. She saved herself from the fear upon hearing new voices call her things such as 'witch' or 'goddess.' She saved herself from the guilt that she should have never felt for merely existing. She saved herself from the memories of the trauma that plagued her when she heard certain sounds or woke up in the night to her own screams. She refused to let herself fall. So each day, she worked harder for herself.

Of course, she was not alone in saving herself. Dmitri was still there, even after all of this time. He was still himself too. There were days, perhaps, when the Leshy inside of him still came through, but it was no longer an unreasonable beast. Dmitri was by her side, allowing her to lean on him on the days when she could not hold herself up. And she was there for him in return, always ready to coax him gently in the right direction or remind him of what was important.

After the battle, and after they had spent some time relishing the life that they had been granted, Dmitri helped Patryk send word to the other villages to collect their dead. Dmitri dragged what remained of their bodies to a separate clearing that was a distance away from the cottage for them to gather. He also assisted when necessary to those who could not travel far if they still wished to grieve and perform proper burial rites. Those who were not collected were few, but they were burned, and Dmitri and Elena said their own words for them. The man responsible for the entire battle was amongst those few, his mother unable and unwilling to look upon her son's corpse. Her stoic response was that he had made his choice.

Disturbingly, the only thing that did not burn from the corpses was a small ornate box with an eye inside of it. Dmitri and Elena could feel the witchcraft surrounding it, so they cast their own spell of unbinding and broke the hex before they disposed of it as well. They could sense the evil surrounding the intention of the eye and would not risk it causing them any more harm. Dmitri was taking every precaution he could to keep them safe.

He had spent time truly working on himself; a god repenting for his own sins. He worked to make amends with the surrounding villages.

While he could not guarantee protection from all elements of the forest, he promised to judge each situation equally. He would not tell the wolves and bears not to protect their territory but would not encourage it. He would not prevent the hunters from killing, though he would not aid them either. He would provide safe passage to merchants and travelers as long as they stayed on the paths. He would protect the forest first and foremost, but he would no longer isolate it and stunt its growth. And he would no longer go out of his way to haunt this forest with an unmatched bloodlust.

After some years had passed, people had even begun to leave small offerings for the two of them inside hollowed trees bordering their villages. The first time it happened, Dmitri had come home after the trees had delivered it and wept in Elena's arms. He often dealt with the feeling of being undeserving of kindness, but as time came and went, he hesitantly began to accept his new role in life and understand that he was indeed worthy of kindness, even despite his sins. It did not erase the pain he had caused people, but it was a step toward penance with those who trusted and now, apparently, worshiped him.

Their small family had only grown the day of the battle as well. The bear that had protected Elena found his way into Elena's heart. Dmitri had managed to save it in the moment, but after the battle, it had not moved very far and seemed to have given up. Elena had insisted they help the bear and would refuse to hear any protests from either Dmitri or the beast.

She spent the following months caring for the creature mostly on her own as Dmitri was unable to intervene much in that regard, though he still took direction from her and helped her gather what she needed. The bear, who she called Medved, slowly recovered and became quite attached to Elena. Once he could move freely of his own volition, he took up residence in a cave near the cottage and began to frequently visit their field, waiting for Elena. The two would walk the woods together and exchange stories—both true and fiction. Dmitri said he had never seen an animal take so quickly to someone but welcomed the devotion that the beast offered Elena for saving its life in truth.

Patryk tapped Elena's arm lightly, signaling a change in direction as they got deeper into the forest. She could most likely find her own way now, but she appreciated his kindness. Elena often met with Patryk and a few others around each solstice to simply check in, gather any supplies that she and Dmitri found themselves needing, and make sure everything was running smoothly for them. She would come sporadically through-out other times in the year as well, but each time, Patryk was always there to welcome her at the border and help escort her back when she was through.

Other times, he would walk with her all the way back to the cottage and visit Dmitri as well. The three of them had become close friends over the years, and the two men, in particular, had truly come to bond with one another despite their rough beginnings.

Patryk was the only human who knew the trick of finding their cottage after Elena had put a powerful enchantment on it. The enchantment was inspired by Dmitri's power and how he could seem to fold the universe in order to step over a border into a completely new area of the forest. So, Elena put an enchantment around the field containing the cottage, making it so that anyone who crossed a certain point of the forest near the cottage simply stepped into a new area beyond it. It was as though they would simply step over the area. She added a minor illusion to make sure that it was not suspicious to anyone who experienced it or came near, effectively hiding their home in a pocket of the forest that was untouchable to mankind. Patryk had been given the ability to effectively be able to see the outline of the illusion and break it long enough to cross inside the border and their home. The border and illusion did not work on beasts such as Medved.

Originally, their meetings had consisted of only one or two other men aside from Patryk, but eventually, around the time of the solstice, people from other villages journeyed to Stapes and took part in the meetings. Eventually, even a few women became interested in joining these meetings. On the Summer Solstice, their meetings were held during a feast on the border of the forest in which Dmitri would provide the meat and food necessary, and then the villagers would cook it. Dmitri and Elena would both attend that one.

On the Winter Solstice, only Elena would attend as she traveled into the village to hold the meeting inside someone's home in order to keep harm from coming to people from the elements. Dmitri's body was bound to the forest, and he could never travel outside of the border for too long, but Elena had more freedom in order to do so. Each time he would always meet her at the border at the end of the meeting to take her home and say a quick hello.

During the winter meetings, Elena often found more women in need who felt more comfortable coming to her alone. It was not that they did not trust Dmitri, but Dmitri's presence in his human form resembled the monsters in their life that they knew firsthand, oftentimes. Elena would provide these women with safety, resources, and protection. She would do anything in her power to help them as best as they would let her. And once she began doing that, more witches that had been in hiding began to come to her of all genders, seeking refuge and help, which Elena was more than willing to provide. No longer would she let magic users feel as trapped and alone as she had once been.

Today had been the Summer solstice meeting, but Dmitri was called to his other duties of the forest and had to step away from the meeting toward the end in order to handle it. Patryk had assured him that he would make sure Elena got home safely, though the three all knew that she had become more than capable of being able to do so perfectly fine . on her own. Elena's magic had grown exponentially though she rarely spoke of it outside of Dmitri. She had worked tirelessly to learn the inner workings of her magic and what she could safely do.

"Did you get everything that you needed?" Patryk asked her softly once they had gotten far enough away from the village.

Elena smiled warmly in his direction. "I did, thank you. Though... I wonder if you might not help me in getting a few more things...?" she asked tentatively, drawing the sentence out slightly.

Patryk stopped walking. "Do you wish to go back now and get them? It is not too late, so the shops most likely have put out the lanterns for the night."

Her cheeks reddened as she kept walking. "No, I would rather the villages not be aware of my request for these items if that suits you."

He raised an eyebrow but began walking after her again. "Do you need ingredients for a spell? I am telling you, Elena, the butcher did not like it when I asked if he had any newts eyes."

Elena chuckled softly and smirked as she remembered the story. "It is not my fault that you did not know that eye of newt was just another way of saying mustard seed."

He rolled his eyes and huffed playfully. "Alright, so am I getting you mustard seed again? Or if it is something else, you had better tell me what it is plainly so that the butcher does not look at me like I grew an extra head on my shoulders."

"No... actually, I will need some material to make clothes. Not much, but soft materials, please."

"Making a new dress then? Or something for Dmitri?"

"Not exactly," she said quietly, trailing off. She smiled a bit to herself. "It just needs to be soft enough for a child, please."

Patryk stopped walking once more, and Elena did as well this time. She smiled as his eyes trailed down to her stomach. She was not showing yet, but she knew Patryk could tell that she would not have told her unless she was certain about it.

"You're...?" he started to ask but stopped as she nodded in confirmation. He smiled wildly and laughed, sweeping her into a hug before gently setting her back down as she giggled. "Elena, that is fantastic! Have you told him yet?"

Elena blushed a brighter red, smiling widely and shaking her head.

"A child!" He exclaimed. "And not just any child but an immortal one. I may be new to this whole magic thing, but I am almost certain from what I have been told that it should be impossible. He is going to be ecstatic! Are you happy?" he asked, smiling down at her small frame.

"I really am," she beamed and couldn't help but let a small tear of happiness slide down her face. She wiped her cheeks quickly and sniffed. "You must think me silly to be crying right now, but it's just... I am going to have a family again. I mean, I already do, of course, but a child is so much different. I am a thousand emotions all at once. We weren't specifically trying for it, but we did, of course, discuss if we would want kids and what would happen if I could bear them. We didn't know... well, I guess we still don't know if the child will be born immortal like us or human, like how we both started, but we will love the child unconditionally regardless. I just wish my parents were here to meet their grandchild."

Patryk's smile softened empathetically. "I know they would be proud of you, Elena. Wherever they are in the beyond, they are surely smiling." Elena had told him her story after they had spent more time together and realized that it had gotten easier to talk about them, even if the sadness still lingered in her chest if she thought too long about it.

Elena smiled and, in turn, gently hugged Patryk again. She was not the biggest fan of physical touch outside of Dmitri, even regardless of gender or if they were human or magic wielders, but Patryk was the closest friend she had. He hugged her back and gave her a small gentle squeeze for reassurance.

"I will get you those supplies. I will also ask around in secret to those whom I trust to see what someone would need to prepare to welcome a child into the world. Don't worry. I won't say it is you. If anything, I will say it is one of those girls you are helping, and you are asking on their behalf. But... why don't you want people to know?"

She shook her head and pulled away from the hug. "It isn't that I never want them to know. I just... don't want them to know yet. Not until Dmitri and I can talk about it and not until we can ensure the baby's safety. It is such a new thing. I worry about word spreading too quickly to manage."

Patryk nodded in understanding but then realized she could not see it. "Of course, I understand completely. You have my word, Elena. I won't tell a soul of it until you want me to."

"Thank you, Patryk."

"Of course. Now come on, let's get you home safely."

They walked together in peace, talking about a variety of different things as they went. Elena could tell that he was now watching her like a hawk, making sure she did not trip and fall or run into anything. He had always acted like the brother she never had, and truly, he had become a part of her small family in that way. Sensing how protective he was now that she was expecting only helped to reinforce that notion inside of her mind.

Once they got to the enchantment border, the two said goodbye before she slowly passed through the shield, feeling the wildflowers greet her excitedly as they brushed along her feet. She walked to the door of their home and felt a warmth inside of her chest. Things had not always been easy, and she knew they would not always be easy in the future, but they had built this life together. She and Dmitri had come from two incredibly broken backgrounds and yet had chosen to fight for each other and for themselves. They decided to love each other despite the fear and uncertainties that love brought.

A few years ago, life had been much different for Elena. If she had learned anything from this, it would be that life was anything but consistent, and change would come whether you were ready for it or not. Life would move forward with or without you, and it would not hesitate to remind you the past was a place you may never return to aside from in memories. However, it would also never stop to remind you that the future is coming too, and while it might be uncertain, it doesn't have to be scary. Change is healthy, and growth is good. And as she opened the door to their home, she could hear Dmitri making sounds as he prepared their dinner and knew one thing for certain; she would never have to face that uncertainty alone ever again.

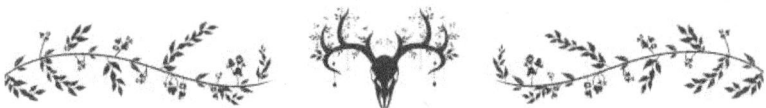

If you loved From Within the Woods as much as I enjoyed writing it, please consider leaving a review on Amazon and Goodreads!

ACKNOWLEDGMENTS

There are so many people who I want to thank for accompanying me on this journey. Most importantly, I want to thank everyone who stayed up late with me at night talking me through all of the doubts and helping me brainstorm. I want to thank the people who were always there for me, encouraging me every step of the way, even when life threw me curveballs. You guys watched me build this story from the ground up, and I will always be so thankful to have each and every one of you in my life. You are all so special to me, and I could have never done this without you.

I would like to thank my family—especially my sisters—who showed interest in my writing and allowed me to read to them. Thank you for excitedly awaiting each chapter and being my first audience, and for giving me the courage to share my work with others. Thank you so much for dreaming big with me.

A big thank you to my editor, Susan Russell, for having the patience of a saint and being so kind to me. Without you, I would not have been able to tell the story that I wanted to tell. Not to mention tolerating my late-night emails and encouraging me, always. I cried over your kindness, even when my grammar was terrible. I promise, one day I will learn to use commas properly (wink).

Lastly, I want to thank myself for saying fuck it and deciding to write and publish a book. When I first began writing this story, it started as a short story that was meant to be a simple tale about two people who chose to work through their pasts—not only to be better for each other, but also to simply be better for themselves. I have always had a deep love for various different kinds of mythologies and folklore, so I wanted to weave that into my story and make it my own. I am not writing this with the notion that is going to change anyone's life, but it is the story I wanted to tell. One of resilience and love, even in the face of trauma. And while I hope that anyone who reads my story finds something to enjoy out of it, ultimately, I wrote this book for myself. So thank you, Tinman, for doing what you set out to do and sticking with it until the end, and finding your heart in it after all. It was stressful and exhilarating in equal measure.

If there is anyone out there doubting themselves or wondering if they can finish the story they want to tell or publish, then trust me, you can. This is your sign that you do what you set out to do, and I have faith in you, friend or stranger. You've got this, just keep going.

www.ingramcontent.com/pod-product-compliance
Lightning Source LLC
Chambersburg PA
CBHW060351260626
47160CB00006B/2269